Kirsty Crawford grew up in Oxfordshire. After studying English at Oxford, she followed a career in publishing, becoming a fiction editor in various publishing houses. She is now a freelance editor and writer, and lives in South London with her husband and son. This is her second novel.

THE SECRET LIFE OF HUSBANDS

Ruth Blackiston has fallen in love with Ned Haskell, and he with her. They are taking the plunge and marriage is just a few months away. But the problem with true love is that it doesn't involve just two people. There's a whole new family of in-laws to meet, get to know — and get on with. Is Ned's mother merely difficult, Ruth wonders, or is there something more dangerous here? Then she meets Ned's close-knit circle of friends. Gradually, Ruth is drawn into Ned's past and all the things that happened to Ned and his friends years before. Is she imagining things? Has Ned really changed? Or are the friends still bound up by the complex, shifting balances that have the power to tear people apart?

Books by Kirsty Crawford
Published by The House of Ulverscroft:

OTHER WOMEN

KIRSTY CRAWFORD

THE SECRET LIFE OF HUSBANDS

Complete and Unabridged

CHARNWOOD
Leicester

First published in Great Britain in 2007 by
Orion, an imprint of the
Orion Publishing Group Limited
London

First Charnwood Edition
published 2007
by arrangement with the
Orion Publishing Group Limited
London

British Library CIP Data

Crawford, Kirsty
    The secret life of husbands.—Large print ed.—
Charnwood library series
    1. Couples—Fiction 2. Parents-in-law—Fiction
    3. Friendship—Fiction 4. Large type books
    I. Title
    823.9'2 [F]

    ISBN 978–1–84617–838–2

Published by
F. A. Thorpe (Publishing)
Anstey, Leicestershire

Set by Words & Graphics Ltd.
Anstey, Leicestershire
Printed and bound in Great Britain by
T. J. International Ltd., Padstow, Cornwall

This book is printed on acid-free paper

To James Crawford

1

'It's fast, isn't it?'

'Of course it's fast.'

'Do you think it's *too* fast, though?'

'Everyone else will think so. No one in the world would advise us to do this.'

'Are we insane?'

'Without a doubt.'

The ring sat sparkling dangerously on the glass-topped cabinet. *It's exquisite*, thought Ruth. Three diamonds were held in place by white-gold claws, icily perfect and alluring. *But what on earth are we doing here?*

The jeweller gazed solemnly at them, too accustomed to this kind of scene to be moved by their flushed cheeks and shining eyes. 'They're brilliant cut,' he said. 'One and a half carats each.'

'It's beautiful, isn't it?'

Ned squeezed her hand. 'Yup. The genuine article.'

'What will everyone say?'

'Who cares what they say? It's what we want that matters.'

'Of course it is.' The ring flashed. She returned his squeeze, a panting breathlessness climbing up her chest.

'Well?'

'I think it's the one,' she said slowly, hardly believing what she was saying.

Ned turned to the jeweller. 'We'll take it.'

They hadn't gone out that day intending to get engaged. It had started in the antiques market, where they stopped in front of a stall selling all kinds of baubles. Ruth was always on the look-out for antique necklaces and brooches, so she paused and examined some of the wares on offer. The woman behind the counter, seeing their faces, had immediately pulled out a tray of what she called importantly 'superb quality vintage antique diamond rings'.

Ruth and Ned laughed with embarrassment and obediently looked over the rings. Ruth pulled one out of its velvet bed: an enormous solitaire diamond on a platinum band.

'Ah,' said the stall-owner quickly. 'I can tell you've got good taste. That's a beauty, isn't it? Rose cut. Real platinum. It's a treasure.'

Ruth held it up to the light where it glinted, and then brought it down and looked at it closely.

'It's got little black dots in it,' she said, holding it out to the woman. 'Is it supposed to have those?'

'Oh, yes,' the stall owner said. 'It's a sign of a good diamond. It's carbon, you see. Diamonds are made of carbon — it shows it's genuine.'

'It's very pretty,' said Ned. 'Shall we go away and think about it, Ruth?'

They walked out of the market together, Ned laughing.

'What's so funny?'

'I don't know much about diamonds but I do

2

know that you're not supposed to be able to see black dots in them. Diamonds *are* carbon but impurities in them are usually pockets of gas, specks or other minerals. Even I know that you want clarity in a diamond — a diamond that's worth having anyway.'

They came out on to a busy road, the traffic hastening past on its way to the ring roads, one-way systems and car parks of Oxford. They stood for a moment, neither saying anything.

'Let's go to the river,' said Ned, at last.

They walked alongside the speeding traffic holding hands, not bothering to talk against the noise, until they reached Abingdon Road, where the cars, joined by the buses that lumbered down St Aldates, were funnelled away towards the outlying city and the dual carriageways.

They went into Christ Church meadow, where the noise and fumes disappeared into peaceful quiet, and wandered towards the river. A rowing eight, training before term started, slid gracefully past. It was a bright day, blue-skied and sunny, but the first dusting of leaves hinted that summer was past its best. Other visitors wandered with them along the wide paths of the riverbank: parents pushing buggies and calling after racing children; couples holding hands, and tourists who took photographs of the rowers and the distant spires of Christ Church, Merton and Corpus Christi.

Ned and Ruth left them all behind and went to a shadier, cooler path, where the Thames became the Cherwell, dark green with low-hanging branches trailing in quiet waters disturbed only by ducks and the occasional punt. They sat on a bench and held hands.

'That ring,' Ned said, his voice more nervous than Ruth had ever heard it. 'Do you want it? Not that one, of course, with its black dots. But a ring. A diamond ring. Do you want one?'

'What do you mean?' Ruth's voice came out high and shaky as well. She thought she knew what he meant but she needed to hear it plainly. The idea of mistaking his meaning was too hideous to contemplate.

'Well . . . I didn't really mean it to happen this way. I had a big plan that involved restaurants and roses and getting down on one knee, but what the hell . . . ' He grinned. 'I didn't know some woman trying to flog us rings would bring the subject up like this, and now it's here, between us. Ruth . . . '

The look in his eyes made her almost frightened and she had an impulse to put her hand over his mouth, because once he said it there would be no going back.

' . . . I know we've only been together twelve weeks. I know you only moved in to my cottage last week. Your father hardly knows me, and your cat still freezes and runs out when I walk into the room — and that's only the start of it. But I think it's right and I have done from the first moment. I think you do too. You do, don't you?'

He was holding her hand tightly, staring intently at her. His nearness filled her with pleasure but she resisted the urge to hug him. Butterflies spun round in her stomach. 'I do think it's right,' she whispered.

4

'Really, truly right?'

'Utterly and completely right. You know that.'

'So why don't we do it? Make it serious.' He paused. 'Get married.'

A whirling sensation took hold of her, making her feel as though she might topple over. She gasped, clenching her fists. What had he said? *Get married!* Intense delight mingled with something else. *Is this it?* she heard a tiny voice asking. *Are you sure? Is this man really the one you want to marry?* A louder voice in her head began to tell her she must reply. *Well? Which is it? Yes or no?*

She felt as though she was standing on a very high diving board, being beckoned in by someone far below. *Jump!* they were saying. *It's lovely in here. I promise.* But she didn't know if she wanted to jump or not. Once she did, there would be no going back.

She realised now she'd been thinking about marrying Ned almost as soon as she'd met him, and had hoped he would ask her; in fact, she had longed for it. The reality of being asked, though, was quite different. She was frightened even while she was spinning inside with happiness. A tiny part of her wished they could put his question back where it had come from and forget all about it.

'Well?' asked Ned. His face was pale and anxious, and she could feel his hand shaking as he held hers. 'Oh God, I've spoiled everything, haven't I? You look horrified. Appalled. Are you about to be sick?'

'No. And no, you haven't. You couldn't,' Ruth

5

said hastily. 'I'm . . . I'm just amazed . . . ' The tiny voice disappeared. She felt wild, reckless and joyful. *What the hell*, she thought. *I'm going to jump*. 'Of course I will. I can't imagine anything more perfect. I can't imagine being any happier than this.'

★ ★ ★

In a daze they went to a proper jewellers on the High Street, with glittering velvet trays behind grilled windows and a brass bell to ring before they could enter. They chose the white-gold band with the three diamonds and as it fitted, Ruth wore it at once. She'd never owned diamonds before; it was odd to walk down the street and see three of them sparkling on her finger, as though she'd come out shopping in evening dress. She kept expecting to be mugged, or for a stone to drop out, or somehow to break it altogether, so she held her hand stiffly, her gaze falling on the ring every few minutes to make sure it was still safe.

Then they went to the Randolph and drank champagne, grinning stupidly at each other and bursting into disbelieving laughter every few moments at the wonderful, foolhardy, exciting thing they had done.

'I should ring my father,' Ruth said. 'It will make it more real if we tell someone else.' Then she gasped and said anxiously, 'What about your parents? They haven't even met me! What on earth will they think?'

'They'll be thrilled,' Ned said stoutly. 'They'll

6

love you almost as much as I do. It's impossible not to.'

Ruth laughed. 'We're crazy! This is ridiculous.'

'It's not so crazy. We've known each other three months, not three hours. In fact, it's the most sensible thing I've ever done.' He leaned in to kiss her. 'I mean it, Ruth. This is the beginning of a wonderful new life. I just know it.'

'Do you?' She gazed back at him, suffused with happiness. It wasn't a mad mistake, she knew that. All the sadness and difficulties of the past were behind her now. Ned was right — it was the end of the old life and the start of something new.

We're going to be so happy. I can't wait.

2

'Ruth, Ruth!'

Ruth paused on the stairway, rested her basket of patient notes on one knee and leaned over the banister to see who was calling her.

Dr Fletcher was standing below, just outside her consulting room. 'Have you got a moment?'

'Of course.'

The surgery was in the lunchtime lull, when the doors were locked and the staff took a brief respite, like swimmers gulping down air between strokes.

Ruth went back down the rickety old staircase, one of the last original features of the Georgian house that had become the medical practice. No doubt it would soon be removed and replaced with something safer, easier for the sick to climb and less vulnerable to compensation claims. Going into the doctor's room, she saw that Dr Fletcher was already back at her desk, sitting in front of her computer screen and tapping away at the keyboard. She turned round as Ruth entered.

'Hello. Thanks for coming in. Sit down.'

'No problem.' Ruth sat down on the chair by the desk.

The doctor gazed at her. Apart from a faint frown, her face was impassive as usual: smooth, oval and expressionless. Her long slender nose and almost lashless hooded eyes made Ruth think of a Tudor noblewoman.

'Shame we didn't take some pictures at the time,' said Dr Fletcher. She got up and went over. 'You took a bit of a bashing, though, didn't you? But I can't see anything here at all.' She cupped Ruth's chin and turned her face up to the light. The touch was smooth and cooling, a pleasantly soft sensation. 'Poor old you.'

'The bruising disappeared a while ago. I've always been a quick healer and it's been weeks,' replied Ruth. 'Anyway, the shock was the worst bit.' For a while immediately after the attack, she had had a pale tattoo of blue-grey and yellow bruises across her cheekbone, and a dark shadow over her jaw as well. They were tender and hurt to touch but the real pain had been at the time, when the boy had gone for her.

'I'm afraid I'm only just getting round to writing up the report. I wanted to make sure I had it down correctly. We have to tell them why we want the family off the register. It was Michael Petheridge, wasn't it? And you didn't do anything to startle or provoke him, did you?'

'Nothing at all. He went at me when I tried to give him his vaccination.'

She remembered what it was like: how he had squealed with horror when he had seen the syringe. She had just pierced the phial, drawn up the vaccine and squirted a fine line of liquid into the air. The next thing she knew, the syringe was flying out of her hand, skittering across the floor, and she was underneath a barrage of punches, fighting desperately to defend herself.

'He's only ten,' remarked the doctor.

'But you've seen him, haven't you?'

Dr Fletcher nodded. Michael Petheridge was tall and fat, always dressed in his thick puffy winter coat, with a glazed look in his eyes. He had the physique of a fifteen year old, and behavioural problems of some sort — Ruth didn't know the details. His mother had sat, exhausted and dazed from the effort of looking after him, hardly able to intervene until Ruth had screamed at her to stop her son. When Michael had been pulled off, Ruth put a trembling hand to her face, already numb from the blows, as hanks of her hair floated down on to her cardigan.

'We're taking them all off the list,' said Dr Fletcher matter-of-factly.

'Oh.' Ruth's natural sympathy was reawakened. Just after the boy had attacked her, she had hated him. But even with the bruises blossoming on her face, she had started to forgive him for it. He was only a child. His early life, she imagined, was nothing like her own. Perhaps it was ruled by the rioting television and packet food and a broken home, void of the things that she herself valued. She wanted to help people like that, do her bit to make life a little more bearable, perhaps steer them on a path towards something better.

But he hadn't wanted her help. He had battered and hurt her instead. He was like that drunk in Casualty who had thought she'd insulted him and tried to whack her over the head with a chair; or the violent woman spaced out on a strange cocktail of drugs who'd seized her wrist in a grip like nothing she'd ever experienced and wouldn't let Ruth take the shards of glass out of her face — 'they're so pretty,' she had said, the blood flooding into her mouth. And then there was the old lady who had clawed at Ruth's face as she lifted her into bed, and plenty of others. They were the ones who didn't respond the way that was expected when care was needed and offered.

What do you do with people who don't want to be helped? wondered Ruth. What do you do when they reject you?

It was partly the unpredictability of the patients, along with the exhausting shift work and the unending routines of hospital life that had made her apply to become a practice nurse in the first place.

She was relieved that Michael Petheridge and his mother were going to be taken off the register. She didn't want to see them any more. There was nothing more she could offer them.

'Perhaps it's for the best,' she said.

'I heard your news by the way,' said the doctor, smiling. 'Congratulations. You must be thrilled. And look at this!' She took Ruth's hand and turned it over so that she could inspect the ring on her finger. 'Gorgeous.'

Ruth smiled. 'Thank you. It still feels very odd wearing diamonds like this.'

'You'll get used to it.' Dr Fletcher's own egg-shaped emerald set in a surround of diamonds glowed discreetly on her finger, over a chunky platinum wedding ring. 'It's been a bit of a whirlwind romance, hasn't it?'

'A bit. We've been together three months.'

'Goodness. That is quick. But if you're sure, there's no point in waiting, is there?'

'Absolutely.'

'Well, congratulations again. I'm very pleased for you. You'll have to bring your fiancé in to meet us all one of these days. Any ideas yet for the Big Day? I suppose you'll be wanting weeks on end for a honeymoon, will you?'

'I've no idea. We haven't planned anything at all. It's all been very sudden.'

'Well, no need to rush. So — ' The doctor turned back to her computer screen. 'I'll email this report to you. Glance over it and let me know if there are any changes you want to make.'

'Will do,' said Ruth. Her interview was over, she could tell. The doctor was practised at bringing meetings to an end, from years of having to get tenacious patients out of the room and on their way. She stood up and clutched her basket of patient notes. 'Bye then.'

Dr Fletcher, her attention fully on her computer, grunted slightly.

Ruth smiled and slipped out, making her way back to the stairs.

* * *

Ruth pulled into the driveway of the Old Rectory and came to a halt in front of the low windows of the dining room. The lights were on and she could see that the fire was burning in the grate.

She walked round to the back door. 'Dad?' she called as she let herself into the kitchen.

'Through here!'

She followed the sound of his voice through the breakfast room and into the hall.

'Where are you?'

'Down here.'

Ruth noticed that the cellar door was open, the glow of its naked light-bulb illuminating the stairs. She went to the door and looked down into the dusty depths. Her father's face appeared round the side of the stairway, smeared with dirt, a cobweb hanging in his white hair. He grinned at her and wiped his hands on his overalls.

'Hello there, lovey. How are you? How was work?'

'All right. But what on earth are you doing down there? Is something wrong?'

'No, no. It's fine. I'm just assessing some possibilities, that's all.'

'Oh dear.' Ruth frowned. Whenever her father started one of his projects, she felt the same sense of anxiety. The Old Rectory was a fine old house of soft grey stone, leaded windows and beams. It sat on the edge of the village, in the shadow of the much grander new rectory, which now belonged to a multimillionaire who had a helicopter and arrived for weekends in a phut-phut of rotary blades. Beside the new rectory, in a leafy, shaggy courtyard with quaintly mouldering graves and yew trees was the church, and beyond that fields and hedgerows stretched away into the distance. The Old Rectory didn't really need much more than care and mainte-nance, but her father couldn't stop fiddling, changing this and that room, redecorating as the

13

impulse took him, according to his own distinct notions of what looked nice. Ruth had a feeling that her mother, who had been so proud of her pretty home, would not have approved.

'I'll come up,' Silas announced, and the little light-bulb went out abruptly.

He gave her a smacking kiss. 'It's good to see you. I hardly know what you look like these days, with you living miles away in that cottage. How's my girl?'

'I'm fine.'

'How is engaged life?'

Ruth grinned. 'Very nice, thanks.

They went through to the kitchen together. Silas washed his grubby hands in the sink, working up a grey lather enthusiastically. 'Did you see the papers today?' he asked over his shoulder. 'Apparently the health minister has vowed to save fifty thousand lives this year. I'm going to try and get Cordy to pull some strings for me.'

'What?'

'Well, you know. Get my name on the list.' He chuckled at his own joke. 'I'd be rather keen on having the health minister guarantee my survival. Might do wonders for the life assurance premiums.'

'I'm sure if anyone can do it, Cordy can.'

'How's Ned? Where is he tonight?'

'He's gone to a poker tournament with his friend Tom. So it's just me.'

'Ah well,' said Silas with evident satisfaction. 'We'll have to muddle on as best we can without him. Cordy's coming later so it will be just us.'

14

Which is how Dad likes it, thought Ruth, watching him rub his hands dry on the towel. Ever since her mother had died, her father had held on to his two daughters, reluctant to let them go or admit that they were now grown women. When Ruth was eight, her father had produced two typed contracts, one for her and one for Cordelia. They said: 'I promise that I will never grow up but will stay a little girl for ever' and the girls had giggled and signed their names. Sometimes Ruth wondered if her father would one day produce the old contract, signed with her careful felt-tip pen signature, the R of her name given special curly edges, and demand to know why she hadn't kept to it.

'Ned's started gambling, you say?' asked her father. 'He needs to watch that. It's the road to perdition. I've seen men lose the shirts off their backs because of cards and the roulette wheel.'

'Really? Who?' Ruth imagined her father in a casino, draped over the blackjack table in a dinner jacket, watching the action.

'I once saw Arthur Harrison lose a significant sum of money betting on cards.'

'How much?'

'A lot.'

'Ten pounds?'

'Closer to twenty, I'd say.'

Ruth giggled. 'That's scandalous. Don't worry, Dad. I'm sure Ned will be careful.'

'He'd better be. A married man has responsibilities, he can't afford to throw cash about like confetti. Now, you must be hungry. Let's see, what have I got . . . Priscilla came in

15

the other day and left some food for me, so I think there's some of that. I could put it in the oven to heat up. There was lasagne. Fish pie . . . ' Silas opened the fridge and inspected the interior.

Ruth went up and peered in over his shoulder. There were dishes of food uncovered, each one half empty, its remains marked by the scoops of spoons. 'You've already been at them.'

'Oh yes. I heat up whichever one I want, and eat it from the dish. Saves washing up.'

'Then you let it cool down and put it back in the fridge — and then heat it up again?' asked Ruth disbelievingly.

'I don't bother letting it cool. I'd only forget it. I just pop it straight back in here. That will cool it even more quickly, won't it?'

She stared at the half-eaten fish pie. 'Dad, you'll kill yourself! Don't you know that's terribly dangerous? You'll get food poisoning.'

'Will I? Now you mention it, I have been having a dicky tummy rather a lot lately.'

'These have to go.' She grabbed the dishes and marched to the bin to scrape them out. 'Prawns! Good God . . . I bet Mrs Jackson had frozen them too. I can't believe you're still alive to tell the tale.'

'I was looking forward to that fish pie,' said her father gloomily as Ruth consigned the remains to the bin. 'Oh well.'

'I can make you a fresh one. Better still, I'll teach you how to make one.'

'I'll never learn.' Silas sounded determined.

'It's just no good. We men aren't meant to be domesticated.'

Ruth raised her eyes to heaven. She didn't want to have that argument again. Her father was convinced that men were biologically unable to do certain tasks, specifically cleaning, cooking and ironing. Even when she pointed out that soldiers were able to do all those things superbly, he refused to concede he might be wrong. 'Women do it best,' he would say stubbornly. 'They see things that we men just can't.' And he was perfectly content to muddle along, letting his daughters sort him out every now and then, or his widowed neighbour, or anyone who felt like doing the things he considered himself excluded from by virtue of his sex. Mrs Jackson didn't help matters either, thought Ruth. She liked to fuss over Silas, and continually confirmed to him that he was right to be so helpless by telling him he could hardly be expected to look after himself.

'How is Mrs Jackson?' she asked, as she put the dishes to soak in warm water and started looking for something to make for supper.

'Fine, fine. Much as always. Mad as a meat axe, of course. She keeps going on and on about how much weight she's lost. It's ridiculous. She hasn't lost an ounce as far as I can see, she's still enormous. And if she really had lost as much as she insists, she'd be a willow wand by now.'

'Poor Mrs Jackson. She is awfully fat, but she does try hard — I hope you haven't said anything mean.'

'Of course I have. It's much kinder in the long run.'

'Oh, Dad! What did you say?'

'Don't worry, I wasn't cruel. I know you think I'm terribly insensitive but I'm not really. She said, 'Have you noticed that I've lost half a stone since last week?' and I said, 'Priscilla, I haven't noticed. If anything you look fatter. Have you had your scales tested? I think they may have a fault.''

Ruth gasped. '*Dad!*'

Silas laughed. 'Of course I didn't. I said, 'You don't need to lose any weight, Priscilla, and you know what we men are like. You could walk in here a redhead with a boob job next week and I probably wouldn't notice.' I have to be nice to the old girl. She's lost that job, you know.'

'Not another one.' Ruth found some cheese and pasta and thought she might be able to make macaroni cheese if there was only enough milk. That would do for them, anyway.

'Yes, she had a job at Windsor Castle. A guide. Showing people round the chapel or something. Anyway, they sacked her. They found her loitering darkly somewhere after hours. I think she was hoping to get hold of the Queen.'

'What on earth for?'

'No idea. You know how Priscilla gets these crazy schemes. Probably wanted to ask Her Majesty if she thought she'd lost weight or something. Anyway, they won't put up with anything that looks vaguely suspicious these days, so that was it for poor old Priscilla. Out on her ear. She never got to see so much as the hem

18

of Her Majesty's coat disappear round a corner. She's got to think of something else to do. I'm benefiting though. She's been over with lots of food lately.'

'Well, that is good.' Ruth started making their supper. She was glad her father had Mrs Jackson to look in on him, and someone to talk to. Mrs Jackson was not the company she would have chosen for herself, but her father didn't seem to mind. It made her feel better about moving out of home and leaving her father alone.

They chatted while Ruth cooked, and when the supper was ready, they took it into the breakfast room to eat at the table. The dining room table was always covered in too much junk to use.

'Keep some back for Cordy,' said Silas, as Ruth doled out the portions.

'She probably won't come.'

'Yes, she will.'

'It's almost eight-thirty. She's bound to have been held up at the hospital. She'll probably just go back to the flat and crash out. I almost wish she would. I hate to think of her driving here so tired.'

It seemed a long time since Cordelia had looked anything other than exhausted, her pale skin verging on grey with dark purple shadows under her eyes. Her long fair hair was twisted carelessly up and away from her face in a straggly bun, and no matter what time of day, Cordy would be yawning, hungry, stressed and generally complaining about her lot as an over-worked doctor with too many patients, too little time and too few resources. Just looking at her sister made Ruth glad that she had decided to leave the incessant activity of the hospital behind.

'She'll come,' Silas said confidently. 'She's off tomorrow, so I've persuaded her to stay here for the weekend. Get her out of that little rat hole she lives in. Why don't you stay as well?' he suggested hopefully. 'Your old room is ready. You could stay here, we can have a nice breakfast tomorrow and go for a walk. There might be some blackberries out. Heh? Isn't that a good idea?'

He was always trying to get her and Cordy here on their own, together, so that they could do the things they used to do as children. Ruth sighed. 'It sounds lovely, but I can't. We're driving up to York tomorrow to visit Ned's parents and we have to get an early start.'

'Oh. I see. Well, I hope you have a good time.' He frowned into his macaroni cheese.

'Don't sulk. You know I can't just drop everything. I have another life now, other commitments.'

'I know.' Silas looked at her a little mournfully. 'I do try and understand, and I'm happy for you, really I am. But I can't pretend it isn't hard for me to come to terms with the fact that one of my little girls is engaged.'

'Dad, I'm thirty. I'm not a little girl anymore. I haven't lived here for years. You should be more worried about the fact that Cordy is thirty-four and doesn't even have a boyfriend.'

Her father shrugged. 'Cordy's all right.

20

Wedded to her job. So — what are these people like? The Harveys.'

'Haskells.'

'All right then, the Haskells.'

'Well — there's Ned's mother Jackie and his father Steven, who's retired like you. And then there's his sister, Susan. I've not met her but she works in London on a magazine and sounds very glamorous. She's a bit older than him. That's all, really.'

Silas shot her a look. 'You're being very mysterious.'

'I'm not.'

'Yes, you are. You're not being very forthcoming. You haven't said what they're like at all. I'm going to be seeing these Haskell bods at least twice a year from now on, since you've decided to get married. I know what happens next. I'll have to lead Neddy's mother on to the dance floor for the first waltz every time we meet. She'll expect old-fashioned courtesies from me: flowers, chocolates and compliments about her hair. I'll have to buy this Steven drinks and ask him about his fishing and did he see the cricket. You may as well prepare me for the worst right now.'

Ruth played with her macaroni cheese, picking up crescents of pasta on her fork and looking at them. She said at last, 'The thing is, Dad, I haven't actually met them yet. Tomorrow is the first time.'

Silas raised his eyebrows. 'Ned's never taken you home to meet his parents? Not even before he proposed? How extraordinary! So how did he break the news of the engagement?'

21

Ruth said nothing.

'*What?*' exclaimed Silas. 'You mean to tell me that they don't even know? I've put the announcement in *The Times*! It was in on Friday.'

'They don't read *The Times*.'

'And the *Telegraph*.'

'They don't take that either.'

'Oh, well, *that's* all right then. So long as they don't realise that it's only about two hundred thousand people who know about their son's engagement before they do.'

'I don't know what you're so riled about. We wanted to tell them in person, so we're going up to tell them tomorrow.'

'Good of you to fit it in before the actual wedding, I must say. What on earth is Ned thinking of? If either of you girls treated me this way, I don't know what I'd do.'

She flushed and put down her fork. 'Please don't start on Ned, Dad.'

'I don't know what you mean, *start* on Ned. I never say anything bad about Ned at all. I'm just startled by this odd behaviour. It looks a bit suspicious to me, that's all.'

'You don't *say* anything — you just imply it. You know how I feel about him. We're getting married. He's going to be my husband. You might think we're rushing into it, that it's too soon, but we know our minds and it's what we want. The only reason we haven't met his parents before is that it's all happened so quickly and they do live quite far away . . . '

'York is hardly the far end of the universe. It's

22

not even Aberdeen. It's not even Edinburgh.'

'I know,' said Ruth, irritated. 'There are lots of places it's not, but the fact is we haven't managed to get up there. I don't want you to take against Ned, you haven't given him a chance, you really haven't. Please — I want us to be happy.'

Silas didn't say anything for a moment, then his eyes softened and he smiled. 'Little Ruthy. It's all you've ever wanted, isn't it? Everything tidy and nice and safe, and everyone happy. I remember when you were small, tucking your little dollies into their cradles at night and giving them kisses, telling them to sleep tight. That's what you're still like, isn't it?'

'Is it?' She felt overwhelmingly tired suddenly. It all took so much effort, so much strength to try and keep things turning, to keep everything on the straight and narrow. 'Just promise me that you'll be good to Ned. And that when you do meet the Haskells, you won't say anything odd.'

Silas looked wounded. 'You can trust me. I'll be charm itself. Mrs Haskell won't know what hit her.'

★   ★   ★

Cordy arrived very late, breathless and rushing as usual.

'God, sorry. I know, it's abominably late, virtually tomorrow already. I was held up, surprise, surprise. I've been on duty since six this morning. Bastards. Is there anything to eat?'

'In the kitchen,' said Ruth, stretching to kiss

her sister's cheek. She was so much taller than Ruth, and about half the weight.

'I'll put it in the oven,' said Silas importantly, as though the meal would then become of his own making. 'Poor Cordy. They work you too hard.'

Cordy sighed as she slipped off her coat. 'Thank God I'm home. You're not going, are you?'

'I will have to go soon. It's getting late. Ned's due back from his poker thing any minute.'

'And I suppose he expects you to be waiting at the door with his warmed slippers in one hand and a mug of cocoa in the other, does he?'

'No,' Ruth said with exasperation. 'Why is everyone so down on us?'

Cordy raised her eyebrows as she sat down. 'Calm down. It's only a tease. No one's down on you or Ned. What's Dad been saying? Has he been as fabulously tactless as usual? Silly old man.'

'He was down in the cellar when I got here. Assessing possibilities.'

'Ah. That's a danger sign, if I ever heard one. Let's hope it isn't anything like the great triumph that is the upstairs loo.'

Silas's last project had been to convert the little box room at the end of the house into another lavatory — but it was virtually unusable because the huge window was without a blind or frosted glass, meaning that anyone in it was starkly visible to people walking past.

'The postman's never been able to look at me again,' remarked Cordy. 'Ever since we locked eyes when he was walking up the drive and I was sitting on the lav.'

Ruth giggled. 'Mum would have had fifty blue fits.'

'Remember when he planned to paint the beams in the dining room pink?'

'Or clad the study in pine?'

They both laughed.

'Do you think he's all right here on his own?' asked Ruth, after a moment. She couldn't help the residual feeling of anxiety about her father, left over, she supposed, from the time her mother died.

Cordy eased her shoes off and stretched her legs out so that she could warm her toes in front of the fire. 'Of course he is. You mustn't worry about him so much. You've got something much bigger to fret about.'

'Have I?'

'Imagine what Dad's going to say in his wedding speech!' Cordy made a face. 'Another objection to add to my long list for avoiding marriage. Now, where's that dinner? I'm famished.'

★ ★ ★

When she got home, Ned was already in bed, warm and sleepy.

'You're late,' he said, yawning, as she came in and started undressing.

'Sorry. Knock-on effect. Cordy was late.'

He pulled the duvet tighter round his shoulders. 'We've got an early start tomorrow. So

25

we miss the traffic.'

'Don't worry, I'll be fresh as a daisy and twice as cheerful.' She went over and sat on the edge of the bed. He turned his face up for a kiss. 'I'm quite excited about it now. Do you think they'll like me?'

'They'll adore you.' Ned tugged at her skirt from under the duvet. 'Come on, get into bed. I want you in here with me.'

'All right, won't be a moment. Did you win, by the way?'

'Oh, yes.' Ned grinned up at her. 'I haven't quite paid off the ring. But give me time. Tom and I are unbeatable together. We thrashed them.'

3

Three months earlier, Ruth had gone to Valentina's party not expecting her life to be transformed in the bar of a noisy drinking joint just off Queen Street. She'd been single for two years and had become accustomed to bowling along on her own, not worrying much about men. Her last relationship had become stifling and dull, and after it ended, she enjoyed the freedom of being able to please herself. The pleasure of being in control of her life was not something she wanted to trade in for anything run of the mill, so she kept the leerers and drunken chatter-uppers at a distance. She was tired of trying to make boring men feel interesting and then fretting about whether or not they liked her.

She stood in the middle of the crowded bar, wishing she hadn't come. It was packed and buzzing with the din of voices raised over pounding music. Everybody seemed to be holding cigarettes and a smoky fug hovered near the ceiling.

I don't recognise anyone, she thought. I could have stayed at home.

But Valentina was one of her nursing pals: they'd been through college and then on the wards together, so Ruth had to show her face. She wished she hadn't spent so long getting ready, putting on her favourite mermaid-green satin top over jeans, sliding her feet into high cork wedges, and applying shimmery eye shadow, mascara to thicken her lashes to a dark brown, and pale baby-pink lipgloss. It seemed like a waste of time now.

I'll look for Valentina, she decided, and fought her way past backs and elbows until she found the birthday girl. Valentina was dressed in a sparkly flesh-coloured wisp of chiffon over tiny white hotpants and high heels that showed off her long brown legs. In one hand she clutched a long glass with three straws poking out of the top and in the other was a cigarette that she waved about as she talked to the man beside her.

'Valentina, happy birthday,' Ruth called over the din.

'Ruthie, *darling*! I'm so glad you came, thank you, thank you.' Valentina swooped to kiss her, smearing lip gloss over Ruth's cheek. 'God, I'm so glad you're here. You must meet . . . um . . . ' She gestured at the man she was talking to. 'He's a friend of Jeff's, they play rugby together. Now,' she said as conspiratorially as she could over the thud of the background noise, 'you two are the cleverest, most charming people in here so you're bound to get on like a house on fire.'

With that, Valentina turned on one stiletto heel and tottered off as she sucked alternately on a straw and her cigarette.

Ruth swore mentally. *Bloody hell. I hate it when she does that*. It was Valentina's least appealing habit. When she didn't want to be bothered with someone, she would do 'the dump': introduce them to a complete stranger

28

with whom they had little or nothing in common, and then walk off.

Irritation prickled through her as she tried to summon brightness and enthusiasm. She was stuck for at least five minutes before she could get away, so she might as well get on with it. *Blast. I don't even have a drink to numb the pain.* 'So, you know Jeff?' Being a friend of Valentina's boyfriend was hardly a recommendation, considering Jeff was a serious meathead, who had little interest in anything but cars, beer and rugby.

'A slight overstatement,' said the man with a smile. 'Last week, during the usually tame and gentle Saturday rugby on the common, a man mountain tackled me with the kind of ferocity I haven't encountered since our school made the terrible mistake of agreeing to a rugby tour in New Zealand. Once I'd recovered consciousness, reset my nose and picked up the teeth scattered round me, he introduced himself as Jeff and by way of apology invited me to this party.'

Ruth felt herself relax a little. *He can talk,* she thought, and then felt nervous. Valentina must have been right — he was probably clever. And now he would think she was clever too, because Valentina had said so, and the two of them would be locked into some kind of *University Challenge* as she struggled to prove that she was worthy of Valentina's description.

What should I do? Discuss how oxbow lakes are formed? Start listing all the kings and queens of England?

'I understand Jeff and Valentina are a couple,' he said politely.

'In a manner of speaking. They certainly do a lot of coupling,' replied Ruth. 'But I don't know if they'll last the distance. I think they exhausted all of Jeff's mental resources some time ago.'

The man laughed. 'How do you know Valentina?'

'We did our training together.'

He looked blank. 'As what?'

'Nurses. We trained in the same hospital. But I'm a surgery nurse in a GP practice now.'

'Oh — a nurse.' He raised his eyebrows with interest.

Ruth waited. Would he make some kind of leering remark about her uniform? Or say 'oooh, Matron' suggestively? They so often did.

'Well, I think you're fabulous — '

'That's very sweet, considering you've only just met me . . . '

'No — all of you. Nurses. You're terrific. My mother was ill last year and the nurses did such a fantastic job. You're all national heroes as far as I'm concerned.'

'That's nice. Better than the reaction I usually get when people find out I'm a nurse. You'd be surprised how many people ask if I wouldn't mind taking a quick look at their sore leg, or waxed-up ear, or the suppurating wound they've got on their side.'

'Don't worry,' he replied. 'There's nothing wrong with me . . . except, now you mention it, I've got a bit of a blister from rugby which seems to be filling with some kind of clear liquid, so if you've got a moment . . . ' He lifted his foot and started peeling down his sock. Then he grinned at Ruth's expression. 'Only kidding. What's your name?'

'Ruth.'

'Ruth,' he repeated slowly, as though trying it out for size. 'That's nice. Ruth. I'm Ned. Why don't we get you a drink, and find a place where we can talk?'

★ ★ ★

That was Ned. He told her that he was an engineer — 'not fixing things, or building them, I design them' — and that he lived in his own cottage in a village on the outskirts of Oxford. His parents lived near York, which was where he'd grown up, along with his older sister. He worked hard but loved sport, which at first made her worry that he'd be one of those dull men who could only talk about football, but it turned out he was passionate about many other things as well: films, books and music, especially indie bands like Belle & Sebastian — 'I see them in concert whenever I can. I may play rugby but I've got an arty, camp little flower-arranging fellow inside me desperate to get out'.

Ruth liked that. 'What made you move down here? Didn't you want to live near your parents?' she asked.

'Not really. After university, my friends all moved round here so I came too.'

'All your friends?' she said, surprised.

'There's a bunch of us, a little set. I don't

mean everyone I've ever met — that would be silly.' He grinned. 'Most people move to London after university, and carry on their friendships there. We happen to have all decided we didn't want to do that. Well, Tom decided — he's my oldest friend — and chose Oxford as the place to be, and then Jeremy got a place at the uni to do a D. Phil, so the rest of us kind of tagged along.'

'Do you like it here?'

He thought for a minute and then nodded. 'Yeah — I really do. I've never craved the city lifestyle. I like the fresh air too much. I thought I'd find the south a bit too soft, but I've got used to it now. The price of beer still depresses me, but apart from that it's all right. What about you? Where are you from?'

'I'm sharing a flat with a friend in Summertown. I've always lived round here — I grew up about thirty miles away from Oxford. I don't know why I haven't moved elsewhere. It just seems to have worked out that way.' As she said it, she knew that it hadn't been as random as she made it sound; she had on some subconscious level decided to stay near her father, driven by a strong obligation to look out for him now that he was on his own. When Cordelia went to Cambridge to read medicine, Ruth had felt the responsibility to stay close to home. It was why she had decided to do her nursing degree at Oxford Brookes, studying the practical at the John Radcliffe Hospital before taking up a job on the wards there. In case Ned thought her boring, she added quickly, 'It's not that I don't like to travel, and I've been to

France and the States and things like that. I had a plan once to nurse abroad for one of the aid organisations, going to trouble spots and helping the people there. Perhaps I still will.'

'Why did you want to be a nurse?'

'Oh, you know — the urge to help others. That idealistic fervour you have as a teenager. Actually . . . ' she paused for a moment and then said, 'if you want to know the truth, it's because I saw the nurses who looked after my mother when she was ill. They were so kind and patient with her. They gave her the tenderness and care she needed, and they comforted her, even at the end when she knew she was about to die. I wanted to be like that. You know — hold people's hands in the dark hours.' She smiled nervously.

Ruth hardly ever told people she'd just met that her mother was dead; she'd discovered that their reaction — awkwardness or embarrassment or a kind of over-wrought grief on her behalf — made her uncomfortable and left her feeling untouched, as though they were all faking something.

Ned frowned and said, 'That must have been terrible for you.' He waited for her to continue if she wanted to.

'It was. A very bad time. I was only thirteen when she died.' She felt that vague uncomfortableness again, as if she were pretending or telling a lie. It was as though she felt she ought to burst into tears or fall down fainting at the very mention of a dead mother, and that if she didn't, she must have not really cared.

She *had* cared, of course. At times she had felt ripped open by the awful grief, but she had worked very hard at subduing it, pushing it far inwards where it couldn't hurt her. In the end, she had succeeded in making it go away.

'It's always tough at that age,' she said lightly, not wanting the atmosphere between them to get too gloomy. 'Most of my friends seemed to have such carefree lives. You know, worrying what they looked like, or whether their allowance would last till the end of the month, or if some boy would ask them out — as though the world would end if he didn't. I really envied them, because it wasn't like that at home. It was a pretty miserable place, as you can imagine.'

She had a sudden flashback to that time, as vivid and immediate as if it had just happened: darkness and closed doors, with her father and sister shut in their rooms closeted away in their own private grief while her mother lay in the ward, wasting away. Laughter, games and noise stopped abruptly and home became full of silence and secrets, as Ruth wondered what she could do to fix the huge and terrible thing that had engulfed them all.

'It must have been a lot to cope with,' Ned said. 'You were very young, weren't you?'

'I got older pretty quickly. Someone had to keep everything going and my dad and sister weren't in the mood. I just tried to make things a bit easier for everyone, I suppose.'

'And now you're a nurse.'

Ruth put on a saintly expression. 'My mission is to heal the sick,' she said in a hushed, nun-like voice. 'And lighten the suffering of others.'

Ned laughed. 'Well, you put me to shame. I spent most of my teenage years being depressed without even having a decent reason for it. I was keen on very melancholy music and penning dire poems about the misery of modern life. I wore a lot of black, sulked around the rec in the holidays, kicking stones and watching people go by while I listened to my walkman. If I'd known you, I could have given you some good sounds to get depressed to. And you'd have been very welcome to my mother.'

'Don't you get on?'

'Oh, well — yes, we get on. She's all right, in her way. We're not all that close, to be honest. I always felt a bit uneasy after the time I asked her what she would do if the nuclear sirens went off with the three-minute warning. It was on our minds a lot in the mid-eighties, do you remember? I was about twelve, I'd read *When the Wind Blows* and frightened myself silly worrying about the bomb. My mum said that when she heard the sirens, she'd march me and my sister out into the road and cut our throats.'

Ruth gasped. 'Really? Why?'

'So we wouldn't have to suffer the after-effects of a nuclear strike, I assume. It was just that extra detail about marching us out that got me. You know, the sirens go off; Mum opens the knife drawer and takes out the big one Dad used for roasts, then thinks, 'It may be a nuclear bomb but there's no point in ruining the kitchen floor. I'll butcher the children in the road'.'

'Perhaps it was so she could be sure of you

getting fried in the blast if the throat cutting didn't work.' Ruth thought for a second. 'But what if it was a false alarm?'

'Exactly my worry. That, and why she didn't cut her own throat and let me take my chances.'

Ruth stared at him for a moment, and he smiled at her. Then they both started to laugh, and the next minute they were both caught up in a fierce fit of the giggles that shook them uncontrollably. The moment one fit seemed to subside, Ruth only had to catch Ned's eye to start laughing again, until tears were running down her face.

'Oh dear,' she gasped, wiping her cheeks. When she looked at him, he was grinning back, his body leaning towards her and his whole face transformed by a smile. She stared at him with the strangest feeling growing in her, making her slightly dizzy and shaken. *Perhaps it's lack of oxygen from all the laughing*, she thought. Ned's face almost seemed to glow, his eyes bright and his smiling mouth growing sweeter and sweeter. She glanced over at her wine glass, wondering how much she'd had to drink and if this was drunkenness catching her unawares. Then, as warmth crept upwards from her stomach, she felt more elated than she had for a long time.

When Valentina came over to their table, flushed and swaying on her high heels, to tell them that everybody was going on to a club and would Ruth and Ned come too, Ruth was startled to see that the press of bodies had gone and that the bar was almost empty. The barman was ushering people out and locking doors behind them. In an instant, she imagined scenarios between her and Ned — heads close over more drinks at the club, dancing together, maybe kissing in a taxi.

'I won't come,' he said.

All of Ruth's pleasant imaginings vanished.

'I might head off as well,' she said, hiding her disappointment and wondering where she would find a cab.

For a moment, her statement hung in the air. There was the distinct possibility that they would now go their separate ways and that all the potential that had been building up would now dissipate, like unused energy. But then he said casually, 'Why don't we go and find some dinner?' and after that, there was no question of their going separate ways ever again.

★　★　★

'Ruth, are you in love?' asked her father accusingly down the telephone.

She blushed furiously even though there was no way her father could see Ned's naked back as he lay asleep in her bed.

'Why do you say that?' she asked, pulling the bedroom door to, so that her conversation wouldn't wake him.

'So you are. It's a good thing you never decided to be a lawyer, you'd be hopeless. Everyone knows 'why do you say that?' means 'yes, you are absolutely right but I don't want to admit it'. I'll tell you exactly why I say that. I have irrefutable evidence. One, you haven't called or visited for weeks — '

'Dad! I phoned on Tuesday!'

' — and two, your flatmate told me.'

'What did she tell you?' Ruth cursed Lizzy's big mouth.

'Just that you've been closeted with some man in your room for a fortnight now, and you never come out except to beam rapturously and request tea, biscuits and so forth.'

'That's not strictly true . . . '

'But it sounds as though it might be quite close to the mark.'

'Well . . . ' She held the phone close to her mouth. She'd been so reluctant to talk about it. She feared it would be like trying to describe a dream: all the radiance and magic would be lost and she would be left with something incomprehensible and rather boring to anyone else. She didn't want this precious new thing exposed to the harsh light of day before it was ready, in case it sickened and died. But another part of her, the part that was dancing with excitement, was desperate to share it as well, and to say, 'The most amazing miracle has just happened! I've fallen in love! Not just ordinary, boring fancying someone, or liking them, or having a laugh, or the things that other people have, but proper love, like books and poems and songs tell you. The kind that just doesn't happen every day — and it's more wonderful than I could have imagined.'

'His name's Ned,' she said at last, aware of how inadequate it sounded, and wishing she knew how to say what she meant.

'Ned.' Her father was silent for a moment. 'As in Sea-goon?'

'That's Neddy.'

'Ned, Neddy. Oh well.' He sighed heavily. 'I suppose I shall never see you again. You'll be spending all your time with this Neddy.'

'Of course you'll see me again. In fact, I want you to meet Ned.'

'Really?' Silas sounded suspicious. 'You said you weren't going to introduce me to any more boyfriends after the last one.'

'Rob didn't really get your sense of humour. He didn't like the way you made up little rhymes about him. Very few people appreciate your terrible jokes, I'm afraid.'

'But this Neddy is up to it, is he?'

'Yes, he is,' said Ruth, and felt her stomach tighten deliciously as she remembered how.

When she went back into the bedroom, Ned was still asleep but on his side now, his eyelashes curling on his cheek and his cherub's mouth half open. She climbed in beside him, shaping herself to the length of his back, and running her hand over his smooth skin. The warm scent of his flesh and the muskiness under his arms aroused her; she put a leg over his and ran her hand round to his stomach.

He breathed in deeply, opened his eyes, and turned over. 'Hi, darling,' he said in a fuzzy, morning voice. 'Have you been up?'

'My dad phoned. He's complaining that I haven't been round for a bit. I know it's horribly soon, but I wondered if you wanted to come home and see the Old Rectory and meet my quaint old father.' She squeezed the firm curve of his bottom. 'Has that put you off? Is it too fast?'

He took her hand and kissed the fingertips. 'Of course it isn't. I'd love to meet your dad. But not today. Today, I want to spend the whole time in bed with you. I reckon we can fit in at least three bouts of delicious sex before lunch.' He kissed her mouth, pulling her in to his bed-warm body.

'We never get out of bed,' she said giggling.

'I know. Great, isn't it?'

The experience of being so entirely at ease with someone she had only just met was strange to Ruth. Her previous relationships had been marked by a kind of agonising diplomacy, in which she tried to work out what her lover was really thinking and stay one step ahead of him, while worrying endlessly about her looks, her body and her sexual performance.

But this was different. From the very start, she had utter trust in Ned and what they had. For the first time, she didn't fret about whether he thought her bottom too big, or her nose too long or her knees too bony. She knew that he found her beautiful and irresistible, and that he'd fallen in love with her; she understood it because she felt the same. She didn't see any flaws in him, but a wonderful miracle of skin and body and scent that pleased her in every way.

It had burst upon both of them with the force of a storm but, rather than battering them with passion, their love had come like a beatific light, to calm them and illuminate their lives with happiness. For Ruth, this love didn't fill her with fear of being used or abandoned, as previous relationships had, but with completeness. She had faith that nothing that happened now could possibly change what he felt for her, or she for him, so she could risk taking him home and introducing him to her family. It occurred to her that Ned might even be more important to her than home.

* * *

She had nothing to worry about: the visit to the Old Rectory was a success. Ned loved the house and her father was on excellent form. Other than insisting on saying 'Aah, Neddy' in a languid Peter Sellers drawl every now and then, he was charm itself and nothing less than welcoming. In fact, he seemed to take great pleasure in the company of another man and more than anything else, tried to keep Ned to himself.

'You'll be interested in this, Ned. Come along and take a look,' he'd say, though there was no reason to think Ned would be any more interested in how to fit tongue-and-groove or install a wall heater than anyone else. He took Ned out for a long and intensive tour of the garden while Ruth cooked the Sunday lunch. As she scrubbed the potatoes, she watched them inching their way round the vegetable patch, her father pointing out sites of special interest, such as the compost heap.

She dropped a potato in the sink, struck by a sense of wholeness. A warmth suffused her. This feeling is close to perfect happiness, she realised: having Ned here in the home I love. And with my father here too. It feels right. I wonder why I didn't notice before how hollow I felt.

After her mother died, Ruth had felt the others' pain almost more than her own. She hadn't been able to bear seeing her father cry, or Cordy alone, hunched over on the bench at the bottom of the garden. She'd tried her best to fill the terrible gap, caring for her father and sister in the only way she knew — by imitating her mother. It had never worked, though, no matter how hard she tried; it made no difference how many meals she cooked or how often she cleaned the house, how much laundry she did, or even when she put her mother's favourite flowers in a vase in the sitting room and made scones for afternoon tea; there was always the sense of something vital missing. Her father and Cordy never turned round, as she'd half hoped they might, and said, 'Oh now we don't mind about Mummy dying because Ruth is here to make everything all right', and so she went on with the same agonising sense of trying her best and failing.

Now, though, she understood that trying to fill her mother's place was never going to work. The real answer was to create a new family and forge new bonds. It made sense to stop seeing her father as the parent and herself as the eternal child. It was her turn to be a grown-up now. She would relinquish the old pattern and adopt a new one, and she and Ned would be the beating heart of it, nourishing the others with their

42

warmth and power.

She plunged her hands back into the cold water and scooped up another potato from the murk, as she began to sing to herself.

⋆   ⋆   ⋆

'When are we going to see your parents?' she asked idly as they lay in bed in Ned's cottage on Sunday morning. They had been engaged for a week now, and Ned hadn't told his parents the news. It was very strange, she thought. Of course, not all families lived by the same rules, and her own voluble, joky family had its areas of silence — perhaps this was one of Ned's. All the same . . . an engagement! It was unusual, surely, not to tell them at once, even if it was only over the phone. And it seemed unfair on the Haskells, leaving them out of all the fun when her own family had had the pleasure of finding out at once, not to mention actually knowing Ned beforehand. When they broke the news, Silas and Cordy had reacted perfectly, with delighted kisses and hugs for them both. Silas broke open a bottle of his very special vintage champagne and insisted on sending a notice to the newspapers. It felt wrong that the Haskells were still living in ignorance. But it was up to Ned, and he insisted that he wanted to tell them in person.

He had twined a lock of her auburn hair round his finger and was inspecting it closely. 'Your hair is such an amazing colour,' he murmured. 'Brown and red and orange and gold all mixed up together. Look at the way it glints in the light.'

'It'll be grey soon, especially with the stress of sorting out your awful mess. Ow,' she said, as he yanked it softly.

'I suppose you want to sort me out — tidy me up. You'll be looking up spells in your mad old books. Three cupfuls of vinegar, a ladleful of bicarbonate of soda, a lemon, some kittens' tails, eye of newt, toe of frog . . . '

'A little respect if you please. My collection of vintage housekeeping books happens to be very interesting *and* useful.'

'Vintage!' Ned laughed. 'You mean old.'

'Come on, you've got to admit this place is a bit insalubrious. My old ward sister would have a fit if she could see the state of your bathroom. *Germs, Nurse Blackiston! Banish, banish, banish!* When did you last clean it?'

'I'm very busy,' he replied obstinately.

'Watching television. Playing rugby.'

'Housework is boring . . . '

'But necessary.'

'Don't go on. You remind me of my mother. Mess never hurt anyone.'

'I'm not talking about mess, I'm talking about fungal growths. Very different altogether.' She looked at him curiously. 'Do I really remind you of your mother?'

Ned gazed up at her. 'No. You don't. You're nothing like her, to be honest.'

'Hmm, is that a good thing or a bad thing? I'm not sure. You don't seem terribly keen to go home and see your parents though, so maybe it's a good thing. So, come on then — stop avoiding the issue. When are we going to meet them?'

'The problem is . . . ' he untwined her hair and pulled her to him, 'I don't think I can stand the four-hour drive without jumping into bed with you. That's why planning has been so difficult. I'm going to have to demand my conjugal rights immediately before we leave and as soon as we get back, or I'm not answerable for the consequences.'

He kissed her hard and then gazed at her. She liked the intimacy of being so close, of being able to see the hazel specks inside his green eyes. How many other people had seen him, really *seen* him, as she had, so that she knew exactly the sprinkling of freckles on his arm and the patterning of the hair in his brows and the way his lashes curled out just so? Who else knew the beauty and warmth of his sweet smell, or that he had such exceptionally pretty feet? *Only me*, she thought happily. Ned had told her about a couple of ex-girlfriends but they didn't matter now. There wasn't anyone else who could feel this kind of connection with him, not in the way she did, just as there was no other man who'd grown as close to her as Ned had done.

'Actually,' he said slowly, 'I thought we could go up next Saturday, if you're free.'

'Of course I am. I'd love to go. The sooner the better, really.' She laughed. 'It's about time.'

She was curious about Ned's family, all the more so because of their absence from his life. There were no photographs of them in the cottage, and no clues at all to what they were like. The phone had often rung when Ruth was there, and Ned had taken it upstairs, emerging a while later to say, 'Just my mother' but adding nothing more.

The only photographs in the house showed Ned and his friends, the same five faces captured over time and in different combinations, subtly changing and ageing. In the loo, there were large clip frames filled with montages of holiday snaps and party photographs. One, in the centre of a large frame, showed them all lying on snowy ground in a circle, the tops of their woolly-hatted heads touching in the centre: four men and one woman, whose dark curly hair was escaping from under her hat. They were smiling broadly into the camera, with cheeks and noses flushed from the cold.

Who took the photograph? wondered Ruth, staring at it. Ned looked the same but his younger face had different and unfamiliar angles.

'Who are these people?' she asked, climbing back into bed, holding the clip frame. 'Are these the famous friends I've heard so much about?'

'Uh huh.' Ned sat up, pushing one of his pillows behind his back. 'That's them.' He pointed at a couple of photographs showing them sitting on a river bank on a summer's day. 'We went for a picnic not far from Tom's house. That's Tom.' He pointed to a fair man. 'We were at school together. Best friends. In some ways it's strange we should be so close, we're from very different backgrounds. My parents worked and saved like mad to send me to a private boarding school; Tom ended up there because he hadn't

46

got into Eton, Winchester or Radley. He's very stubborn. The more they told him to work for his Common Entrance, the less he could be bothered. So he turned up at my school.' Ned pointed at the other figures. 'This is Jeremy. Scary and brilliant. And this is Luke. Also brilliant but much less scary. And me.'

'A bunch of clever boys. And who's this?' Ruth pressed her fingertip on to the image of the girl sitting cross-legged on the grass. She was slender, her hair falling loose about her neck in heavy curls. She wore jeans and a vest top; her bare pale shoulders were hunched over, with her hands tucked under her thighs. She was laughing, her eyes closed and mouth wide in silent glee.

'Oh. That's Erin.'

'The only girl allowed?'

Ned laughed. 'Maybe. The only girl who could be bothered with all of us.'

'Why? Were you freaks?' They looked quite normal to her.

Ned shrugged. 'A bit insular, maybe. Not that keen on outsiders.'

'How did you all meet?'

'Ah, the fateful moment. When we got to university, Tom and I decided to develop our theatrical sides, after he'd made a sensation as Miranda in the school production of *The Tempest*.' He pointed at Tom's blond fringe. 'Girly hair, you see. And he looked pretty good in a dress, I have to admit. Some of the sixth form were quite flustered by him. I'd had stunning success as the master of the ship with my line, 'Good, speak to the mariners: fall to't yarely, or we run ourselves aground: bestir, bestir'. After that, I was hungry for more — for a part with more than two lines, anyway. So the two of us bowled up to a Fresher amateur dramatics club run by a very camp young man called Alasdair, and were promptly put into a little group to improvise a playlet. I can't remember exactly what we did — something painfully predictable, I think. A spoof Noel Coward or something. The others in our group were Luke — he's the short one — and Jeremy and Erin. And we kind of gelled. You know how you're supposed to spend your second and third years at uni trying to drop the friends you made in your first week . . . it wasn't like that for us. We got closer and closer. We went on holiday together — as you can tell from all the photos — shared flats, went out, did more plays, you name it . . . '

'And now you even live in the same part of the world, more than ten years later. That's amazing. I can't think of many groups of friends who are that dedicated to each other. Fran, my best friend from college, moved to Manchester about six months ago — it never occurred to me to go with her.'

'Is it that strange? I know plenty of people who keep in touch. Anyway, you have lots of friends around here — all those nurses you know.'

'But that's because I've always lived here, and the girls I met at college stayed on to work in the Radcliffe because that's the way the system works. It's not quite the same deciding to move en masse to the same town.'

'We're not in the same town. Luke and his wife Abigail live over the other side of Oxford. Jeremy's in digs in Walton Street. Tom and Erin are down the road in the next village. If we all have to move apart, I suppose we will. It just suits us at the moment.'

Ruth looked at the photograph again. 'So Tom and Erin ended up together?'

Ned nodded.

'When am I going to meet these best friends of yours?'

Ned pushed the clip frame away, and turned towards her, nuzzling in to her shoulder. 'I want to keep you to myself for as long as I can,' he said playfully, and softly bit the skin on her arm. 'I don't want to share you with anyone.'

4

They got up early on the Saturday morning for the trip to York. Ned was stern-faced and silent because, Ruth assumed, he was intent on the journey. She sensed that it was important that they weren't late and that everything should go as smoothly as possible.

In the shower she looked at her engagement ring, the hot water bouncing off the white diamonds, wondering if perhaps she should take it off for this first visit. It seemed a little presumptuous, or too obvious a reminder that the bargain with Ned was signed and sealed with a ring, without the need of approval from his parents. It was a potent symbol of how late in the day they were being allowed in to the proceedings.

I'll take it off, decided Ruth. *To be on the safe side*.

Back in the bedroom, wrapped in her towel, she slid it off and put it on the chest of drawers. Her finger, which had seemed so overdressed for the past few days, now looked naked, and she didn't like that. The idea of leaving the ring sitting there all day without her was not appealing either, so she put it back on. *I'll take it off later*.

It still felt unbelievable that she was engaged to be married at all. Once she had accepted Ned's proposal, things began to take on their own life. An outside force had become involved against which she was powerless, the force of tradition and expectation, of simply *what one does*. They had the ring, but that was just the start of it all: there suddenly seemed to be a million things to organise if they really were going to do this peculiar thing and get married.

She got dressed in the bedroom, watched by Maisie, her elderly tabby cat, who was curled up on the bed, licking a paw from time to time.

'How do I look, puss?' Ruth asked, as she turned in front of the mirror to examine her reflection. Sensible and respectable, she hoped, in a plain black skirt, shirt and lacy cardigan with a ribbon round the waist. Too demure? Too boring? It was so hard to know when she had no sense at all of the people she was about to meet.

When she'd tried to picture Ned's family, Ruth had taken the few details he'd given her and fleshed them out with her own imaginings. They had always lived outside York, and had had aspirations for him, Ned said, working hard to send him to a private school, which had almost ironed out his accent to standard public-school RP, but had left him his short 'a' and 'o'. He had been the first in his family to go to university. Ruth imagined his parents as good hearted and industrious, full of homely wisdom and warmth. Unconsciously, she had attributed to Ned the background she would have liked him to have; she envisioned a bright and cheerful home, rich with the scent of home-cooking. His parents she cast as stalwarts of the local community, Jackie red-cheeked and plump, capable and cheerful, wearing an apron to the shops. Steven she saw as perhaps a local magistrate or bank manager, respectable and respected. The sister, Susan, was plain, a duller version of Ned's solidity, spinsterish and librarianish, conveniently out of the way in London.

'Ruth, are you ready? We have to get going,' shouted Ned from downstairs.

'Coming!' she called back. She took a deep breath and gave the cat one last stroke. 'Wish me luck, Maisie.'

★ ★ ★

On the motorway, as the car smoothly covered the miles between Oxford and York, the apple-cheeked mother and the rose-covered cottage began to appear more and more ridiculous. Of course it wouldn't be like that.

'Tell me what they're like,' Ruth said, glancing at Ned as he drove. 'I need to be prepared.'

He only shrugged. 'You might as well make up your own mind now. There's only another hour to go and then you'll meet them for yourself. Whatever I say will be wasted.'

'Come on. What should I expect?'

Ned said nothing.

'I don't understand,' exclaimed Ruth good-humouredly. 'You always tell me everything. They can't be that bad, can they?'

Ned looked exasperated as he stared ahead at the road. 'I don't know what you want me to say,' he snapped. 'For crying out loud. I didn't ask you for a full report on your family, did I? I

52

just waited to see what they were like. Can't you leave it?'

Ruth retreated into herself, hurt. They never quarrelled or argued and, until now, harsh words between them were unknown. She watched cars slide past as Ned overtook them, and they carried on in silence.

★ ★ ★

The house stood on smooth tarmac in a curve of other identical modern brick houses. In front of it was a long green lawn with perfectly shaped borders and round cuts around the base of trees. The grass was so perfect that Ruth almost expected to see a sign telling people to keep off it. The little border plants, each with a stretch of dirt between it and the next, had small pink flowers and purple shiny leaves, only just distinguishable from the brown soil.

They walked up to the front door.

Ruth felt her mouth dry with nerves. She clutched the bag she was carrying a little harder and squeezed Ned's hand.

'Don't worry, you'll be fine,' he said.

'You won't leave me on my own, will you? I should have brought some flowers or something.'

'It'll be all right.' He rang the door bell, which sounded two long descending chimes. A shadow approached the frosted glass panel and Ruth smiled broadly in preparation.

The door opened and a woman put her head round it slowly, almost timidly. Ruth was surprised. She hadn't realised that she'd drawn such a complete mental picture of Ned's mother until she saw her now. The real thing was completely different to what she had expected. The woman in front of her was short and slim, wearing neutral clothes: navy trousers, a white shirt and a cardigan. Her hair was dyed but not garishly: it was a honey blonde with silvery lights, carefully blow-dried under into a smooth bob that curled inwards to her chin. She had round, brown eyes and wore a small set of spectacles with an almost invisible titanium frame. When her gaze landed on Ruth, it was vulnerable and questioning.

'You must be Ruth,' she said, in a small, soft voice. Then she looked at Ned, a broad smile creasing her face. 'Hello, son.'

'Mum.' He leaned forward and kissed her on the cheek.

'Hello, Mrs Haskell,' Ruth said, politely, wondering if she should try and kiss her as well.

Ned's mother stood back into the shadow of the hall. 'Come on then,' she said, 'you'd better come in.'

As they went down the hall, Ned's mother said, 'You must excuse the state of the place.'

Ruth couldn't understand what she meant. She had rarely been in a place so tidy. Side tables stood along the hallway, each holding a little collection of photographs and china ornaments. Pictures in gilt frames were hung at careful intervals. They passed a glass cabinet full of little dolls in national dress that looked as though they were frozen dancing cheerfully to inaudible music.

'This is the lounge,' said Ned's mother as she led the way into a large room towards the back of the house.

'It's lovely,' said Ruth. She felt a little cold and imperceptibly shook her shoulders. 'What a beautiful home you have.'

It was, like the hallway, pristine and carefully arranged. The furniture was heavy and matching, covered in a beige damask with fringing around each arm and wing. Contrasting cushions were artfully placed in thick piles on each seat, as if to dissuade anyone from sitting on them. The carpet was also pale, the kind daring you to drink a cup of coffee or a glass of red wine, or to wear shoes on it straight after a walk. The curtains too were fringed, draped and pelmeted, held back by large tasselled ties. Round side tables covered in beige silk displayed more photographs; Ruth caught a glimpse of Ned in his graduation robes. A crystal chandelier with several tiers of glass drops hung from the centre of the ceiling. There were more cabinets full of jewel-coloured glasses and tea sets, and a huge, gilt, twirl-edged mirror hung over the gas fire.

'I do my best,' said Mrs Haskell in her soft voice. 'It is hard to keep it nice, but it does matter to me. Do you really like it?' She sounded almost anxious.

'Yes, I do,' Ruth answered firmly. 'You've made it look lovely.'

They took their places, sitting stiffly on the unyielding cushions. 'Would you like tea?' Mrs Haskell asked. 'We'll have lunch soon but I imagine you'd like a cup of tea after that drive.'

'Oh yes,' Ruth said quickly and with a kind of forced jolliness she sometimes used with patients. She could tell that she was holding herself unnaturally and longed for the awkwardness of the meeting to wear off so that they could all relax.

'Steven!' Jackie bellowed, making Ruth jump. 'Steve! Bring the tea!'

A moment later, a tall, plain man with a grey moustache, wearing grey trousers and a white shirt, wandered in carrying a folded tea tray.

'Hi, Dad,' Ned said, with a smile.

'Hello there, son,' said Steven Haskell, looking as though he hadn't expected to see Ned in the lounge at all, but was pleased with the surprise. 'How are you?'

'Good, good. Yeah, I'm fine. And you?'

'Oh — I'm well. Nothing wrong with me.'

'This is Ruth,' Ned said, gesturing at her. She sat bolt upright, like a dog hoping for praise, a smile broad across her face.

'Hello, love.' Steven seemed to see her for the first time. He nodded at her and smiled but made no move to approach her. 'Very nice to meet you.'

'Put the tray over there,' Ned's mother ordered, gesturing to a spot beside her, 'and then bring in the tea.'

Steven extended the tray on its long, flimsy metal legs and put it where directed. Then he went out again.

'How are you, son?' Jackie Haskell said, in her strangely soft voice. It didn't sound natural, Ruth thought, but as though she'd been trained to bring it down to a half whisper. 'How's work?'

'Good.' Ned slung one leg up over the other and examined the sole of his boot. He twiddled with the laces. 'I'm doing well.'

'Are they treating you right?'

'Oh yes, no problems there.'

'And the cottage?'

'Fine.'

Jackie looked at Ruth, her large brown eyes blinking slowly behind the glasses. 'You've moved in to the cottage, haven't you?'

'Yes,' Ruth replied. She felt embarrassed to be so much a part of Ned's life without ever having met his mother. *We just have to get through this bit*, she thought. *Then it will all be fine*. She remembered Ned saying, 'They'll adore you' and clung on to it even though neither of his parents looked much like the adoring type.

'Do you like it?'

'It's lovely.'

'Perhaps you'll have an easier time persuading Edward to keep it tidy than I've had.'

'Who?'

Jackie stared at her for a moment, and her mouth twitched. She rested her hands carefully on her knees. 'Edward.'

'That's me,' said Ned. 'Edward's my real name.'

'Oh.' Ruth laughed nervously. 'Of course. How silly of me.' She'd seen post addressed to Mr E Haskell, but no one had ever called him anything but Ned, as far as she knew. 'He's not too bad, really.' She smiled at Ned, eager for his support. Then she remembered the bedroom the way they had left it that morning: the duvet heaped in the middle of the bed, the sheets crumpled, dirty clothes in a pile on the floor — and felt embarrassed. A flush crept up her face and she felt a prickle of sweat under her hair.

'Those are lovely.' She gestured towards the cabinet filled with coloured glass. Jackie followed her gaze and then softened. She looked proud.

'Yes, they are nice, aren't they? One thing I do like is nice things. You see that set of liqueur glasses? Handmade, they are. I bought them in Prague — handmade original glass. I bartered the man right down as well.'

'They're beautiful,' said Ruth sincerely, and at that moment the jewel-coloured glasses really did seem to be beacons of loveliness. 'I bet they look lovely on a white tablecloth.'

'We've never used them. They're only for best.'

Steven Haskell came back in with another tray, this one loaded with a china pot, milk jug, sugar bowl, cups and saucers and a plate of biscuits. He decanted all this on to the first tray and then sat down on a chair near the door as though ready at any moment to dart back off if ordered.

Jackie poured the tea ritually, carefully putting the strainer over each cup. She passed one to Ruth, first dropping in two cubes of sparkling white sugar and stirring.

'Thank you,' said Ruth, even though she didn't take sugar. She took a sip: it was insipid, so milky that it tasted of malt, and sickly sweet. *I'll have to drink it*, she thought. She was certainly far too cowardly to say anything about it; she had a horror of being rude or demanding in other people's homes.

There was a polite but uncomfortable pause as they all sipped their tea. *When is Ned going to say something?* she wondered. *When is he going to tell them?*

'Edward says you're a nurse, Ruth.' Jackie put her tea cup back on its saucer with a little clink.

'That's right,' she answered brightly. 'I work in a GP practice in Oxford. I haven't been there terribly long though — before that I was a casualty nurse for three years at the John Radcliffe, which is a very old hospital. It's absolutely enormous but because it's so old, the rooms are far too small, hardly enough space to turn round, let alone run a busy emergency unit. I left there because the shift hours were just too demanding after a while.'

Jackie nodded, saying 'mmhm, mmhm' through closed lips and when Ruth paused, she cut in quickly. 'You must be a very caring person.'

'Well, I don't know about that . . . I do my best, I suppose — '

'Did Edward tell you I was sick last year? I've not been well at all. People don't understand. They look at me and they think I can cope. They see my outside and they think I'm made of steel but I'm not. I'm very stressed. My blood pressure is sky high and I suffer terrible pains. Last night — Steven will tell you, won't you, Steven — I was almost screaming with pain. It's here' — she pressed her stomach, and then her back — 'and here.'

'That sounds very distressing,' Ruth said slowly, thinking *what does she want me to do?*

Does she want me to diagnose her? 'What does your GP say?'

'Oh, him.' Jackie waved a hand scornfully. 'He doesn't know what he's talking about. He doesn't know what it's like! All doctors are the same. Murderers.'

'That may be a little bit harsh,' said Ruth, wondering where the conversation was going.

'Come on, Mum,' said Ned, smiling. 'Don't talk rubbish. Dr Portman's all right.'

'He's an old crook. Happiest when he's killing off anyone over fifty.' Another thought seemed to strike her and she leaned towards Ruth, her eyes concerned. Her voice dropped back to its whispery state. 'Edward says your mother's dead. Was it her you got your ginger hair from?'

'Um, no. My grandmother, I think.'

'Well, it can skip a generation, can't it? How old was she when she died?'

'She was forty-one.'

'Oh, that's nothing. That's younger than I am. Poor woman. What was it?'

'Ovarian cancer.'

Jackie's face crumpled as though she was in pain. She moaned softly. 'Oh that's terrible. That's just awful. You must have been just a young thing, too. Oh, Ruth. She must have been in torment leaving you. She's probably guarding over you from heaven. Think of the joy she brought you, don't dwell on the grief. She was the angel who came into your life and left too soon. Give me your hand.' Ruth held out her hand towards Ned's mother, who grabbed it between her own cool, smooth palms. Then her expression changed, and she frowned, turning Ruth's hand over. 'What's this?'

The engagement ring glinted in the light of a lamp.

'What's this?' demanded Jackie again, her voice harsh.

Oh God, thought Ruth, cursing herself for forgetting to take off the ring. Ned shifted awkwardly beside her.

'Well, that's what we came to tell you about, Mum — '

'Are you engaged, Edward? To someone I've never met? Are you *engaged*? When were you thinking of telling me?' Jackie's tone climbed the scale with indignation.

'I came to tell you now — '

'How long has this been going on?' The brown eyes were no longer damp and puppyish but hard as pebbles. Anger contorted her mouth.

'It was only the week before last,' said Ruth, eager to placate her. She was about to explain but Jackie sucked in her breath loudly.

'The *week* before *last?* That is disgusting! Your own mother!' She turned to Ned. 'You've hurt me deeply, Edward.' She gasped as if in pain, rose to her feet and walked out of the room unsteadily, one hand clutched dramatically to her chest. Ned got up, shot a look at Ruth and said, 'I'd better go after her. Don't worry. I'll calm her down.'

A minute later, Ruth was alone with Steven Haskell, still sitting smartly in his chair by the door like a footman on duty.

'You mustn't mind her,' he said. 'She'll be

fine. Well, that's splendid news. I wondered when our boy would settle down. You seem like a very nice girl. Let's see that sparkler.'

Ruth held out her hand, smiling timidly. 'Do you think Mrs Haskell will be all right?'

'Oh yes. Don't worry. We'll ride out the storm and it'll be calm again. All forgotten. Ooh, this is nice. Real diamonds, is it? They can do wonders with cubic zirconia these days.'

They sat together for forty minutes, Ruth asking polite questions about the garden and the local area, all the time feeling slightly sick and unhappy because the visit had taken this unfortunate turn. *Why didn't Ned tell them about the engagement right away?* she wondered. *Why didn't I take off the bloody ring? Will she hate me for ever? Oh, for crying out loud — it couldn't have gone any worse than this.*

She looked up anxiously when Ned came back. 'Is everything all right?'

'It's fine. She wants to see you.'

He led her into the hall and up the stairs.

'Is it really all right?' she asked urgently in a whisper.

'We've had some histrionics but it's okay now.' He took her to a door, knocked gently and opened it. 'Here's Ruth, Mum. In you go.'

Ruth went forward into the gloom. Jackie was on the large double bed in the centre of the room, covered in a blanket. The curtains were closed and the room was in semi-darkness.

A small voice from the bed said, 'Come over here, Ruth. Sit on the bed.'

Ruth went over and sat down on the edge of

the mattress. Jackie's hand came out from under the blanket and rested on her knee.

'Are you all right?' Ruth asked in her best bedside voice. 'How are you feeling? I'm sorry it was all such a shock for you.'

'So you're going to marry our Edward . . . ' Jackie's voice was soft again, high and whispery. 'I don't understand the way things happen today. It's all very different to when we were young. But I want what's best for my boy, Ruth, I'm sure you understand that. You will, one day, when you've children of your own. You only desire their happiness. Now I've got one question for you and then we'll go on.' There was a pause. Ruth waited, tentative. 'Are you expecting? Is that why it's all happening like this?'

'Oh! I . . . ' Ruth laughed nervously. 'Um — no. No. I'm not pregnant.'

'Are you sure?'

'Yes, yes, I'm sure.'

'It must be true love then, mustn't it?'

'I hope so,' said Ruth, smiling, catching a hint of sarcasm in the feathery voice.

The cool light hand patted her. 'Ruth — you must think of me as your mother now. We need each other, I can see that. You can be my daughter. And I can be your mother.'

Ruth was confused. Didn't she already have a daughter?

'Would you like that, Ruth?'

'Of course I would. It's very important to me to be close to you and your husband.'

'I want you to call me Mum. Will you do that? Will you call me Mum?'

Ruth knew absolutely that she didn't want to do that, but now did not seem to be the time to disagree. 'Well . . . '

'Will you?'

'Of course.' Why can't I ever say what I mean? she wondered, agonised.

'We must be close. I need that, Ruth. You're a nurse. And you're educated. I look up to you, Ruth. I admire you . . . '

'Oh, please don't,' cut in Ruth. 'Really — '

'I think I can trust you. Can I?'

There was a pause. Ruth looked down at the round brown eyes that glinted in the half light behind the spectacles. 'Of course you can.'

★ ★ ★

'That didn't go as smoothly as it could have, did it?' said Ruth, when they were back on the motorway heading south. Jackie had stayed in her bed while her husband served up the roast chicken and vegetables. All through lunch, Ruth had felt the weight of Jackie's absence, imagining her lying upstairs in her gloomy room. The other two didn't seem to notice; Ned and his father chattered away through the meal, and then with coffee while they watched some sport on the television. Then it was time to go home.

'I suppose not, no. The thing is, no matter how we did it, it would have been difficult. There was no easy way of breaking the news.'

'Why on earth not? Why isn't she happy for you?'

'Look, it's just complicated. That's all. You

know what mothers and sons can be like. No one good enough, and all that.'

'I suppose so,' she replied uncertainly. 'But she was all right with it in the end? What did you say to her?'

'I just calmed her down. It was not knowing that got her. And the fact she'd never met you. She's a bit protective of me, that's all.'

'I *told* you we should have gone before.'

'I know, I know.'

'I bet she'll think it was me who stopped you.'

They drove along in silence for a while, Ruth remembering what it had been like to go into that darkened bedroom, with Jackie on the bed under her blanket like the big bad wolf pretending to be grandma. 'It was as though she had an attack of the vapours, like a Victorian mama.'

Ned said nothing for a moment, then in a tetchy voice, 'She was just a bit upset, that's all. You've got to see it from her point of view.'

'Of course, of course,' Ruth said hastily. She'd caught a tone of defensiveness and didn't want to sound critical of his family. *But it was your fault*, she couldn't help thinking, *for not telling them in the first place*. She didn't say anything — what was the point in arguing about it? A picture of the Old Rectory was suddenly sharp in her mind: she could feel its warmth and worn quality, the sense of lives lived inside it. The place had a humanity about it, as though age and experience had brought with it calm and wisdom. She thought about the open friendliness of her father, and contrasted that with the cool,

65

concrete atmosphere of the Haskell home. *Lucky me*, she thought. *Even when terrible things happened, there was always home. But poor Ned, growing up in that cold, creepy house. I bet he was never allowed to make a mess.*

'Do you think they liked me?' she asked at last.

'I'm sure she did. But don't worry about it. Honestly.'

'It seemed all right by the end, anyway.' She wanted to mention Jackie asking her to be a daughter to her, but she could sense the frostiness and impatience in Ned's voice. *He doesn't want to talk about it*, she thought. *He's touchy about it.*

Ned pushed a button on the CD player and they didn't speak again until they got close to home.

5

'Hello, Ruth? It *is* Ruth, isn't it? I hope you don't mind me ringing up like this out of the blue. I'm Erin. Ned's friend. Has he told you about me?'

'Oh. Hello . . . yes, yes, of course he has.' The girl in the photographs. She was on the other end of the telephone line. Ruth imagined her as if she'd stepped straight from the picture of the group by the river bank: slim, tanned shoulders, a vest top and jeans, corkscrew curls about her neck. Nineteen years old.

'It's rather naughty of me to phone you like this without any warning, but I'm afraid I just couldn't wait any longer. I haven't seen Ned for weeks and I guessed that he might have found a new playmate — and then we hear that he's engaged. Naturally we're all horrified.'

'Really?' Ruth felt clumsy, caught on the back foot. She ought to be able to bat back a breezy witticism in return but she couldn't think of anything.

Erin laughed. 'I'm joking — well, sort of. We *are* horrified that we haven't even met you yet. And Ned knows he's supposed to get our permission on this kind of matter. Luke had Abigail thoroughly vetted by us for months before he even dreamed of mentioning the M word. So we want to get started right away. I've talked to the others and we insist that you come out tonight and meet us all. I know you're not doing anything else because unless Ned is out with us, he never does anything on a Saturday night. You're not, are you? You haven't converted him to clubbing or all-night cinema or anything, have you?'

'Um, no, I don't think we're doing anything . . . ' She'd had a lazy morning reading the papers and had cut out a recipe that appealed to her. She was going to go into Oxford to the Covered Market and find a pheasant to cook for their supper.

'Good. Then we'll see you at the Fox and Hounds at eight o'clock. All right?'

When Ned came downstairs, his hair still wet from the shower and his feet bare, Ruth called out, 'Looks like we've got a date for tonight.'

'Really?'

She came through from the kitchen. Ned was scratching Maisie under the chin, and she was responding with an enthusiastic purr. 'Erin just called. She wants us to meet them at the Fox and Hounds tonight.'

'Oh.' Ned continued rubbing the cat's chin, frowning. 'Do you want to go?'

'It's about time I met them, isn't it? After all, you still see the boys at rugby, and Tom at your poker nights. They must wonder if I really exist.'

'I suppose so.'

Ruth went over and slid her arms round him. 'Well, you don't sound very eager. These are your best friends.'

'I am eager.' He kissed the tip of her nose. 'But I've kind of enjoyed these last few weeks, just the two of us.'

68

'I know. It's not nice, letting the big bad world in on us, is it?'

'I feel like we've got everything we need here.'

'We've got to venture out some time.'

'Have we? Can't we just stay here forever, and make everything else go away?'

'We would slowly but surely go insane.'

'Maybe. But I'd rather be mad with you than sane without.'

'I am rather hoping we can strike some kind of mean.' Ruth laughed. 'We can't stay insulated indefinitely. And I want to meet your friends, it's important to me. I want to put some voices and characters to the pictures you've got all over the house. They must think it's very peculiar that you've got engaged to someone they haven't met.'

'Yes, no one seems to like that much. I had no idea it was so important to everyone,' Ned said ruefully.

'Your parents, your friends . . . anyone would think you wanted to run away from them all.'

'Of course I don't. Let's go to the pub tonight then. Actually, it will do us good to get out of the house.'

★   ★   ★

She took the park-and-ride bus into Oxford and went to the Covered Market. The butcher shops were full of game, splendidly swathed in fur and feathers of russet, brown and grey. A little girl with her mother was crying at the sight of a dead rabbit hanging from a butcher's hook, its paws

69

crossed and tied like a villain's, its eyes closed. 'The p-p-poor b-b-bunny,' she sobbed.

We could always have rabbit instead, Ruth thought. She knew a particularly delicious recipe with mustard and white wine. But she decided to stick to the pheasant idea instead and went in to find a good one. Coming out, she was tempted by the delicatessen across the way with its jam and butter biscuits and was wondering whether to buy some pudding, when she heard her name.

Valentina was coming towards her waving a cigarette. 'Oi! Mrs Beeton! What's for dinner?'

'Hello, my sweet. What are you doing here? It's pheasant. I'm making it with prunes.'

Valentina made a face as she kissed her. 'Um — sounds delightful. I'm sure it will be marvellous but I'll stick with my Tesco's lasagne, thanks. Now, come for a coffee. I'm meeting Isabelle later. Stay, and we'll all have fun.'

'I'll come for coffee but not for Isabelle. I have to get back.'

'Oh yes.' Valentina smirked as she led the way to the café. 'You owe me big time.'

'For what?'

'For services rendered, darling! I hear you pulled *massively* at my birthday party. I only went and found you Mr Right! Show me your hand.' She inspected the ring as they found a table and sat down. 'Very posh. It's all coming right for you then? Cushy number as a practice nurse and a wedding dress to buy.'

'It's pretty good.' Ruth tried not to look pleased with herself but couldn't help grinning broadly.

'I'm happy for you, darling. You deserve it.'

'What are you up to?'

'I'm a ward manager now. Team of nurses reporting their every move to me. But I'm thinking of giving it up.'

'Is it the back?' Nurses were notorious for their bad backs, caused by years of lifting patients.

'Nope. I'm going to volunteer for service abroad. I'm going to Sri Lanka to work out there. That's the plan anyway. Or Pakistan. Or Darfur. Wherever I'm needed.'

'What a fabulous idea. That's what I always planned to do,' said Ruth. She frowned. It felt as though Valentina had chosen the path her own life might have taken if she hadn't met Ned.

'I know, darling. You gave me the idea. I've just done a course in tropical medicine in London with some study leave.' Valentina puffed out a stream of cigarette smoke. 'I've got to get out. Get back to basics. Remember what it's all about. We're so bogged down with admin here, I can't even look the patients in the eye I'm so busy writing down every little thing in case something goes wrong and they sue. You know what swung it? Isabelle told me that in Casualty there are lawyers handing their cards to patients, *encouraging* them to sue us if they possibly can.'

'Really?' Ruth was horrified. 'What a nasty little scam! They do that here? It sounds like something you'd hear about happening in America.'

'That's the way it's going. Some things are changing for the better, but the legal aspect most

71

certainly isn't. I want to go somewhere where the person I treat gets better and is glad to be better — not planning some sort of compensation windfall because they don't like the kind of bandage I use.' Valentina stared at her for a moment. 'It's not too late, Ruth. You could do it too, if you like. If this bloke really loves you, he'll let you.'

'Oh, no . . . it's not that.' She felt confused. She'd once planned to go away, hadn't she? So why, when she tried, was it so impossible to imagine leaving?

★   ★   ★

'That was a delicious dinner. Pheasant is my new favourite and I'm a signed-up prune-o-philiac. I'm a lucky man. How did you learn to cook so well?'

They were walking the dark half mile to the pub along a back lane, arm in arm.

'I taught myself. From those old books you're so scornful about.'

'I'm sure they contain the wisdom of ages. Anyway, if it means you carry on making grub like that, I don't mind how many you have.'

'Maybe I'll teach you to cook.'

'That'd be great. I'd like that.'

She squeezed his arm, smiling even though he couldn't see her. He was so open to new things and new experiences, he didn't consider himself too good for anything. It was one of the many things she loved about him. That, and the way he sang along unselfconsciously with the soft-voiced

72

singers he preferred, like Nick Drake or Elliott Smith; and the way she could hear him laughing at the television when he sat there watching it on his own. She loved to see him dreaming as he washed the dishes, or hear him splashing in the bath after rugby, making a soup of mud and grass. Every day she seemed to find something else that reminded her how happy she was with him, and how lucky it was that he had been there, waiting for her.

As they strolled on, she tried to quell her growing apprehension. After all, hadn't she just learned that things that seemed a good idea in theory were less appealing when put into practice? Meeting the Haskells had made her view Ned in a subtly different light for a while, and he had become a kind of stranger because he was so profoundly entwined with people she'd found it hard to connect with; it had taken her a few days to recover and reclaim her own Ned.

It could be the same with his friends, she thought. *They might put a distance between us. He might not be the same Ned with them that he is with me.*

She had an urge to stop walking and tell Ned that they should go home at once and treasure their solitude for as long as they could. After all, they had no need to step out of the warm and delightful intimacy that they shared. Once they allowed the world in, that would be that. From the start, when she had visited the cottage she had turned off her mobile and Ned refused to answer his telephone. Their excursions were walks, alone in the surrounding fields, talking endlessly as they tramped along the footpaths. There was so much to say and so much of their lives and opinions to tell each other. They weren't interested in anyone else. Now, as they neared the pub, she didn't know whether to mourn the end of their exclusive and intense affair or to welcome in the parts of Ned's life she was so curious about.

It's too late to go back now, she thought. *Anyway, I must make a good impression, I want them to like me. I'm sure their approval matters. Not enough to stop Ned loving me,* she told herself hastily. It was a small fear that niggled — that the influence of his friends might be more powerful than she knew.

The pub was solid yellow-grey Cotswold stone, its upper storey completely swathed in thick ivy. The wooden door, lit by a vast iron lantern hanging above, let them into a low-ceilinged bar with an uneven flagstone floor and panelled walls, with wooden settles pushed up against them.

Ned said, 'They'll be through here, in the comfortable bit.'

Past a low-beamed doorway that Ned had to bend right down to get through, there was another room, this one also wood-panelled but with padded benches tucked into booths.

'Hey, Ned!' was the first cry, and then there was a chorus. A crowd of people seemed to have leapt to their feet at the far end of the room, and were shouting and beckoning them over.

When they reached them, there weren't as many of them as it had seemed: three men and two women, strangely familiar from the photo-graphs but with the disconcerting complexity of real life. They absorbed Ned into their circle, hugging him and congratulating him on his engagement, rebuking him jokily for being away for so long. Ruth waited for their focus to move to her, as she knew it would.

'So you're the mystery woman.' This was from the man she knew was Tom: fair-haired, blue-eyed and with a closed-off face. 'We don't know what to make of Ned here getting engaged like this. We've all talked about it and we'd like you to take a series of simple tests: psychometric, graphology, phrenology, a lie detector. Just the usual.'

Ruth smiled politely.

Ned said, 'Okay, introductions. Everyone, this is Ruth.'

Everybody chorused a greeting. She continued smiling and nodded, thinking *I'm so stiff! I must look like the Queen, nodding like this.* She wanted to be as relaxed and easy as the rest of them.

Ned indicated a tall, shabby-looking man with a high forehead under receding brown hair, and a piebald beard. 'Jeremy. A man devoted to the study of the classics.'

'Hello, missy,' said Jeremy. He smiled in a curious, one-sided way, and his fingers fidgeted with an unlit rolled-up cigarette.

Ruth said, 'Hello, very glad to meet you' with another little nod of her head. Now that she had the idea she mustn't act like the Queen on walkabout, she couldn't stop it. *I'll be asking him if he's come far, at this rate.*

Ned pointed at a short, plumpish couple in the corner. 'Luke and his lovely wife, Abigail.'

Abigail reached out a hand, which Ruth took and started to shake, but Abigail pulled her close, landing a smacking kiss on her cheek. 'Oh, you poor, poor thing. Fancy taking on Ned for life. Our hearts are bleeding for you, darling. You look too young and innocent for all this.'

'Don't do it,' added Luke solemnly. 'I regret getting married. Too late now. Can't afford a divorce, can I, darling?'

'No, worse luck.' Abigail smiled, her face warm. 'I'd take you for every last penny. You'd be in a caravan in Whitstable before you knew what had happened. Ruth, you're very welcome. Ned, get your fiancée a drink at once. In fact, order some of the filthy champagne they sell here and we'll all celebrate. Come and sit by me, Ruth.' She shifted her plump bottom closer to her husband, making a tiny gap for Ruth.

'Wait, I haven't finished. This is Tom,' said Ned. Tom, hunched in the corner, said, 'Hi.'

'And Erin,' added Ned, 'who you've already spoken to. There. Now that's done, I'll go and get those drinks.'

'You can't imagine how pleased I am to meet you,' declared Erin.

Ruth had been aware of her since the moment she'd seen Ned's friends. It was impossible not to be. Next to Erin, the others appeared faded while she sat glowing against the dark panelling of the wall. It had been easy to see in the photographs that Erin was unusually attractive, but in the flesh she was beautiful, properly beautiful, with abundant rich black hair and dark-blue eyes in a bewitchingly Irish-looking combination. Her white skin was vivid, enhancing her dramatic colouring, and she was slim and supple, with elegant, long-fingered hands. She had a way of gathering up her tumble of curls and twisting them around the back of her head, so that one couldn't help but admire the Pre-Raphaelite mass of dark hair, and the slim white wrist and hand that held it.

Ruth was disconcerted; Ned had not prepared her for someone like this. If she had felt like the Queen a moment ago, she was now the stumbling flower girl entrusted with a bouquet, nervous in the presence of royalty.

'We're so glad Ned has met you,' Erin said warmly. 'We want to hear all about you.'

'Come on, sit down.' Abigail patted the sliver of seat next to her.

'Come here,' said Erin decisively. 'There's more room next to me.'

Ned went off to get the champagne, and Ruth was immediately bombarded with questions. At first, she was stilted and formal but soon began to relax; the others were friendly and receptive, interested in her and what she had to say. She began to regain her confidence. When they learned that she was a nurse, Tom said, 'Tell us the most gruesome thing you've ever seen.'

'You're so morbid!' exclaimed Erin. 'Ignore him, Ruth.'

'No, come on. What's the worst thing?'

'One of the oddest things I saw was a man

come into Casualty and try to murder his wife,' said Ruth. 'He'd already stabbed her once, which was why she was there. Then he came pounding in with a bloody great knife to finish her off.'

They gasped and laughed.

'Did he do it?' asked Abigail.

'No. We've got security guards now. He didn't get far. We had an armed police response, though. Lots of drama there. But every day had its dramas, some worse than others.'

'What's the worst problem Oxford's got?' asked Jeremy, lighting his little cigarette. 'Booze? Student suicide? Sexually transmitted disease?'

'Oh no. Drugs. This city has one of the worst heroin problems going. When I was in Casualty, every other week a car would screech to a halt outside, a body would be chucked out, and off it would screech again.'

'Dead?' breathed Erin.

'Overdosed. I got quite used to doing resuscitation in the car park.'

They looked at her with respect.

'And the saddest thing?' asked Tom, ignoring Erin as she protested that he wasn't to ask such dreadful questions. 'What's the saddest thing you had to do?'

Ruth said, 'The saddest thing is when a child dies. When you have to tell the parents. There's nothing worse.'

There was quiet for a moment, then Luke said cheerfully, 'Well, it's very useful to know a nurse, I must say. Especially as I've had a pain in my back lately. Do you know anything about backs, Ruth?'

When Ned returned and sat next to her, squeezing her hand under the table where no one else could see, she was already charmed by his friends. After a while, the concentration on her eased; they began to talk among themselves as well as to her, and then she was able to blend into the background and listen to their easy banter, jokes and friendly one-upmanship. She was fascinated to see this other side of Ned, and the way he was so much a part of the group, knew its idiosyncrasies and how to behave inside it.

'I've got something to tell you, something I bet you don't know,' Luke announced. There was a general moan of good-natured derision.

'Luke is convinced he is a man of great mind,' Ned said to Ruth. 'Don't let him frighten you.'

'No, come on, this will interest you. I just found this out today.'

Ned whispered, 'He reads and edits Wikipedia for fun. He's always coming up with these gems of useless information.'

'What's Wikipedia?'

'It's an on-line encyclopaedia you can add your own entries to.'

'Ned, listen,' called Luke. 'Did you know that there is a word in Russian for a fawning scrounger — *sheramizhnik*? And where do you think it comes from?'

'No idea,' said Ned.

'Listen carefully, I'll say it again.' Luke said slowly: 'Sher — a — mizh — nik.'

'I don't know about you lot, but I'm none the wiser,' remarked Tom. 'Say it as slowly as you like.'

'Okay, think of French . . . it's from *cher ami* — my dear friend. And the reason that the French for 'my dear friend' became Russian for 'fawning scrounger' is that when Napoleon's soldiers were starving to death in the bleak Russian winter, having lost their supply train and been roundly beaten, they would beseech the peasants for food, begging and calling them dear friends.' He said dramatically, '*Ah, mon cher ami, aide-moi!*' and then in a guttural Russian accent, 'You *sheramizhnik*, get out of here!'

'That *is* interesting,' said Ruth, genuinely impressed.

Everyone laughed, and she flushed, wondering what she had said.

'A virgin!' exclaimed Jeremy. 'Unused to the ways of Luke.'

'Watch out,' added Tom. 'Don't encourage him.'

Abigail leaned over. 'I wonder if you would be interested in a wife swap — only permanent. Luke has many, many more interesting snippets to share with you, and I wouldn't mind a rugby tackle with Ned . . . ' She raised her eyebrows suggestively.

'Now, now,' declared Ned. 'Ruth's out of bounds. No teasing for at least another month, until she's used to all of you.'

'We've been allowed to tease his other girlfriends,' protested Luke, but was silenced by a nudge from Abigail.

Erin smiled at Ruth. 'You mustn't worry about us. It's all hot air, we promise. We're so glad Ned has found someone as wonderful as he is. Have we toasted the couple yet? Come on.'

They raised their glasses, and Ned put an arm around her as his friends called their names.

★ ★ ★

'Hello, it's Erin.'

'Hi, how are you?' Ruth nestled the phone under her chin and poured some cold coffee from the cafetière into her mug. After the meeting in the pub the night before, she'd already decided that she wanted to be accepted into their group but she was tentative about shoe-horning herself in, so an unsolicited call from Erin was a good sign.

'I'm fine. Are you busy today?'

She looked around at the kitchen. Ned had got up early, made himself a bacon sandwich, glanced at the papers and gone, leaving the grill pan dirty on the side, the bread out, crumbs everywhere and a ketchup-smeared knife on the bench. She'd intended to put on some music and clear up, give the place a good clean, get a load of washing on and then perhaps sit down with some coffee and the paper and look at the Saturday crossword. 'Nope. How about you?'

'I'm dying to get out of the house actually. Why don't we meet up at the café on Blythe Street? Then we can meet the boys afterwards at the pub.'

'That sounds lovely.'

'Good,' said Erin with satisfaction. 'Shall I see you there in forty minutes? I've got to jump under the shower.'

'It's a date.'

Erin was already sitting at the café when she got there. Her hair was bunched at the nape of her neck, her head bent over a wodge of paper while she waited for Ruth.

'Hi.' Ruth sat down next to her. 'Sorry I'm late.'

'You're not. Don't worry. Besides, I need to read this script.'

Ned had told her that Erin was an actress. 'She had real talent,' he had said on the way home from the pub. 'Unlike the rest of us, who just liked showing off. She actually got an agent to come to a student play and watch her in a production of *Macbeth*. She was the most incredible Lady Macbeth you can imagine: you could absolutely understand why Macbeth leapt to do her bidding. Then she was working professionally before we even graduated. But that's Erin for you. She's pretty determined when she knows what she wants. She may not quite have made it to Hollywood but she's done more than okay.'

An agent and a career in acting only heightened the glamour around Erin. Ruth looked at the script, impressed. 'Is it good?'

Erin wrinkled her nose. 'A film. I don't think I have a hope, but it's worth going up for an audition just to meet the director. He's supposed to be on the up.'

'Is it a good part?'

'It's all right, I suppose. I don't think I'll get it because my agent tells me they've called in just

82

about every hot young thing in London for a reading, and I'm not quite in that league.'

'Yes, you are,' said Ruth loyally.

Erin looked rueful. 'It may say twenty-nine on my CV, but it ain't quite the truth.'

'You could pass for twenty-five with no trouble.' It was true, she thought, with a tiny edge of envy: Erin had a luminosity and purity of skin that made her look almost childlike at times. She certainly didn't look as though she was in her mid-thirties — in fact, she looked even better than she did in Ned's photographs. Her face had filled out a little and it suited her. But there was something ageless about her. Perhaps she would go on looking just the same for ever, until there would be one sudden collapse into old age, like Dorian Gray withering in seconds when his portrait was destroyed.

'Do you really think so?' Erin touched her cheek softly with the back of one hand. 'I think I'm looking like an old crone.'

'No, you're not. I was thinking just the other day that I must find out what you put on your face, because you look really . . . dewy. Like an advert.' It was odd to be bolstering Erin's confidence, she thought. There she was, a mess of insecurities herself, having to prop up this stunning woman. *Why do we do it to ourselves?* she wondered. Only the other day she had found a photograph of herself taken at a party eight years before and had been surprised to see that she had been slim, bright eyed, fresh skinned — well, pretty. And yet at the time, she'd spent miserable hours criticising herself for being fat and ugly. Would it always go on like that, never really knowing or appreciating what you were until it was gone?

'You're very sweet. And you can rifle through my bathroom cabinets any time. I spend the most ludicrous amount on cosmetics. But my accountant tells me that it's all tax deductible, so that's all right.' Erin leaned back in her chair and signalled the waitress for another coffee. 'It really is a waste of time going to this audition, I haven't got a hope. Part of the trouble is not being in London. I ought to be there, showing myself where it matters, networking, going out with my agent. But Tom would never hear of moving there. He'd never dream of moving away from here, from his friends.'

'It's not far to London.'

'I know, I know. But it's not the same as being there. But I couldn't ask him. He's put so much into his work here. It would be madness to leave it all now. Besides . . . ' She smiled at Ruth. 'He would never leave Ned and Jeremy and Luke. And neither would I. I don't know why I'm even talking about it, it's never going to happen. I'd better resign myself to zooming up the M40 at a moment's notice when I'm summoned.'

The waitress came over with two frothy cups of coffee.

'Could I have an almond croissant, please?' asked Ruth.

Erin sighed as the waitress walked away. 'They do make gorgeous croissants here. Lucky you. I mustn't have anything like that, don't let me be tempted whatever happens. This film audition is next week and I don't want to look like a vat of lard next to all those beanpoles.'

Ruth was conscious of her full chest and the thighs splaying comfortably on her seat. Erin was slender, with a graceful, ballet-dancer build. I'll only eat half the croissant, she promised herself. But when the sugar-dusted crescent of pastry sat before her, with its squishy centre of sweet almond paste, she couldn't resist it.

Erin sipped delicately at her coffee. She was one of those people who was effortlessly elegant, Ruth thought. She looked the kind of woman who knew where to buy the best cashmere, the most wonderful black trousers, the obscure label of jeans that the beautiful and famous wore. Today she was simply dressed in a white shirt with a pale blue sweater over it, slim trousers in a heathery tweed and boots. She looked wonderful and every item seemed ten times more expensive and exclusive than anything in Ruth's wardrobe, even though it might have come from a market stall. *It must be the way she wears her clothes,* thought Ruth. There was an air of being constantly observed about Erin, as though she was always performing and always knew she was being looked at, not because she craved attention but because people couldn't help giving it to her.

She put her head on one side, and stared at Ruth, her velvety blue eyes unreadable. 'So how did you two meet — you and Ned?'

'Nothing spectacular, I'm afraid. At a party, a friend of mine's birthday. I wish it was more interesting. We got on, went out for dinner, went out again and then before long, we were

85

dating . . . ' It sounded so pedestrian, nothing like the magical flowering, full of ecstasy and excitement, that she remembered.

'Oh, come on. That sounds boring! There must have been a thunderbolt. When did it happen?'

'No — no thunderbolt. Just a realisation, beginning very quietly and building up. You know that long chord fading to nothing at the end of 'Sergeant Pepper'? Like that in reverse.'

'So you realised that you'd met your soul mate?' One of Erin's perfectly shaped brows lifted.

'I suppose so, yes. That other side of yourself you're supposed to be looking for. It felt so . . . right. There's no other way to explain it.'

'You two have certainly signed up for the long haul together pretty fast. You must be sure of it.'

'We are.' Ruth ran the bowl of her teaspoon through the white froth on her coffee, collecting the melted chocolate. Her engagement ring caught the morning sunshine and glittered. *What does she want to know?* she wondered. *Does she think we're wrong for each other?*

'Well, that's lovely. And it's about time. Ned deserves to be loved properly. He's capable of a lot of love himself, you know. I'm glad you've allowed him to love in the right way.'

'What do you mean?'

'Love isn't all just hearts and flowers, is it? People can love destructively as well. The way stalkers do, or those people with that syndrome that makes them fall intensely in love with a stranger and see messages from them on posters and in the clouds. They can fall in love with murderers and terrorists. They can love in pain. They can love when they don't even want to.'

No wonder she's an actress, thought Ruth. 'Has Ned done any of those things?'

Erin laughed. 'It's just an example. He hasn't been so lucky with romance, though. None of his girlfriends have been serious.'

'The great thing about love is that you only have to be really lucky the one time. You only need one love.'

'Of course you do. In a perfect world.'

'Don't you think that?'

Erin shrugged. 'It's a wonderful idea. But people don't stay the same all their lives. They grow and change. Someone who is perfect for you at one stage of your life might be quite wrong for you later, and someone you overlooked when you were younger might metamorphose into your ideal partner. It seems to me that if you marry at eighteen and are still in love at eighty, you've beaten greater odds than winning the lottery. I don't mean to sound cynical — it's just what I think.'

Ruth nibbled slowly on her croissant. *We will*, she thought. *We'll beat the odds.*

'I can see you don't believe me!' Erin cried. 'You're at that stage where you can't imagine not being wild about each other forever. Do you know the Rupert Brooke poem 'Love'?'

Ruth shook her head.

'Perhaps now is not the time to read it. Maybe after you're married. But you're full of the astonishment of hand and shoulder. When you read it, you'll see what I mean.'

Ruth felt a surge of resentment. *It sounds like she thinks we're doomed,* she thought. *What on earth does she know? No one knows what we're like together.* She wanted to tell Erin that she was wrong but she couldn't think of how to say it the right way, so she said instead, 'The strange thing is how people find it so hard to accept that we don't need to slog through two years of being a couple before we get engaged. We know what we feel. We know we've found the right person and now we just want to get on with things. I wish people would stop asking me if I'm sure.'

'You've got to remember that you and Ned are a new couple.' Erin's voice was mellifluous, her actress diction putting a crisp bite into every word, making everything she said sound loaded. 'I know that to you it all seems as though it was written in the stars, but the rest of us know Ned as someone else, someone separate from you. It's going to take a little while for everyone to adjust. You can't be surprised if it doesn't happen immediately.'

Ruth felt rebuked. Erin laughed, seeing her discomfort, and cocked her head on one side, her slender white neck in a graceful attitude. 'Now, don't worry. We all adore you, Ruth, and Ned is a changed man since he met you.'

'Really?'

'Oh yes.'

'How?' She was insatiably hungry for information about Ned, and for how they, Ruth and Ned, were perceived by others. She wanted the

ratification of others recognising their relationship, and liked the little voyeuristic thrill of
briefly seeing themselves through someone else's
eyes.

Erin thought for a moment. 'He's much more
confident. In himself. I can see it. He's lost some
of those little nervous habits he had. And of
course, he's glowing with that inner light you
have when you're in love, obviously having
glorious sex all the time, and it's all fabulous.
Like you. You're shining over there like a little
light bulb.' She smiled at Ruth. 'Enjoy it. This bit
is wonderful.'

'It *is* wonderful.' Ruth smiled broadly, unable
to keep her happiness hidden. Just hearing Ned's
name still gave her a small inner thrill of delight.
'I'm so lucky. I can't believe this has happened to
me.'

'You're really madly in love, aren't you?'

'Yes,' said Ruth honestly.

Erin laughed, her practised actress's voice
making it a liquid tumble down the scale. 'It's so
sweet! And to think . . . it's strange for me, for all
of us, because we know dear old Ned, and we
love him, but seeing you gripped in your passion
. . . well, it feels as though Ned, who I see all the
time grubby in his rugby kit or cross at the
traffic, has just been unveiled as Prince
Charming.'

Ruth felt stupid for a moment, as though Erin
was telling her that she was in the grip of an
illusion that would soon shatter. Then she
recalled Ned's face, his smell and touch, and
instead was filled with triumph that she had been

clever enough to see what was really there while everyone else had been too blind.

'But you and Tom must have been like this when you got together,' she said.

Erin smiled again. 'Of course. I know exactly what you're going through.'

★   ★   ★

Ruth and Erin got to the pub before the men arrived, but they came in a few minutes later, muddy and red faced, talking loudly about their rugby game.

Ned and Tom came over to the women's table. Ned's front was smeared with grass stains and he was carrying mud-encrusted boots in one hand. He went to Ruth and kissed her, his lips tasting salty with sweat. 'Hi, darling.' He leant over and dropped a kiss on Erin's cheek. 'Hello, Curly.'

'How was the game?' Ruth asked, wanting to hug him but held at bay by the mud.

'Brilliant. I was man of the match, wasn't I?'

Tom sat down opposite Erin, picked up her hand and kissed it. She smiled at him, and he said to Ruth, 'He certainly was. Ned took the most terrific pass. He did three feints, in the form of the most graceful pirouettes ever seen outside Sadler's Wells, and then zoomed away up the field and landed a try.'

'Did you?' Ruth said, excited by Ned's skill and physical ability.

'That was quite a good move, I have to admit, but I didn't win the whole game single handed.'

'Not for want of trying,' said Tom. 'What'll it be? I'm buying.'

They're such contrasts, Ruth thought. Tom was shorter and stockier than Ned, with blond hair in a thick, dead straight mop that fell into his eyes. At first sight, he looked very handsome, with his fair hair and blue eyes, but the longer Ruth looked at him, the less she admired his looks. His eyes were slightly bulbous and their blue a little too pale to be attractive. His features were regular but she didn't like the narrow, pinched quality of his nose, his thin upper lip and the way his mouth in repose turned downwards.

He doesn't smile much, Ruth thought. *Even though he's always making jokes. Ned has told me a hundred times what a funny man Tom is. I haven't quite seen it yet.*

Jeremy, as muddy as the others, came up to the table, a cigarette clenched between his lips. He was even taller than Ned, with a thin, angular face and a gawky way of holding himself; Ruth liked his strange charm, even though she'd barely spoken to him. His elliptical way of talking made any kind of conversation a challenge. 'Howdy,' he said to Erin. 'How's tricks?'

'Hi,' said Erin with a smile. 'I'm good. How are you?'

'Dandy.' He glanced at Ruth. 'Hello there, missy.' Then turned his attention to the men. 'Thanks for the game. Are we on for next week?'

'Same time, same place,' said Ned.

'Excellent.' Jeremy darted a glance about the

table as a general farewell. 'See you later.' He turned on his heel and walked off, heading out of the pub.

'Where's Luke?' asked Erin.

'He's sloped off,' Ned said. 'Abigail let him out for the rugby on condition he was back by twelve.'

'I hope you boys know how lucky you are, having such understanding wives as Ruth and me,' Erin said lightly.

'Fiancée,' corrected Ned. 'Ruth's my fiancée.'

Erin slid her dark-blue gaze round to Ruth. 'Of course she is. But that's almost the same, isn't it? Have you two set a date for the big day yet?'

'We thought just after Christmas.' Ruth instinctively reached for Ned's hand. 'Nobody likes the dark days of January. We thought a wedding would be just the thing to cheer everyone up.'

'That's only four months. You've got a lot to do in a short time, haven't you?'

'There's not that much — and as January isn't a traditional month for weddings, we don't have to worry about everything being booked up.'

'And is it church? Civil?'

'We haven't really discussed the finer details . . . '

'I would have thought that's rather a big detail.' Erin smiled at Ned. 'Do you want to get married in the eyes of God? Or just the law?'

Ned said, 'The chances are it will be Ruth's village church, where she was baptised.'

'Sounds lovely. We must get together again, Ruth, and have a good old chat about it. I want to hear all your plans. Now, Tom . . . ' Erin stood up. 'We'd better be on our way ourselves.' She looked at Ned. 'You're coming next week, aren't you?'

Ruth looked at Ned, puzzled. 'Are we?'

'Didn't Ned mention it? We quite often have supper at our place on a Saturday. Once a month at least. It's a bit of a standing arrangement,' said Erin, 'so I just assumed . . . well, everyone else is coming.'

'We'll be there,' Ned said. 'We'd love to. Wouldn't we, Ruth?'

'Of course.'

'Good,' said Erin, satisfied. She put her hand on the top of Ned's head for a moment and said softly, 'You've been away too long.'

6

'What do you think?' Ruth asked hesitantly, as she and Cordy washed up the plates in the Old Rectory.

'Very nice,' said Cordy stoutly.

'Hmmm,' said Ruth, torn between wanting everything to be just right, and needing to confide in her sister.

'Although, if I'm honest — '

'Yes?'

'I can't say she's what I would want for a mother-in-law.'

'Oh dear. I was worried you'd think that.'

'What on earth was wrong with her? I couldn't make her out at all. One minute she was the life and soul, all giggles and chat. Then she got all morose and a bit depressive. She was practically asleep on the sofa at the end. And that thing she said about you!'

It had been an unavoidable duty to invite the Haskells to meet her family and Ruth had had to force herself to arrange it. Ever since the visit to York, she'd felt fearful of Ned's family and sure they thought that she was somehow to blame for Ned not telling them about the engagement immediately. But she also wanted to smooth out the misunderstandings as quickly as she could, and replace the memory of their first meeting with another, more benign one. So a family lunch at the Old Rectory it was, a prospect that had made her even more nervous than the trip to York.

As far as she could tell, Jackie had enjoyed herself. They'd arrived bang on the dot, and Jackie had been girlish and almost flirtatious at first. She'd pounced on Ruth with every appearance of great affection, kissing her and whispering 'It's lovely to see you again, dear!' into her ear, holding her hand whenever she had the opportunity and referring lovingly to 'my new daughter' at regular intervals. But her eyes had a certain glassiness, her attention wandered and she sometimes lost track of what she was saying, fading off into nothing.

Silas was at his charming best and completely at ease, handing out pre-lunch drinks of his own blend of Bloody Mary, which had generous amounts of salt, pepper, sherry, large dollops of horseradish and sticks of celery floating in it. He seemed to get on well with both of Ned's parents and his jokes made them laugh even if sometimes they looked as though they didn't quite understand what he was talking about. Steven also seemed unaware of any awkwardness while Ruth spent the whole time on tenterhooks, trying to interpret Jackie's behaviour and make sure she had whatever she needed, hoping that she was being attentive and caring enough to make up for the first blunder. When Jackie had stared with bewilderment at the Bloody Mary and its leafy celery, Ruth had quickly replaced it with a gin and tonic which seemed much more to Jackie's taste.

It had been during lunch when Steven said,

'So, have you two fixed a date then?'

'We're thinking about January,' replied Ned.

Jackie made a face. 'Oh no. It can't be January. That's bad luck, I'm sure it is. Anyway, you can't do it so soon. There isn't time for Ruth to lose enough weight.'

Everyone looked at Ruth, who blushed scarlet.

'Mum,' said Ned, an edge in his voice. 'Ruth doesn't need to lose weight.'

'Well, just a little bit.' Jackie looked about the table at everyone, her brown eyes wide with injured innocence.

'What?'

'She's a bonny girl as she is,' said Steven politely.

'We men like a woman with curves and a bit of meat on her,' declared Silas, trying to be loyal and cheer Ruth up, but making it worse.

'Ah, for goodness' sake,' said Jackie crossly. 'I didn't mean she's ten-ton Tessie! But she could do with dropping a bit.'

Cordy was looking at Jackie with frank disgust and Ruth saw her draw in a breath. *She's going to say what she thinks*, Ruth thought in panic. She could see this visit going the same way as the last one. She didn't care what Jackie said about her — she'd nod and agree happily if her future mother-in-law said she was a dead ringer for the Elephant Man — as long as they kept the peace and no one got angry.

'I'm on my wedding diet already,' she proclaimed, getting to her feet and beginning to collect the empty plates. 'It wouldn't be a proper wedding without a diet. Have you heard of the

GI? They say that's the best for long-term maintenance ... ' Gabbling away about blood-sugar levels, insulin and cravings, she felt that she'd managed to deflect the worst of it, but the afternoon never quite regained its good humour. After lunch, Jackie had seemed very sleepy and it wasn't long before Steven suggested heading off home, for which Ruth was greatly relieved.

'Why didn't Ned defend you?' asked Cordy now, plunging another plate into the hot water.

'He did.'

'Not much. I'd have told her where to get off. Imposing her body fascism on you, not to mention being despicably rude. You absolutely do not need to lose any weight. You're a perfectly normal, healthy woman. Honestly, it makes me furious, it really does. You didn't believe her, did you?'

Ruth thought for a moment. Had she? Why didn't she feel as cross as Cordy? Probably because, like almost every woman she knew, she secretly wished she could be thinner and was sure she'd look much better if she were. Besides that, she was beginning to realise that Jackie was accustomed to saying exactly what she thought without any kind of filtering process that might take into account other people's feelings. It was something she was going to have to make allowances for, she could see that. Jackie obviously didn't think she was bound by the rules of politeness that most people obeyed. Ruth was prepared to put up with that for the sake of good relations.

She said, 'I think Ned's a bit protective of his mother. I think she's a bit . . . vulnerable. Touchy. She has problems with her nerves, Ned said.'

'You mean she's spoilt. That husband of hers reminds me of a seeing-eye dog — you know, faithful, silent, negotiating obstacles for his mistress without a sound. Is she on anything? Painkillers? Antidepressants?'

'I don't know. She might be. Why?'

'Come on. Didn't you think she looked like she might be on pills or something? She did to me.' Cordy looked at her carefully. 'Try and keep your distance a bit, Ruth. Don't let your need to win her approval blind you to what she's like.'

'I don't know what you mean,' Ruth said, hurt.

'You're defending her. Making excuses for her. You were the one she was so horrible about.'

'Well — you have to take circumstances into account, don't you?'

'Maybe.' Cordy shrugged. 'Just watch out, that's all.'

★　★　★

Ruth moved a couple of the pictures off the chimney piece and put up two of her and Ned. She'd gone out in her lunch hour and bought pretty frames for them, wanting to put something of herself into the cottage. She had some leave to use up before Christmas and planned to get some paint and fabrics and do some decorating.

'Does it need it?' Ned had asked, surprised, looking about at the tatty walls and ancient dusty light fittings.

'Er — yes. Can I?'

'Darling, do whatever you like. I have no eye for colour.'

'From living with all that beige all your life probably.'

Ned had laughed. 'Very likely. But tell me what you want me to do, and I'll help.'

They had decided to take leave at the same time and spruce up the cottage, and Ruth was getting quite excited about it now, hunting round shops and department stores for bits and pieces.

She stood back to look at the effect of her new frames. One photograph had been taken at the Old Rectory by Silas, who had wrestled with the digital camera for a while before taking a decent photograph of Ned and Ruth sitting together at the roots of the big oak tree on the lawn. They were smiling broadly, their eyes shining, Ned's arm round her shoulders.

That's us, she thought, staring at it. It was reassuring to look at it. It gave her confirmation of their togetherness.

The dinner party at Erin and Tom's had been enjoyable but it had undermined some of her newly acquired confidence as far as belonging to the circle of friends went. She'd never spent an evening feeling quite so much an outsider. It wasn't that they meant to exclude her; it was just that she had nothing to offer to their reminiscences and private jokes, and her only possible role had been to listen and laugh, even when she didn't really understand what was funny.

They passed the conversation between them, from person to person round the table, sometimes tossing it across to someone unexpected, or having a two-person rally for the others to enjoy before resuming the game. The only person who wasn't required to take part was Ruth. Instead, she listened, trying to follow what they were talking about and wishing she could keep up with the jokes that seemed to fly about so fast.

'Have you heard what Jeremy's got in his bath?' demanded Tom, pushing away his plate. The group was curiously formal, seated around the dark wood dining table by candlelight. The house was a 1930s red-brick villa with bow windows and a generous garden. It was bigger than Ruth and Ned's little cottage, and the rooms had more substance, with nooks and cupboards and skirting, designed with a more modern life in mind. It was furnished in Thirties period, with contemporary touches and little twists, like the bright pink carpet in the sitting room and the multicoloured glass cocktail cabinet, that should have jarred but worked brilliantly. Just the kind of thing that someone like Erin would be able to pull off, thought Ruth.

When they arrived, Erin had come bursting out of the kitchen, exclaiming, 'Is that my Ned? Ned, come here quick, I need your help!' and Ned had gone off obediently, leaving Tom to show Ruth into the sitting room and offer her a drink.

'You can have the good gin if you like,' he'd said graciously. 'I usually keep it for Jeremy. He won't touch anything else.'

Ruth had taken it and sat awkwardly with him, grateful when the others arrived.

'What's in Jeremy's bath?' asked Abigail now.

'Water?' suggested Luke. 'Or am I being ridiculously naïve.'

'Tell them,' said Tom, with a chortle, pouring out more wine and passing the bottle to Ned.

Jeremy, opposite Tom at the far end of the table, shrugged. 'It's not as odd as you're making out.'

'It is. Tell them.'

'I have a dead fox in my bath,' Jeremy said at last. There was a general outcry.

'Oh God, why?' exclaimed Erin. 'How dead?'

'Are there degrees of deadness?'

'No, I mean — how long dead?'

Jeremy shrugged. 'It looked quite fresh when I found it on the road.'

'Why do you want a dead fox?' asked Ned, which seemed a reasonable question to Ruth.

Jeremy made a furious face at him. 'Because it might come in *useful*, that's why. I've tried to preserve it by filling the bath with ice cubes but it's made it very wet. I was hoping to get the pelt off somehow — I've always wanted a fox fur — but I may have gone about it the wrong way. It's looking a bit bedraggled anyhow. Not quite the lustrous brush I've dreamt of. A fox's tail is actually quite thin when all the fur is matted down, as you'd see if you came over.'

'Why didn't you put it in the freezer?' asked

101

Erin. 'That's what you do with mohair. Or is it angora?'

'I don't think my housemates would have liked it. And besides it wouldn't fit.'

'But they don't mind it in the bath?' Abigail said in disbelief.

'They're not *too* happy.' Jeremy made his furious face again, and pulled his tobacco tin out of his pocket. 'Such a fuss they're making, the old turds. Just when I'm trying to write about that arse Cicero as well. They have no sympathy for a man in torment. I can't be expected to think about the pompous tedium of *De Finibus Bonorum et Malorum* and how much a fox is smelling at the same time.'

'Perhaps you should throw it away?' ventured Ruth.

Jeremy turned and looked at her, puffing a bit through his nose. 'I fear, young miss, that that is what will eventually happen. But it seems such a *waste*, doesn't it?'

'You need something smaller that takes up less room. I'll buy you a dead rabbit,' said Ned. 'You can keep it in a bucket in your room. Avoid all that nasty recrimination from your ignorant co-habitees.'

Jeremy grinned at him as he gathered up shreds of tobacco in his long fingers. 'Ah, my friend. You put the Ned into refined.'

It seemed to Ruth that between the men, vying with their undoubted affection for each other was a competition for something, but she couldn't work out what it was. To be the funniest? she wondered. Or the cleverest? But that didn't seem right. The biggest competition is between Tom and Jeremy, she decided, watching them in the candlelight as they faced each other over the glowing mahogany. Where do the other two fit in? The women were excluded from the contest it seemed, but Erin seemed to preside over it, calm and unruffled like a queen watching her champions.

All the time, Ruth was reminded of how intimately their pasts were entwined; everything seemed to spark off a memory.

'Do you remember that time in the Prado?' Luke said, over pudding. 'When Ned had to run for the toilets?'

'You spent bloody hours in front of the Goyas,' Ned protested. 'I couldn't wait any longer.'

'Well, you should have,' Luke replied. 'Because I could have told you the Spanish word for toilet.'

'I thought that was the way to the bar. I kept seeing signs for beer.' Ned laughed.

'That is *cerveza*,' said Luke, loftily. 'You were seeing the word *servicios*, which is in no way the same.'

'Not to you. But it looked pretty similar to me. And every time I saw it, I got more and more desperate for a pee. Bloody hell. Thank God I found an English guide who pointed me in the right direction.'

'You only had to ask me,' Luke said.

'You were discussing the finer points of El Greco's use of pink with Jeremy, weren't you?'

'I like to call it his raspberry ripple period,'

remarked Jeremy, rolling another of his small fragrant cigarettes on the table.

Erin put in, 'I preferred the tapas afterwards. Remember that place with all the plants and that black paella?'

Ruth imagined them all, slim, tanned and barely out of their teens, travelling round Europe together on one of their holidays. It made her wish she had known them then, so that she could have joined in.

'Remember that place in Rome?' asked Luke. 'The grilled lamb? My god, that was wonderful. La Sabatina or something. Near the Jewish quarter.'

'Of course. The enormous open grill and the old man hunched over it, turning all that different meat,' said Jeremy.

'La Sabatina?' Erin echoed. 'I don't remember that. When did we go there?'

'*You* didn't, darling,' said Jeremy dryly. 'You weren't there. It was the day you and Tom got lost. Remember that?'

There was a strange, uncomfortable pause.

'Oh.' Erin laughed, with only a trace of discomfort. 'Of course I do. Well, I wish we hadn't missed the grilled lamb, I do love it. Where did we go from Rome? Was it Naples?'

Abigail said, 'I've heard these bloody stories so often I feel like I know the itinerary of your European tour better than you do. You went to Naples, sweetie, and it was closed and there was the rat on the pavement and the campsite on Vesuvius with the clouds of sulphur. Shall we talk about something else? Don't forget poor old

Ruth hasn't a clue what you're on about.'

'Let's play a game,' said Tom.

The others chorused their agreement. 'Scrabble?' suggested Luke. 'Drunk scrabble? Or foreign scrabble?'

'I'm rather keen on that twentieth-century general knowledge one at the moment,' remarked Tom.

'That's another thing,' said Abigail in a low voice to Ruth. 'This lot are crazy about games. You'll never get away from an evening here without playing something. I'm terrible at it, so don't worry. They all get carried away between them.'

'It's true,' said Erin, hearing the end of the conversation as she topped up Ruth's glass. 'If there are points, and a winner at the end, we'll do it. Do you remember — ' she turned to the rest of the table ' — our bridge craze? Once we sat up for two whole nights without stopping, playing endless rubbers of bridge, taking it in turns to sit out.' She shook her head. 'I think that's why I mucked up my end-of-term exams. Stupid.'

'But fun,' said Jeremy. 'Addictive.'

'Come on then, foreign scrabble!' announced Luke.

'Just because you can speak three languages,' grumbled Ned. 'Let's do ordinary scrabble. Break Ruth in gently. In fact, I think we should do it in teams or we'll be here all night.'

'Will you be on my team, Bear?' wheedled Erin, putting her hand over Ned's. 'You know lots of three-letter words and I'm *hopeless*.' She looked about at the rest of the table. 'What do

105

you think? Two teams? Shall we split the couples up? It seems fairer that way, doesn't it?'

'I'll get the board,' said Tom, getting up.

'And Ruth can be on my team,' announced Jeremy, smiling at her. 'Come over here, miss, and sit by me.'

⋆ ⋆ ⋆

In bed later, both of them a little drunk and lazily talkative, Ned was anxious that Ruth had enjoyed herself.

'I liked it. I like learning about your life before you met me,' she insisted. 'Even if we did lose the scrabble.'

'Jeremy was not happy,' said Ned with a laugh. 'He hates losing.'

'You and Erin seemed to make a good team.'

'Ah, well, we had Luke. The secret weapon. He can always make a word out of any combination of letters.'

Something had been nagging at her. She remembered what it was. 'What did she call you? Before the game.'

'Oh. It's just an old nickname. Sometimes I was called Bear at uni. Edward, and all that. Teddy. Bear. I think that's how it went.'

'No one calls you that now, do they?'

'Not really.' He said after a moment, 'Do you like Erin?'

She thought. She had mixed feelings about Erin, she knew that, torn between admiration and a kind of jealousy — not for Erin's glamour, beauty and style, but for everything she'd known and shared with Ned. It was as though she owned a piece of him. 'I hardly know her, but she seems very nice. She's been lovely to me.'

'It's always been difficult for Erin. She's one of the boys really. She hasn't had many girlfriends. I think other women find her a bit scary.'

'Because she's so beautiful.'

'She's striking,' Ned said slowly. 'And she gets attention. That's why she's an actress, I suppose. She can't help it. And that puts some people off.'

'It doesn't put me off.'

'I know. Because you are a generous person and you don't have a jealous bone in your body. But not everyone is as wonderful as you — in fact, no one is.' Ned dropped a kiss on the end of her nose.

'Are she and Tom happy?' Ruth asked suddenly.

'I don't know. I suppose so.'

'How long have they been together?'

Ned frowned. 'Um . . . let's see. It's about ten years now.'

'How long have they been married?'

'Oh, they're not married.'

'But she wears that ring.' Ruth had noticed it particularly: a beautiful platinum band with six glittering diamonds set deep into the metal.

'It's a kind of wedding ring — the kind you wear when you're not actually married but as good as.'

'But she said that thing about wives the other day — about Luke not having an understanding wife like her and you said I was your fiancée but no one said anything about Erin not being a wife either.'

Ned lay back on his pillow, staring at the ceiling, running one hand through his hair. 'I think she's come to think of herself as a wife.'

'So you all just pretend along with her.'

'I wouldn't say that. It's just . . . I don't know . . . she's an actress. She can pretend convincingly. In the end, you believe in her.'

Ruth frowned. That didn't seem right somehow. Was Ned saying that Erin had the power to change reality and make them all accept it? 'What I don't understand is why they *aren't* married. I mean, Erin is obviously a very desirable woman. I'm surprised Tom hasn't done his best to snare her.'

'Marriage isn't really Tom's scene. And he takes a long time to make up his mind. I think Erin's given up on ever getting him down the aisle. I don't know if she even really cares. She knows Tom well enough. If he could, he'd exist in the same state for ever. He only moved into that house because Erin threatened blue murder if he didn't sell the tiny place they were in for years before that. We were all pretty amazed when he gave Erin that ring in the first place. Not like him to make a gesture that committed him to something indefinitely. But I think he was a bit more keen on the whole permanent thing back then, probably just to be sure that she wasn't going to go back to Jeremy.'

'Jeremy?' asked Ruth, surprised. 'Your Jeremy?'

'Yes. Didn't I say?'

'No, you didn't.' She was exasperated. Why

did men never seem to appreciate the drama of people's lives and how interesting they were? 'Are you telling me that Erin and Jeremy used to be a couple?'

'Oh yes, for years. All the way through university. But then she and Jeremy broke up, and she and Tom got together.'

'That's all. Simple as that.' Her voice had a touch of sarcasm. 'There must be more to it than that. Tell me about it.'

Ned turned his eyes to the ceiling. 'Oh lord, you're going to make me pick over every single bit of it, aren't you? It's a long story. I'm tired. I'll tell you everything tomorrow, promise.' He yawned hugely. 'I don't know how much use I'm going to be. I'm not very good at it.'

'Try.'

'Okay. As long as you let me go to sleep now. Promise?'

'It's a deal.'

★   ★   ★

As they headed out the next day, Ruth thought that one of the things she most loved about Ned was how he enjoyed walking. He had no time for cars and only owned his battered old Volkswagen because he had to; he attached no value to it. If he could possibly walk or cycle instead of driving, he would. She'd always found boyfriends who loved cars slightly ridiculous: their excitement over engine size and gadgets made her want to laugh and, in the end, bored her.

Their cottage was at the far end of the village,

a mile along the main road, long after it had left behind the common, the primary school and the rows of shops and pubs that formed the heart of the village. The road went out between hedgerows and through woods, a mud-spattered, wilderness-edged ribbon leading to the next village, where Erin and Tom lived.

They marched along smartly in their coats and scarves, breathing in lungfuls of sharp air. The autumn was now upon them; they could no longer pretend it was just summer with a hint of chill. Although there were still warm, blue-skied days, the frosty bite in the breeze increased just a little more each day. There were already heaps of crackling leaves underfoot, the shop signs swung in strong gusts of wind, and the beech trees around the common were losing their lime-green freshness and fading quickly to yellow. They followed the pavement out of the village and then tramped along the roadside, Ned on the hard surface and Ruth picking her way on the high grassy verge, her hands thrust in her jacket pockets.

'Come on then,' prodded Ruth. 'Tell me all about it.'

Ned began to explain, hesitantly at first and then getting into his stride. 'We were all a bit amazed by Erin, I suppose, and a bit frightened of her. Tom, Luke and I had been at all-boys' schools and had barely spoken to a woman. Then Erin came along, wanting to be our friend, and tell us how clever and funny we all were. It put us in a bit of a spin, to be frank. After all, she could have anyone — all the guys were interested in her — and she wanted to be with us. I mean, we weren't outcasts or anything, but we weren't at the forefront of fashion. We were flattered — all of us.'

'Did you all fall in love with her?'

Ned shot her a sideways glance. 'We were all a bit starry-eyed for a while, but it wore off pretty quickly. Besides, it was obvious at once that it was Jeremy she was interested in and the rest of us accepted that — well, except for Tom, but no one knew it at the time.'

'Why Jeremy?' It puzzled her; they didn't seem a natural fit. Jeremy, tall and gawky, surely lacked the polish that someone like Erin would find attractive.

Ned shrugged. 'Who knows what people see in each other? But my theory is that Jeremy is clever and a touch eccentric, and Erin is very attracted to clever, unusual people.'

'*You're* clever,' said Ruth quickly, defensive on his behalf.

'I'm not really in Jeremy's league. He's always been effortlessly brilliant.'

'Well, what about Tom? Is he clever?'

Ned thought for moment. 'He's clever enough. But he's also difficult, and that's what Erin likes. She likes a challenge. Men are usually all over her, so she likes someone who treats her a bit mean. And there are other things she likes about Tom as well — his background. His family. The whole package.'

'How did she get together with him?'

'Don't know really,' he said carelessly.

'Oh come on, you must know something.'

'Not really.' He puffed out a breath. 'I don't know enough about what went on, to be honest. One day Jeremy and Erin split up — I think she said she wanted to take some time out to think about the future. Then, suddenly, after our holiday in Europe, she and Tom got together.'

'Did Jeremy mind?'

'If he did, he's over it now.'

Ruth thought about it. It seemed strange to her, that the group should stay so intact despite a change of partners. Surely it couldn't be as amicable as it looked.

'Did you know how Tom felt about her?'

'I had an idea. There had been signs. We were all living together at the time, anyway.'

'*All* of you?'

'Me. Tom. Erin. We shared a flat.'

She hadn't known that. The story seemed more and more tangled. Something prickled at her, worrying her with a nasty edginess. 'What about you?' she asked, almost nervously.

'What do you mean?'

'Did you . . . were you ever in love with Erin? Not just starry-eyed, but really in love?' She was suddenly afraid of what he might say. Ned put an arm round her and pulled her close.

'No,' he said. 'I was a bit dazzled for about five minutes when we first met, but ever since then, we've been friends and that's it. That's why she and I are such good mates, because there's never been anything like that between us and there never will be.'

'But why? She's so beautiful. Don't you find her attractive?'

'Nope. It's never crossed my mind.' He stroked a finger down her nose as they walked. 'You're the most attractive woman in the world. Please don't think for a moment that I could ever prefer someone over you.'

'Don't be silly.' She pushed him playfully. But inside she was relieved. For a minute, she'd felt a horrible shiver of fear, and she was delighted to have it laid to rest.

* * *

Ruth put her key up to the lock, trying to hold all her shopping and open the front door at the same time, when it unexpectedly opened and Ned was standing there in his fluorescent cycling jacket.

'Oh thanks,' she said, smiling. 'I was about to have a spillage.'

Ned took some bags from her and carried them through to the kitchen, saying over his shoulder, 'I'm just off out, actually.'

'Where to?'

'Erin called. Her heating's not working. Apparently it's freezing in her house.'

'Can't Tom fix it?'

'He's working late. So I'm just going to pop over — see if I can locate the problem.'

She tried to hide her exasperation. 'When will you be back? What shall I do about supper?'

'Dunno. Should be back soon. I've got the radiator key so I'm going to try bleeding them, see if there's an air lock or something. See you later.' He headed out of the front door, slamming it behind him.

Ruth sighed crossly. Am I imagining it? she wondered. Is it the way I think it is, with Erin always summoning Ned to her, and he leaping to do her bidding like some kind of indentured servant? Or am I being too touchy?

Perhaps she was oversensitive. She had to guard against behaving selfishly, insisting Ned devote himself entirely to her; he had known his friends far longer than he had her. She shouldn't be surprised if it took a while before the balance of power shifted. Besides it was in his nature to help anyone in distress — it was another reason why she loved him.

Maisie came through the cat-flap, climbing in delicately and whisking her tail out of the way before it shut with a snap.

'Hello, girly, hello my Maisie,' said Ruth, crouching down to stroke her. The cat wove in and out of her legs, purring. It had taken a while but Maisie seemed to be settling in at last. At first too fearful to venture out, she was now happy to slide into the garden so, with some relief, Ruth had put the litter tray away. It was no fun coming down to it in the morning. Now that Maisie was so old, she wasn't as pernickety and neat as she had once been, and a scattering of litter all over the kitchen floor was most unattractive first thing.

'You're doing all right, now, though, aren't you? This is home now, isn't it?' crooned Ruth. She put some cat food down, and poured herself a glass of wine. Glancing at the clock, she saw that it was nearly seven o'clock. 'Any moment now,' she muttered. She turned on the radio and wondered what to make for supper. A few minutes later, as she'd expected, the phone blared out. It happened every other night, sometimes on consecutive days, and she tried to avoid answering it if she could, leaving it to Ned, because she never quite knew who she would be picking up the phone to. Sometimes it would be an abrupt stranger who said, 'Is Edward Haskell there?' and when she said he hadn't got in from work, would say, 'Could you tell him Mrs Haskell called, please? Thank you.' Or a sweet-voiced, tender woman would say, 'Ruth, is that you? It's Mum. How are you?' It was mysterious. When she tried to make a joke of it to Ned, he'd frowned and said, 'Just ignore her.'

But it was difficult to ignore someone who called the house so often, seemingly with no memory that the last time they'd phoned, they'd pretended not to know who had answered.

She was tempted to leave it, but it was hard to resist a ringing phone. It demanded to be picked up, like a screaming child. 'Hello?'

There was a long pause, as though the person on the other end had not decided what to do in the event their call was actually answered.

'Ruth.'

'Yes.' She stumbled mentally over saying 'Mum', so she said brightly, 'How are *you*?'

'It's Edward's mother.'

'I know. Hello.'

'Is he there?'

'No, he's just popped out. If you call a bit later, you'll get him.'

'This wedding. What's happening?'

'Well . . . we've only just started making plans really. Nothing concrete.'

'Where are you having it? I've waited long enough for you two to get yourselves sorted out, and I'm not waiting any longer. I spoke to the man who runs our club, and he told me that they often put on wedding parties. They do a lovely deal for you — a whole spread for up to a hundred, a bar, a disco — and it's very reasonable. So I've put down a provisional booking for next summer but they want a deposit.'

'Oh . . . ' Ruth was stumped. She hardly knew where to begin. She struggled for words. 'We . . . I . . . that's very kind of you but . . . it's just . . . '

'Do you want me to pay the deposit?'

'No, no. I'd better talk to Ned first.'

'He'll be delighted, if I know him. But you need to tell me the date and let me have this cheque.'

'All right,' she said, wishing she could just say *how kind but there's no need, we're making all the arrangements ourselves*, but she couldn't. Dealing with someone so unpredictable but whose opinion of her mattered so much was frightening; the backbone she had when dealing with difficult patients turned to jelly and failed her.

'Call me back later,' said Jackie curtly, and put the phone down.

Ned came in half an hour later, cold-cheeked from the gusty night outside. 'Brrr. That wasn't too much trouble. Don't know if I've fixed it but I gave it the once-over.' He saw her face. 'What's wrong?'

She told him what had happened. In the time since Jackie had called, she'd managed to work herself up into a fit of anxiety. She could now see the wedding she'd imagined some time in the New Year, married from the Old Rectory in the familiar church next door by the vicar she'd known all her life, steamrollered and replaced by a summer do somewhere in the north, where she would feel like a stranger.

'You've got to tell her,' Ruth said desperately. 'I don't want her taking everything over. Will you?'

'Of course I will.' Ned spoke soothingly, trying to calm her down. 'Don't worry about it. She's like this sometimes, she's a bit impatient and when she starts fretting over something, she'll suddenly take action.'

'I don't understand why she would do that without asking us.' Ruth sat down at the dining room table, her shoulders hunched. It seemed to her that such rudeness must be an act of hostility. *She's telling me she doesn't like me,* she thought. It seemed to be the only answer.

'It's just provisional, isn't it? It probably seems like a wonderful idea to her — she knows the people, trusts them not to rip her off, thinks she can get a good deal. She's only doing it to help.'

'But it doesn't help!' Ruth felt that Ned was being obstinate, putting a harmless gloss on his mother's invasion. 'This is *our* wedding. I'm delighted if she wants to use her club for a party

117

or something, but it's not for us.'

'I know. I'll tell her. We just need to keep her in the loop a bit. It will stop her from getting anxious.'

'I don't understand it, though,' Ruth persisted. She had kept her anxieties about Jackie to herself for long enough and now she wanted Ned to give her some answers. Surely he must know why his mother behaved in the way she did? So why did she feel that the whole thing was about soothing *her*, making her feel like the unreasonable one? 'Why does she do it? I wouldn't dream of imposing on someone else like that.'

Ned's face took on the shut-off look he developed so often when they talked about his mother. 'Ruth — don't go on about it. Mum's not perfect, I know that. She has her own way of doing things that don't always conform to what other people think is right.' He shrugged as if to say 'there's your answer'.

'And you just let her? Don't you ever tell her when she's crossed a line?' She remembered suddenly the way that Ned had said almost nothing when Jackie had insulted her at the Old Rectory lunch. 'Is she allowed to do whatever she likes?'

'There are things you don't understand,' Ned said sharply.

'Shouldn't you tell me what they are, seeing as she's going to be my mother-in-law?'

Ned turned away, his shoulders set in the way that she was learning meant he refused to say anything more. She felt anxiety rush through her: she hated the way that Jackie was coming between them. *I must make it all right*, she thought. *I'll have to win her over.* For a wild minute she wondered if she should give in and agree to have her wedding at Jackie's club but the mental image that floated in front of her mind's eye made her want to giggle with slight hysteria. Her anger began to subside into a weary confusion. 'I just don't know what I've done to annoy her,' she said at last, in a weak voice that signalled she wanted to make up.

Ned turned back to her. 'You haven't done anything. She's just . . . it's just the way she is, all right? You just have to be careful how you deal with her.'

'I really want her to like me. I'm trying so hard, you know I am. Whenever she calls, I talk to her and listen to everything she's got to say . . . '

'I know. And you're brilliant. She likes you very much, really, she does. But, like I say . . . ' He frowned and sighed. 'She's just the way she is. Carry on the way you are, it will be fine.'

Ned was being deliberately evasive but Ruth could tell that he was not going to be drawn any further on the subject. She had no choice but to leave it. *I'll sort it out on my own*, she decided. *I know I can win her over if I try hard enough.*

Later, he took the phone into the spare room and came out after an hour looking exhausted.

'Is everything all right?' asked Ruth anxiously. She'd been hovering nearby, catching the rise and fall of Ned's voice but unable to follow what was going on. There hadn't been any shouting as far as she could make out, so Ned's diplomatic skills must have been effective.

'Yup,' he said gruffly. 'Don't worry about the club, it's not going to happen. But we ought to go ahead now and make our arrangements so she can't carry on doing stuff. She's worrying away at it like a dog with a bone and she won't be able to let it go until we can present her with what we've decided.'

'Thank you.' Ruth hugged him, relieved. 'We'd better start planning then, hadn't we?' She grinned up at him, her mood happy now that her anxiety had passed. 'It'll be fun. I'll get some bridal magazines and we can start deciding what we want.'

He groaned good-naturedly. 'I'm happy to do whatever you want.'

'But I want it to be what we *both* want.'

'I know — but you tell me what you want first, and we'll see if I agree, which I probably will.'

'You're no fun,' said Ruth, pouting, eager to make up with him. He'd gone in and fought the battle for her and he'd won it. She was sorry now that she had overreacted.

'Aren't I?' he said, kissing her ear.

'Mmm, well, sometimes you are . . . '

'Maybe now, perhaps?'

She kissed him back. I won't worry about Jackie, she promised herself. I won't even think about her.

7

Erin drove with the same kind of effortlessness she brought to everything, Ruth thought. It was just that the sight of her steering with only the pressure of one slim wrist balanced on the top of the wheel, her other hand on the gear stick, made Ruth wish nervously that she was just a bit less casual as they hared down the country lanes, taking blind corners at a reckless pelt.

'It's very kind of you to do this,' said Ruth, trying not to look at the speedometer.

'No problem at all,' said Erin, with a smile. 'It's the least I could do.'

Ned and Ruth had been painting the sitting room when Erin had called and, for once, hadn't asked to speak to Ned. She and Ruth had chatted for a while before Erin asked, 'Now, how are you getting on with your wedding dress? Have you found anything?'

'Not yet. I've been looking but nothing so far.' She and Cordy had been out on one expedition and Valentina had gone with her on another, but they'd had no luck. They'd first tried the traditional dressmakers in Oxford, the kind who supplied dresses to all the county girls. Their rails were crammed with stiff ivory silk and satin creations, all with big skirts, trains and lots of buttons, designed to be worn with a tiara, an antique veil, and a rich groom. Ruth felt like a fraud in them. Then they'd gone to the department stores and the specialist high-street shops, but those dresses weren't right either. There was something standard about them — nothing challenging, all perfectly nice, but nothing special either; they would do the job adequately. Despite their ordinariness, though, they were not cheap and Ruth was beginning to be depressed. It was not as though she had a set idea of what her wedding dress should be. She was, she thought, easily pleased, but nothing she had seen was right.

'Then you have to come with me. I know the perfect place. I'll be right over.'

Ruth had left Ned painting the woodwork, scrubbed the paint off her hands, and waited for Erin to collect her in the Mini Cooper.

'It's a place I heard about,' she said, as they headed out towards one of the remoter Gloucestershire villages. 'It's in the middle of nowhere and a bit bizarre but I was told about it by one of the costume designers on a TV thing I did. Apparently it's incredible. They use it for movies and photo-shoots quite a lot.'

When they arrived at the small shop, it was evident at once that it was indeed different. The window was crammed with things from top to bottom, each more sparkling and glittery than the last: necklaces, fans, shoes, embroidered veils, earrings, bracelets, silk flowers, jewels for the fingers and the hair and the wrists, and two stunning gem-encrusted corsets.

Ruth was open-mouthed. 'These fabrics are beautiful! My goodness, I was looking for a pattern just like that floral basque for the bedroom curtains. But — are you sure? I mean, this place looks as though it might be for someone a little more . . . er . . . dramatic than me.'

Erin laughed. 'It is a bit like a fantasy dressing-up box isn't it? But we haven't seen the dresses yet. Anyway, a bit of sparkly colour is nice in the depths of winter. Let's face it, you can go two ways: the snow queen in white, with fake fur everywhere — very Narnia but perhaps a bit done — or the bright beacon of light, glamour and colour.'

'Are those the only two ways?' ventured Ruth. 'I'm not sure if either of them is right.'

'Well, let's go in and see.'

Once inside, they could see that the window was the eye-catcher, the extravaganza designed to lure one in. The interior was a little more restrained, although there were still plenty of beautiful things. Ruth was drawn to some exquisite jewelled flowers, violets made of amethyst rimmed in twisted gold, like something that Fabergé would have made for the Russian Imperial family.

'Where would you wear these?' she asked Erin, who was already exclaiming over some Madame de Pompadour shoes of silver damask silk with white satin rosettes.

'Those could be worn in your hair, like this!' boomed a voice behind her, and Ruth turned to see a tall, imposing woman, dressed in a long black velvet robe, her hair hidden under a fur hat and her eyes the false cornflower blue of coloured contact lenses. She stepped forward from the darkness at the back of the shop like a bear emerging from its lair, and took Ruth's hair up into one of her hands, smoothing it with the other. 'Oh, this is beautiful hair. This colour — the most wonderful auburn! These violets would be stunning against this. Look.' In a deft movement, she twisted Ruth's hair upwards and arranged the ornament on her head; holding it with one hand, she took the jewels in the other; they were mounted on long pins, and she quickly skewered them through Ruth's hair so that they were held in place — the flowers glinting prettily on the side of Ruth's head. 'There! Beautiful, aren't they?'

'They are,' breathed Ruth, turning her head so that she could see the effect.

'That does look wonderful, Ruth.' Erin emerged next to her, staring at her reflection.

'Is this for a wedding?' asked the woman. 'You're getting married, aren't you?' She indicated the ring on Ruth's finger.

'Yes. I am.'

'You have come to the right place!' the woman exclaimed. 'Here you will find the dress of your dreams, I promise you that. I am Xenia Yasparov and I design the finest things in the world. You would be amazed by the people who come to me. I am not at liberty to reveal exactly who they are but they are international royalty! Princesses! Queens! And stars of the world of music and the stage.'

Ruth bit back the urge to giggle. She had no idea if this was true but it was certainly an effective act. The name she was sure was invented, and probably everything else as well.

Erin said, 'My friend is getting married in January in a church. She hasn't found anything suitable yet.'

'She will now,' Xenia Yasparov said confidently. 'I have everything you will need.'

Ruth was not convinced at first: the designer led her to a rail of clothes and showed her what looked like a morass of lace and fake flowers. She could see pink pompoms stitched to lurid blue veils, and chintz bodices, like something from a Regency farce, with dangling long laces. She was persuaded to try on an Elizabethan style dress — 'so suitable for the winter! And edged in real mink. Please don't tell me you object' — but the fur-edged neckline, the tight corset and the heavy fabric dotted with seed pearls made her feel as though she were going to a fancy dress party.

'You look magnificent,' breathed the designer solemnly. 'Like a young Elizabeth the First with that red hair. I think you should wear it.'

'I might look a little out of place.' Ruth turned and looked in the mirror, hoping she'd be strong enough to resist the designer and fearing that if she weren't, she'd have to persuade Ned to get married in a doublet and hose.

'Then remove it at once!' cried Xenia. 'You must feel nothing less than the star, than the ultimate! Come, I have other things . . . '

They looked at frothing white confections that made Ruth think of Cecil Beaton's Thirties photographs of the Queen Mother, and at flounced crinolines and body-hugging Fifties-style sweetheart dresses.

'Do you want white?' Erin asked, as they put back another organza creation.

'I'm not sure. Perhaps not. I know it's traditional but . . . '

'Oh!' said Xenia, suddenly. 'I have the thing, the very thing. I don't know why I didn't think of it before. Wait.' She disappeared into the murk at the back of the shop and emerged again a moment later with a gown carefully draped over one arm. 'This is new — a prototype. But I may as well have designed it with you in mind. For it is perfect.'

She held up the dress: it was a silk sheath of the palest green, cut on the bias and looking shapeless on its hanger. Over it was a long silk coat in the same delicate shade — like a pale green waterlily — but embroidered all over with silver thread and the most intricate and beautiful pattern of chinoiserie: minute jewel-coloured, iridescent birds hidden among silver and green vines and tiny, delicate silken flowers.

Erin gasped. 'It's exquisite!'

'It is,' agreed the designer proudly. 'You must try this. I think it will fit. I make my prototypes bigger than most other designers, because I am tall myself.'

'I don't know . . . ' Ruth said doubtfully. 'It's gorgeous but I don't think it will suit my shape. It looks more like your sort of thing, Erin.'

'Just try,' coaxed Erin.

'Try,' echoed the designer in her deep voice.

She was wrong. She had thought that the

126

bias-cut silk would be unforgiving to her curvy shape but instead it gave her the voluptuous silhouette of Jean Harlow, clinging to all the right places. Over it, the embroidered coat toned down the outrageous sexiness of the sheath, creating a demureness that was appropriate for a church bride. She stood in front of the mirror, marvelling at her glittering reflection.

'You look wonderful,' said Erin, her voice a little choked. 'Oh dear, look at me. I'm all teary. You look so romantic, like a fairytale princess!'

'But do I look like a bride?'

'You couldn't be anything else.'

Ruth couldn't take her eyes off the shimmering clothes. 'Should it be white?'

Xenia said, 'I could make it in white . . . but I would have to order the fabric to be specially made. It would take many months.'

'Why white?' exclaimed Erin. 'It's nonsense these days! All that virginal rubbish. Next you'll be telling me you want to love, honour and obey. It's not as though you're in scarlet, either. This pale green is fabulous — it makes me think of the edge of white hydrangea petals. It's so elegant. And with your colouring . . . look at you!'

It was true that her skin, often washed out by strong colours, was creamy and her hair glinted richly, still twisted round its jewelled violets. For the first time, she didn't feel cast into the shade by Erin.

'And shoes,' purred Xenia. 'Look at these . . . ' She slid some pale green velvet slippers with tiny silver heels under Ruth's feet. 'Perfect.'

127

'It does look amazing,' murmured Ruth. She saw herself standing in the door of the church, a jewel against the ancient grey stone. It was what she'd dreamed of, only she hadn't known. She turned to Xenia. 'How much?'

'For the dress and the coat? Oh dear . . . that is my prototype. It will take some time to make the dress up for you.'

'But this one . . . it fits perfectly. This is what I want.'

'I'm not sure.' The designer frowned. Panicked, Ruth felt the desperate yearning for something that appears to be in reach and is then taken away.

She tried not to show her emotion but looked appraisingly in the mirror again and said slowly, 'If you would be willing to sell the prototype, I'd be very grateful. I don't think I can wait for you to make up another dress and there isn't really anything else I like.'

Xenia thought for a moment. 'Well, it would mean I would need to start again from scratch on this dress. But perhaps if you would also buy the hair jewels and the shoes, it would then be worth my while.'

'How much would everything be?'

Xenia named a figure that made Erin draw in her breath with a hiss and Ruth feel a little faint. It was three times more than she had planned to spend on her dress.

'Would your father help you?' Erin asked in a low voice.

'I don't know. He might. My mother left me some money as well, which I'd always planned to

128

use for my wedding. I suppose I could call on some of that.'

'Look at it this way — that includes the shoes and the hair — you don't need a veil with this dress. And I'll do your hair and make-up, you know I'm good at that. And as it's not white, you can always wear it again.'

'Of course, I could wear it again,' she said, looking longingly at the dress. She couldn't now imagine getting married in anything else. She looked up at Xenia Yasparov. She felt reckless. This was her wedding dress, after all. 'I'll take it,' she said.

★ ★ ★

'Thank you so much for taking me there,' she said to Erin, as they drove back home. 'It means a lot to me.'

'You can't go shopping for your wedding dress on your own! It was all fun for me. I like nothing better than looking at very expensive dresses. It's just a shame that your sister couldn't go with you.'

'Cordy never can get away in the day. She's far too busy.'

'Is she your bridesmaid?'

'I suppose she will be. I haven't asked her yet. Oh, God, that's another thing. What on earth is she going to wear, with me in that dress?'

'Put it this way, she's going to find it very difficult to upstage you. If I were you, I would look for something in the evening wear department. Something quietly dressy. In grey, perhaps. Or a kind of khaki.'

Ruth laughed. 'It sounds pretty horrible, the way you describe it.'

'You should be the centre of attention. The bridesmaid has a job to do, she doesn't need frills and furbelows.'

'Well, I've still got a couple of months. I'm sure we'll find something in the meantime. I really do appreciate your help, Erin. I mean it.'

'You're very welcome. Any time.'

★ ★ ★

'How did it go?' called Ned as she let herself in the front door. She seemed to have been away for hours. But at least she had done it — she'd found the dress. It had been worth taking the whole day to do it.

'Fine, fine.' She went into the kitchen, where Ned was sitting at the kitchen table, a beer in one hand, his tee-shirt sweat stained. 'Hard day painting the woodwork?'

'Harder than you'd think actually. And I did the bookcase in the bedroom too.'

'You're a star. Thank you. I promise I'll get the curtains made up for the sitting room. That can be my job.'

'Don't hurry on my account.' He grinned up at her. 'So . . . did you find it?'

'What?' she asked innocently, getting herself a drink of water.

'What,' he repeated scornfully. '*What*? The dress, of course! Come on, tell me everything.'

'Yes, I found one. I think you'll like it. It's a

huge yellow meringue with a matching bonnet. I look a bit like those loo-roll dolls, with their crinoline dresses. I'm even thinking of getting a matching parasol.'

'And maybe a goat you can lead on a yellow string,' said Ned, laughing.

'What a good idea!' She sat down opposite him. 'Or perhaps you could just wear a goat costume and I could lead you about.'

'Too accurate a representation of our relation-ship.' He took her hand and kissed it. 'I wouldn't want our friends and relations to see us like that.' He gazed at her for a moment. 'Mmm. You are beautiful, do you know that? You look radiant today.'

'Do I?' She was still brimming with the excitement of finding her dress, and of it now being her secret.

'Yes.' He leaned over and kissed her gently on the lips. He tasted faintly salty, from the sweat of his exertions with the paintbrush. The gentle soft kisses became stronger and longer, until they were utterly absorbed in each other.

Ned pulled away for a moment. 'Let's go upstairs,' he whispered. Together they half-walked, half-stumbled out of the kitchen, giggling between kisses as they went up to their bedroom. They sank down together on the bed. She loved this moment and the way he made her feel: it was so pleasurable she couldn't imagine ever feeling anything less than this deep warm bliss, as he wrapped her in his arms and enveloped her. Even though their love-making was now familiar, she felt the same pitch of excitement and wonder as she had the first time. Everything about him pleased her: his strong limbs and flat stomach; the pattern of freckles on his arms; the soft sprinkling of hair on his chest and the sweet musky smell that seemed to impregnate his skin and hair. She ran her hands over his buttocks and up his strong back as he murmured his pleasure at her touch, and returned her caresses.

When the first peal of the telephone came, they hardly heard it, they were so lost in each other. It was only when the shrill sound had echoed through the house for the third time that Ned pulled away from her.

'Shall I get it?'

'Leave it. It can't be anything urgent. They'll ring back.'

'Perhaps I ought to get it . . . ' He stretched over her and reached for the phone on the bedside table.

'Don't. It's probably Tom — ' She bit her lip in annoyance as he picked up the handset and pressed the button.

'Hello?' He closed his eyes briefly. 'Oh, hi Mum.' Rolling off her, he lay on his back and put a hand up to his forehead, rubbing it just above his brows. 'No, no . . . this is fine. Yep.'

Ruth lay still, not wanting to give away her presence so close to Ned. She tried to quell her irritation with him, and listened instead to the distant tinny voice inside the handset. She couldn't make out any words, just a little constant buzz of sound. Instead, she tried to decipher what was being said from Ned's side of the conversation.

'Yeah, she's fine . . . yeah. Well, I don't know, I haven't asked her. I told you the date . . . it's the eighteenth of January . . . '

It's about the wedding, thought Ruth. She felt a pang of guilt that she hadn't been in touch with Mrs Haskell to discuss it. Ned had passed on the date and Ruth assumed that would be enough for now.

' . . . I know, I know . . . no one's expecting that . . . you don't have to do that. Honestly, Mum . . . ' He was silent for a while, listening, his eyes closed. ' . . . Yes, I understand but I don't think that's the case . . . Uh huh. Okay. I'll ask her now.'

He covered the mouthpiece and said in a low voice, 'What are your plans for Christmas?'

Ruth was taken aback. She'd hardly thought about Christmas. She was so taken up with the wedding plans, she had almost forgotten Christmas would happen in between. Besides, what was there to plan? The same would happen this year as happened every year.

'My plans?' she whispered back. 'I just thought I'd do what I always do — go to my father's. I'm always there from Christmas Eve till New Year.'

Ned took his hand off the phone, turning away from her again. 'I think we'll go to Ruth's, Mum.' There was another long pause as the metallic voice started up again. 'Okay, look, I'll talk to her about it. Okay? I'll call you back when we've decided. Yeah. Bye.'

He clicked the phone off, looking annoyed.

133

'I didn't really think. Was she cross? I just assumed we would go to my place.' It was impossible to imagine Christmas anywhere other than the Old Rectory, with the fire ablaze, the tree covered in the familiar old ornaments, including the battered things that she and Cordy had made at primary school, and all their old rituals. There would be oysters, tiny hot sausages and cold Chablis for Christmas Eve supper, carols on the radio and then whisky macs to warm them up for the walk to Midnight Mass, even though the church was only two minutes away. The next day, after stockings were opened, there would be presents round the tree, a lazy breakfast and then Ruth would make Christmas lunch for the other two, usually beef or venison or, if she were feeling particularly traditional, a goose. Then there would be a long walk around the village, bumping into old friends who were also walking off their lunch, before they dropped into Mrs Jackson's for tea and Christmas cake. Ruth realised she could not bear the thought of any other kind of Christmas but this — this *was* Christmas.

'Mum's kind of protective of Christmas too. She likes to do it her way. It's always us. Me, Mum and Dad and Susan, and a couple of relations. Mum's brother used to come every year up until a few years back when there was a bit of a row and he doesn't come any more. But other than that, it's just the same.'

'And she wants us to go?'

'She expects us to go.'

They lay together quietly for a moment,

thinking their own thoughts. Ruth said quietly, 'Was she upset about the wedding too?'

Ned sighed. He reached for her hand and pressed it to his chest. 'She's got . . . ideas, about how things ought to be done. And I think she's a bit over-excited, she's dying to get in and organise it all.'

'But . . . it's *my* wedding. And I am the bride, and we're paying for it ourselves. She has your sister, doesn't she? Won't she be able to organise your sister's wedding?'

'To be honest, it doesn't look like Susan is going to get married any time in the near future. And even if she did, I don't think Mum would get much of a look-in. They're not on the best of terms. I imagine if Susan ever did get married, she'd do it as far away from home as she could.'

'Why don't they get on?'

'Oh. You know. The usual. Hardly anyone gets on with their mother, do they? Especially daughters.'

Ruth didn't know. She remembered getting on well with her own mother; nearly all her memories were of laughter and affection. But then, she hadn't negotiated the tortuous terrain of adolescence with her mother. Perhaps it would all have gone wrong there, as it seemed to with so many others.

'Do you think . . . do you think that if we spent Christmas with your mother, she might hold off a little on the wedding?' asked Ruth, her voice tentative. She wanted to do the right thing, and she very much wanted Ned's parents to like her. But it was also her wedding, and she didn't

135

want to start compromising it.

'She might. I don't know. I can't promise anything.'

'Wouldn't Boxing Day be any good?'

'I don't think it would.'

'Well . . . how about if she and your dad came to the Old Rectory for Christmas?' she said, inspired. 'There's loads of room! They'd love it — it's so cosy and Christmassy, like something out of a children's story. Why don't you suggest it?'

'She wouldn't do it,' answered Ned gently. 'It's her thing. Her day. She's in charge. She would hate it if she was the guest.'

'Oh.' Ruth imagined Christmas in that cold, pristine living room. It made her heart sink, and a mantle of depression descend on her. 'Then . . . I suppose we ought to go. I'm sure Dad will understand. We'll go to him on Boxing Day instead.'

This, she thought, was what happened when you became a couple. You joined a new family at the same time as staying in your own. And now there were two loyalties and two duties. It would be turn and turn about now; there would only be Christmas at the Old Rectory every other year. Dad and Cordy would be on their own, and then Cordy would find someone and she'd be off as well, and perhaps Dad would be on his own, with no one to make his Christmas lunch at all. The thought was unbearable. She felt furious that she was being made to give up something she loved so much.

She turned on her side away from him,

scrunching the pillow under her head, bunching it hard with her fist. He rolled towards her and put an arm over her shoulder, resting his head against hers.

'Thanks,' he said. 'Do you mind very much?'

'No,' she said in a small voice. 'No, it's fine.'

* * *

Ruth warmed the speculum for a moment between her hands, even though the latex gloves proved a bit of a barrier.

'Now it might feel a bit uncomfortable but it shouldn't hurt,' she said as she approached the woman on the gurney. The patient lay there looking anxious and vulnerable, dressed only on the top half of her body. Ruth smiled at her. 'It'll be over in a flash. Now, put the soles of your feet together and lower your knees as far as you can.'

'It's like Pilates,' joked the woman, trying to overcome her embarrassment. 'This must be odd for you, having to look at hundreds of . . . ladies.'

'To be honest, I don't even think about it,' said Ruth. 'It's quite automatic.' She went through the familiar routine of taking a smear of cells and transferring them to the slide for the lab. 'All done.'

'That *was* quick. The last one I had was horrible. You're much better.' The patient sat up in relief, reaching for her clothes.

'Thank you very much. You should get a letter letting you know the results in a few weeks. Do let us know if you don't hear anything. It has been known for results to get lost or bogged down.'

'Is that it?'

'That's it. You probably won't need to do it again for quite a while.'

'Thanks then.' The woman dressed quickly and let herself out, while Ruth put the speculum in to sterilise, filled in the necessary paperwork and updated the computer system. Then — what was next? She checked the appointments. An eight-week-old due for its first vaccination. She liked those: a sweet cuddly baby to enjoy for a few minutes. It would usually grin and chortle at her, watching as she prepared the small needle and phial, and then, unaware of what was to come, observe her gather up a podgy thigh with one hand. The shock and surprise that transformed its little face as she jabbed the needle in always caught at her heart, and the wails of pain that followed frequently reduced the tender new mother to tears.

She remembered that boy, Michael Petheridge, who had attacked her, and wondered what had happened to him. They must have had the letter now, telling them to find a new surgery. Ruth felt sorry for the poor woman. How often had that happened? How much help did she get with that brutal boy?

The phone rang and she answered it quickly. 'Nurse Blackiston,' she said curtly. External calls were often marketing companies trying to flog her things and she dealt with them sharply.

'Well, hello, Nurse. I've got something horribly

138

painful I'd like you to look it. I've heard you've got the most wonderful cooling touch and I'm desperate for some relief.'

She smiled. 'Hello, my love.'

'Hi, sweetness. How's your day going?'

'Just been doing a smear.'

'Ah. Girl-on-girl goings-on in the doctor's surgery? How saucy.'

'If only you could see the plain mundanity of it, darling, it would ruin the whole thing for you, I'm sure. How are things with you?'

'That's what I was calling about. You know the McTavish account? They've brought the deadline forward. It's going to mean some full-on work for the next week or so. I'm only at very rough blueprint stage and they want to see finished designs for the dispersal unit at a presentation next week. David just broke the news to us all.'

'Oh, honey. That's bad luck.'

'Yeah. So don't expect to see me for the next few evenings. But we've been promised some time off in lieu, and a small bonus if we meet the deadline, so we can do something really nice afterwards. Okay?'

'Okay.' She said in a babyish voice, 'I'm going to be lonely.'

'Can't you have someone over? I don't like to think of you on your own in the cottage. Or you could go to your dad's. Or see Valentina or one of the other girls.'

'Maybe I'll ask Cordy over. She hasn't seen the cottage yet.'

'That's a good idea. I'll text you when I'm on my way home.'

'All right, darling. Hope it's not too grim. Good luck.'

'Thanks, honey. Bye.'

★　★　★

'Am I late?' asked Cordy breathlessly, as she came through the door. 'I am, aren't I? Those slave drivers made me late, as usual.'

'You know you are. But if we agree seven thirty, I never expect to see you before eight. That's why I asked you for seven. You're just about on time.' Ruth took her sister's coat and hung it up.

'Always thinking ahead.' Cordelia grinned. 'Brrr, it's bloody freezing out there. My car heater doesn't work. I nearly froze to the steering wheel.' Her cheeks and the end of her nose were flushed red. 'Nice and toasty in here, though. Oh, this is nice! Ruth, you are funny! You've been decorating, haven't you?'

'Yes,' said Ruth. 'Why? What's so funny?' She glanced about at the fresh paintwork, the new curtains and the way she'd put everything just so, and felt a small sting of hurt. Was it comical in some way she couldn't see? It looked perfectly all right to her.

'It's just the way . . . everywhere you go, you set about recreating home. It's so loveable and you can't even see it.'

'No I don't! It's not the same as home at all.'

'Not the way it is now — the way it was then. Before Dad got going with the tool box and the paint pots. Anyway, don't be wounded. It looks

140

gorgeous. Very homely and pretty.'

'I haven't had it all my own way,' Ruth said, leading the way into the sitting room.

'Yes, I can see that this used to be a bachelor pad. Look at that stereo!' In the corner of the room, a small mountain of matt-black technology held the sound system. 'Where are the speakers? Crumbs! They're like the stones of Easter Island.'

'The television sound goes through them as well.'

'Yes, well, the TV is something else altogether. A flat-screen plasma! Must have cost a fortune.'

'Ned bought it before he had a wedding to pay for. I'm not too keen on it over the fireplace like that, but I'm not sure where else it could go.'

'No, you're more of a mirror-and-a-pair-of-candlesticks girl, aren't you?'

'Am I that predictable?'

'You're just traditional, that's all. Where's Neddy? And can I have a drink? Gin, if you've got it.'

'You can have one gin and that's it. Or a glass of wine with dinner. You're driving. Which is it? Come through to the kitchen.'

'Aye, aye, nurse.' Cordelia followed her into the small kitchen. 'I'll take the gin. Make it a large one. This is a lovely little home, it really is.'

'I'm fond of it,' said Ruth, trying to hide her pride in the cottage. Their hard work repainting had lightened and freshened the place, as had a thorough clean. She'd got out her sewing machine and run up curtains from old fabrics she'd found in junk shops and antiques markets

141

and warehouses that sold vintage paraphernalia. The sofa had been re-covered in a bolt of raspberry and sand-coloured Mulberry check that, to her delight, she'd found in a seconds fabric store, and antique lamps brought warmth and cheer to the room, along with the other bits and pieces she was always finding for the cottage. Ned teased her that she was like Katie Brown in *Calamity Jane*, making Doris Day's wood cabin all sweet and feminine with gingham curtains and flower pots.

'That window seat!' he'd said, when she'd turned the low stone sill into a comfortable place to sit with cushions of faded floral prints. 'Talk about a woman's touch — which, incidentally, is my favourite kind.'

She'd cleared away rubbish and old magazines from the bookshelves and put out some of her collection of second-hand hardbacks, their worn fabric covers in dark green, navy blue and maroon stamped with tarnished gold lettering. Her old favourites were there too, and some classics to keep the tone up. Clearing out one of the shelves, she'd found a book of Rupert Brooke's poetry, the flyleaf inscribed, 'To Bear. Let's be neo-Platonists together. All my love, Curly x x'.

Curly was what Ned had called Erin once. She remembered Erin's comment about a Brooke poem and turned to the index to see if she could find it. When she'd located it, she read it over.

Love is a breach in the walls, a broken gate, it began. It was a sonnet of cynical despair on the way love vanishes. *Astonishment is no more in*

*hand or shoulder, but darkens, and dies out
from kiss to kiss. All this is love; and all love is
but this.*

That's what she meant about the hand and
shoulder thing, thought Ruth. That we're still in
the grip of our illusion. Is it true? Is it inevitable
that we'll lose our pleasure in each other?

A sadness swept over her. She noticed that a
line of the poem had the faintest of pencil marks
underneath it, as though it had been put there
with the lightest touch, or rubbed out, leaving a
trace behind. It had underlined the words *They
have known shame that love unloved.* She ran a
finger over the print as if to feel the indentation
of the pencil. Brooke had died young, she
remembered. He had written that famous line
about a corner of a foreign field being forever
England. And he had had his heart broken by
the sound of it. She put the book back on the
shelf, next to her other volumes of poetry, and
went on cleaning.

As well as decorating, Ruth had a quiet
mission to get rid of the more hideous of Ned's
possessions, including a talking ice cream scoop
that particularly offended her. 'Ding-a-ling-a-
ling!' it would shout when she inadvertently
touched it in the drawer. 'Iii-ce creeeeam!' It was
silent now, in the shed, buried under some
garden sacks. Now, without the beer mat
collection, grease-encrusted pots and dead
plants, the kitchen looked calm, homely and well
equipped.

Cordelia took the gin and tonic that Ruth had
poured her. 'Ooo, thanks. Yum yum. So where is

the man himself? The bridegroom-to-be?'

'Working late.'

'Having an affair already? Most husbands wait until they're actually married.'

'Ha ha. He's got a horrible deadline on. I've been on my own the last three evenings. But the end is in sight, he says. It'll all be over after the weekend.'

'Good stuff. Nice to know he can provide for you, anyway.'

'Dinner will be ready soon. Let's go and sit down.'

They went back to the sitting room, Cordelia throwing herself down on the sofa while Ruth put another piece of wood on the fire. Cordy started chatting about work and the men there. 'The doctors, honestly. You've never seen anyone work and play so hard in your life; they're all chain-smoking, drug-addicted alcoholics, they really are. And the married ones are always eyeing up the nurses and the single ones are sleeping with as many as they can. Even the women are pretty bad. You've never known anything like a hospital for a hotbed of sleazy goings-on.'

'Sounds much more exciting than our surgery. I take it you haven't got your eye on anyone?'

Cordelia shrugged. 'I had a cheeky snog the other day, after a night out with some of the crowd. But I don't think it will come to anything; I think he's moving down to King's soon. Quite a nice radiologist. Six foot seven. Officially a giant, apparently, which would be a good talking point. You know — me and my

144

giant. 'Do meet my giant — he may be big, but I promise he's friendly.' Oh well. To be honest, I'm too busy to even think about anything more than a quick kiss and fumble and see ya round.'

'Sounds a bit sad, Cordy. Are you sure you aren't lonely?'

'Lonely?' Cordelia rolled her eyes. 'I'd love some more time to myself! I'm hardly ever on my own.'

'Well, you know — someone to share things with.'

'Nah. I'm not like you. I'll be happy when it comes along but I'm not going looking. Besides, you know how I feel about marriage. Legal bondage.'

'Talking of my legal bondage, there was something I want to ask you.' Ruth leaned forward. 'I don't want to be all gushy, so I'll come straight out with it. Would you be my bridesmaid? Not really my bridesmaid, that sounds too twee. I never wanted a flock of children in pixie outfits or knickerbockers. I mean that I'd like you to be my best woman. Ned's asked Tom to be his best man and I want you to be mine.'

Cordy's face lost its joky expression and froze.

'If you don't want to, that's fine,' Ruth said hastily. 'I'm sure you hate the thought of being trussed up in a dress . . . '

'No, no! Don't be silly . . . I'm just bowled over, that's all. I can't believe you want to ask me.'

'There's absolutely no one else whom I would ask,' Ruth said simply. 'No one who means as much to me as you. And as Mummy isn't going to be there, I'd like you to be as involved as possible.'

Tears sprung to Cordelia's eyes. 'Oh Ruthy . . . Thank you. I'd love to be your bridesmaid. It's a real honour.' She sniffed and rubbed quickly at her eyes. She looked up, back to normal. 'Unless this is your revenge for me burying your Sindy that time, and you're going to make me look like a pig in a dress.'

'Well, now you mention it, there are a few scores to settle.' Ruth grinned. 'I was thinking polished apricot satin with a drop waist and puffed sleeves . . . '

'I'd do it for you,' declared Cordelia in mock-heroic tones. 'I'd brave the peachiest of meringues to make your wedding day all you've dreamed of.'

'Thanks, love,' said Ruth, and gave her a hug. 'Let's have this shepherd's pie, shall we? I want to tell you about my dress.'

They had their supper, and went back to relax on the sofa.

'I'm going to have to get a move on,' Cordelia said, looking at her watch. 'Another Friday night getting to bed before eleven p.m. Anyone would think I was sixty-four, not thirty-four.'

'You've got to catch up on your rest when you can.'

'S'pose so.'

The phone rang. Ruth leaned over to pick it up off the side table. 'Probably Ned,' she said, answering it. 'Hello?'

There was silence at the other end.

'Hello?' She turned to Cordy and said quietly, 'It must be a marketing call. Someone in Calcutta will ask me if I want a new mobile phone in a minute.'

'Hang up,' urged Cordelia. 'It's hell getting them off the phone.'

'Hello?' said Ruth again. For a moment she wondered if it might be her father. He was still grappling with a modern phone and sometimes pushed buttons he wasn't supposed to. 'Is anyone there?'

Then she heard the distinct sound of heavy breathing, and a low growl.

'Hello?' she said again, now a little fearful. The growl came again and this time there was a word inside it, but she couldn't make out what it was.

'Who is it?' she said sharply. 'Who is this?' She clicked the phone on to speaker mode, so that the heavy breathing could be heard in the room, and made a face at Cordy. They listened for a moment as the eerie breathing with its throaty growl filled the room.

'It's a dirty caller. Bloody weirdo!' called Cordy, leaning towards the phone. 'Piss off!'

The sound stopped for a moment and then began louder, and the nasty snarl resolved itself into a harsh voice that shouted, 'You FUCKING BITCH.'

Shocked, Ruth clicked the phone off. The silence in the room seemed to ring with the vicious words. The sisters looked at each other, shaken.

'God, that was like something out of *The Exorcist*,' breathed Cordy. 'Remember when that horrible voice comes out of the little girl, after she's turned all green? Ugh. It was creepy. It must be some prank caller.'

'Do you think so?' Ruth tried to quell her fear.

'Bound to be. A one-off. Someone dialling randomly. Probably a kid getting some kicks on a Friday night. Are you all right? Do you want me to stay? You look a bit freaked.'

'No . . . no. I'll be fine. You're right. It's just a weirdo hoping to get a woman on the end of the line.'

'Nasty, though,' observed Cordy. 'There are some strange people in the world, aren't there? Who knows why they do these horrible things.'

★ ★ ★

When Ned crept into bed much later that night, Ruth was still awake. He got in beside her and she turned to him, nuzzling into his naked chest.

'I'm so glad you're back,' she whispered into the darkness, his warm scent acting like a sedative, calming all her fears and making her feel safe and comfortable again.

'Why aren't you asleep, sweetie?' he said, kissing her forehead. She smelt his minty breath, fresh from cleaning his teeth.

'I had a nasty phone call.'

'Really, who from?'

'Don't know. Anonymous.'

'What did they say?'

'Nothing really. Nothing too obscene. Just swore at me. I hung up as fast as I could. Cordy was here — she heard it — and she thinks it was just some nutter.' A thought occurred to her. 'You know who it might have been? Remember when I was attacked in the surgery? Dr Fletcher said she was going to get the boy off the register. It could have been the mother in a fit of anger. Perhaps she got my number from somewhere.'

'That's probably it.' Ned yawned. 'Poor little girl,' he said gently. 'Don't worry. I'm here now. You'll be fine.'

8

Ruth stood at the back of the waiting room, taking a breather for a moment. One of the receptionists had brought in some disco lights and they had been flashing an incessant red, blue and yellow until Ruth thought she might be liable to start fitting if she stayed near them any longer.

She watched the midwife and the extremely fat receptionist bopping in the middle of the waiting room to 'I Will Survive', and reached out for another mince pie from the paper plate next to her. She wasn't hungry but there was something about these parties that made her keep pushing down the snacks until she had the unsatisfied fullness that came from party food. In the other hand she had a mug emblazoned on the side with the benefits of something called Niacapazam. Goodness only knew what that was: there were so many drugs on the market these days, they were going to have to start publishing the medical dictionaries in ten volumes. The mug held a poisonous attempt at mulled wine that got most of its heat from a hefty proportion of brandy and two minutes in the microwave on high. It didn't have the usual spicy flavour Ruth associated with mulled wine, but rather the gritty twang of cheap red livened up with a few cloves and a stringy piece of orange.

How soon can I leave? she wondered. She could already feel the effects of the wine, even though she'd tried to prevent the over-eager receptionist who'd brewed it from refilling her mug every few minutes. A muzzy headache was beginning, and she was thirsty. So much for the joys of Christmas.

'Hello, Ruth.' Dr Fletcher came up, still wearing her party hat from lunch. It was dark purple and managed to look more regal than anything else, sitting straight on her smooth blonde hair, where anyone else's would have slid down at the back, or over one eye. The queenly effect was spoiled by a tangle of coloured streamers from a party popper that sat in a bunch in the crown and dangled over the side past one of Dr Fletcher's emerald earrings. 'How are you? How are the wedding preparations? It's pretty close now, isn't it?'

'A month,' replied Ruth, smiling. 'There's so much to do, I really had no idea.'

'That's weddings for you. Are you doing it all yourself? My mother did everything for me. All I had to do was turn up. I even wondered whether, if I didn't do that, she'd just step in and marry Declan for me.'

'My mother's dead, so it's all me,' said Ruth lightly. 'But I don't mind — I rather like being in control. And there are plenty of things I'm not bothered about. I don't need classic cars or horse-drawn carriages because we live right next to the church. If it's raining, Dad can just drive me round. And the reception is in the local pub, where they do delicious food.

So I'm not fighting with caterers.'

'I take it you're not having a smoked salmon, chicken à la king and peach melba medley, with dancing in a marquee afterwards?'

Ruth laughed. 'Oh no. It's all very down to earth. We'll be having roast beef and mashed potato. The wedding cake is one of those towers of profiteroles, so we'll knock that down for pudding.'

'It sounds like you're amazingly in control. Well done. I bet you'll have a lovely day.' The doctor turned to look at the surgery staff dancing and talking in the semi-darkness. 'January feels like an age away, though. It's hard to believe that we'll all be back in two weeks, with Christmas and New Year over once again. I've got all of Declan's family coming over from Ireland — it'll be an absolute riot. Thank heavens we all get on wonderfully well, or I'd probably be on my way to leap off the tower of the University Church right now. My mother-in-law is an angel and I'll have to wrest the kitchen out of her control or she'll do everything. What about you — are you going anywhere? Or are you and . . . '

'Ned.'

'Of course — Ned. Are you going to have a blissful little lover's Christmas together, not getting out of bed all day and feeding each other lobster?'

That's what we should have done, Ruth thought. We should have insisted that we wanted to be on our own this year. Too late now, I suppose. 'We're going to Ned's parents,' she

152

said. 'They live near York.'

'Oh. It's very pretty round there.'

'Yes.' She tried to hold her tongue but couldn't. 'Actually, I'm dreading it. I've never spent Christmas anywhere but home and you know what it's like — everyone has their own little customs and habits. I'm worried I'm going to be a bit of a spare part.'

'Do you get on with Ned's family?'

Ruth said nothing for a moment, then lamely, 'His mother can be a bit difficult.'

'Ah. I see. Bad luck. A grim mother-in-law is one of life's less pleasant burdens. I hope it gets better for you.'

A thought struck her. 'By the way — do you remember the Petheridges, that boy who attacked me and his mother? Did you ever get them off the register?'

'Yes, I remember them. We did get them off in the end. Why?'

'Can anyone get my phone number from the surgery?'

'Of course not. Is there a problem?'

'Oh, no. No. I just wondered.'

Dr Fletcher picked up a mince pie. 'Did you like your secret Santa present?'

'I must show it to you — it's hilarious. I've never been given anything so odd. I got a pair of large chocolate breasts with a lacy bra painted on it in white chocolate. I can't think what the person who bought it was thinking.'

'I was thinking of a kind of hen night gift,' remarked Dr Fletcher. 'But I can see that it might look strange out of context.'

'Oh! God, I am sorry. It's lovely . . . they're lovely. I'm sure they'll be delicious. I love chocolate.'

Dr Fletcher smiled. 'Don't worry. If it's any consolation, I got the exact same packet of bath salts I gave as secret Santa last year. Some receptionists have very long memories.'

★ ★ ★

Ruth came out on to the main road, pulling on her coat and breathing in the fresh evening air with relief. The cool December night refreshed her after the long afternoon partying with her colleagues, and the sight of people bustling about being Christmassy cheered her up. There is nothing quite like this time of year, after all. The lights were up, festooned and flashing on every lamp post — stars and reindeer this year. The shops were alive with their late-night, last-minute rush of customers. By Martyrs' Memorial, a cluster of carol singers were warbling 'Ding Dong Merrily on High' with all the harmonies. A bright-faced little boy in a Santa hat came up to her with a bucket, collecting for charity on behalf of the singers, so she found a pound coin for him and dropped it in.

She looked down towards Cornmarket and wondered if she should do some shopping. Nearly everything was done; she'd got into the habit of being one of those annoyingly organised people who got everything bought in October, before the rush started. The only thing she hadn't got was a present for Jackie Haskell, and that was because she had no idea what her future mother-in-law might like. She'd bought gardening gloves for Ned's father, which seemed like a good bet, and a Royal Horticultural Society book of plants. She'd told Ned to get something for his sister and she had the feeling that the large box that had arrived from Amazon the week before contained most of Ned's Christmas gifts. But Ruth had felt that she ought to get Jackie's present, and that it needed to be a good one. A thoughtful one. One that showed consideration and care, and that would set the tone for their relationship.

'What does your mother like?' she'd asked Ned.

'I don't know really,' he replied.

'That's very helpful. What do you usually get her then?'

'Um . . . just something small. She likes perfume. I get her that sometimes.'

'I can't give her that — it's not special enough. There must be something else. Does she have any hobbies?'

Ned looked blank. 'She watches television, goes out with her friends. She does a little bit of gardening. She cooks — you could get her something for the kitchen?'

'I'm not doing that!' exclaimed Ruth. 'And you'd better not turn into the sort of husband who gives me saucepans or a new washing machine for Christmas.'

'All right, keep your wig on. Message received. You know I'm not like that. Honestly, I wouldn't worry about Mum. She doesn't really expect anything.'

Ruth had sighed with annoyance. Sometimes he could be so dense, she thought. A loving mother might make excuses for her darling son not getting her a particularly original gift but she was very likely to think differently when it came to her daughter-in-law. And imagine the embarrassment if the Haskells spent a huge amount on something lovely for her, and she handed over a cheap bottle of scent. It would be unbearable.

Now more than two months had gone by and she'd been taken up in the daily round of work and in thinking about the wedding, and was still no closer to having a present for Jackie.

On impulse she set off down the street, and into the bookshop on the corner of the crossroads. Pretty choral music was playing, tinkling down from the speakers above the heads of the searching shoppers. The displays were colourful and enticing, from the latest celebrity autobiography to the Booker Prize winner offering its badge of membership to informed literary circles.

What would she like? wondered Ruth, walking among the shelves. Crime? Thrillers? Something gentle? A royal biography? A humorous book, or perhaps a collection of writings . . . ? Everything seemed possible but nothing quite right. She decided to play it safe and buy something she liked herself, something mainstream but good. Intelligent but accessible. In fact, she knew just the thing . . .

Ruth left the shop, pleased. A good, solid romantic novel made a satisfying weight in her plastic bag. She'd read it herself in the summer and liked it enormously, so she splashed out and bought it in hardback. Still, it wasn't really enough to qualify as a proper present. Mrs Haskell — she really must think of her as Jackie, if not as (oh dear, must she?) Mum — would be able to see exactly how much she'd spent because it was on the dust jacket, and in reality she hadn't even spent that because it had been reduced in a promotion.

She followed a stream of golden light emanating from the department store across the road and found herself inside among the cosmetics and handbags on the ground floor. There must be something here she would like, thought Ruth. There was just about everything after all, from designer goods to cheap plastic stuff, something for every taste. Perhaps a jumper, or cashmere gloves, or a scarf . . . but all that was a bit hackneyed, and besides, buying clothes for someone you didn't know very well was a tricky business.

As she walked about, Ruth wondered whether, after all, one of those Christmas boxes of an expensive scent with matching bottles of bath oil and body lotion might not be a bad idea, when her eye was caught by a glass case sparkling with jewellery. She went over to it. On top of the case were carousels of earrings, from chunky clip-ons to tiny gold studs, with everything in between. Earrings weren't right, she thought. A bit too personal. Besides, were Jackie's ears pierced? She

157

couldn't remember. Glancing over rows of bracelets and necklaces, she was drawn to the far end of the case, where lines of brooches were laid out on a piece of black velvet. On a cushion of its own, a crystal-encrusted brooch glittered, reflecting hundreds of colours as the bright overhead lights caught its stones.

'Do you need any help?' asked a shop assistant, startling Ruth as her head suddenly appeared close to her own over the case.

'I was looking at that.' She pointed.

'Oh. The bow. Yes, it's lovely, isn't it? Would you like to see it?'

'Yes please'.

The assistant carefully lifted the cushion out of the case and put it on the glass top in front of Ruth. She could see now that it was a bow shape, a gold base covered in crystals that looked like diamonds.

'You've probably heard of Swarovski,' said the assistant importantly.

'Of course,' answered Ruth, although she hadn't.

'These are Swarovski crystals. This brooch will be a collector's item.'

'Will it?' said Ruth in impressed tones, though she was dubious that it would.

'It is for yourself?'

'No, a present.'

'It would make a divine gift. I can see a big smile on someone's face when they open this on Christmas Day. Your mother, perhaps?'

'How much is it?' As the little stones sparkled and glittered, sending out rays of pink and white light, Ruth could imagine Jackie Haskell opening it on Christmas Day, and being impressed. It looked right, somehow. It looked as though it would fit with all the beige silk and pelmets and tasselled cushions.

'It's one hundred and fifty-nine pounds, ninety-nine pence.'

Ruth gazed at it. It was far more than she'd intended to spend. But it looked so right to her. It seemed to be saying *I'm the one. I will buy you the way to her heart.*

She looked up into the heavily kohled eyes of the assistant. 'Do you gift wrap?' she asked.

★ ★ ★

Out on the street she felt the satisfaction of a job well done. She'd chosen good presents, she was sure of it. Now she could relax. As long as Ned picked up the bottles she asked him to get from the off licence, then they were all set for Christmas. It was odd not to have to be planning menus and ordering meat and rushing off at the last minute to get forgotten Christmas crackers.

She turned her back on Cornmarket and started walking up St Giles towards her car. Tomorrow she must post those last cards — thank goodness she was off all Christmas. The other surgery nurse was doing the Christmas and New Year shift this year. Ruth decided she'd take advantage of the clear time to concentrate completely on the wedding preparations. After Christmas it would only be three weeks until the day itself, so she had to get a move on.

Two figures were walking towards her, their heads close. They were dark shapes in their winter coats until they got quite close and began to resolve themselves into features and details. They were both familiar, she thought, as they neared her. Then she realised why.

'Ned?' she called.

Ned looked up and saw her. He smiled. 'Hey, Ruth — there you are!'

'Hi, Ruth,' said Erin. Ned and Erin stopped as Ruth came up to them. Under the streetlight, she could see Erin's long hair falling in a dark cascade over the antique Astrakhan coat she wore, a frill of pink cashmere scarf emerging at the neck.

'What are you doing here?' she asked Ned. His work was on the outskirts of the city on a trading estate and he only ever came in to Oxford in the evening if he was meeting her. It was disconcerting to come across him unexpectedly like this.

'Didn't you get the email?' he asked, frowning.

'What email?'

'It came round to all of us — I was sure your name was on it. I checked.'

Erin said, 'You were definitely on it. Are you sure you didn't get it?'

'We were at our Christmas lunch all day. I haven't been in my office since this morning.'

'Well, that explains it.' Ned smiled and put an arm round her. 'We thought we'd all meet up for a Christmas drink before we go our separate ways for the festive season. It's a bit of a

160

last-minute thing. Erin suggested it.'

'It occurred to me that it was a bit ridiculous we hadn't arranged it before,' added Erin. 'We're going to the pub.'

'Where were you going then?' asked Ned.

'I was on my way home,' said Ruth, still feeling affronted that she'd been left out of things so easily. 'Why didn't you call me when I didn't answer the email?'

'I did,' protested Ned. 'I left a message on your voice mail.'

She pulled her phone out of her bag and saw that she had a message. Then she remembered turning her mobile to silent in the cloakroom before they'd had their lunch. She'd forgotten to change it back. 'The sound's off.'

'There you are. I just assumed you'd meet us at the pub.'

'But I was on my way home.'

'Well, I would have called you when you didn't turn up, wouldn't I? But it doesn't matter, because here you are. Now we can go together.' He hugged her tight. 'Aren't you pleased that work's over? I'm bloody ecstatic. Let's go and celebrate.'

She was mollified. Her spirits began to rise again. She wanted to tell Ned about finding his mother's present but didn't like to with Erin there. Instead she said, 'Have you done all your Christmas shopping, Erin?'

As they turned into Broad Street and passed the elegant Sheldonian Theatre, Erin told them what a miserable failure she was at getting her shopping done.

'I'm going to do it all mail order next year,' she declared, 'in May. I can't believe I inflict this torture on myself year after year.'

They followed the small winding streets round between two colleges, dark now that term had ended except for one or two glowing windows, and went down a narrow passageway to an old tavern that nestled hidden away from the main streets. The pub itself was small with low ceilings and large fireplaces, but the two courtyards on either side of it were full of tables provided with warmth and light by braziers of hot coals. It was buzzing with people out celebrating the end of work and the beginning of Christmas. Some office lunch parties had obviously stretched on into the evening and there were tables of tired, red-faced workers, still eager to keep going, some of them singing raucously and cajoling others to join in.

They found a table at the back of the courtyard, by the stone wall that was now softened and crumbling with the ivy climbing all over it.

'I'll go to the bar,' Ned offered. 'What will you have?'

'Mineral water for me,' said Ruth. 'I suppose I'll be driving us home later.'

'We could get a cab home. Come on, Ruth, it's a party. We can leave your car and come in tomorrow in my car and pick it up.'

'What about your bike?'

'We can fit it in my car. Or we can come in by bus, you can drive home and I'll cycle.'

'What a palaver for the sake of a drink or two. I've already had some mulled wine. I don't much feel like more.'

Ned looked sulky. 'What about you, Erin?'

'I think Ruth's being very sensible. No point in everyone getting off their heads. I'll have an orange juice.'

'You girls,' he grumbled. 'Well, I'll be glad when the boys get here. Honestly . . . ' He wandered off into the courtyard towards the bar.

'How's everything? The wedding preparations? What's been happening?' asked Erin. 'It's been ages since I've seen you. Weeks.'

'I suppose I have been busy,' Ruth answered. 'Work's been rather frantic. The other surgery nurse was off sick for a while. And then there's the wedding . . . '

'Tell me all.'

Ruth felt reluctant. 'I spend my whole day thinking about it. If it's not finding a dress for Cordy, it's deciding what kind of flowers I'll have. With that dress, it's not easy thinking of something that won't be too much.'

'Don't have a bouquet. Have a jewelled handbag instead. Or something really plain — like white roses. You can always take a florist to see the dress and get them to suggest something.'

'Oh God, we're discussing it! Aargh! Let's stop. Those are good ideas, though, thanks.'

'We got our invitation,' Erin went on. 'I thought it was utterly charming — not many people make their own these days.'

'You really thought it was all right?'

'Oh — beautiful! I had no idea you were so talented.'

'I like to get the scissors and glue out occasionally.'

'If you ever get tired of nursing, you could do it professionally. Really.'

'Thank you.' Ruth felt the warmth of pleasure at being praised.

'No wonder I haven't seen you in so long. It must have taken hours.' Erin leaned in confidentially. 'By the way — last thing about the wedding, I promise. I just wanted to say that Ned's asked me, and I'm absolutely delighted. Of course I'll do it.'

'Do what?'

'Read at the wedding. Ned asked me this evening. I'm thrilled you want me to be a part of your day and I promise I won't let you down. I'll practise like mad!'

Ruth was confused. When had that been agreed? They had talked about the readings at the wedding, and decided that they would chose a reader each, but Ned hadn't said anything about choosing Erin — although Ruth assumed she would be on the shortlist.

'Well — I'm so glad,' she said quickly, not wanting to show her surprise. 'Of course we'd like you to be a part of the day. Did Ned tell you which reading you were doing?'

'He said you had chosen that beautiful piece from the New Testament — the sounding gong and clanging cymbal one. The greatest of these is love. That one. I love it. I know everyone has it, but I don't think that makes it any less wonderful.'

'Yes, that one. Right.' Ruth nodded. They'd certainly discussed having that reading. Ned had obviously decided it was the one. 'Good. Good.'

'Hello, ladies! This corner is a bit chilly, isn't it? The nearest brazier is over there.' Luke appeared over Ruth's shoulder, giving her a smacking kiss on the cheek before squashing in next to her on the bench. 'we'll have to rely on body warmth.'

'I'm sure Ruth will get far more of yours than she strictly needs,' observed Abigail, who was as short and plump as her husband. 'Hi, girls. It's been a while.'

'Hi, Abigail.' Erin gave her a broad smile and offered up a white cheek to be kissed. She kissed the air in return. 'Lovely to see you.'

Abigail came round to kiss Ruth hello as well. 'How's the bride-to-be? Cold feet yet?'

'Not yet!' said Ruth brightly, thinking, *What's wrong with me? It's Christmas, work is over, I'm out with friends — I should be happy.* But her spirits were slowly sinking.

'I've still got mine, and I've been married five years,' remarked Abigail as she crammed herself in next to Luke. 'Every year I can't believe we're still toughing it out. Can I, sweetheart?'

'She spent the whole reception telling everyone what an appalling mistake she'd made, and how she hoped she'd be able to sneak off on her own on the honeymoon,' said Luke in a wounded tone.

'I did not,' protested his wife. 'I wanted to go

off with the best man — '

'Ned,' put in Luke.

'He was single then, Ruth. But he was having none of it. Loyalty to friends or some such nonsense. Oh, here's the utterly glamorous Tom. Hope he sits next to me. Luke, can you move over to the other side?'

'Ruth.' Tom kissed her in that way he had, darting a quick brush on to her cheek as though he didn't like to touch her. He saw Ned arriving with the first round of drinks. 'Ah,' he said, a curiously nasty tone in his voice. 'Here's *Bear*.'

Ned flicked a glance at him and looked uncomfortable for an instant, before saying amiably, 'Sorry I haven't got a drink for you new arrivals. Do you want to do the honours, Tom?'

Did I imagine that tone? thought Ruth, watching Tom go off to get supplies for the others. Why do I feel like an outsider again? she wondered. I see these people all the time. Erin helped me choose my wedding dress. I know them, I like them . . . and yet . . . She wasn't quite sure why she felt unhappy, only certain that she wanted very much to get Ned on his own, to talk over the day and catch up, and ask him why he hadn't told her he was going to ask Erin to read at their wedding. She knew what he would say — she could almost hear him, and it would be perfectly reasonable.

'I knew you wouldn't mind,' he'd say, 'and the perfect opportunity came up. She was so happy. Isn't it great?'

And she didn't mind, she really didn't. Only why hadn't he told her first? She sat there sipping her water, listening to the banter between them all, fighting against the depression that was growing stronger all the time. After half an hour, she could bear it no longer and got up.

'Just going to the loo,' she muttered. Ned shot her a smile. She got herself out of the tight wedge along the bench, and made her way through the crush of people in the courtyard and round to the ladies. Once shut safely in a cubicle, she sat there a while feeling shaky and tearful, though she didn't know why. She wanted very badly to be at home, in the safety of the cottage, just her and Ned. But she could tell that wasn't going to happen. Luke had just bought him his third pint and he was well away. He was cutting loose, she could see that, and he deserved it. He worked hard. That special project, the McTavish account, had exhausted him. He was only just starting to recover. And she knew that the strain of the wedding was probably not helping, although she tried to take as much as she could off his shoulders. And now there was Christmas to get through . . .

She felt tears well up again, and used all her strength to suppress them. That wouldn't help. She had to stay grounded and not let it get her down. What did she have to complain about after all? This was meant to be the happiest time of her life.

Sniffing, she prepared to return to the others. Leaving the ladies, she walked out of the bar, and bumped into Jeremy.

'Evening, miss,' he said, grinning down at her.

She blinked at him for a moment, hardly recognising him, then came to. 'Oh — Jeremy. Hello. They're all at the back.'

'Are they?' He took his familiar tobacco tin out of his coat pocket, which she noticed was hanging off at the side. From the tin, he plucked a little roll-up and stuck it in between his teeth. 'And how are you?' He lit it with a small brass lighter. 'I don't often see you on your own.'

She hardly saw Jeremy at all, if she thought about it. He was the most elusive of the group, the most self-contained. He was, as far as Ruth knew, single, and lived in a house share in Jericho, an artistic kind of community in a converted old chapel. There he pursued his doctorate in some kind of classical study, though she'd never found out what. Now she knew he'd once been out with Erin, she looked at him through new eyes, imagining the two of them together. It was not an easy image to conjure: although there was something imposing about him, he was too shabby and with the air of being an oddball to be her match.

'No. No, we don't meet much, do we?'

He puffed out a cloud of sweet smoke. 'You work in that doctors' place near the Playhouse, don't you?'

'Yes, that's right.'

'We should meet up some time. Do you have a lunch hour? We could go the Ashmolean or something. Soak up some culture.'

'Yes. That would be nice.' She felt bewildered.

Why would Jeremy want to spend time with her?

'Okay. Well. Maybe we will. When the horrors of the festive season are over and we're all back to normal.'

'We've got the wedding after that.'

'Of course you have. You're going to plight your troth to our Ned. Very brave.'

'Why is that brave?'

He gazed down at her for a moment and then said, 'Very brave to think you can last the distance. Very brave to think that marriage is somehow going to make you less alone in life. People always seem to be under the illusion that a lover, or a spouse, or a sibling or a child will somehow combat the immense loneliness of existence. A basic if understandable error. Howling loneliness is just our lot.'

'You're a cynical bunch, aren't you?' blurted out Ruth. 'If it's not Abigail and Luke telling me how they can't stand each other, it's you and Erin telling me love doesn't last and I'm a fool for thinking it does.'

Jeremy laughed. 'First off, Abigail and Luke are the exception to what I said. I don't think I know any couple more suited to each other and more successful at fighting off the great void of despair and terror by clinging to each other. But I'm interested to hear what Erin said. Has she warned you off Ned?'

'Of course not.' Ruth felt suddenly disloyal to Erin, as though she'd blabbed a secret. 'She was just realistic about how you can fall out of love as well as in.'

'She should know.' Jeremy raised an eyebrow

at her, and puffed on his little roll-up. 'Come on. Let's go and find the others. The clan awaits.'

★ ★ ★

It seemed like hours before everyone decided to go their separate ways, and when they did there were multitudes of kisses and Christmas wishes to get through before they could finally say good bye and make their way north to find Ruth's car.

Ned was staggering slightly but happy. He draped one arm heavily round Ruth's neck. 'That was great, wasn't it? Aren't they great?'

'They're all great.'

'Did you have a good time?'

'Yes,' she said, thinking that she just wanted to get him home.

He stopped and faced her, taking both her hands in his. A rowdy group of revellers passed on the opposite side of the street, jeering at them and shouting 'Snogger!' and 'Giver one!'

'Ruth, Ruth,' he said earnestly, gazing into her eyes. 'I love you, you know that, don't you? I really do love you. You're amazing.'

'I love you too.'

'No — no. I mean it. I want you to believe me. You're the best thing that's ever happened to me. I've been so miserable, you don't know. You can't know. But not any more. Do you believe me?'

He was drunk, she could see that. But she also knew he was telling the truth. The stress and anger of the previous few hours began to melt away, leaving her sane again. She went to him

170

and slipped her arms under his coat, hugging him tightly.

'Of course I believe you. And I love you too. I'm so happy we're getting married. I know we can get through anything together.'

9

Perhaps, she thought, as the car turned into the long concrete driveway, it wasn't going to be so bad. She couldn't help her spirits lifting as Christmas approached, and now that she had resigned herself to being away from home for the day itself, she'd decided to look on the bright side. Besides, if she didn't start off with at least an attempt at being positive, it could hardly improve.

Ned was taciturn as they approached the house. It had been the same the last time they had visited; being here seemed to bring out this particular side of his nature. Whenever he was under stress or cross or depressed, he retreated inside himself, having less and less to do with his surroundings. It made Ruth furious when they were arguing; at a certain point he would switch off and refuse to say another word, listening stony-faced to her torrent of words, his lips tight. The familiar signs were there as they got closer and closer to his parents' house: a certain stiffness round his eyebrows and shoulders, and a descent into monosyllables.

He must be stressed, she thought. He's worried about how it's all going to work out. But he needn't worry, he knows I'm going to do my best. He knows I'd never in a million years do anything else. I must make it as easy for him as I can.

Steven Haskell answered the chimes. 'Hello, you made it! How was the traffic? Any hold ups? Did you stop along the way? Hello, my girl,' — he kissed Ruth awkwardly on the cheek — 'ah, hello, son.' He shook Ned's hand heartily. 'Glad to have you here.'

As they crowded into the hall, Jackie Haskell emerged from the kitchen, wiping her hands on an apron.

'Hello,' called Ruth, cheerily. 'We're here!'

'So I see.' Jackie smiled at her. 'I won't come too close, I've been cooking. I expect I've got the smell in my hair. Hello, son. Where's your luggage?'

'This is some of it,' said Ned, dropping the overnight bag. 'The rest is in the car.'

'With the presents,' added Ruth. 'Isn't it pretty and Christmassy here?' The hall was festooned with Christmas cards, each one attached to a line of green twine by a tiny festive peg. 'You've got so many cards.'

'Some are from last year,' said Jackie. 'I get them out to make up the numbers. No good having spaces on the string.' She went over and started looking inside some of the cards. 'This one is from my brother George. He can't be with us this year sadly. His wife isn't at all well, though she's been dying for years according to her, so there's no knowing the truth of that. This is from Mrs Briscoe. Mrs Mendelson. Mrs Darling. Some of Steve's old work colleagues. This is from Hannah Taylor — I know her from the club we go to on Thursday nights.'

173

Ruth nodded as they walked along, Jackie reading aloud from each card.

'This will be familiar to you,' Jackie said suddenly, opening a small card with a single silver star on the front. 'To dear Mr and Mrs Haskell and family,' she read, 'with much love and many Christmas wishes from Erin and Tom. Kiss, kiss.' She paused and turned to look at Ruth. 'That's nice, isn't it?'

'Very nice.'

'I was wondering where the card from you was.'

'From me? I suppose — as we were spending Christmas with you — I thought . . . I tend to send cards to people I'm not going to see over Christmas.'

'We sent you one.'

That was true. A card had arrived in late November. She remembered now. 'Of course you did, thank you.'

Jackie said nothing for a long moment. Then she turned to Ned who was coming back into the house with more luggage, including the box of wine they'd brought. 'Do you want tea?' she asked.

Ruth saw her opportunity to make up for her error with the Christmas card. 'Mrs Hask . . . Mum, we've brought along some wine.' She went to the box and opened it, bringing out the Veuve Clicquot. 'Look — some champagne for Christmas Day. And we brought some claret and a bottle of port as well.'

Jackie stared at the bottle Ruth was holding towards her, with its bright orange label. 'Very

174

nice, I'm sure,' she said coolly. 'Steven has laid some bottles down for Christmas. You'd better give it to him.'

'All right. I will. I hope it's what you like.'

'I'm sure it is.'

Ruth threw a helpless look towards Ned. He was expressionless.

'I'll make some tea,' said his mother, and went back into the kitchen.

'That didn't go well,' said Ruth, 'but I haven't quite worked out why.'

Ned shrugged. 'Forget it. I'll take your bag to the spare room.'

'Aren't we together?'

'I'd take a sizeable bet that we're not.'

'Oh no!' she wailed, as quietly as she could. 'We can't really be in separate rooms, can we? We *live* together. We're both over thirty. We're getting married!'

'Mum is quite old fashioned. She wouldn't like it before we are actually married.'

Despite her best efforts, Ruth felt her heart sink. Perhaps it was going to be too much for her, especially now that the source of her strength, Ned and the warmth of his body, had been taken away from her.

Oh my God, she thought, suddenly deeply homesick. At this time on Christmas Eve she'd usually be at home, going round the garden looking for a couple of good sprigs of holly to put up over the fireplace, or getting her father to chop some logs for the next day. She would feel cherished, among her loved ones. What on earth was this going to be like?

★ ★ ★

She had her answer soon enough. It was dreadful. With each step, Ruth seemed to put a foot wrong, never quite understanding where she had gone awry. As Christmas Eve wore on, she felt as though she were in some other universe, where the exact opposite of everything she expected happened.

She was indeed in the spare bedroom, a bare, cold room with a single bed pressed against the wall. Pacing around it a few times, she took a deep breath and told herself that it couldn't last indefinitely; she would be out of here in thirty-six hours maximum. Just two nights in this horrible place and she'd be home again.

'Bear it,' she told herself. 'Bear it, be nice, and it will all be over, and Ned and I will be back home, far away from all this.'

She went downstairs, wondering what happened here on Christmas Eve, taking with her a bag of carefully wrapped presents. She'd bought a chic paper that looked like plain brown parcel paper, until it picked up the light and tiny veins of gold shimmered inside it. Round that she'd tied a golden string so that the presents looked like old-fashioned packages. Understated but glamorous, she thought. And Jackie's special gift was in the department store purple glossy paper, with a big purple bow on top.

'Where's the tree?' she asked gaily, coming into the sitting room. 'I can't wait to see it.'

Ned and Steven were sitting on the sofa, their heads bent over sections of the newspaper. They looked up as she came in and, in answer to her question, looked as one to a corner of the room.

Ruth had a strong urge to laugh, but managed to stifle it. Thank goodness Jackie was in the kitchen and couldn't see her face. She'd been expecting a big fir tree dripping with decorations. Instead she saw, perched on a side table, a small, rather pathetic artificial tree, sporting threadbare ruffles of gold tinsel on its metal arms. Hanging off the end of the sorry branches were some padded decorations that looked like pin cushions pretending to be German biscuits: brown with red and white squiggles embroidered on them.

'Oh,' she said lamely. 'Isn't it lovely?'

She heard a faint snort from Ned. Steven said with a tone of excuse in his voice, 'We've had that for years. It's got sentimental value, you know? And none of those pesky pine needles that need cleaning up.'

'No. Very sensible. I'll just put these down here.' The other presents were on the floor under the table, covered in bright paper decorated in sleighs, Santas and red-nosed reindeer. Ruth bent down and added hers to the pile, then went over to the fireplace, where there were more Christmas cards stood on the mantelpiece. There was also a printed card, plain white with black type. It read:

Mr and Mrs Blackstone
request the pleasure of your company
at the wedding of their daughter Ruth
to Mr Edward Haskell

And underneath were the time, date and place of the wedding. In the corners were printed horseshoes and bells and at the bottom, a tiny bride in a bell-shaped dress next to a groom in a black top hat.

'What's this?' asked Ruth, surprised. She picked it up, frowning. 'It looks like an invitation to our wedding.'

Steven coughed uncomfortably. 'Oh, yes . . . '

She turned to look at him. 'Didn't you get the one I made?' She'd spent long hours at the kitchen table hand-lettering the invitations and embellishing them, each one a little different. She laughed. 'This isn't even my surname.'

Ned got up and came over to have a look. He sighed wearily and turned to his father. 'Dad?'

'You know what she's like, son. She likes things done properly. The invitation was very pretty, Ruth,' he said, with a touch of pleading in his voice, 'but my wife . . . she likes shop things a bit more than homemade things. She doesn't think all that much of stuff you don't buy. So you'll have to indulge her a bit, dear. I know what you were doing, but she didn't want the neighbours to think you couldn't afford proper invitations. We saw those machines at the station, the ones where you can print out your own cards, so she thought it would be a bit of harmless fun to make a version of your invitation.'

Ned put an arm round her, and said quietly, 'She's a bit bonkers that way. Don't worry about it. I'm sorry.'

'It's fine,' said Ruth, her voice tight. 'But it's

even from my mother. Your mother knows very well that she's dead. Was that a bit embarrassing for the neighbours to know about as well? Perhaps they thought I couldn't afford a mother.'

Steven laughed. 'That's the spirit. I knew you wouldn't take it personally, dear. It's just a bit of fun.'

Ruth put the card back on the mantelpiece, still shocked. Where was the one she had made so carefully? In the bin? Then, as she looked at it, it suddenly seemed ridiculous. She pictured Jackie casting away Ruth's handmade card and hotfooting it off to the station to make an invitation that she considered acceptable, and laughed.

Ned hugged her. 'You're my best girl, do you know that?' he whispered.

She kept on laughing, replaying her mental image of Jackie running down the street to the station, determined to have everything the way she wanted it.

★ ★ ★

Once she'd begun to see the funny side of it, it was hard to stop and everything became tinged with the ridiculous; but at least that way it was easier to bear. It was clear that there would be no Midnight Mass, with its comforting roster of familiar carols and general feeling of joy and celebration. Instead there was supper in front of the television, and Jackie calling for her favourite Christmas drink.

'You have one, Ruth,' urged Jackie, relaxed and good humoured now that the evening meal was over. 'You'll like this. Steve, get us two Advocaats and cherry.'

Two revolting-looking drinks arrived: a small base of red, topped with a glassful of something thick and bright yellow.

'That's the stuff,' said Jackie happily. 'I don't drink much — but I do like my Advocaat and cherry brandy.'

Ruth sipped at the liquid. 'Mmm. Unusual.' It wasn't as horrible as she'd expected, and made her think of cold custard with a dash of cough medicine.

'This is the Dutch national drink,' said Jackie.

She's made that up, thought Ruth, imagining households all across Holland celebrating the festive season by calling for their red and yellow cocktails. No, it was impossible. This was so strange and semi-foul, it could only have been concocted here.

'I think it's called a Bleeding Heart,' remarked Steven, who had got some ale for himself and Ned.

There, thought Ruth. That doesn't sound Dutch. 'Lovely,' she said, wondering if, at this rate, they would engrave that on her tombstone: *Here lies Ruth. Everything was lovely.* 'What's it made from?'

'Egg yolks,' said Ned, with a grin.

Ruth looked at the yellow liquid, feeling faintly revolted. '*Raw* egg yolks?'

Ned laughed. 'Have you ever tried drinking a cooked egg yolk? Of course, raw.'

'Come on, Ruth, drink up,' Jackie urged. 'Or I'll have yours.'

Once she got used to the taste, her drink slipped down quite easily, and when Jackie called for another, and then another, she joined in. Things gradually seemed easier; there was no need for conversation with the television on and they all found a camaraderie, laughing together at the Christmas comedy specials. Ruth felt her strength returning. Perhaps it was going to be all right after all.

She made her excuses and went to bed at eleven, leaving the others in the sitting room. Pattering along the corridor to the bathroom in her pyjamas, her toilet bag in her hand, she felt like a teenager staying over at a friend's house. She went to the loo, cleaned her teeth and brushed her hair, gazing at her reflection in the mirror.

I'm a little drunk, she thought, leaning closer to her reflected face. Her green eyes looked over-bright and bloodshot. Well, so would you be after four advo-whatsits and cherry brandy. She laughed at herself. 'Where's your Christmas card, Ruth?' she asked. 'Whoops!' She clasped a hand over her mouth. 'Silly me! I forgot. Bad Ruth. Nice champagne, Ruth. Only thing is, I prefer a raw egg and medicine. Did you make that invitation yourself, Ruth? How cheap and disgusting! I'd prefer something different, so I think that's what I'll have.' She leaned in close to her own face again. 'What am I doing?' she breathed. The mirror fogged with the heat from her mouth. 'How on earth did Ned come out of

181

those two? And is he really any different? He must be. He is. I'm sure of it.' With one swoop of her fingertips, she wiped away the mist on the glass. 'Or else I couldn't do it.'

*　*　*

Ned's sister arrived at eleven o'clock the next day. Ruth and Jackie were in the kitchen when the door bell rang.

'That'll be her,' said Jackie, and went back to peeling potatoes.

Ruth was sitting at the kitchen table, having helped clear up the breakfast things, wondering why no one was acting at all as though it was Christmas Day, when things like presents happened. Ned had crept into the spare room in the early morning armed with a stocking for her, and they'd swapped their small gifts: books, CDs and the little things they both wanted. Ruth got a pair of deliciously soft cashmere bedsocks. She gave Ned a new belt to replace the fraying old thing he'd been using. But sharing a chocolate orange with him over a cup of tea in bed was the only Christmassy thing that had happened. Was that it? she wondered.

She perked up with interest when she heard Steven answer the door. Here was a possible salvation. After a few minutes of chat in the hall, Ned's sister put her head round the kitchen door. 'Hi, Mum,' she said. 'Happy Christmas.'

'Hello, Susan. Season's greetings,' said her mother.

Like her mother, Susan Haskell was blonde,

182

her well-groomed head shimmering with high-lights. She was also small, slender and very well dressed in expensive clothes, not at all like the spinsterish figure Ruth had imagined. 'Oh, you must be Ruth. Glad to meet you. I'm Susie.'

'Hello.' Ruth smiled at her, warming to her already.

'You've made good time then.' Jackie turned briefly to her daughter and then went back to her potatoes.

'Roads were wonderfully clear. I bet everyone else was being sensible and enjoying a lie-in.' Susie's voice was rich and deep, with a northern accent that was stronger than Ned's. 'Having a nice day?'

'Very nice, thank you.'

'Super. Well, I'm going to put my presents under old Will o' the Wisp — have you seen our Christmas tree, Ruth? He's older than I am. Someone should put the poor thing out of his misery — and then I'm going to have a fag. I'm desperate.'

'Not in my house you're not,' snapped Jackie.

'No, Mum,' said Susie amiably. 'I'm going outside on the patio. And I'll remove all the evidence.'

'No black marks on the paving.'

'Not a speck. D' you want to come, Ruth?'

'Yes, please,' said Ruth eagerly. 'I don't smoke, but I'll get a breath of fresh air with you.'

'I don't know how much fresh air there'll be with old Fag Ash Lil there,' said Jackie, nodding in Susan's direction. 'She's a walking health hazard.'

Susan winked discreetly at Ruth. 'I'll see you outside in five. Put a coat on, it's perishing.' She sashayed out of the kitchen.

★　★　★

When Ruth joined her on the patio, Susie was already puffing happily at her cigarette, a soft black shawl wrapped around her shoulders.

'Welcome to the Family Grimm,' she said cheerily as Ruth approached. 'How are you finding it?'

'Not so bad.'

'You wait. It'll get worse.' Susie laughed. 'You've probably already sussed that Mum's an odd character. I don't want to put you off or anything but you'll have your work cut out. But,' she shrugged, 'I could be wrong. She might change her spots and be an angel with you. Anyway, listen to me. I haven't even said congratulations on your engagement. Well done on seeing something in Ned. I can't say anyone else has.' She said everything with such jovial good humour, it was hard to know what she meant seriously and what was a joke. 'I'm sure he's a terrific bloke. I just can't help thinking of him as a moody teenager with BO and spots.'

'You don't seem to see much of the family,' ventured Ruth, pushing her hands down into her coat pockets.

'I do my duty. Twice a year,' declared Susie. 'I'll do it in good humour and I'll do what's expected. Christmas and a birthday — his, hers, mine, whoever's. But after that . . . ' She shook her head vigorously. 'Nope. My life's my own. I worked bloody hard to get where I am — without much help, I may add, seeing as I didn't get sent to a private school like Ned — and I'm damn well going to enjoy it. I'll do your wedding too, and be the life and soul. But there's no point in pretending that I'm close to my family because I'm not. As you might deduce, I've got problems with my mother; I've been through many years of counselling, I know why I'm angry, and I can now look her in the face and smile, knowing I'm leaving at the end of the day and that I owe her absolutely nothing.'

She's very open, thought Ruth. Considering she's only just met me.

Susie said, 'I'm telling you all this now, because I'll be one of the few people who know what you're talking about when she does something outrageous. It won't happen today, or even this month. But one day it will. I should think you'll be little Miss Golden Girl today, though, now that I've turned up.'

Susie was right. Jackie went upstairs and came down dressed in her Christmas best, a red dress and matching high heels, make-up and jewellery and her voice brought down to that soft, winsome whisper.

'Did you know Ruth's a nurse, Susan?' she said, arranging the candles on the table. 'Isn't that wonderful? I always admire people like Ruth so much — they're so selfless, aren't they? They don't care about clothes or money or luxury goods, they work for the good of mankind.'

'You can't admire them more than I do,

Mum,' said Susie cheerfully.

'Ruth's done up Edward's cottage so beautifully. She has such good taste.'

Ruth knew Jackie hadn't visited the cottage since she'd moved in, but Susie was obviously more than capable of dealing with her mother, so she stayed on the sidelines and listened to them instead.

'Ruth's so pretty, isn't she, Susan? It's a lovely natural look. She doesn't need hair dye, or make-up, or expensive clothes. Isn't she lucky?'

Ruth noticed she didn't praise her artistic skill in making handmade cards. Susie defused everything her mother said with a bright reply and a grin at Ruth. When everything for lunch was ready, Christmas at last began.

'Shall we open Ruth's bottle?' suggested Jackie. 'Susan, Ruth brought a bottle of real French champagne as a gift. Isn't that nice? It's very generous of her, isn't it? Then we can open the presents.'

'Ooh, Veuve. That'll do,' remarked Susie as Jackie brought the bottle back from the larder. 'That's going to perk Christmas up.'

'Steven!' shouted Jackie through the kitchen door. 'Come and open this bottle, will you?'

Steven obediently came in and wrestled the cork out of the bottle, while Jackie shouted 'mind the ceiling!', 'mind the cupboards!' or 'mind the windows!' depending on where he pointed it. Eventually it came out with a small but satisfying 'thwop' and the obligatory gush of white froth.

'This is the high life,' he said as he poured out

the foaming liquid. 'I call this living! Here you go, Susan, one for you. Ned, here's yours.'

When they were all armed with a glass of golden fizz, they trooped through to the sitting room for the gift opening. The pile of presents under the table looked large but when it was all distributed, there wasn't all that much. In Ruth's house, everyone went to great lengths to wrap as much as they could, so that there would be lots to open, even if they were only tiny things — one year, her father had individually wrapped every piece of a chess set so that Cordy had thirty-three little presents to unwrap — and they fell upon their gifts, opening them quickly and exchanging hugs and kisses of thanks.

Here, each present was handed out, and the recipient was observed, every reaction noted, as they unwrapped it.

Ruth's present from the Haskells was small and light. She wondered what on earth it could be and when her turn came round to open it, she did so with an expression of rapt pleasure. 'This is very exciting, I've got no idea what this is . . . ' then as she revealed the contents, she saw a plastic cube filled with pot pourri, two small lavender pillows of the kind kept in underwear drawers, and two bars of lavender soap. 'Well, how lovely. That's just what I need. Thank you.'

'I made the bags myself, Ruth,' whispered Jackie, as Ruth went over to kiss her dutifully. 'Do you like them?'

'They're beautiful,' she replied stoutly. 'Thank you, Steven.'

'You're very welcome, love,' he said, as he

accepted the peck on the cheek she gave him.

Is that it? she wondered, with the dreadful feeling that she would now look like some flashy spender when Jackie opened her presents. Then she felt guilty for expecting more. *Don't be greedy, Ruth*, she rebuked herself. *It's a very nice present.* Except as she looked at it, she remembered what Steven had said about Jackie not thinking much of things that didn't come from shops.

The turns kept coming. Susan's present from her mother was identical to Ruth's except rose-scented instead of lavender — 'You shouldn't have, Mum,' said Susie, not bothering to hide her sarcasm — but Ned had two parcels from his parents. One was a pair of rugby boots, which he was clearly delighted with. As he opened the other, Jackie said, 'That one's for both of you, really.'

This is the real present, thought Ruth with relief, as she leaned over to join Ned in pulling off the wrapping paper. It was a home brewing kit. They stared at it for a moment.

'Thanks, Mum,' said Ned, frowning slightly. 'What made you think of that?'

'You'll be a married man soon,' said Jackie gaily. 'If you brew your own beer, you won't need to go to the pub, will you? You can stay at home with Ruth.'

Susie laughed, as Ruth said, 'What a brilliant idea,' and tried to hide her puzzlement over how this present could be construed as a joint gift. She hadn't had great hopes for her presents but even so, she couldn't help feeling deflated as she

188

looked at her little pile. Only Ned's gift to her, a beautiful silver charm bracelet, could cheer her.

But she needn't have worried about her own gift for Jackie. It was the last one opened, after Susie's presents of a box of Fortnum and Mason chocolates for each of them had been doled out. Jackie, she suspected, had purposely left it till last.

Her reaction was extreme. She moaned gently as she opened the first parcel and stared at the book inside as though she had never seen one before, breathing 'A book! A book!' with such delight that Ruth felt a little uncomfortable. She pushed it quickly aside, though, in favour of the shiny purple package in front of her. As she pulled off the bow, she sighed. When the box was revealed, she gasped. When she took off the lid and saw what was inside, she screamed at the top of her voice and then began to cry. 'It's the most beautiful present I've ever had in my life, Ruth,' she said, tears spilling from her eyes. 'I've never seen anything so lovely.'

'You're most welcome,' said Ruth, wondering if this could be an even worse outcome than Jackie rejecting her gift.

'It must have cost a fortune!' breathed Jackie, taking it out and examining it. She turned the little bow over in her hand. 'Are these real diamonds?'

'They're crystals,' said Ruth hurriedly, flushing. 'Swarovski crystals.'

'Crystals,' sighed Jackie, as though this were even better than diamonds. 'Imagine. I'll wear it now.' She pinned it carefully to her dress. 'There.

Isn't it beautiful, Susan? And it will last for ever.' She flicked a glance at the box of chocolates next to her.

'It's stunning, Mum. Definitely the nicest thing you've ever had. And probably ever will have. Isn't Ruth clever?' She sent another subtle wink in Ruth's direction. 'Now if that's over, I'll go and get a bag for the rubbish.'

Ned smiled over at Ruth encouragingly and mouthed, 'You're brilliant.'

A success then, she thought, relieved. *Thank God*.

* ★ ★ ★

Jackie's good mood lasted for the rest of Christmas Day, over the lunch, and through the afternoon. She'd made a traditional feast of turkey and all the usual trimmings, and afterwards brought out a Christmas pudding flaming blue with brandy. They ate and drank until they were sleepy and woozy, sitting around in the afternoon gloom with the television glowing in the corner of the room.

'Thanks for a lovely Christmas, Mum,' said Susan at last, getting up. 'I'd better be on my way if I'm going to get back at any kind of decent hour. I reckon I've worked off that champagne and the glass of wine with lunch, so I'm off.'

'Bye, bye,' mumbled Jackie from the sofa, her eyes drooping. Her empty wine glass was on the coffee table next to her. 'Drive carefully. Mind how you go. Go'bless.'

Ruth went to the door to say goodbye to Susan.

'That's me done for another year,' she said, pulling on a smart pair of black leather driving gloves. 'Good luck, girl. I'll see you at your wedding. And look' — she pressed a small business card into Ruth's hand — 'call me anytime if you need to. Bye, Dad! Bye, Ned! Happy New Year.' She walked off into the darkness with a jaunty step, leaving Ruth to go back inside the brightly lit house, envious of the other woman's freedom.

★　★　★

The following morning, she woke feeling cheerful. Christmas Day was over. Soon they would be on their way, their duty done, with something she considered could be counted as a success under their belts. This boded well for the future and, most particularly, for the wedding.

She and Ned were downstairs early, and made breakfast.

'Where do you think your mother is?' asked Ruth, when they'd finished. She glanced at the clock. It was ten o'clock already. She'd hoped to be on her way by now. It was going to be quite a drive from York to Oxford, and they'd be lucky if they got to the Old Rectory before dark.

Ned looked up from his coffee. 'Well, she was pretty plastered last night, wasn't she? That's why we got our night of passion. I don't imagine she'd have woken for anything short of a twenty-one gun salute next to the bed.'

Jackie had come to after her doze, and started drinking again enthusiastically, finishing off the wine and then requesting some more of her favourite yellow and red cocktails. By the time they were watching the late movie, she was clearly dead drunk and beginning to snore in her seat. Steven had taken her upstairs not long afterwards. There hadn't seemed much point in Ruth and Ned not sleeping in the same bed — and Ruth felt with all the brownie points she'd won with the brooch, she could risk a bit of Jackie's displeasure over the bedroom arrangements.

'She'll be down,' said Ned. 'Don't worry about it. It's only because Dad's not here to wake her up. He's gone to play his Boxing Day golf. She'll be down any minute.'

But it was half past eleven before Jackie came downstairs in her dressing gown, her hair messy. Ruth's good spirits were evaporating fast as the minutes ticked by, each one reducing her day at home by another degree. Jackie was clearly in a foul mood; Ruth was sure that a mix of champagne, claret, Advocaat and brandy was not going to make anyone feel jolly the next day.

She grunted in response to Ruth's greeting, and got herself a large glass of water from the tap. Then she went over to the kettle and switched it on.

Say something! Ruth mouthed at Ned over the kitchen table.

'Mum, we've got to be at Ruth's dad's today,' said Ned lightly, 'so we'll have to make tracks quite soon.'

192

'I know,' Jackie said irritably, getting the teabags.

'We're all packed up, so we might have to head off shortly.'

'All right, all right!' she snapped. 'You could stay for a bit longer, you know, after I slaved for you all yesterday. Are you just going to scarper off, now you've had your Christmas?'

'Now, come on, Mum, you know that's not the case.'

'Oh do I? Well, it doesn't look like it to me. Can't you even stay for a bit of lunch?' She poured the boiling water into her mug.

Ned looked apologetically at Ruth. She made a pained face at him.

'Well . . . ' he said.

NO! mouthed Ruth. *We have to go!* She felt desperate, with the wild feeling that any minute now she was not going to be able to help herself, but would leap up and run out of the front door as fast as she could.

'Is twenty minutes too much to ask?' Jackie turned round to face them, haggard with the force of her hangover, the polished, good-humoured creature of the previous day quite gone.

'No,' said Ned, giving in.

'What about you, Ruth? Can't you stay for half an hour and have a bit of lunch with me? I'll be all on my own with Steven out, won't I?'

'Yes,' said Ruth, unable to stand up to her either. 'Of course we can.'

'Your father won't mind, will he?'

'I suppose not.'

'That's decided then. You'll stay for lunch.' Jackie looked satisfied, though she was unable to raise a smile. 'Where's the bloody paracetamol?' she mumbled.

Ned stood up. 'I tell you what, I'll go and pack up the car. So that when we've had lunch we can zip off sharpish, and get a good start.'

'All right,' said Ruth, depressed. She could see that it was going to be at least another half an hour before they got away. Ned went out and she heard him run up the stairs to get the bags.

'I'm taking this upstairs,' said Jackie, clutching her mug of tea, 'while I get dressed.' She went to the door and turned round to look at Ruth. 'By the way, don't forget to settle up before you go.'

Ruth blinked at her, puzzled. 'Sorry?'

'I worked out your share and it came to thirty-eight pounds sixty. You can leave me a cheque if you don't have the cash.'

'My share?'

'Of the cost of Christmas. You don't expect Steven and me to foot the bill for everything, do you? All that Advocaat you drank doesn't come cheap, you know.'

'Oh — no. Of course not. I'll write a cheque, then — I don't think I have enough cash on me.' When Jackie put it like that, it sounded almost reasonable. But, really, a bill for Christmas? Was this for both of them, or just her?

'Good.' Jackie turned back to head upstairs. 'I didn't want you to slip off without paying up, that's all.'

Ruth stared after her, open-mouthed.

In the car on the way to her father's she was furious. 'She did it on purpose!' she cried, almost weeping with frustration. 'It's after three o'clock and we've got miles to go! We won't be home before nine o'clock tonight at this rate.'

'I'm sorry.' Ned shot her an apologetic look before turning back to the road. 'I don't know if she meant to . . . '

'Of course she did!' She banged the dashboard with a fist. 'She was in a dreadful mood so she decided to spoil our day. And she knew I'd wanted to spend Christmas at home in the first place! And then to ask me for money.'

'That is bad,' agreed Ned. 'I'll have a word with her about that.'

'After we brought wine worth over a hundred pounds, and I spent a fortune on that bloody brooch — '

'And she really loved it. It made her day.'

'I bet it did! She gave me something worth tuppence ha'penny. I bet she couldn't believe her luck.'

'Ruth, come on, she's not that bad.'

Ruth bit her tongue, trying to calm down and be reasonable. She didn't want to come across as a materialistic person, totting up the worth of gifts when the whole idea was the spirit in which they were given. After all, Jackie hadn't asked her to spend so much, had she? She'd probably expected something just as small as the gift she'd given.

But in her heart, Ruth suspected that Jackie

195

had known very well that she would push the boat out.

'It's all right for you. Those rugby boots are just what you wanted.'

'It's only because she doesn't know you. Next year, it will be different. She'll make it up to you.'

Ruth shuddered at the hideous thought that next year she might be back in that cold house, enduring another round of present opening.

'I'm sorry we're going to be late. It's only because she doesn't want to be on her own. I hardly ever see her. She wants to make it last as long as possible.'

'What about that invitation? What about that?'

Ned said nothing for a while. Finally he sighed, and said, 'I know that to you, it must seem odd — '

'*Seem*? It *is* odd, Ned. I'm sorry if you don't think so, but it is . . . '

'All right. But that's the way she is. Things matter to her.'

'Do you think they don't matter to me? I spent hours on those invitations.'

'It's just easier if you let it go.'

Ruth stared out of the window and did not reply.

'Darling?' He put his hand on her knee. 'I know she's a bit difficult but she really doesn't mean it in the way it comes across.'

'If you say so,' she said, but it was hard to make it sound as though she meant it.

★　★　★

196

When the car finally pulled to a halt in front of the Old Rectory, she felt as though she'd never been so glad to see it in her life before. The windows were bright, and when the front door opened and her father came out to greet them, she dashed out of the car and over to him as fast as she could.

'Oh Dad,' she said into his jumper, as he hugged her. 'I'm so glad to be here. I'm sorry we're late.'

'Good Christmas, was it?'

'It was worse than you could ever imagine,' she said in a small voice, hoping Ned couldn't hear her. 'I was desperate to get away.'

'Poor Ruthy.' Silas laughed, making his chest rumble against Ruth's ear. 'I knew you'd miss us all. Cordy and I had a very pleasant day — we're glad you're here, though.'

'Me too,' she said sincerely.

'Let's go inside. You look like you need tea and Christmas cake.' He led her by the hand into the bright warmth, and Ruth followed, feeling as though a great weight had been lifted off her.

10

January was always bleak but this year it seemed that the weather was worse than usual: the countryside was battered by storms and sunk in gloom and darkness most of the time. The days were short, the few hours of grey light hemmed in by night.

What a month to get married in, thought Ruth, as she drove to work. Most mornings it was hard to believe that the sun had risen, it was so dark. The wind whipped through the bare branches of the trees and there was an icy drizzle in the air. Everywhere was dank, damp and depressing. Oxford was glowering in the cold weather, the streets virtually empty except for the odd hardy soul who didn't mind being lashed by rain and beaten by the wind that raced among the buildings like a joyrider.

New Year had been quiet, by the standards of years gone by. They'd gone round to Luke and Abigail's. The others had been there too, with the exception of Jeremy who was still away. There'd been dinner, and then games: charades and other parlour amusements. At midnight, everyone had cheered, kissed each other and sung 'Auld Lang Syne' and then, within an hour, they were all on their way home. Not like those wild parties in my twenties, thought Ruth. Seeing in New Year's Day looking grey and haggard but still dancing. Well, I'm older now.

Who wants to be hanging round nightclubs watching the young things strut their stuff?

It felt as though, now she was getting married, those pastimes were no longer needed. They were, after all, just mating rituals. At the heart of most nights out had been a desire to meet someone — that had been the point of all the dressing up and the preening and the anxiety about how she looked — and she thought it was the same for everybody else. Now that she had found her mate, and that part of her life was done and decided, her leisure had a different aspect. It was now about a certain quality of time; she considered an evening out with Ned, talking and eating without either of them having to worry about cooking or cleaning up afterwards, as one of the best ways she could spend her time. Or Ned would book tickets at the arthouse cinema in Oxford and take her to see off-the-wall documentaries and little known Iranian films. She'd taken home a leaflet from the Playhouse the other day, when she'd seen that some London shows were going to pass through on their national tours, wondering if they should go.

That was the life she had dreamed for herself, really. A quiet, civilised existence, in which she loved and was loved, and had the perfect companion with whom to pass her days and nights. She remembered what Jeremy had said about the folly of trying to stave off the terror of loneliness and death by having a partner, but it seemed to her that, as the terror and death were non-negotiable, it was perfectly reasonable to stave it off as much as possible. And if it were impossible to imagine being someone else, it helped to ameliorate the confusion and difficulty of being oneself if one felt loved. Ruth smiled to herself: she was no nihilist, that much was plain. Nihilists did not become nurses. Nihilists did not get married. She thought of a story her father had told her; when she and Cordy were little, their mother heard them having an argument in the back of the car. Cordy was eight years old and had declared that she hated boys and would never get married.

'Don't you want to get married, Cordy?' asked four-year-old Ruth.

'No!' declared Cordy, crossing her arms.

'But don't you want someone to talk to, and go out to dinner with?'

Their mother had thought that this was very funny, and had wondered how Ruth had got the idea that marriage was just talking and going out, when she and Silas almost never went out. To Ruth, it still seemed as though that was pretty much the point of marriage; and if she ever got to a point where she didn't want to talk to Ned, it would be a sorry state of affairs.

These days, though, there was only one topic of conversation, and that was the wedding. She was trying not to become boring about it, but she couldn't help it. Even though she'd planned what had seemed to her almost the simplest wedding in the world — what could be less complicated than a service in the church next door, followed by a meal in the pub down the road? — the sheer detail of it all was bogging her down. A service didn't just mean putting on a dress and turning up. It meant marriage classes with the vicar, and somehow persuading Ned to go to them; it meant choosing hymns, readings, prayers, anthems and organ pieces to come in and go out to; it meant flowers, and service sheets (which font? How many pages? A ribbon on the front or a sketch of the church?) and payment for the choir; it meant arranging banns to be read, and payment for the licence and a gift for the vicar and . . . on and on and on it went, each thing bringing with it a bill. Her savings were dwindling as she wrote cheques for deposits. Although they'd agreed to split the cost, Ruth seemed to be stumping up for most of it, simply because she was making all the arrangements. Perhaps it was also that Ned knew she had a nest egg saved for her wedding from the money her mother had left her. But then, she reminded herself, he was paying for the honeymoon.

On those dark evening journeys home from the surgery, she hoped that they were going somewhere light and warm. She wanted to see the sun. She craved heat on her skin. Ned had promised not to tell her where they were going; she just wanted to arrive there without any of the burdens of sorting it out. And it would be his gift to her, this surprise location. When they got there, it would mean that the wedding was over and done with, that they were successfully married and that now they could get on with beginning the rest of their lives together.

He was doing a good job of keeping it a secret;

she hadn't stumbled on any brochures or mysterious large ticket-sized envelopes. He hadn't left a website open on the computer, giving away their destination. She was sure he must have told other people — Tom and Erin must surely know, and probably Luke and Abigail too — but they all knew that Ruth wasn't to be told. She liked that. It was good to have one part of the day that was hidden from her.

Occasionally she felt a prick of conscience that Jackie and Steven Haskell were left out of the arrangements almost entirely. But, honestly, she had no idea what they could do, especially so far away in York. And as parents of the groom, all they really had to do was turn up; tradition dictated that there was not much of a role for them. On top of that, they hadn't offered any money at all towards the cost of the day. That was fair enough, but in the circumstances Ruth couldn't really see why she should go out of her way to include them. Besides, the business with the forged invitation bothered her: it showed how intransigent Jackie was, how she had a fixed idea of what was right and would not tolerate anything else. She was fearful of letting someone so controlling into the delicately personal business of planning a wedding.

There'd been a sticky moment the other night when Jackie had rung. Ruth had got into the habit of not answering the phone but letting the answer machine pick it up. It was partly because she didn't want to talk to Jackie, but also because she had the lingering memory of that nasty call and didn't want to be on the receiving end of any abuse. She felt the usual wash of relief that she hadn't answered when Ned picked up the phone and said, 'Hello, Mum.'

Jackie had wanted to know how many invitations she would be getting for the wedding. How many people was she allowed to invite? There were her far-flung relations to be thought of, not to mention all her friends from her club, and the next-door neighbours on either side.

'How many people is she allowed to invite?' said Ruth, incredulous when Ned told her. 'None! This is *our* wedding, we decide who is invited. She's a guest. None of the other guests have rung up enquiring about how many pals they're allowed to bring along. I'm not having her cronies whooping it up at my wedding — people we've never met before and never will again.'

It seemed extraordinary that someone wanted to treat her special day as a way to give their friends a treat. She didn't want to look at her wedding photographs in years to come and wonder who the people in them were. Everybody there ought to be a proper part of her and Ned's lives, or what was the point? Weddings were so expensive these days, it was not as though she could have an open house, getting the world and his wife along. Numbers had to be limited and that was that. The bingo club, or whoever they were, would just have to content themselves with looking at the photographs.

She left it to Ned to break the news. She didn't want to get into fights about anything but she also felt intractably stubborn on this issue:

this was *her* wedding, her and Ned's. No one was going to take it away from her.

★ ★ ★

In the week before the wedding she had the sense of being pulled very tight, so that every nerve was straining. The closer they got to the big day, the more minute were the details that demanded her attention. The pub rang to ask what kind of cloakroom facilities she would require and to find out exactly what time on the wedding day the warehouse would deliver the wine, and how long she needed the champagne to chill and the red wine to breathe. To keep track of it, she had a spreadsheet on her computer that looked like the details of a military campaign, listing exactly what time everything should happen on the day, from the arrival of her bouquet at the Old Rectory, to the assembling of her profiterole wedding cake in the upper room of the pub.

'This was meant to be simple!' she wailed to herself, as she phoned the dressmaker who was making the waistcoats for the ushers to find out when the last alterations would be finished and when she could drive over and collect them. Xenia Yasparov had finished the last details of her dress the previous week and it was now hanging on the back of the spare room door, inside an ornate protective cover. Ruth hadn't bothered to tell Ned not to look at it. She'd be surprised if he even noticed it was there.

It didn't help that Ned had told her worriedly

that his mother was ill: Jackie had taken to her bed with an unspecified illness, insisting she was in great pain and might have to go into hospital at any moment.

'I don't know what we should do,' Ned said, anxiety in his voice.

'What do you mean?'

'Well — what will we do if she actually does go into hospital? I don't know if we could go ahead with everything.'

'You don't mean — cancel the wedding . . . ?' Ruth was aghast.

'If she went into hospital and was diagnosed with something serious, I don't know that we'd have any choice.'

Ruth, panicked and angry, bit back her words but she wanted to tell him that she would expect the moon to turn into green cheese before Jackie was actually diagnosed with anything seriously wrong. As far as she could see, all of Jackie's symptoms were the result of self-imposed histrionics and drinking too much too often. It seemed to Ruth, now that she had witnessed her at Christmas, that many evenings in the Haskell house ended up with Jackie slurring her words, repeating herself and eventually slumping down on the sofa into a drunken sleep. It began to make sense: the unpredictability, the mood swings and the different personalities that rang up, depending on how many cherry brandies Jackie had indulged in that night.

She wondered if Ned and Steven had noticed. How could they not? And yet, no one ever said anything about it. Even after Ned had sat for an hour with the phone clamped to his ear, not having to say a word in response to his mother's ramblings, he didn't comment on it when he finally got away. Ruth wondered if it was simply not a problem — or if they were just so used to it that they hardly noticed it anymore.

When Ruth picked up the phone one evening, she knew at once she had a sober Jackie on the other end, soft-voiced and very sorry for herself. Ruth listened to a long, self-pitying speech about how much she was suffering and how no one understood.

'I don't know how I'll make it to the wedding. I think it's probably cancer,' she said weakly.

'You're so brave,' Ruth comforted her. 'I'm sure you're fine but if the doctor does decide to be on the safe side and take you in, well . . . It'll be hard not having you there, but I know you wouldn't want us to cancel everything now.'

There was a long silence and then Jackie said, 'No, of course not. I wouldn't hear of it.'

A few days later, she was up and about, to Ned's relief and Ruth's secret amusement. Perhaps, she thought, I'll be able to handle her after all. It was one small victory and it heartened her, even though she was frazzled with the amount of organisation still to do.

The last thing she thought she could handle was going to a party.

'We've got to go,' insisted Ned. 'It's Tom's birthday.'

'But I'm exhausted,' said Ruth. She was aware that she was difficult company for Ned at the moment, and sometimes she was frightened that he would turn around and say, 'This wedding has turned you into a monster. I don't think I want to be married to you at all. It's all off.' But she felt so strained by the burden of arranging everything that it was difficult not to snap, or get cross, or show that she was finding it stressful.

'Then a party is just what you need. Anyway, it's not a big thing, just a meal out in town.'

'But it means finding a present, a card . . . and we can't really afford to go out.'

'Ruth — would you relax? Come on, let's have a break from the bloody wedding for five minutes and think about someone else for a moment. Tom's very kindly agreed to be my best man and organise my stag night on Saturday. I think the very least we can do is pop along to his birthday dinner.'

Ruth was mollified. 'You're right. I'm being ridiculous — I am sorry, honey, I just can't help it at the moment. Of course we'll go, and I'll be able to hand out the ushers' waistcoats at the same time, so that's one more thing to tick off the list.'

★ ★ ★

The dinner was downbeat, as though everyone was conserving their energies for the bigger party to come. The venue was an old-fashioned restaurant tucked down a back street in the city centre, a place with wood-panelled walls, huge fireplaces and wonky leaded windows. They were in a private dining room away from the main restaurant; there was one large refectory table and the friends sat round it, occasionally swapping places to talk to someone else. Ruth found herself next to Abigail, who was keen to hear all about the wedding preparations, although whatever Ruth mentioned Abigail couldn't wait to tell her version of the same thing. It was strange, thought Ruth, that no matter how much you thought you had made your wedding your own, it was essentially the same as everyone else's: a ceremony and a party. It was just the detail that varied and even that was pretty much the same.

'So our cake had to be transported by three taxis!' Abigail was saying, as the waitress cleared away the pudding plates and brought round the coffee. 'It was absolutely ridiculous but Luke had insisted on five tiers and no one had thought about how we were going to get it to the castle . . .'

Then she was interrupted by Tom, who sat up straight in his chair at the top of the table and tapped his glass with his fork. The chatter round the table subsided and everyone listened obediently.

Once he had their attention, Tom sat back in his chair, casual and yet elegant, his thick blond hair disarrayed and a speckling of dark stubble around his jaw.

'A speech,' he said, grinning. 'I'm getting into practice for Ned's big day. This won't be a long one, promise. Unlike the reams I've got prepared for you, Ned. There isn't terribly much to say, really. Just thank you all for coming to celebrate me crawling one year closer to my dotage, and for the presents. Very kind of you all.' He paused and stared at the table for a long moment. Then he coughed, and stretched out a hand towards Erin, who was staring at him with shining eyes. 'There is one other thing,' he said slowly.

They're getting married, thought Ruth. *They're announcing their engagement.*

A huge smile spread across Erin's face and she squeezed Tom's hand.

'It's a very strange announcement to be making really, but we didn't really know how to say it. I suppose I'd better just come right out with it. You see . . . '

The expectation around the table almost crackled.

'You are all going to be aunts and uncles.'

There was a gasp and a sigh and a burst of laughter and delight, as the news sunk in. A flood of chatter followed, cries of congratulations and questions: 'When is it due?' and 'How did you keep that a secret? What about morning sickness?' and 'Do you know what you're having?'

Ruth saw Ned get to his feet and rush to Erin to hug her, and then turn to Tom and shake his hand, laughing. He put a hand on his old friend's shoulder and said something that made all three of them laugh. Ruth caught a glimpse of Jeremy's face. He was observing the other three intently, a half smile twisting his mouth at one corner. His long fingers fidgeted with his napkin. *What's wrong with him?* she thought. *He can't be jealous, can he? After all this time?*

'Oh, isn't that fantastic?' said Abigail excitedly.

'A baby. It's about time we started breeding, isn't it? Fancy Tom and Erin going first. I thought her career wasn't going to let her start having babies for a while yet.' She leaned towards Erin who was still talking to Ned, now crouching between her and Tom. 'When is it due, Erin?'

'Early summer,' Erin called back, her face still aglow. 'June.'

'Congratulations, darling. That's fabulous news.'

'Thanks, Abigail.'

'Congratulations,' echoed Ruth, smiling. But inside she felt mean and vile because for some reason the news didn't make her happy. In the most selfish way, she felt angry that the excitement of her wedding, that she'd worked so hard for, had just been eclipsed.

★　★　★

By Saturday night, she had forgotten that her initial reaction to Erin's pregnancy had been so ungenerous. It was only momentary anyway — she was soon agreeing with Ned that it was wonderful news. Besides, she had a lot to think about. The prospect of her wedding, now only a week away, filled her mind and gave her a feeling of sick anticipation — 'what will go wrong? I want everything to be perfect' — mixed with the heady excitement that at last she and Ned would be married.

Ruth's hen night was hosted by Cordy and, against Cordy's instinct which tended towards nightclubs, costumes and saucy toys, was very quiet. Six close friends for dinner in her sister's flat was all she wanted. All of them — Cordy, Fran down from Manchester, Valentina, Isabelle, Abigail and Erin — brought part of a meal and a bottle of champagne and they ended the evening drunk — except for Erin — and dancing in Cordy's tiny sitting room, singing along to the karaoke machine she'd hired specially.

The night before the wedding, in keeping with tradition, Ruth left the cottage she shared with Ned and went back home. Although she knew that this was hardly the last time she would stay in the Old Rectory, she had a strong feeling that she would never again be quite the same person, and she looked at all the familiar rooms, furniture and pictures as though she was seeing them in this particular way for the final time.

Cordelia cooked supper for the three of them and they ate in the breakfast room, trying to stay calm.

'It feels like the night before an execution, doesn't it?' said Silas.

'Dad!' cried Cordy. 'It doesn't in the least.' She glanced at her sister. 'Does it, Ruth?'

'It doesn't,' said Ruth, slowly. She put down her fork, leaving most of her supper untouched. 'But it feels so horribly serious that every time I think about what's going to happen tomorrow, I get butterflies.' The things that Erin and Jeremy had said to her had begun to play through her mind. She was certain that she and Ned were absolutely right for each other, but could they last? Was it naïve and stupid to think so?

211

Unwanted doubts and fears, stirred up by the others' comments, were making her unsure of herself.

'I'm sure everything will be all right,' replied Cordy stoutly. 'The rehearsal went well, didn't it?'

'The rehearsal was fine — and at least Ned's mother turned up for it, even if it was at the last minute — but that's not what I mean. I mean that tomorrow I'll be *married*. Swearing to stay with Ned for life. My whole life. I don't even know if I'll still like the china I picked for the wedding list in five years. It just feels so . . . *momentous*.'

'I don't know why you need to get married at all,' remarked Cordy. 'Most people just live together nowadays, and don't need some legal ceremony to tell them they can. It seems to me like a much more realistic arrangement. You're absolutely right, you can't tell whether you're going to love someone in ten years time, and the chances are you won't.' She waved a hand at Ruth apologetically. 'I'm sure you and Ned will, but it just seems ridiculous to put all this pressure on people to swear to stay together their whole lives when people live so long. I can see that in the past, your chances of both making it were pretty low, so 'till death us do part' made a sort of sense. But now . . . ' she shook her head ' . . . I don't know why we still do it. Five years ago, it was non-stop weddings for all my friends. Now, the divorces are starting. Why do we bother?'

Silas coughed, a sure sign that he had

212

something to say. He sat back and folded his hands over his old, frayed jumper. 'What you don't understand, Cordelia,' he began.

Cordy rolled her eyes to heaven and muttered, 'Here we go.'

Silas continued regardless. 'What you don't understand is that there is a huge difference between standing up in front of all your friends and family and saying 'I vow to stay with you until death', and between two people saying to each other, 'Let's stay together until one of us feels like moving on, probably in about five years.' You feel quite different after you're married. I don't know why — perhaps it's purely psychological — but you do. Once you walk away together after that ceremony, you're now one. A unit. You've stood up before the rest of society and said, 'We are now a new family, a permanent fixture, an indivisible team'. I was very young when I married your mother and, like Ruth is feeling here, I wondered if this person were the right one for me, even though I knew I could search forever and find no one better, because it is frightening — terrifying even — to commit your future in this way. But what is the alternative? To live alone your whole life? We humans aren't made that way, we're not meant to live alone — it's a path to loneliness and depression, even madness. Or to go from one relationship to another, always having to start again, addicted to that initial rush of falling in love but never able to build a life or share a history together? At some point you have to take the risk, and you have to make the promise that it's permanent, or it's worthless.'

He turned to Cordy. 'When you talk about love, it seems to me that you're talking about all that romantic stuff — stomach churning like you're on a rollercoaster ride, moonlight and roses and all that. But real, married love is something else. It's the deepest friendship of your life. It's the safest place you know — it's the home of your heart. It is where you are utterly yourself and completely loved, and in return you offer love, tolerance, respect and trust, and do your best to earn those things from your partner. Yes, it is an enormous task, and many, many marriages are not lived that way and never can be, and they won't last, but it's what you must aim for, or what's the point? Those things — love, trust and respect — don't just come from your emotions, the fickle feelings of desiring someone, or feeling cross or tired, or excited. It comes from your will, because you can make yourself love someone — and believe me, there will be times when you have to work very hard to keep on loving, when things are difficult and money is tight or when the other person is behaving like a mule — and from your heart, because that's where your goodness resides.' He leaned over to Ruth and put a hand on her arm. 'I've seen you and Ned together and I believe you two have what it takes. Don't forget to guard it because it's precious. But don't be afraid to take what you need from it in order to flower in your life, because Ned will be your wellspring, just as you will be his.'

He patted her gently, and smiled.

'Oh Dad,' said Ruth in a choked voice, wiping her eyes that were full of tears. 'That was beautiful. It suddenly all made sense. I know I'm doing the right thing.'

'I know you two think I'm just a silly old man,' said her father, 'and not a little mad, but I have lived a bit. And my own marriage was very happy. I wish the same for you, Ruth. And you too, Cordelia, when the time comes.'

Cordelia said, 'Sorry, Dad, it all sounds super, it really does, but what sentimental tripe. It's all greeting-card nonsense that doesn't begin to address how two people are supposed to spend a lifetime together. But far be it from me to be the wicked fairy at the feast. If anyone can do it, you can, Ruth. I do believe that.' She smiled at Ruth. 'Early bed for you?'

'Yes,' agreed Ruth. 'I think that would be best.'

No matter what Cordy said, her father's words had worked. Her nerves were calmed and she felt ready to face the day ahead.

11

'Ruth, are you ready? It's almost time.' Cordy's voice floated up the stairs.

Erin stepped back and looked at Ruth, who stood before the long mirror staring at her reflection in the glass with a calm but dazed expression.

'I think you're ready, don't you?' asked Erin, looking pleased with her handiwork. Ruth's make-up was a triumph of Erin's practiced actress's hand: she knew exactly how to emphasise the features so that Ruth would look beautiful both at close range and at a distance. Walking into the church was like making an entrance on the stage, explained Erin, and no bride should look washed out or pallid; but neither should she look like a pantomime dame, with blackened brows and bright red lips. 'So we'll avoid those, shall we?' Instead, with a subtle blend of colours and highlights, dark pencils and rosy glosses, Erin had brought out Ruth's high cheekbones and green eyes, making her look flawlessly pretty. She had lifted the auburn hair up and secured it away from Ruth's face with the gold and purple violets from Xenia Yasparov.

Ruth turned to look at her, her face bright. 'Thank you for this,' she said. 'It's perfect. I'm ready.'

★ ★ ★

She went carefully down the narrow stairs, finding her balance in her heels, her pure white bouquet held carefully in one hand. Cordy and her father waited at the bottom and when they saw her, their expressions told her that her appearance was what she had hoped.

'Crumbs, Ruth,' breathed Cordy. 'You look amazing.'

Her father couldn't say anything for a moment. Then he said gruffly, 'I wish your mother could have been here today. She would have been very proud.' In his normal voice, he added, 'Fancy having a green wedding dress!'

'It's *eau de Nil*,' said Ruth, smiling. 'Not green. Don't let anyone say green.'

'The coat's gorgeous,' Cordy exclaimed. 'Like beautiful old wallpaper.'

Ruth laughed. 'I'm glad you two aren't the people I asked for advice. Old green wallpaper!'

'It's jolly pretty, your oh-dee-neel,' said Silas quickly. 'You look beautiful, sweetheart. I've never seen a more glamorous bride.'

★　★　★

It seemed that January had taken a rest from pounding the country with storms and the day was clear and bright, with a hard edge of frost. The photographer, who'd been waiting patiently in the kitchen while Ruth got ready, took some pictures of them all standing before the fireplace, Silas looking unusually smart in his morning coat and dark grey striped trousers, Cordelia in the silver dress she and Ruth had chosen together, with a lavender-coloured sequinned shrug over her shoulders and a small bouquet of pale purple and white roses — and Ruth between them, feeling like a movie star in her silk dress and embroidered coat. Erin left to get to the church before them, and, when the photographer had got the necessary number of pictures, they left the house to make the short walk to the church.

As they walked in the brisk, cold air, Ruth was astonished by the deep calm within her. All the tensions and fears of the last few weeks had gone — *well*, she thought, *there's no point in worrying now, there's nothing I can do about anything* — and she felt relaxed. The only thing in her mind was Ned; he was all she could think about: that he was waiting for her at the church, and that soon they would be married, the one unit that her father had talked about the previous night. She wondered how he was feeling, and hoped that he too had the profound inner certainty that she now felt.

The church was grey gold in the bright early afternoon light, mellow against the stark fields behind it. It was so quiet, Ruth thought, as they approached. There was no one to be seen.

'Where is everyone? Did anyone come?' she whispered.

'They're all inside,' reassured her father. 'Waiting for you.'

Now she could see the vicar, just inside the door of the church. She stopped briefly on the doorstep as she heard the organ strike up and said anxiously, 'Do I look all right?'

218

Cordy smoothed a hand over her sister's hair and plucked at the coat so that the seam was straight. They both took a deep breath. 'Everything's just right.'

The vicar came out and said, 'Ready? In we go. Don't worry, he's here. And he appears to be sober, which is a great advance on many of the bridegrooms I get here. He also didn't arrive in his own combine harvester, as my last one did.'

Silas offered Ruth his arm and smiled, and they began their procession into the church.

★   ★   ★

People had told her that the day would go quickly but even so, Ruth was startled by the speed of events. Everything seemed to fly by in a blur although she willed herself to remember every moment and imprint it in her mind.

The walk up the aisle was like passing through a tunnel of faces. The church was usually sparsely attended and it looked different so full of people, all turning towards her and smiling with love and encouragement as she passed by. She looked at some of them, but mostly at Ned, who was standing waiting for her at the top, Tom next to him. The other thing she noticed as she passed was that Jackie was standing on the groom's side, facing resolutely forward so that she couldn't see Ruth approaching.

She's wearing black! thought Ruth, as she saw the large hat and plain suit that her mother-in-law was sporting. But as she walked past her, she saw that it was dark navy blue, with a white rose and giant triangle of fern pinned to the chest. I'm not going to think about her, she promised herself. This is only for me and Ned.

★ ★ ★

The service was as beautiful as she'd hoped. The choir sang as well as a small church choir can be expected to sing; no one objected at the vital moment; Ruth didn't trip over a grating and fall down as she feared she might. Her father read from the Song of Solomon in a loud monotone: 'Your lips distil nectar, my bride; honey and milk are under your tongue; the scent of your garments is like the scent of Lebanon' . . . it made Ruth want to laugh. Erin stood at the lectern, elegant and glamorous in a leopard-print opera coat and pill-box hat, and read the piece from St Paul in a voice of honeyed smoothness. When she came to the end, she slowed melodramatically, turned to gaze at Ruth and Ned, and proclaimed in round tones, 'Faith, hope and love . . . But the greatest of these — ' she paused, as though overcome with the moment — 'is LOVE!'

The vicar spoke to the congregation about the great step the couple were taking, and how they would need all their friends' and families' support in the years ahead. And then it was time to step forward, clasp Ned's hand, and be married.

As they spoke the words to each other, he looked in to her eyes, smiling. He took her hand and slipped the ring on her finger, speaking the vows loudly and confidently.

It's all right. It's all wonderful, she thought, as she put the band on to his finger in return.

Then there were hymns and prayers, but it seemed like only moments later that the organ pealed out Handel's Music for the Royal Fireworks and they were walking back down towards the open door and the yellow winter afternoon outside.

★   ★   ★

They had been going to walk to the pub, but to her surprise, there was a hansom cab waiting outside the church, its side lamps festooned in white ribbons, a grey horse in the harness and a uniformed coachman on his perch behind the roof.

'What's this?' she said, laughing. It was everything she'd been trying to avoid, with its air of pretend tradition. What was it about weddings and Christmas that made everyone wish to act like Victorians? Close up, though, the cab was impressive, two huge cartwheels supporting the carriage, which glowed with black leather and brass. The horse stamped on the hard ground, blowing steam from its nostrils with a snort.

'I thought you might like it. And I wanted us to have a few moments on our own,' said Ned.

They climbed in as the photographer buzzed about them, clicking madly away at this photo opportunity: the bride and groom in their carriage, glowing with their newly married status. The guests, emerging from the church behind them, exclaimed at the sight. Ned tucked a fur-lined rug around Ruth's knees and knocked on the roof of the cab. Obediently the driver clicked the horse into motion, and turned the cab round.

As they moved away from the church, past the crowd of tourists sighing happily at the sight of the bride in her carriage, Ruth heard her mother-in-law asking loudly, 'But when are we having the formal group photographs?' and she giggled.

Ned hugged her and they kissed with a fizzing excitement. 'Hello, wife,' he said. The word that once sounded mundane to her was now impossibly glamorous.

'Hello, husband,' she replied and they kissed again.

⋆ ⋆ ⋆

Ned had arranged that they take a tour of the village in the carriage, and all along the way, people waved and cheered, and cars tooted congratulations when they saw the ribbons.

'I'm going to have a red face,' said Ruth, laughing. 'It's jolly cold.'

'You're beautiful. I couldn't believe my eyes when you came into the church. I was stunned.'

'I thought you looked a bit sick.'

'Are you mad? I was just scared in case you realised what you were doing, and made a run for it.'

'Was this what you expected?' She touched her dress.

'You mean, did I think you'd be in a yellow meringue?' He laughed. 'I knew you'd pick something wonderful and unique. You look fantastic.'

★   ★   ★

By the time they arrived at the old pub, the congregation had made their way from the church and were waiting for them in the large upstairs rooms. They climbed the stairs and entered to a burst of cheers and clapping, and were passed glasses of champagne by Tom, and the celebrations began.

It was like floating on a cloud of approval, thought Ruth. Everywhere she looked, she saw smiles and love and pleasure at her happiness. The speeches were about how wonderful she was, and how wonderful Ned was, and how happy they were going to be. Her father had written a comical poem about Ruth's childhood that made everyone laugh, and then spoke so warmly and lovingly about her that she wasn't the only one sniffing a little when he'd finished.

Ned did his duty with a speech thanking everyone, and he presented Cordy and his mother and his sister with huge bouquets. At the end, he spoke simply of his happiness.

'Ruth is pretty amazing for taking me on. I'm proud she's agreed to be my wife.'

'More fool her!' shouted Luke, while everyone cheered and clapped. Tom's best man speech was witty and clever, as she had known it would be. And through it all, she was aware of Jackie

Haskell sitting nearby. Despite the darkness of her suit, she seemed in a good mood. The winsome Jackie, evident on Christmas Day, was on show again, a slightly sickly smile permanently on her face. She kept her head cocked in an attitude of sentimental pleasure throughout the speeches, and wiped her eyes with a handkerchief when Ned presented her with a bouquet of flowers 'for being such a wonderful mother'.

Cordy leaned towards Ruth and whispered, 'Her retirement present — your services are no longer needed!'

'Shh,' said Ruth, worried someone would hear. She had noticed that the crystal-encrusted brooch that she'd given Jackie for Christmas was glistening on her lapel, and at once felt guilty for thinking badly of her in the way she did. 'She's not so bad.'

They finished the toasts, and everyone drank more. Ruth and Ned circulated, greeting their friends and family, stopping at tables to talk and have photographs taken. Susie Haskell, resplendent in black velvet and a stunning red silk Spanish shawl, stopped her and said, 'Love your dress, Ruth. Congratulations. It's been a lovely day, and I don't say that lightly.'

Then, as the atmosphere mellowed further, the pub staff cleared away the tables and made room for dancing. Ruth and Ned swayed and spun together on the empty dance floor to the first dance — Ned had chosen 'Embraceable You' — and then they were joined by other couples carried away by the romance of the occasion.

My wedding day is nearly over, thought Ruth, high on the champagne and the excitement of it all. There was also the sheer relief that nothing had gone wrong and that all the arrangements had worked smoothly. She stood at the edge of the room to catch her breath from all the dancing. Her embroidered coat had been discarded and was hanging over a chair, but she was still warm just in her silk sheath. Her father was dancing with Cordy, his movements a bit strange but more polished than she would have expected. Ned and Abigail were be-bopping to the rock 'n' roll. The dance floor was crowded with people enjoying themselves.

She wove her way through chairs to the door and found her way along the corridor to the ladies'. In there, she looked at her reflection in the mirror: she had stood up remarkably well to the long day, considering. The morning, when she had been so polished and perfect, seemed like an age away. Now her hair was a little awry and tendrils had escaped from the pins, but it gave her a romantic air, she thought. There was a bright pink flush along her cheekbones — champagne rather than good health, she guessed.

She heard the flush of a lavatory and Jackie Haskell came out of the cubicle. She swayed over to where Ruth was, an over-sweet smile on her face.

She's drunk, thought Ruth, recognising the signs from Christmas Day: the lumber in the walk, the head wobbling slightly and the slow

225

blinking of the eyes. I don't know how to deal with her when she's like this.

Jackie joined her at the basin and put her handbag down heavily on the surround.

''Lo, Ruth. You're my daughter-in-law now, aren't you? Welcome to our family. I hope you'll be very happy here.'

'Thank you,' answered Ruth, carefully neutral. She felt at once very sober.

'I didn't say, did I?' Jackie put her hand to her mouth in mock horror. 'I'm so naughty! You always have to tell a bride how nice she looks on her wedding day. And you do, love. You look lovely. It's like . . . it's like a nightie, isn't it? Pretty, though. A lovely green nightie.' She looked suddenly serious and she said, 'You want to be careful, though. What people will think. Not wearing white on your wedding day. People are wicked, they really are. They say dreadful things behind your back. They say things like, the bride's got this or that condition, that she's pregnant or worse. She's not really a nice girl. There was a woman we knew who got married in yellow. They said she had syphilis. She had to wear a pearl choker round her neck to hide the signs.'

Ruth felt her smile begin to fade. *She's trying to rile you. Don't let her get to you. It's all nonsense.* But it pierced and deflated her happiness all the same.

'This is very nice, though. Did you notice I wore it?' Jackie stroked the little glittering bow that sat high on the lapel of her suit. 'It was very generous of you, Ruth. Really you shouldn't have spent so much on me. A hundred and sixty pounds! That's a lot of money, isn't it?'

'That's all right,' Ruth said shortly. 'How did you know how much I spent?'

'I took it into a store in York and they looked it up for me. Swarovski, you said. So they found it for me without much trouble. I was very pleasantly surprised. Well, you have to know. For insurance. Don't you?' Jackie smiled at her again, that sickly insincere tight-lipped grimace, cocking her head.

How do I get away? How can I do it without being rude? She turned away from the other woman and tucked some of the loose tendrils of hair behind her ears. 'I'd better get back. Ned will be wondering where I am.'

'You get back. After all, it's your big day, isn't it? You don't want to miss it, standing here in the toilets with your mother-in-law. Besides, you've got places to be, haven't you? I bet you can't wait to get on your way. They say that Thailand is wonderful at this time of year.'

With a final smile, Jackie picked up her bag and walked out, leaving Ruth impotently furious, leaning on the hand basin for strength.

★   ★   ★

She went back out, striding through the reception, wanting to find Ned. She was full of anger — how dare that woman spoil the surprise? She must have known Ned was keeping it a secret. But she couldn't wipe out the knowledge now: it was like being told who had

227

done the crime before you reached the end of the book. And it was dreadful, because she'd come so close to being kept in ignorance so that she could enjoy finding out on the flight or at the airport or from Ned.

Bloody woman, bloody, bloody woman, she thought furiously. In the main room, a soft, slow dance was playing. She looked for Ned and saw him among the people on the dance floor. He was dancing close to Erin, who had her arms snaked about his neck. They were moving slowly in time to the music, and he was gazing down into her face, listening as she spoke to him. Ruth wanted to go up to him, to pull him away and claim him back. Why wasn't he dancing with her? This was her wedding day, and he was her husband. They should be together.

She was about to storm her way on to the dance floor and grab him when a lazy voice in her ear said, 'Isn't that sweet?'

Ruth turned to see Jeremy, unusually dapper in a morning coat, even if he'd taken off the jacket and let his tie hang loose. 'You seem to be making a habit of surprising me,' she said as lightly as she could. She couldn't take her eyes off Ned and Erin turning languidly on the dance floor. 'How are you?'

'I'm very well. And I thought your wedding day was charming. I offer you my warmest congratulations.' He bowed slightly and it reminded her how old fashioned he always seemed to her. 'Erin read beautifully, didn't she? I'm always touched when she reaffirms the Biblical values — you know, faith, hope and charity. Or, as the new version has it, faith, hope and love.'

They stood in silence for a moment. This is all wrong, thought Ruth. What am I doing standing here with Jeremy? I know where I should be.

The whole day had been an affirmation of what she felt in her heart: that she and Ned were now one. Something in her was pulling her towards him, as irresistible as a magnetic force. She wanted, needed and desired to be close to him, and she knew that if she got close to him, he would turn to her, smile, embrace her, pull her close to his heart, and she would have the reassurance she needed so badly.

I must be drunk, she thought wretchedly. *I shouldn't feel so insecure. I shouldn't let Jeremy keep me here.* But, nonetheless, her ridiculous sense of politeness kept her standing beside him as he lit a cigarette.

'They've always been close,' Jeremy said finally. 'He's always known what she's thinking. I envied that, because I never did. Perhaps Ned's secret is that he understood her better than she understood us.'

'What do you mean?' she asked. Another couple moved into her vision, blocking out Ned and Erin.

'What do I mean?' echoed Jeremy. He spat a tiny piece of tobacco out on to his lip, and stroked it away with a fingertip. 'I mean — that.'

The floor seemed to clear in front of them. Ruth saw clearly: Ned reached down with one hand and very gently stroked Erin's belly. She smiled at him and he said something in her ear.

'That connection,' said Jeremy languidly. 'He had it much more than the rest of us.'

Ruth couldn't stand it another minute. She left Jeremy behind and advanced on to the dance floor, forcing her way between the dancers until she reached Ned and Erin. Reaching out, almost with all her strength, she grasped at Ned's arm. He turned, saw her and smiled with pleasure.

'Ruth! There you are. Where have you been?'

'We've been looking for you,' said Erin.

'Ned, can we go now?' she begged. 'Please, I'm ready. Can we go?'

He looked surprised. 'Of course we can, darling. It's almost time anyway.'

'You haven't thrown the bouquet yet,' said Erin.

'You have it,' said Ruth wildly. 'It's over there — on the chair. Please, take it, it's yours.'

'The taxi isn't here yet,' Ned said, now a little concerned. 'Your bags are still at the Old Rectory.'

'Then let's go, we'll go and collect them and they can send the taxi there.'

'If that's what you want . . . '

'It *is* what I want.'

They left quietly, weaving their way among their guests and saying good bye before sliding away. Most didn't even realise they'd gone. As they went, Ruth saw that her father was still dancing. Only Erin came to wave them off, with Ruth's wedding bouquet clutched in her hand.

*   *   *

230

When the airport announcer asked all passengers for the flight to Thailand to make their way to the gate, Ruth feigned surprise and delight, almost managing to convince herself that she hadn't had the vaguest suspicion of where they might be going.

'Are you pleased?' Ned asked anxiously. 'Is it what you wanted?'

'It's wonderful. It couldn't be more perfect.' She clasped his hand tight, feeling the unfamiliar hardness of the wedding ring round his finger. When they finally got on to the plane, she was overcome with relief and a deep sense of exhaustion.

It's just us now, she thought. No friends, no family. Just Ned and me.

★ ★ ★

They went to a luxury resort on an island off the coast. It had been hit in the natural disaster a few years before but no one would have known: there were no traces of the destruction, and to Ruth, it was idyllic, a mixture of burning blue and gold and the cool, air-conditioned relief of their hotel room. The wedding had wearied them both, and each day they woke up exclaiming about how glad they were that it was over. They talked about the day again and again, recalling details and sharing their different experiences of it. The only things Ruth kept to herself were the encounter with Jackie, and what she had seen when Ned and Erin were dancing together. It seemed a little dreamlike now, and not

231

something she wanted to think about.

Occasionally, as she lay by the pool, toasting in the sunshine, feeling the tiredness seep out of her, she thought about Jackie and wondered how she would handle her in the future.

Don't worry about it, she told herself. *You're married now and there's nothing she can do about it. She'll probably calm down now. Anyway, she lives miles away and has her own life. It will only be an issue once or twice a year when we have to go and see her. I'm sure I can handle it.*

When she did replay the scene in her mind, she had lots of witty and cutting replies she wished she'd said. *L'esprit de l'escalier*, she thought. The brilliant retorts you think of after the event.

Over dinner one night, she cautiously broached the subject of Ned's mother, saying, 'Have you ever thought that your mother might be drinking a bit much — and that's why she feels so ill all the time?'

Ned looked uncomfortable. His skin had taken on a healthy golden glow from the sunshine, making his eyes look brighter, and his hair was burnished with blond where the sun had lightened it. It made her want to run her fingers through it, and touch the rosy warmth of his cheek. 'Do you think she has a problem — in your professional opinion?'

'I've no idea. I'd have to know her much better. Do you think so?'

'She does drink a bit, but she seems to have it under control. I don't think she's an alcoholic anyway. She's perfectly able to go without it as far as I can see. She's not swigging vodka at ten in the morning or anything. It's just social drinking and the occasional evening glass of wine or a cocktail.'

'Cherry brandy.'

'Well — yes. And I can't blame her for it, sometimes.'

'Really? Why not?' She tried to sound casual but her interest was pricked. Perhaps, at last, Ned was going to start opening up about his mother.

'She's had a hard life in some respects.'

'What respects?'

'Well, her father died when she was young. She was very close to him and I think it affected her quite badly.'

'Poor thing,' said Ruth, and waited for more. Somehow that didn't seem an adequate explanation for Jackie's destructive personality, not only towards other people but towards herself.

Ned continued, 'She had a difficult relationship with her mother, and then she and Susie did not get on at all, even though they're more alike than you'd think. There was a lot of conflict there. I came along late, after she didn't think she could have more children, so she's always babied me, given me lots of attention, made me her favourite. You know the sort of thing, you've seen it.'

'Adored you. Too much. It's hard to live up to that kind of love.'

'Maybe. Yes, I suppose so. She's never really been able to let me go. But — well — I can't help feeling sorry for her.'

'You feel guilty that she loves you so much.' She wanted to add 'when you don't love her back the same way' but she didn't. It seemed too mean. She could see his discomfort. She could understand his reluctance to talk about Jackie: how did you begin to explain her schizoid personality? It was the kind of thing you had to let people discover for themselves, let them work out their own strategies for coping with her unpredictable nature and the puzzle of who they would encounter today: the sweet, motherly Jackie, who wanted nothing more than to be their closest, dearest friend, or the rude one, or the coarse one, or the drunk one, or the one who thought she was being persecuted by her friends and neighbours.

'Perhaps,' said Ned slowly. 'I'm no analyst. I just try and keep everything going in a way that we can all live with. I don't see why that should change.'

The waiter came with their food, and they talked about something else.

There's no reason why anything *should* change, thought Ruth as she lay on the sun lounger by the pool. We'll just go on avoiding her most of the time, putting up with her when we have to. There's no need to make a fuss about it. If Ned doesn't want to talk about it, we won't. I can easily live with a few nasty jibes from my mother-in-law without troubling Ned with it. She's jealous of me, that's all. It will calm down when she understands that nothing's changed, that Ned's still available in the way he was before. And it's part of the territory, isn't it?

She turned over in the baking sun and resolutely put Ned's mother out of her mind.

⋆　⋆　⋆

'Honeymoon?' people would say. 'Ah, that's wonderful. Congratulations. Enjoy it.'

In the resort's luxurious restaurants, they were sent bottles of champagne by smiling fellow diners, who could see from their air of absorbed bliss that they were newlyweds, and waiters automatically led them to the tables with the most romantic view; holidaymakers looked on fondly when they held hands; and every night there were two white roses on their pillows.

'I could stay on honeymoon my whole life,' said Ned dreamily, as they walked along the hot white sand, or swam in the pool.

They felt complete only when they were together. Ned could hardly bear to let Ruth out of his sight even long enough for her to order drinks at the bar. They craved each other constantly. In the weeks before the wedding, they had been so tired and stressed that they'd almost forgotten to kiss each other good night. Not now: they were so full of each other and so keen for more, it was as though each time they touched each other, it only increased their appetite instead of sating it.

They spent the morning in bed, and went back in the afternoon, and then fell upon each other again after dinner as though they hadn't already made love several times that day.

'It's what we're supposed to do,' Ned said, kissing her neck as they lay between the cool sheets. 'It's our honeymoon. I read somewhere that if you put a penny in a jar every time you had sex for the first two years of marriage, and then spent the rest of your married life taking a penny out every time, you'd never empty the jar.'

'Oh, that's sad,' said Ruth. She leaned her face against his arm, inhaling his scent. 'Will that happen to us? I don't want it to. I want it to be just the same.'

'It won't happen to us,' Ned said confidently.

'We did the right thing, didn't we? Are you glad you married me?'

'Of course I am.'

'You don't wish you'd married any of your old girlfriends?' She said it knowing it was a stupid question, but she wanted to hear the answer, even if she knew what it was.

He laughed. 'I'm constantly wondering why I didn't. Let me see — who would I rather have married? There was Jasmine. Lovely girl. Bit tiring because she was a multiple orgasmer. I only had to touch her and off she went, brrrrrrrrr. Like a clockwork toy that never wound down.'

'Isn't that nice, a multiple orgasmer? It must make you feel like a splendid lover.'

'It does at first. Then you realise you're actually a bit bored while they're juddering away ceaselessly, having a whale of a time. Or perhaps I should have married Teresa. We went out for a whole year before I finally realised she was deeply stoned almost all the time. I wondered

236

why she found me so hysterically funny and couldn't stop eating.'

'There must have been one of your girlfriends you liked.'

'Of course there was. I was in love with one or two of them, but it didn't work out, and we went our separate ways, and then I met you.'

'Very in love?' Ruth persisted. 'Tell me who you were very in love with.'

'You silly sausage.' Ned nuzzled into her, holding her tightly. 'Why do you ask me these questions? You women, I don't know. We've had a beautiful wedding day, we're on the most romantic honeymoon ever, we're at it like rabbits day and night — and you're wondering if perhaps I wish I'd married someone else.' He laughed.

'It does sound stupid when you put it like that. I suppose we just need a lot of reassurance.'

'Then I will just have to reassure you again,' he said, and kissed her slowly and sweetly.

★　★　★

On the plane home, they were both quiet. Neither of them wanted the beautiful hot, lazy days to be over.

'It was wonderful, wasn't it?' Ruth squeezed Ned's hand. 'We must never, never forget how it felt.'

'We won't,' he promised. 'It just feels so bleak to be going home.'

'I know what you mean.' The things that had been resolutely pushed out of her mind were beginning to haunt her again. The people who had shrunk away in her imagination during their time in Thailand were looming large. This was the life she had chosen. Now she would have to get on with it.

12

'Will this weather ever end?' asked Rhonda, the receptionist, as Ruth passed by with a basket full of patients' notes. 'I've never known it so bad.'

'It's bound to get better,' Ruth replied. 'Spring is nearly here.'

'Bring on global warming,' the other woman grumbled. 'Why do they keep going on about it, and we get weather like this? Rain, wind. I feel like we haven't seen the sun in months.' She nodded at Ruth. 'You're all right. You've still got your tan.'

'Have I?' Ruth inspected her bare lower arm. It looked pale to her, nowhere near the dark golden glow she'd had on her return from her honeymoon. If she thought hard, she could almost summon up a memory of the sun on her skin and the heat seeping into her bones. It must be an illusion, she told herself. She knew that there was no physical memory: the body could no more recall the heat on its skin than it could toothache or how an apple tastes. It was only the mental process that went alongside the physical sensation that could be recalled. Perhaps that's why we don't get bored of eating or kissing, she thought, because each time, in a small way, it's like the first time.

'Are you finished for today?' Rhonda asked.

Ruth nodded, putting her basket on the shelf for filing. The surgery was closed, and the place was back to its quiet, calm out-of-hours demeanour, the way it was early each morning and late each evening. In between, it belonged to the shuffling elderly, the squealing, screaming, running young, and everyone else who needed it. Now it was theirs again.

Rhonda pulled out the aerosol that she kept under the reception counter and sprayed the air with it fiercely. 'We had a stinker in earlier,' she explained. The chemical burn of artificial lavender stung Ruth's nose. 'Poor old boy. Don't know when he'd last had a bath but — pooh! He really honked. Lots of wee in it, too.'

'Charming,' Ruth replied.

'You feel sorry for them, of course,' said Rhonda, 'but we're still human and we've still got noses. I just feel sorry for Dr Potter. He had to get up close and personal.'

'That's me done,' said Ruth. 'I'll see you tomorrow.'

'Did you see you've got a holiday jab? Someone's off to Nepal and needs the full blast.'

Ruth nodded. 'I'm all prepared. Bye, then.'

She pulled her coat on and went out into the cold, wet darkness. Weren't the nights supposed to be getting lighter now? Every year it was the same — the winter seemed to stretch on and on, even after the crocuses and snowdrops appeared. They were false friends now, not announcing the arrival of spring but bravely showing how far away it still was as they succumbed to frosts and disappeared.

I must take Ned to the bluebell wood when they all come out, she thought, avoiding the black spray sent up from the road by passing traffic. When will that be? Easter, I suppose.

The bluebell wood was not far from the Old Rectory, in a piece of land protected by a wildlife trust. At a certain moment each year, it donned its imperial dress: a carpet of purple that shimmered and shook in the spring breeze. Silas would take the girls to see the full glory of it, explaining that they couldn't pick armfuls of the flowers as they wanted to, but must leave them where they were.

'You're not allowed to take wild flowers,' he would say. 'They're not to be removed. You can enjoy them here, but they must stay where they grow.'

Just one, thought Ruth one year, and she plucked a small triangular stem out of the ground and hid it in her pocket. When she took it out at home, it no longer looked like part of that triumphant, proud mass, but a crushed, wilted, lonely thing, its bells flattened and dull. The beauty it had possessed in the wood was gone. She felt so awful, to have taken it from its home and family to this ignoble death, that she cried with guilt and sadness, and buried it in the garden so that no one would ever know what she had done.

The cottage windows were bright, showing that Ned was home. She was glad. Married life, she had already decided, was wonderful. She could understand now why married people were so eager to convince others to do it. Once, she had assumed it was so everybody could be as imprisoned as they were but now, she thought, she could see what it was. Her father had been right: the change had been perceptible from the moment they'd left the church. It was as though an invisible thread had been tied between her and Ned, and no matter how much it stretched and how far apart they were, it was still there, almost tangible, connecting them and pulling them back together.

Two months married, she thought, laughing at herself, and here I am, an expert on the whole thing already.

The sight of Ned's broad back and tall frame in the kitchen made happiness swell gently through her. *I hope I always feel this way. I will, won't I?*

He turned and smiled at her. 'Hi, darling. How was your day? I'm making dinner.'

This easy domesticity nourished her soul, she thought, as they talked about their work, and then took their food to the table and ate together.

'Oh, there is one bad thing,' Ned said, his mouth full.

'What?'

He made a face. 'We have to go away on a management training course this weekend. Absolutely grim. I can't believe that David has fallen for all this nonsense, but apparently he has and we all have to go. He planned it ages ago and I'd completely forgotten about it. But it's all of us, going to some adventure camp to learn team bonding and how to interact with each other in a positive, team spirited way, you know the kind of guff.'

'Doing little tasks in teams, drawing on white boards to show the value of communication, giving each other little envelopes marked 'this is not a buck' — that kind of thing?'

'Add in a bit of paint-balling and I think you've got it.'

'Might be fun. I'd have thought you'd be in your element running round the woods playing soldiers.'

'Ruth,' Ned looked hurt, 'please. I'm not a child. I'm a grown man.'

'I know. That's just the point.'

'Okay — yes, it might be quite fun. The only thing that these weekends really achieve is making you get on better with your work colleagues. Expensive and time-consuming way to do it, if you ask me.'

'So I'll be on my own.'

'Friday to Sunday. Sorry. I don't have to tell you how much I'd rather be here with you, doing all the nice weekend things. Maybe you could have Erin round.'

'Maybe.'

Ruth hadn't seen a lot of Erin since the return from honeymoon. It was curious, the way a pregnancy seemed to separate someone off from the rest of the human race who weren't nurturing embryos inside them. Ruth wasn't sure if she should call Erin, or drop round, as if she might be busy concentrating on making the baby, sitting somewhere quietly and visualising tiny fingers forming and miniature organs growing, knitting little bones together in her mind. 'Perhaps I'll ask her.'

243

'Do that. I'm afraid we're going to have to venture out of our nest at some point.' He smiled at her. She knew that was what they had been doing — reverting to the earliest weeks of their love affair and shutting out the world, reluctant to let anybody into the life they had created behind their door, a place that seemed utterly complete in itself.

'I'll sort out the wedding presents,' said Ruth. Boxes had arrived from the department store, oversized and packed with other smaller boxes, hidden among drifts of polystyrene chips like prizes in a giant lucky dip. They'd opened most of them already, but the china was still carefully packed away. 'And make a start on the thank-you letters. And that will virtually take care of my weekend.'

* * *

It was horrible coming home on the Friday night to the cottage, knowing it was empty and that she'd be without Ned for a whole weekend. The time seemed like a vast gulf, or a desert she was going to have to cross alone.

She went to bed early, with a book and a mug of herbal tea. It wasn't so long, she reminded herself, since this was the way she spent every night. It wouldn't be so hard to get through it, would it? But, lying curled towards the bedside light, she found that the bed at her back seemed empty and cold without Ned's presence, and if she thought about it, a shiver came over her along with a deep need for him.

Go to sleep, she told herself. *It will be Sunday evening soon enough.*

In the morning, she felt brighter and more able to cope with the solitude. The fears of last night felt rather silly but she still had a niggling ache of loss as she went through the day. I'll use it as well as I can. Get all these annoying things out of the way.

Once she'd dressed in her old clothes and started tackling the wedding presents, stamping on empty boxes to flatten them and filling bags with discarded chips and wrapping, she'd got the bug.

I may as well give this place a good spring clean, she thought, hands on hips, gazing about. The day was brighter than it had been for the last few weeks, shafts of bright light illuminating the dust and dirt about the place. It needs a bit of attention.

The time she spent with Ned still had a sense of luxurious self-indulgence, and they hadn't been ready to buckle down to the work of keeping house: so far, it had been about breakfasts in bed and long baths, cosy dinners, and curling up together to watch the television, and not about the practicalities. It would have to change, she realised that. The domestic routine couldn't be ignored. Cleaning everything out would be a good way to use up her time, and start afresh.

Armed with rubber gloves, bin bags and a bucket of cleaning materials, she began to work her way round the house. The radio babbled away while she dusted and cleaned and sorted and discarded. It was therapeutic, she thought, this kind of work. The results were so immediate and so calming.

When the downstairs was done, she moved further up, changing their bedding and airing the room with the window wide to let in the fiercely fresh spring breeze.

She went into the spare room, a room they hardly used except to get to the computer which was set up on a desk just inside the door. Beyond that was a collection of Ned's things, reminders of his life before her: old sports kit; an exercise bike; boxes of tapes and mementos. The bed was scattered with magazines and books, and the wardrobe had old clothes, more boxes and even childhood toys stuffed inside it.

We waste this space, she thought, looking about it as though for the first time. It's a perfectly nice room and it looks like a junk shop. The window showed a view over the garden and the fields at the back of the house. She could see the dark green smudges of hedges and the blacker smears of woodland further away. This would be a good room to use for other things, rather than just sidling in to use the computer. She could hang damp clothes in here to air, or do the ironing here and stop clogging up the sitting room with the ironing board. She could put a fresh eiderdown on the bed, and a little lamp on the cabinet and make it look welcoming and cosy, ready for a guest, like a proper spare room.

That was what she would do — clear this room out. Put some things in boxes to go into the loft. Throw out things Ned would never even remember he had, let alone miss. Like those frightful tracksuit bottoms . . .

She went about her task energetically, sorting things into piles, stripping off the bed — 'when was *that* last done?' she wondered aloud — and tidying up. She cleared a path to the wardrobe and started jettisoning the contents, heaving up boxes and pulling them out. They were full of litter: papers, books, comics, birthday cards, notebooks, bank statements; the detritus of years.

She pulled one open to look inside it. Surely these things could be rationalised — there were about six boxes here and they could easily be turned into four, or even three. Then Ned could take them and hoist them up into the roof where they could be kept out of sight. She peered into the box; it was another morass of paper — postcards, letters, notebooks. She pulled a handful out, wondering when Ned became such a hoarder. Beneath this she saw a school exercise book with childish letters written neatly if shakily on the front: Edward Haskell, they said. Class 3BT.

Smiling, Ruth lifted it out and flicked through it. There were pictures drawn in a child's hand — stick men with spiky hair shooting at each other with enormous guns; or curious animals behind a criss cross of fencing; houses with heavily drawn plumes of spiral smoke coming from the chimney. Underneath the pictures was more erratic writing, occasionally corrected with red in an adult hand: *this weekend I went to*

247

Ben's house and we played on his jungel jim and we had jam on toast and we played football and then I went home and . . .

How sweet! she thought. It tickled her to think of Ned as a little boy, an adorable, mischievous, energetic child; and herself somewhere, a small girl, learning her own lessons and writing her own accounts of afternoons and weekends, as time worked inexorably to bring them together. She sat down and read slowly through it.

My mum was cross, he had written under a picture of an angry mother figure, its yellow curly hair standing up on end and spiky-fingered hands on its stick hips.

Poor little Ned, with that woman waiting for you at home every day.

We went to my grandmas and it was nice. I ate one bag of crips and then another bag of crips.

She plucked another book from the pile. Ned was older in this one, the writing clearer and more complex.

The boy went to the race track and he saw the cars wizzing round the track very fast. He wished that he could drive a car as well. Then the red car stopped beside him and the driver said . . .

Stories and make believe, and at the end, the teacher's comments in round red pen: *Good. Well imagined. Write out 'experience' ten times* and underneath ten valiant little scrawls as Ned fixed the word into his nine-year-old mind.

She pulled another exercise book. It had an adult hand scrawled across the front. *Ned Haskell*, it said. *Notes.*

The first page was neatly titled and underlined: _The Workings of the Human Eye._ _The eye is made up of optic nerves, the cornea, retina and . . ._

Biology A-level, she remembered, That was one of Ned's exams. She flicked on. The biology stopped after a couple of pages and rough notes began: scrawlings, jotting, sketches. Then a few pages of closely written handwriting. She started to read it almost before she knew what she was doing.

Today was another typically shit day. I couldn't even get myself together till well after lunch so I missed the lecture I was supposed to go to, which doesn't bode well for my course-work mark this term.

Lecture? she thought. At school?

Then I went into town and wandered about a bit before finally bowling up at the Union in the hope of seeing her. Hung about like an arse trying to look like I was fascinated by the vending machine and then by the women's rowing results pinned up on the notice board. Apparently Esther Cox has been selected as cox for the first eight. Crazy, huh? Now they just need to find eight girls with the surname 'Meaty Rower' and they'll be all set. While I was pondering the delightful Esther's career, I saw her _come in._

University, thought Ruth. He's at university. This is a diary. I must stop reading.

Marriage did not mean access to all areas, after all. It didn't mean diaries were allowed to be read. The same rules held true for marriage as for any relationship. Private areas had to be offered, not invaded. Wasn't that right? No one had explained it but she assumed that was how it worked. She would not dream of opening post addressed to Ned without his permission, and she'd expect the same of him. And diaries, after all, were sacred.

But then, it's years old, she thought. How on earth would Ned mind if I read it? Nevertheless, her stomach tingled with the sensation of something forbidden. I must stop. But who is this? Which girlfriend is this? The multiple orgasmer?

She came over to me. It's so hard to describe the effect she has on me. It's like she's surrounded in a halo of beauty and when she gets near me, it kind of lights up my life. I can't see anyone or anything else in the room. She was wearing a red top, a long skirt and boots, and a bunch of amber necklaces that looked stunning.

We sat down and had a coffee together and she had one of those long, weird conversations with me when I just don't know if either of us understands what the other one is trying to say. I spent most of the time frowning and staring at the table and wondering if I should just come out with it.

She sat there, telling me I'd been treating her oddly lately and why didn't I want to talk to her any more and was it something she'd done? Then, she stared up at me with those enormous, luminous eyes and asked me if I still wanted to be her friend. She said that she wasn't sure sometimes if I even liked her.

Liked her! Christ! She doesn't know if I like her, and sometimes I want to rip my heart out because it's fucking me up, being so in love with her and not able to say anything.

Ruth already knew. Her hands were beginning to turn clammy and she could feel her heart racing and her breathing getting heavier. Her scalp prickled.

Then Jeremy came up, casual as fuck, kissed her and told her they needed to get back to his. We're all going to Luke's party later and she's getting ready at J's place because all her stuff is there. It's kind of torture to think of her there, walking round his bedroom, getting into the bath, putting on her clothes. Even worse is what happens when they get back together. It makes me want to vomit just thinking about it so I don't think about it. I pretend they've got a totally platonic relationship.

I don't know how to handle parties when she's there. No wonder they all think I'm a moody bastard. I end up going to the kitchen or the garden or someone's bedroom, or some other sad place where there's no one else, drinking myself stupid and convincing myself I have to tell her — then staggering off to find her and do it. But I never, ever can. Something even more powerful than a bottle of vodka stops me. Why? But this party might not be so bad because Manda is going to be there and Tom told me she is quite keen and has said she is not averse to my very slight charms, so I might be able to drown my sorrow in her instead of alcohol.

The entry ended. Underneath was written:

251

Erin, I have to confess something that I suspect you know already. I find it difficult being around you not because I don't like you: in fact, the reverse is true. I'm deeply, profoundly in love with you and I need to know if you can ever feel the same way about me.

Ruth felt dizzy. What was this? It was proof, written proof. Ned had loved Erin. He had, and yet he had said that he had never felt that way about her. *Never?* This diary had been written some way into his university life. It was clear he had felt deeply about her.

She felt sick, and raddled with jealousy and fear.

I knew it, she thought, all the time I knew it. How could he not love her when she was so beautiful and glamorous and feminine, and everything a woman ought to be? Wretchedness filled her. I'm second best, she thought. I was what he settled for when he couldn't have her.

Now that she had opened the door to Ned's private thoughts, she couldn't stop herself, even though she knew she ought to put the book down, back in its box, reseal it and leave the room. She flicked through the pages of his notebook: the different inks and varied handwriting showed that it covered a period of time. All the entries concerned one thing: Ned's deep and unrequited love for Erin. But — did he ever tell her? Did she ever know? I have to find out, thought Ruth. She sat down and began to read.

Ned had kept his diary erratically: days of consecutive entries would be followed by one a month later. He would write long, intricate

252

reports, only to break off halfway through some event and not go back to it. Or one or two lines would cover a week. Some were written when he was drunk, and some were poems, most of which were heavily altered. One was crossed out in thick, angry lines and next to it was written *God, this is SUCH CRAP.*

Ned, she thought, her heart going out to him. She could see it so clearly. She remembered the photographs from the albums and she peopled her imagination with the younger versions of Ned, Erin and Jeremy. Ned was thin, and gawky, his face looking too long, his hair shaggy; he wore jeans and tee-shirts proclaiming the name of bands he liked, with a drab old coat over the top. Tom was more James Deanish, his thick fair hair falling in his eyes or swept away in a quiff, wearing a dark duffle and black jeans. Beside them, Jeremy looked like a precocious adolescent imitating his elders, a beatnik philosophical type in ancient pinstripe suits over black polo necks, a cigarette always in his teeth. The suits made him look slender, and his limbs overlong, like one of the Beatles in their early photographs. Luke, already rounder than his friends, was a typical public schoolboy in his checked shirts, jumpers and chinos. And then there was Erin. It almost hurt to summon up her image from those photographs: lithe, elegant, always looking perfect, no matter how the camera caught her, the dark curls spilling over her shoulders and the navy blue eyes sparkling in that luminous face.

I'm going to tell her, vowed Ned in one tortured entry. *I'm going to ring her up and ask*

253

*her to meet me. Then I'm going to tell her that
I'm sorry to stick my ugly feelings into her
world, that I don't particularly want to betray
my friend but that I have to tell her how this
fucking passion for her is tearing me up. I
already have no idea how I'm going to exist in
the holidays when we have to be apart for the
entire summer. Home seems like death.*

At the same moment as she felt light-headed
with fear, she wanted to reach out to Ned and
hug him, tell him she knew how he felt and how
dreadful and amazing love was.

As she read on, she could see that he hadn't
told Erin how he felt; that at every moment
when he had planned to, something went wrong,
or Erin needed to weep on his shoulder about
her relationship with Jeremy, and he let her do it
and gave her everything she needed while he
creased up inside with longing for her. It was his
second year of university and his love for Erin
had been growing steadily since he had first met
her, and it was becoming more and more
agonising for him. The passages in which he
spoke of his physical longing for her made Ruth
occasionally slam the notebook shut, appalled at
herself for reading what was so obviously not for
her eyes, or anyone's. When he described how he
yearned to kiss her hair, to stroke her face, to
undress her and make love to her, it had, to
Ruth, a kind of nobility, even though he berated
himself in the next line for feeling this way about
his friend's girlfriend. Reading it made her feel
sly, weak and gutterish. But she couldn't stop.

It was obvious that he dreaded going home to

York. He was considering anything at all that might take him away from his parents' house, when Luke came up with a plan. They would stay on after term ended in the house he owned, find jobs, earn money and then go travelling round Europe, the five of them together.

It had been for Ned a wonderful solution but still an agonising one. Now he would see Erin every day for weeks, but more than ever he would be aware of her relationship with Jeremy and that she was unobtainable, someone else's precious possession. As they travelled, cramming themselves into one small car and taking turns to drive across the continent, they would stop at campsites, and Ned would experience the nightly agony of seeing Jeremy and Erin crawl into their two-man tent together, hear them giggle and laugh, see the torch go out and imagine what they were doing next, although he never heard a thing.

I'd do anything for her, he vowed. I'd devote myself to making her happy. I would be completely and utterly hers. Can't she see it? Sometimes I think everyone must know. When Jeremy ignores her, or puts her down in front of the rest of us, it's all I can do not to leap in and defend her, challenge him, say, 'What the fuck are you doing, don't you know what you've got? I'd die for what you have.'

And, all along the way, he felt Jeremy's superiority keenly. As they visited capital cities, galleries and museums, it was Jeremy who suggested where they should go and what they should see, who told them about the lives of the artists, the kings and queens who had built the palaces they saw, the wars that had been fought, and the saints who had died or founded churches or performed miracles before the masses.

If Jeremy or Luke give me one more fucking lecture on art, I'll punch them, wrote Ned. But he loved it too: Ruth could sense the way he was sucking up information, longing to educate himself to be more like his friends. And if he was racked with the pain of his unrequited love, there were also many good times, and much laughter, as they made their way from to town. They seemed to fall into two camps: Jeremy and Luke, leading the way, dictating the itinerary, talking loudly about what they knew; and Ned and Tom, smoking and drinking together, looking for bars rather than galleries, a melancholy pair making black jokes and sitting up late outside the tent when the others were asleep. Between the two, Erin moved easily, welcome in both. Sometimes she would creep out of the tent she shared with Jeremy and sit with the other two, cadging cigarettes, and laughing at their dark humour. And then, in Rome, Ned wrote a long entry.

Strange day today. We went to the Forum. Erin said it would be closed. I said 'how do they close the bloody Forum, put a giant blanket over it?' We went in and walked about. It was incredible; kind of gives you a chill to imagine what went on there and makes all those stories so real. Jeremy told us about various great moments that had happened there, and he was so vivid and interesting that quite a crowd gathered about him. Lots of tourists wanting to find out what the hell they were looking at. When we'd done the Forum we went to the Coliseum, fighting our way through Italians dressed as gladiators and Caesars, with shabby red cloaks and fake gold laurels, wanting to charge us to have their picture taken. The Coliseum is creepy; I stood on one of the upper tiers and imagined looking down into one of the bloodbaths that happened there. The floor is gone so you can see the network of passages that ran underground, where they would herd the animals and prisoners before they came up above ground to fight to the death. I could almost hear the screams and cheers of the crowd, and imagine the wealthy citizens of Rome getting their kicks out of suffering and slaughter.

We split up and wandered about. I found Jeremy on one of the lower tiers and he asked me if I'd seen Erin. He said they'd had an argument, though not what about, and that she was upset. He looked pissed off. So we went off to look for her but there was no sign, until I saw her and Tom on one of the upper levels, leaning against the wooden balustrade, their heads close, talking intently to each other. We called up but they didn't hear. Then they turned and went back down into the darkness of the stairs.

We found Luke but couldn't find Erin or Tom again. We waited outside near the arch of Constantine, where we said we would meet if we got split up, but they didn't come.

Eventually we went back into town, and found a bar where we had some lunch. Then we went to the *Campo dei Fiori* and Jeremy insisted that we start ordering *vino tinto* and before long he was quite pissed and very bleak. Luke and I tried to keep him off the wine as much as we could. I wanted to find out more but he wasn't giving anything away.

Went back to the campsite in the evening. Tom and Erin got back very late. They said they'd lost us at the Coliseum, and waited somewhere else for us, and then decided not to waste the day and had gone to the Borghese villas. Jeremy was furious. Not an enjoyable evening at all.

That must have been it, Ruth thought. The beginning of Tom and Erin.

Spoke to Erin today, wrote Ned in his next entry. *Asked her what happened yesterday. She was very evasive. But she said Tom had told her that he would always be there to help her. I don't know what to make of this at all.*

In the course of their holiday it was decided that Ned and Tom would share a flat together the following year. There was no mention of Erin living with them, or of what the others would do, but Ned was evidently pleased with the arrangement.

Tom is my closest friend, he wrote. *It will be cool to live together.*

But did he know? wondered Ruth. Did Ned tell Tom about his secret passion? Did Tom admit that he was wooing Erin and that she was nearly his? Weren't these two supposed to be best friends?

The notebook ended before the holiday did,

though they were close to the last leg of their journey. Ruth closed the paper cover. She felt as though she'd been hauled back through time, and taken on a speeded-up tour of someone's life. But this wasn't all — where was the rest? There must be more notebooks, more explanations, more descriptions. Now she'd had this taster, she was hungry for more, and curious enough for her conscience not to trouble her any further. Now she wanted and needed to know, and here was the treasure trove right in front of her.

She spent hours going through the boxes, pulling out letters, notebooks, postcards and photos, piecing together Ned's life and his relationship with Erin. She found letters from her to him, written in a smooth, plain hand. They made Ruth's stomach churn again. Erin wrote to him as Bear and her letters were intimate, chatty and inventive, occasionally cut through with anxieties about life, work and university.

Dear darling gorgeous Bear, she wrote, *do you miss me as much as I miss you?*

Or:

I'm sitting here, thinking about you, wishing you were here too. I'm lonely today and I need you to make me laugh and forget about all the bad, grim things that are happening in the world.

But what was she thinking of? thought Ruth. She was outraged on Ned's behalf. These are like love letters! If you didn't know, you would think that they were a couple. How can she write to

259

him like this? She must know how it reads! Perhaps she thinks that because she's with Jeremy, she can write like a lover and not be misinterpreted. But poor Ned . . . She imagined him opening these letters, reading them, hoping, feeling that she *must* feel something for him.

To my darling dearest Bear. Are you thinking about me today? Here's what I'm doing. I'm sitting with my books in front of me, watching the clock tick down to when this bloody essay is due, and I'm writing to you instead of doing it. That's extremely naughty, isn't it? But I've got Bear on my mind and can't help it. Tell me what you're doing . . .

It was the third year of university. Ned and Tom were living together along with another student; Erin was living in a house with some girlfriends, Jeremy and Luke were in their own digs.

Ruth found diary entries scattered through notebooks. It seemed that Ned and Erin were growing closer. *She wrote to me today. A letter comes almost every day. But when we see each other with the others, we don't even speak about it. It is like there is something incredibly secret, a bond, growing up between us. I don't understand it. What does it mean? It must mean that she feels the same way, doesn't she?*

There were so many letters, closely written across two sheets, ending with streams of crosses and *All my love, Curly*; or anonymous postcards — one had a poem on it in Erin's hand:

Oh Bear
Are you there?

Do I dare
To care?
Shall we share
This spare
Pear?

Ruth didn't understand. Did Erin know how Ned felt? She must have known: the careless intimacy in the letters and cards assumed it. Or that was how it appeared to Ruth.

Poor Ned, she thought. As she read, it felt as though her own love story with Ned had ceased to exist and she was transported back into the past to live his experience with him. She didn't know if she wanted him to win his girl or not. The girl was a slippery character, she thought. From the letters it seemed that the girl was keen for her Bear to stay faithful to her, even if she had no intention of returning the compliment.

She found notes from Jeremy, almost illegible and when she could read them, incomprehensible with their in-jokes and obscure references. There were only a few letters from Tom, perhaps because he and Ned lived together and there was no need for correspondence. One was sent during a holiday.

Ahoy, it read. I discovered the remains of a pornographic magazine today, half burnt in the ashes of the bonfire at the bottom of our garden. It must have belonged to my esteemed father. Pulled it out and spent a good hour looking at the naked Paulines and Sheenas, with their burnt bushes and charred tits. Well, well. Who would have thought the old man had so much blood in him?

261

The letter went on, dark, elliptical and strangely impersonal. It could have been written to anyone.

That's how I find Tom now, she thought. Mysterious. He hardly ever addresses a word to me. Sometimes I wonder if he realises I'm there, or if he's auditioning me for a walk-on part in his life and one day I'll be allowed to pass the audition and be noticed.

It made sense that Tom's writing should be as obscure as he was himself. She found only one reference to Tom in Erin's writing.

Have you heard from that wicked piper's son? asked one letter. *I made him muffins for his birthday and left them for him at his lecture but he never said anything and I don't know if he got them. You wouldn't do that, would you, Bear?*

It was, she realised, almost too dark to read in the spare room. The afternoon was darkening. She had been sitting there for hours, surrounded by mounds of paper. What should she do now? She was exhausted from the emotional experience and, she realised, hungry and thirsty. Looking about, she realised that she was back in the here and now; Ned's and Erin's voices, which had come so clearly across the decade or more since they had spoken, were silenced. But her present was irrevocably changed by this knowledge of the past: Ned was no longer her Ned, but another Ned. This Ned had nursed a passion for years for his friend's girlfriend, a woman who'd belonged first to Jeremy and then to Tom — she had found no diary entry dealing with that event, which must have shaken Ned's

262

world — and had never been able to fulfil it. What had happened to his love? Had it just gone away?

Or perhaps — she felt fear crawling over her skin and a hollow, sick feeling inside — it had never gone away. Perhaps he'd damped it down out of necessity, but if Erin ever so much as gave him a hint that he could now be successful with her, it would flame up again as powerful as it had ever been.

'Oh, Ned,' she whispered. 'Is that why you never told me?' She pressed her hands to her face and rocked slightly, trying to take in what it meant.

13

She woke on Sunday morning feeling groggy, her eyes gritty. Then she remembered that she'd been unable to sleep until the early hours as she thought over and over about what she had learned.

With each hour that had passed she had grown more frightened. Going back over everything that had happened between her and Ned, she saw it now in a different light. Now he was not her Ned, but the Ned who truly belonged to Erin.

Everything from the time they'd met, to the wedding and beyond . . . she remembered all of it. He'd asked Erin to read — it was the passage about love. He must have wanted her to do that in particular, it must have had meaning to him. Perhaps it was a message to her . . . No, she was being stupid. It couldn't be true. She believed in Ned, she was sure he meant everything he had said to her, that he wanted to marry her and loved her.

But, but, but she would reply to herself. He loves you because he can't have Erin. If he could have her, would he still love you? Would he?

Every piece of evidence seemed to show her that he would not.

Be careful, she warned herself. You're talking yourself into this.

But still she couldn't help it.

When she had got up and had breakfast, she went upstairs, taking each step slowly as though approaching something of great significance. Opening the door of the spare room, she saw that it was as she had left it yesterday, with Ned's past scattered all over the floor. She wanted to go back to it. It felt as though she had been away on a long journey, to somewhere quite different with new but familiar people, and then, like the children jumping back out of the wardrobe from Narnia, discovered that she'd not been away any time at all. The voices from the summers and the university terms years before were still calling to her, wanting to tell their story in that elliptical way through their letters and cards. It was odd to think that if they had been a few years younger, none of this would exist. There might be postcards and birthday cards, but all this everyday chat would be over email, and lost on abandoned hard drives or sitting somewhere in the ether, unaccessed.

She went in and stood for a moment, looking at the mess at her feet. And in the wardrobe, there were more boxes. What secrets did they hide? Did she have time to go through them all before Ned got back? He had said their course was over at four and then he would have to drive all the way back from the middle of nowhere . . .

She was disgusted at herself. 'What am I doing?' she demanded out loud. 'This is terrible!'

In a sudden frenzy, she crouched down and began gathering up all the books and papers, throwing them back into the box. I'm not going to read any more! she told herself. It will make me mad if I'm not careful. I can't go there.

She wrestled the box back into the wardrobe and slammed the door on it. The spare room was now almost as she had found it yesterday.

'What a waste of time!' she shouted, furious. 'What a waste of bloody time.'

★   ★   ★

The house was full of Sunday quietness. She went about silently, finishing the jobs she had started yesterday, making lists of things to do in the week ahead, planning the shopping. Inside her head, her imagination was alive, playing out scenes, dressing up characters and putting them into little dramas, some she had read about and some she invented as she went along. It was impossible to stop herself, even though she was maddening herself by it. Even when she tried to focus on something else, suddenly she would be seeing a party. Erin was dancing with Tom. Ned was on the sidelines watching jealously. Then he and Erin were in the garden of the house, or in a spare room, and he would grab her and say 'I love you' and she would reply, 'Oh my Bear, I love you too,' and he would kiss her . . . NO. Stop, she ordered herself.

This was like Pandora's box. The things released could not be put back. Knowledge, once gained, could not be unlearned. She had lost her innocence and the Ruth of yesterday morning felt like another, happier, better person, a more honourable person, who did not sneakily read diaries and letters not meant for her.

266

When Ned came home, what would she do, she wondered. Confront him? But to tell him what she knew would mean admitting that she had invaded his past, and read his most private thoughts in a way that was inexcusable. She'd make herself completely unlovable at the same moment as demanding that he prove his love for her, or at least defend it.

She would act normally, she decided. She'd do her best to forget and put it all to the back of her mind and, somehow, make it all go away. Ned wouldn't guess. She wouldn't allow him to. Things were different now — it was ridiculous to act as though nothing had changed. Ned had married her, he loved her, she knew that. And Erin was expecting a baby with Tom. Life had moved on. She had to push away the knowledge of all the fiery love that had burned so hard all that time ago, and forget it.

*   *   *

'Ruth?'

'Up here.' She heard him bounding up the stairs, and turned over in bed to face the door.

'Are you asleep?'

'No. Just reading.'

'Hi, darling. How are you? I missed you.' Ned came over and sat on the bed, putting an arm round her. He pulled her towards him and kissed her. 'Mmm. That's what I needed.'

'Hi, sweetheart. I've missed you too.'

'Did you get my texts?'

'Oh yes.' There'd been two on Saturday night

267

and a couple more as he'd made his way home.

'I couldn't really phone. It was non-stop.'

'Did you enjoy yourself?'

'You know, I did, actually. I really didn't expect to, but it was quite good fun, running about on all our team-building exercises and staying up late playing games.'

'And did it work?'

'Boy, did it. You will not see more of a team player than me. I can now approach everything in a sensitive, inclusive way, concentrating on getting the job done at the same time as making sure everyone is able to play to their strengths and feel appreciated. I'm now officially ideal middle management material, with a certificate in paint-balling to prove it.'

'Sounds like you were a very good student.'

'A plus.' He grinned and kissed her again. 'What did you do?'

She stared back at him as though trying to imprint everything about him at this moment on her mind: those green and hazel eyes she knew so well, the sweet smile, the strong arms and hands that she loved to feel about her. She was seized by a compulsion to say, 'Ned, I know, I know all about it, I know everything!' but she damped it down and instead thought, I've been so stupid. I've ruined everything.

Despite his dear familiarity, Ned seemed like someone subtly different, changed in some fundamental way; and yet, even though she felt her knowledge and fear between them like an invisible wall, her love for him welled up afresh. It was as though, at the same time as seeing him as a stranger, she also knew him much better and more intimately than she had before, now that she had read his thoughts and travelled with him through the agony of his love. She felt surprised that he couldn't read it in her face, but he gazed back at her, smiling, unaware of what she was thinking.

She said slowly, 'I didn't do much. Some cleaning. I had a quiet time.'

A quiet time filled with noise and fury and stories and voices.

'Did anyone come round?' he asked, taking a strand of her hair and twirling it round his finger.

'No. I was on my own.'

'Did you miss me?'

I spent the entire time with you, she wanted to say. Impulsively she threw her arms around him and hugged him tight. 'Of course I missed you,' she mumbled into his shoulder. 'I love you.'

He laughed, a comforting warm buzz against her ear. 'I love you too. We're not very good at being apart, are we?'

'No.' She wished she could push all her sorrow out of her body, and cleanse herself of the jealousy she could feel growing inside.

'Then let's not be again.' He nuzzled her hair. 'It's all right. I'm back.'

★ ★ ★

'There's a call for you,' said Rhonda, her voice tinny down the telephone. 'Someone called Jeremy Forbes. Do you want to take it?'

Ruth went very still. 'Yes,' she said. It felt as

269

though she'd waited a long time to answer but it must have been only a moment. 'Put him through.'

She heard the click of Rhonda patching the call through, and then Jeremy's breathing coming down the line. He didn't realise he was connected. There was still time to press her finger down on the plastic lever and sever the call. She heard him fidget slightly and cough. 'Hello, Jeremy?'

'Ah, you're there. What are you doing today?'

'Work. Nursing the sick.'

'Even nurses get lunchtimes, though.'

'I suppose we do.'

'Well, what are you doing? What time are you off?'

'Surgery closes at twelve thirty. I usually try and get some paperwork done.'

'Excellent. Meet me outside the Ashmolean at quarter to one.'

The Ashmolean Museum was virtually next door. She could, she supposed, get her work done before she went out. 'All right.'

'Good. I'll see you then.'

★   ★   ★

'Did you know that this is the oldest public museum in Britain?'

'I didn't know that.' She looked up at the grand neoclassical façade of white and caramel stone, ornamented with stone medallions. 'It doesn't look that old.'

'This isn't the original building,' Jeremy

explained as they walked across the courtyard to the magnificent main doors. 'This is very much in the style of the National Gallery and the British Museum, and that's because it dates from that golden age of philanthropy in the nineteenth century, when these enormous institutions were set up for the benefit of the public. They were intended to help the masses educate themselves, so that they could ennoble their souls by looking at art and the relics of mankind's glorious past. In fact, this collection started off as a little heap of curios, animal skins and man-made bits and pieces, amassed by Jacobean explorers. A family called the Tradescants charged people to see it at their house in Lambeth. They bequeathed it to Elias Ashmole, the collection moved here to Oxford and grew and was displayed to the public free of charge — which was pretty radical for 1683. It's been many things in its time but everything has now been neatly organised, with the natural history and ethnic artefacts shipped out to the Natural History and the Pitt Rivers museums, and Anglo-Saxon jiggery pokery, and coins and pottery brought in, so that you have the delightful Museum of Art and Archaeology.' As they walked under the portico, Jeremy added, 'When I take power as mighty Emperor, which I expect will be any day now, I intend this to be my headquarters. I'll keep the paintings and porcelain, some silver and the statues, but I'll decree some new home for everything else. I'm not that keen on coins.'

Ruth laughed. 'Perhaps they could move it all

to Buckingham Palace, if it's no longer needed.'

'Even the coins are too good for that monstrosity. No, I'll keep Buck House for tourists to walk around — after I've had my pick of the pictures.'

'Don't you want to move to London when you're Emperor? It's traditionally the heart of power, after all.'

'I would like to stay in the heart of learning,' said Jeremy solemnly. 'It's going to be a pretty different country after I've been in charge for a few months, I can tell you that.'

'For the better, I hope.'

'But of course. There's no better government than benign dictatorship, and I intend to be the benignist of all, whether people like it or not.'

'But power corrupts,' said Ruth. 'Won't you be corrupted by your absolute power?'

'I'm going to make a plan to stop that happening but I'm not sure what it is. It might be, like the Caesars, to have someone whose job it is to remind me that I'm mortal and fallible. Now.' He stopped in the main hall. Galleries opened up before them, and a graceful staircase curved away, classical sculptures set in the alcoves along it. 'What would you like to see? What floats your boat? Art? Porcelain? Statues? Medieval knick-knacks?'

'I don't know,' said Ruth. She could imagine now how Ned felt on the tour of Europe. It felt as though she were signing up for a lecture, and she didn't want to appear too ignorant. 'Art?'

'Art. Lovely. I know — we'll go and look at the Dutch still lifes. Then we can do the Pre-Raphs, which I know you'll like.'

'I have seen paintings before, you know,' said Ruth drily. 'I've even heard of the Pre-Raphaelites. I'm not a total ignoramus.'

'I'm sure you're not. Come on.'

The Dutch still-life paintings were in the gallery at the very top of the museum, and arched glass roofs let in the natural light above sea-green walls.

'I love these,' confided Jeremy. 'The detail is extraordinary. It was the beginning of something very special — artists began to find inspiration in the ordinary things of life. A glass, an apple on a plate, a pewter mug on a sideboard. They began to see that there was as much, or more, to learn in the domestic scene as any grand vista of a mythological story, or the flights of angels and invocations of heaven in their religious allegories. They began to examine life as it is, not as we pretend it is in our stories of gods and saints.'

They walked among the paintings: vast ornate bouquets of flowers rendered in rich colours and intense detail; the detritus of meals and card games on mahogany tables; strange twisted arrangements of dead game birds and fruit. Jeremy pointed out paintings he liked, and whispered to her details of artists as they passed their work. He stopped in front of one entitled 'Still Life with Strawberries and Cherries'. 'There, look at this. It's perfect, isn't it?'

Against an almost black background, a porcelain dish containing pink and red strawber-ries sat wonkily on a table top. Dark red cherries were scattered about, a stem of them beside the dish, and a silver spoon lay bowl down among the strawberries, its handle on the table. Behind, an ornate glass was half-full of yellow wine.

'It looks simple enough, doesn't it? Some fruit and a glass of wine. But look at the extraordinary detail, and the felicity of the arrangement — the way the dish is tipped slightly to one side, and the cherry stem thrusts out into the black at the side of the picture. And look at the contrast of textures. How does he make the strawberry so obviously a strawberry — organic, palpable, water-rich red skin — and the china dish so obviously cold, hard and impervious to touch, when he uses the same medium to recreate both? And look at the glass. Against that solid black background, how do you portray something transparent? See how he does it — by using light. By working almost in negative. You can't see the glass at all. If you look at it, the wine is almost floating unsupported in mid-air. It is only the reflection of light against the rim and side and the stem that create the glass at all. See how he's created the whole illusion of a solid object sitting there with only three thin lines of white and a downward smear. It is really . . . not there. Can you see?'

She stared at the painting as he talked, and as she gazed at it, every brush stroke deepened and became so vivid that she seemed to see almost inside the painting; she began to comprehend what made it what it was, and to see the different style of stroke, and thickness of paint, and slim lines of silvery white put just so to give meaning, texture and depth to what were, in the end, only coloured daubs on a piece of canvas. She felt as though she could touch the leaf on the cherry stem and feel its papery brittleness, or dip a fingertip into the dish of strawberries and take it away moistened with their juice.

'That will do,' Jeremy said abruptly. 'You've seen enough. Let's go.' He began to stride out of the gallery and she turned, surprised, and went after him.

'What do you mean? It feels like we've only just started,' she said, catching up with him.

'There's a way to look at art,' he explained as they went downstairs, Ruth going at double-time to keep up with his long legs. 'Most people do it wrong. They go to a gallery and they stare for a long time at the first five or ten pictures they see. Then they start to get tired, and spend a little shorter in front of each one. They start looking at the name of the artist, and if they don't recognise it, they move on. They carry on like this until they're virtually running through the galleries in order to get to the gift shop — but they are still under the apprehension they've just 'done' the gallery. What you want to do is — do you want coffee, by the way? Have you had lunch? Let's go to the café — what you want to do is see only one or two paintings, but *really* see them. So that they live in your memory, and you'll always remember what it was like to look at them. If you ever see a postcard or a reproduction of that painting now it will startle you, as though you've seen something incredibly familiar. You've learned it and felt it and believe in it. I don't want you to ruin that by getting vague in front of other pictures. Ah — here we are. Now, you must come back every other day and look at another painting the way you looked at that one. Think of all this richness sitting here, waiting for you, day after day, and you never come to it!'

Ruth was ashamed. He was right. Perhaps she should try and enrich herself a little more. They got themselves coffees and sandwiches and took them to a table under a vaulted arch.

'How's married life, missy?' Jeremy asked as he unwrapped his prawn sandwich. 'Are you enjoying it?'

The art lecture is over, Ruth thought. She had been apprehensive before she'd arrived. Meeting Jeremy so soon after reading Ned's diary felt odd, like meeting an actor just after seeing him in a film. He had no idea of how she perceived him now, or that she was longing to ask him about his past and his relationship with Erin, and if he'd ever known how Ned had felt about her. As soon as she'd seen Jeremy, though, all those thoughts had gone out of her head. He had a way of absorbing all your attention and emptying your mind of anything but what he was saying. Now, in front of their café lunch, he had focused back on Ruth and with that came everything that had been filling her thoughts for the last few days.

'Married life is wonderful. I can highly recommend it.'

'Good. That's what old Forbes likes to hear. I've been a little worried about you at times. You seem to languish a little.'

'Do I?'

'On the outskirts, you know. I know we can be a bit fearsome when we're all together. It's hard for others to get a word in and if they're a little bit mousy, like you are — '

'I'm not mousy!'

'Glad to hear it. But that's just the thing, isn't it? You seemed all quiet and shy and retiring to me, because you don't really get a chance to shine when we're there.'

'Perhaps that's true.'

'That's why I've been meaning to get you on your own for a bit, so we can get to know each other away from the bustle. I've hardly had a chance. And I wanted to make sure you were all right, you know — coping with all of this.'

'I'm not the only outsider. There's Abigail. She wasn't one of your gang, was she? But she seems to manage.'

'Abigail's all right. Tough as old boots. I've never had a moment's worry over her. And she's got Luke right where she wants him. It's a bit different with Ned.' He looked up, his brown eyes serious. 'He's always had an intense relationship with the rest of us. He seems to need us a bit more than we need him.'

'What do you mean?'

Jeremy shrugged. 'I'm sure it's different now you're here. But don't forget Ned and Tom have been best friends since school and Ned's always looked up to him.'

'Has he?'

'He adores him — can't you tell?'

'He hasn't talked much about him at all. We

see him quite often, I suppose.'

'Perhaps his magic is wearing thin. The longer I knew them both, the more alike they became, or at least the more like Tom Ned became. It was quite sweet, really, the way Ned copied him — if there was something Tom wore, it wasn't long before Ned had one just like it, or at least similar. They listened to the same music and read the same books, they shared a kind of linguistic code between them which came from obsessively quoting their favourite films and comedy. It was almost like a love affair.' Jeremy flicked another glance at her. 'Of course, it was a love affair that could never come to anything. It was destined to fail. Ned could never have Tom in the way he wanted. I'm not saying Ned was gay — I'm sure you know better than anybody that he isn't — just that he had a kind of hero worship for Tom that was either going to be cruelly shattered in some way, or would have to fade and die in order for Ned to live his own life.'

'Which one do you think it was?' Ruth asked. She was listening intently, sure that Jeremy was trying to tell her something more than simply what he was saying.

'Actually, perhaps neither of those things has happened. Perhaps it lives on yet, though not with the same intensity. Ned had the kind of regard for Tom that meant he wanted to *be* him, if he could. He did his best to imitate him in every way. The other option is, of course, that he found someone else to worship.' Jeremy flicked a look at her. '*You*, for instance.'

'Me,' said Ruth cautiously, making the word neither a statement nor a question. Jeremy seemed to imply that she, Ned's wife, was only a candidate for the position, that Ned might have a shrine to someone else. What is he trying to tell me? she wondered. She had to beware of twisting everything she heard to make it fit her own theory. 'I don't know that worship is entirely healthy. It's not what I'd want from Ned.'

'Wise words. After all, all idols have feet of clay, don't they? I'm terribly fond of Ned — I hope I'm not giving the impression that I'm not.'

'No, of course not,' said Ruth, thinking, I'll decide about that later when I've heard what you've got to say. I don't know if you're really a friend to Ned or not — we'll see.

'Perhaps it's his background, his childhood, that's made him so insecure. I blame that vile old witch who brought him into this world.'

'His mother adores him.'

'She adores him the way vampires adore their victims. Which is all very well for the vampire. I don't think Ned emerged from his childhood feeling he was worth particularly much. I can imagine Mrs Haskell stamping down whatever she saw of vitality and independence in her little boy, making sure he was docile, obedient and exactly what she wanted. It didn't give Ned much faith in himself. Those are the people who are most likely to need heroes and passions to give their lives meaning. They need to be told how to fill out the corners of themselves. Tom is entirely different. He's a cherished younger son with a parcel of older brothers who kicked him around a bit and made him stand up for himself. He's from a bohemian, liberal, unusual family, and even though he's probably not the most brilliant of them, he still dazzles someone like Ned. And he's very powerful, a powerful personality with the kind of charisma you don't find all that often.'

Dazzle, thought Ruth. That's what Ned said about Erin — that he was dazzled. She wanted to jump up and find her car and drive to Ned's office and fold him in her arms and tell him that she didn't want some pale imitation of Tom, that he was brilliant and dazzling enough for her.

She had an urge to stand up for Ned. Feeling as though she had pinned on his colours and was going into the lists on his behalf, she said, 'It seems to me that if anyone has an intense relationship in your little group, it's you and Tom. After all, he stole Erin from you, didn't he?'

Jeremy said nothing for a while. He carefully ate his sandwich and then wiped his fingers on the paper napkin, and sat back. Finally he said, 'Of course you've heard all about that. It would be silly of me to think you hadn't. Tom didn't *steal* Erin from me. No one could make Erin do a single thing that she didn't want to. But I will say that he won her from me, and he mounted a long and clever campaign. Erin values certain things in a man. She values independence of mind, originality of spirit and a kind of reserve, almost an unobtainablity. Tom spent many months, years, even, working on all the things he knew about her, and playing to exactly what he knew would appeal to her. Then, when his time came and the breach in the wall was there, he made use of everything he had prepared.'

Breach in the wall. The words echoed in her mind and then she recalled the Rupert Brooke poem Erin had quoted to her: *Love is a breach in the walls, a broken gate.* She remembered the line that had been lightly underlined: *They have known shame who love unloved* . . . Well, that made sense now, didn't it? 'You make it sound so heartless. It can't have been the way you make it sound. Tom must have loved her.'

'I'm sure he did, and I'm sure he does.' Jeremy shrugged again, as though all this was really beneath his notice now. 'You can see why of course — there aren't many men who can resist Erin. She has what all men want: beauty, and spirit.'

'And you don't hate him for having her?'

'We are gentlemen. We have never talked about it and I doubt we ever will. I simply accept that in this particular instance, he was the better strategist. He won the game and walked off with the spoils.'

'That's a very peculiar way to talk about your ex-lover. It's as though your friendship mattered more than your relationship. It's rather cold.'

'I didn't get upset about it, because I knew that there was no alternative. It wasn't as though I could keep her. I'd already had my chance with Erin, I was already conquered territory. She had no fire in her belly for me any more. She is a colonialist, an imperialist. She wishes to go out and win more possessions, convert them and find more.'

'A moment ago, she was the possession. Now she's a crusading army.'

'That's the mystery of relationships. We are all both the possession and the owner at different times.'

Ruth sat back and stared at him. 'I don't understand why you're talking to me like this. What are you trying to tell me, Jeremy? You're the kind of person who has a reason for everything they do. You've been trying to get me on my own for weeks so you can plant seeds in my mind, haven't you? The only thing I don't understand is what you want to achieve. If you intend to turn me against Ned, or Tom, or Erin, it's not going to work.'

He laughed. 'You've quite opened up, haven't you? It's been difficult to get so much as a word out of you until now. I wish we could talk all afternoon but I'm sure you have to get back.' He thought for a moment and then added, 'The thing about the five of us, the thing I believe keeps this little club of ours together, is that we are utterly fascinated by ourselves. We're addicted to our own soap operas and by the changing balances of power: we like to see who is getting close to whom. All I want you to do is be on your guard, that's all. Either you'll be sucked into it, or closed out — unless you are very clever indeed. Now. I want a cigarette and it's forbidden in here, so let's go out and I'll walk you back to the surgery.'

* ★ ★

A steady flood of patients that afternoon kept Ruth occupied. She was glad; as soon as she was on her own, she couldn't stop herself thinking about what Jeremy had said to her, replaying phrases and analysing them, trying to draw out the meaning she was sure was there.

She drove home thinking about it, like a detective caught up in a difficult and complicated case, amassing evidence that would lead her to some kind of answer. But what was she looking for? Someone guilty of something? A clearer picture, she decided. More understanding of what had happened in the past, so that she would know Ned even better. But she was aware that the fluttering fearfulness that possessed her whenever she thought about it revealed that, underneath, she was expecting to find out something much more present and pertinent.

Ned had loved Erin, that was not in doubt. Ned, according to Jeremy, revered Tom and longed to emulate him. It made the fact that Erin had chosen Tom all the more poignant. It must have cut Ned to the core to find out about it. How on earth had he reacted? She had found nothing in his notes and letters that referred to it.

Poor Ned. He must have been through hell.

But even as she pitied him, she was wracked with jealousy that he'd felt such passion for Erin — and with fear that his passion wasn't dead, only sleeping.

It started to rain as she neared the cottage,

heavy dense drops so that roads were soon rippled with small rivers and the wipers were going at full pelt. She pulled into the driveway, and made a dash for the front door, her bag held over her head to protect it from the downpour.

As she approached, she saw a figure in the porch. Getting closer, she realised it was Erin.

'Thank you so much,' Erin said, following Ruth into the hall. 'I'm such an idiot, locking myself out. I don't know what I was thinking of — it's my pregnancy head, it's making me into a complete fool. I decided I'd go and get something from the village shop, picked up my purse and walked out. I didn't take my keys or my phone or my umbrella and Tom's not back for ages, so I thought I'd walk down here and see if you were in.'

'That's fine. Really. Have you been waiting long?'

'Only twenty minutes or so.'

'You shouldn't be out in this weather, especially in your condition.'

Erin was wearing a black belted cardigan over her swelling stomach. 'Don't worry, I'm not that delicate. It would take more than a bit of rain to worry me or the bud.'

'I'll get you a towel for your hair.' Ruth went upstairs to the linen cupboard. When she'd first seen Erin, she felt horror grip her, as though Stalin or Dracula had appeared on the doorstep, but now, confronted with the reality of the other woman, her fears seemed ludicrous. The Erin of years gone by vanished and the present one — pregnant, friendly, unselfconscious — took

284

her place. It was impossible to feel about this Erin what she did about the one who wrote semi love letters, signed Curly with half a page of kisses underneath. Ruth felt calmer, almost normal for the first time in days, as though actually having Erin here released her from an evil enchantment. Coming back down, she said, 'You must have walked along the road to get here, in the pouring rain. It's dark. You could have been knocked down by a car.'

'I know I said I had a pregnancy head but I'm not a complete idiot,' said Erin affably, taking the towel. 'I was fine. I could do with a cup of tea, though, and a biscuit if you've got one. I can't stop eating sweet things.'

'How is everything?' Ruth said, struck again by the oddness of seeing people she now felt she knew more intimately than they realised. 'How is the baby?'

'It's absolutely great,' said Erin with satisfaction. They went into the kitchen and Erin sat down while Ruth made tea. 'I went for the twenty-week scan just the other day. It was incredible to see it, I can't tell you — the amazing thing is that you expect to see a still picture, like all the scan photos you get shown. You know, little white jelly bean with tiny arms and legs. But at this stage you can almost see features, and the incredible thing is that it's moving, wiggling about, turning somersaults.' Erin giggled. 'It put its thumb in its mouth while we watched.'

'How sweet,' Ruth said. 'And everything was all right?'

'They said it was all as it should be.'

'I'm very glad.' Ruth meant it. 'You're looking marvellous.'

It was true: Erin was fulfilling all the requirements of the ideal mother-to-be, with colour in her face, a lustre to her hair and a general air of wellbeing. 'I *feel* marvellous. Perhaps it's the pregnancy yoga I'm doing. I'm lucky, though. I'm having a very easy time of it. No morning sickness, just some tiredness in the early days, and now full of beans and everything going like a breeze. It probably means I'm in for a very difficult birth — there has to be a catch somewhere, doesn't there?'

'It doesn't always follow.' Ruth passed her the mug of tea. 'There's not much you can do about it, anyway.'

'I'm starting ante-natal classes soon, so it will be birth plans and methods of pain relief and what to do when. Honestly, it's like going back to school to sit an A-level, with only four months to do all the coursework before you have to take the exam whether you like it or not.'

Ruth laughed. 'You're certainly in for it now. You can't send it back or change your mind.'

Erin stroked a hand over her stomach. 'I don't want to send it back, I want it to get here as soon as possible. I can't wait. You're on your way, though, aren't you, bud? When you're good and ready, you'll make your appearance.'

'It must be very exciting,' said Ruth, envious for a moment of the contentment she could see radiating out of Erin.

'I couldn't be more excited.'

'And is Tom?'

Erin looked away and shrugged. 'Sometimes he is, and sometimes he isn't. It's always hard to tell with Tom. He's a mysterious character.'

'Surely if anyone knows him, you do.'

'Yes. If anyone does.' Erin gave a little laugh and sipped her tea. 'You'll have to come shopping for baby things with me, Ruth. Tom doesn't seem very keen on that aspect of fatherhood.' She looked up at Ruth. 'When is Ned back?'

'I don't know. Soon, I suppose.'

'Oh.'

They were quiet for a moment. 'Did I tell you that I have a job?' Erin asked.

'No. What is it?'

'Nothing special but it's nice to have. I can't imagine what other kind of job I'm going to get right now. I've got a commercial for television. I have to go to Germany for filming. It's for a pregnancy aid — a supplement or something like that. I've got to waft about looking pregnant and happy and healthy.'

'That's good . . . isn't it?'

Erin laughed. 'Well, it's not exactly Hollywood but it'll do. It's going to be shown all over Europe, so there are benefits. Plenty of repeat fees.' She sipped her tea. 'And by the time I'm back, you might even have your new neighbours.'

'Sorry?'

'Your new neighbours. The Haskells.'

Ruth shook her head, puzzled. 'I don't know what you mean . . . '

Erin looked mortified. 'Oh God — hasn't Ned

287

told you? I just assumed he had. I spoke to him today and he told me then.'

'Told you what?' Ruth allowed her irritation to show in her voice.

'About his parents. That they're selling their house and buying one just down the road from here. I'm sorry, Ruth. I thought you knew.'

14

Our first row, she thought, miserably. A tiny part of her was standing outside herself and watching as she raged at Ned. This part of her observed what was happening, but couldn't seem to control what she did.

They faced each other across the sitting room, occasionally moving so that they circled slowly round in the course of their argument. Ned began apologetically but soon became exasperated and then angry. Even as she stormed and shouted, Ruth longed to tell him that she was not furious but miserable and afraid. But she couldn't do it, and they went on circling each other and going over and over Ruth's grievances.

'I only told her first because she happened to call right after my mother. It was natural to tell her, and I had no idea that she was going to tell you before I had a chance to!'

'Why didn't you call me to tell me? I was at work. You hardly ever call me during the day!'

'Because we're both busy! We email each other all the time. I didn't call you because this was the kind of thing I thought we should discuss face to face. I wanted to break it to you gently and I *also* didn't want your day ruined the way mine was.'

'But you shouldn't have told her before you told me! Do you know how that makes me feel? As though I'm not important.'

'That's just not true — '

'How often do you speak to Erin?'

'I don't know. Every few days, I suppose. She quite often calls me.'

'Why don't you tell me when she rings?'

Ned looked bemused. 'But . . . why? She's always done it. Look, she's sitting there at home with nothing to do half the time. She's an unemployed actor, drinking her coffee, reading her magazines and waiting for a phone call to summon her to an audition. When she feels like a chat, she calls me — or Tom, or Luke, or Jeremy. That's the way it's always been.'

'Her little band of admirers.' Ruth couldn't help the sneer creeping into her voice. 'Her faithful disciples, always ready to tell her how marvellous she is. Why haven't you said? I had no idea she called you all the time. Do you know how awful it feels, thinking you have secrets from me? It was the same with the wedding.'

'The wedding? What are you talking about?'

'You asked Erin to do a reading, and you never even told me you'd decided to ask her, or which reading. It might have been nice if we'd been able to ask her together! But instead, she tells me out of the blue that she's so happy to be doing a reading, and I'm sitting there like an idiot trying to guess what you've said to her, so it doesn't look as though you can't be bothered to tell me what you've planned for our *own* wedding.'

'I must have forgotten . . . you never said anything. We'd agreed that we'd ask her, hadn't we?'

'Do you know how it makes me feel?' Ruth

demanded, her voice high with rage. 'It feels like you're carrying on behind my back.'

'Ruth! How can you say that? I didn't tell you because I had no idea it mattered and to be honest, I don't even remember when I talk to Erin or I don't talk to Erin, because it happens all the time and it means what it's always meant — that we're friends.'

You're lying, you're lying, thought Ruth furiously. I know you weren't always friends. She dangled the chance to confess in front of him, suddenly hoping that he would take the bait, and tell her everything and set her churning fears to rest. 'Is that all you and she have ever been — friends? After all, there's not been a time when she hasn't been going out with one or other of your mates. Didn't you ever wish that you'd had a chance as well?'

Ned stared at her for a long moment. There was silence in the room, all the more profound for the shouting that had preceded it. Then he said slowly, 'No. I don't wish that.'

'Did you ever wish it?' Ruth persisted.

Ned sighed with aggravation. 'Ruth, I don't understand where all this has come from. You're blowing an innocent remark out all proportion.'

'Why won't you answer me?'

She could see Ned lose his temper and he spat out, 'For Christ's sake, I will not have you dictate to me like this! Erin is one of my oldest friends. I've known her a lot longer than I've known you. When I heard this news about my mother, and she called me, it was only natural that I should tell her. Why the hell shouldn't I? Does being married to you mean I've got some kind of censorship over what I'm allowed to tell my friends about my life? Fuck that! Erin knows my family, she knows how I feel about it, she understood how the news affected me. For God's sake, why are we arguing about how you found out? The real issue is that we're going to be living virtually next door to my parents and we have to work out a way to deal with it!'

'Why don't you ask Erin?' said Ruth in a cold voice, hating herself for it but unable to stop. She was quivering inside with hurt at what Ned had just said. He's confirmed it, she thought miserably. 'She obviously understands you a great deal better than I do. Perhaps you should have married *her*.'

Ned muttered something under his breath, and strode to the door, picking up his coat on the way out. 'I'll see you later,' he said, as he slammed the door behind him.

Ruth stood where she was, frozen in front of the fireplace, feeling tears building up behind her eyes. She had the uneasy sense that she had engineered Ned's departure. She sank into a chair, her hands shaking slightly. He hadn't denied it. She was his *wife*. Why did he have secrets from her? Why didn't he just say 'Yes, once I loved Erin, but I don't any more'? It would lay the ghost. It would destroy this awful thing that was coming between them and poisoning everything they had. But he didn't, thought Ruth miserably. He won't tell me, and there can only be one reason: he still loves her.

She felt a kind of inner quake that seemed to

release something, and hot tears were suddenly dripping down her face. The phone rang out, shrill and mechanical in the silent cottage. Ruth jumped, and looked at it. The face was illuminated and flashing. Ned, she thought, reaching out to it.

'Hello?'

'Hello Ruth, it's Mum.'

Mum? she thought, confused for a second before she identified the low whispery voice. 'Oh. Jackie. I mean, Mum. Hello.'

'Are you all right? Is this a bad time? I called to tell you my news, about our move.'

Ruth's misery sat cold and heavy in her chest. It exhausted her. At any other time, she'd have put on a bright and cheerful voice and pretended to be glad that the Haskells were leaving York to move near to her. But Jackie had offered her a way out and, although she would normally have protested that she was fine, she decided that, for once, she would use it. 'Actually, it *is* a bit of a bad time. Ned and I have just had an argument and I'm feeling rather low. Would you mind if I call you back later or tomorrow? I'd love to hear all about it then.'

There was a chilly silence down the line and then Jackie's harsh voice said, 'I see. Very sorry to have bothered you.' And the phone went down with a click.

'Oh shit!' said Ruth aloud, looking at the dead handset. 'Shit, shit, shit!'

★ ★ ★

293

Ned came back late, when Ruth was in bed. The light was off and she pretended to be asleep. He didn't try and wake her, but slipped quietly in next to her, his smooth long back curved towards her, and sighed. He went to sleep without kissing her for the first time since they were married.

★   ★   ★

'Only masochists come into Oxford to shop on a Saturday morning,' remarked Erin, as they walked into the mall from the multi-storey car park.

'When else is there?' asked Ruth, side-stepping to avoid a six-year-old girl maniacally skipping towards her. She was doing her best to seem as normal as possible. In fact, she'd been relieved when Erin had rung that morning and asked if she felt like going on a baby-fest trip into town. The evening after her horrible row with Ned, Erin had phoned and, after the initial hello, had asked to speak to Ned. He'd taken the walkabout phone into the spare room and chatted to her there, while Ruth hovered in the kitchen, glancing upwards to the ceiling, wondering what they were talking about but unable to bring herself to try and listen. Ned came down with the phone half an hour later, and appeared to take a kind of grim pleasure in not saying anything about his conversation.

It made her wretched, this atmosphere of distrust that had crept into their relationship. Erin's phone call that morning had been welcome — she'd pounced at the opportunity to restore something of the old normality: Ned going out to play rugby with his friends and the women joining forces to amuse themselves. A secret part of herself also wanted to be with Erin in an almost masochistic way, to observe her from Ned's point of view and admire her graceful beauty, the slim wrists and white hands, the mellifluous voice and easy charm that were so evidently captivating.

'When else?' echoed Erin, as they strolled under the harsh shopping-mall lights. She made pregnancy look like a fashion accessory, her bump sitting neatly above her skinny jeans, a wholesome-looking roundness under pink cashmere. From the back it was impossible to tell she was pregnant at all. 'Darling, I'm an actress. And with my work schedule, I can go shopping virtually any time I want. The strange thing is, it always ends up being rush hour or Saturday or when everything is closed. I just don't know how to manage my time. I've had so little training in punctuality. I *am* hopeless, aren't I?' She laughed lightly.

'I couldn't have come with you any other time. I'm afraid I've got very dull, regular hours.'

'I wish sometimes that I did something regular and worthwhile as well.' Erin sighed. 'Acting is such a silly job, isn't it?'

'You'll soon have more to do than you can handle,' said Ruth, nodding at Erin's bump.

'Do you think so?' asked Erin, in the placid way of a mother-to-be whose image of her baby was of a peaceful slumbering infant curled delightfully on her chest.

'Oh yes.' Ruth had seen enough wild-eyed new mothers in her surgery to know that the reality was quite different. 'Now, where shall we go first?'

When she had started looking for wedding things, a whole world of bridal paraphernalia opened itself up to her. It had always been there but she had simply never seen it. Now, she found, it was the same with baby and nursery equipment: how on earth had she missed great swathes of the shopping world devoted to infants and their multifarious needs? In the department stores, whole floors were crammed with cots, chairs, changing tables, buggies, prams, baths, rails, bedding, toys, bottles and endless clothes. Did one tiny baby really require so much? Erin consulted a long list that she carried about with her, muttering things like, 'Muslins. Apparently I need at least fifteen' and 'Hand held or electric breast pump, do you think?'. She stowed packets of tiny white vests and all-in-one suits into her basket, tiny sponges and miniature socks; the larger goods she ordered to be delivered closer to the birth.

Outside the department stores, they found boutiques devoted to expensive but beautiful baby clothes, and toy shops with vast ranges of goods designed to stimulate and educate a baby from the moment it arrived in the world.

'All this is giving me a feeling of mild anxiety,' confided Erin. 'I feel like I ought to get *everything* just to be on the safe side.'

'Don't forget you'll get lots of gifts when the

baby arrives,' said Ruth, holding up a tiny rainbow-striped cardigan. 'Isn't this cute? And there really isn't much a newborn needs beyond food and warmth and a safe place to sleep.'

'Of course I ought to ask you about all of this,' observed Erin, picking up a baby monitor. 'You're a nurse, after all.'

'There's a bit of difference between being a midwife or a maternity nurse, and what I do. I'm not trained for all that. I was on a maternity ward for a while as part of my training, and I did some theory at college, but it was years ago.'

'Oh well,' said Erin carelessly, putting the monitor back. 'Never mind. Shall we go and get some coffee? I need a break. And I urgently require cake.'

They went to a small, fragrant café that served vast pieces of passion cake alongside frothy mugs of cappuccino.

'That's just the thing,' said Erin, scooping up cream-cheese icing on the edge of her fork. 'You wouldn't believe how I've craved sugar lately. It must be my body telling me something.'

'To make the most of it, probably.' Ruth stirred the sprinkles of chocolate into the hot milk.

Erin laughed. 'Maybe. I can't deny I'm enjoying letting myself go a bit, but I'm going to be the size of a house at this rate. Imagine what kind of a diet I'm going to have to go on straight afterwards.'

'But then there's breastfeeding. You have to take in extra calories every day to make milk. It's not the time to be denying yourself anything.'

'Except perhaps my three daily KitKats.'

'When are you off to Germany?'

'Next week. I won't be away long, it's only a few days' filming. Tom is under orders to paint the nursery while I'm gone. I don't want the bud to be subjected to paint fumes so I've insisted he do it while we're away.' Erin looked at her hard. 'Are you all right, Ruth? You seem a bit down.'

It wouldn't be so bad if I didn't like her, thought Ruth, but Erin was never anything less than open and friendly. When she was with Erin, the whole thing seemed a bit absurd, like a fantasy she'd made up for herself. She's the last person I can talk to about it, Ruth thought miserably, even though she'd probably talk good sense. Unless I'm being a fool and can't see through her act.

'I'm fine.'

'How's Ned? Is he all right? I saw him last night, he dropped in on his way back from work.'

'Did he?' Ruth's spirits swooped downwards and she felt wretched. Ned hadn't said.

'Yes. And he seemed rather down as well. I don't want to be nosy, and tell me to shut up if you want to, but . . . is everything all right between you?'

Why did she want to know? What was her motive? Ruth's mind raced, trying to find possible answers. If Ned was still in love with Erin, it was not despite Erin pushing him away; she'd made summoning him to her side for the slightest reason an art form. Why did she do that? It wasn't as though she treated Luke or Jeremy the same way. It was only Ned she

298

crooned over, only Ned's hair she stroked, only Ned she called every day. This wasn't normal friendship, Ruth could see that now. Why on earth hadn't she seen it before? Ned loved Erin and she . . . what did she feel for him? It was in her power to set Ned free, so why didn't she? And what did that mean about her relationship with Tom, the man whose baby she was having? She looked at Erin for a moment, suddenly seeing the girl who'd teased Ned and toyed with him and led him on. Her liking for her began to diminish.

'Is it?' persisted Erin. 'Is it all right?'

'Yes,' answered Ruth slowly, looking straight into the wide blue eyes.

'Good. I know what it is, though, that's making you both miserable.'

'Do you?'

'I don't blame you. I'd feel the same in your position.'

'Would you?'

'I think it's outrageous behaviour. She called me the other night and told me all about it. Apparently she's had this scheme going for months.'

She means Jackie, thought Ruth. 'She called you?'

'Oh yes. She does every now and then.'

Is there any part of my marriage you're not involved in? Ruth asked silently. Anger was building inside her.

Erin continued, 'She tends to let things slip to me a bit. She told me that her house had been on the market since before the wedding and they found this new place just after Christmas.'

Ruth was shocked, diverted for a moment from her thoughts about Ned and Erin. 'They never said a word to us!'

'She said it was going to be a lovely surprise for you. But I think it's because they knew Ned wouldn't like it.'

'But . . . ' Ruth frowned helplessly. 'If they know he doesn't want them to live near him, why are they doing it?'

'My theory is that Jackie is pretending to herself that Ned would like it and that it's just you who might kick up a fuss. It's an excuse, of course. I'm sure she knows deep down that Ned would never want his parents living in the same village, but now she can make her move and it'll be harder for you to protest, because it will look like it's your influence, not Ned.'

'I still don't understand why . . . '

'She says it's to be close to her grandchildren.'

'What grandchildren? We've only been married a few months.'

'Jackie seems very aware of the fact that your father lives nearby. She doesn't want any baby brought up knowing your side of the family better than Ned's side.'

'This is madness! What can I do?' Ruth slammed her spoon on to the table with anger. 'I feel like she's going to control my life.'

'Controlling things is all she knows. She's always tried to control Ned, and he's always been fleeing from her as fast as he can. At university we all laughed about it, the way she wouldn't leave him alone: constant phone calls and visits. She even made friends with his landlady and kept tabs on him that way. And she treated the rest of us like we were *her* friends, not Ned's. She still calls all of us frequently, sends cards and gifts, acts hurt if we don't keep in touch for a while. She was a bit suspicious of me until she realised I wasn't going to try and go out with her precious son, then I could do no wrong. So don't think that you started all this off, because she's always been this way.' Erin leaned towards her. 'Do you want my advice? Jackie seems to have quite a strange attitude to you. Sometimes you are perfect, at other times she seems very suspicious of you and your motives and what you're doing to Ned. I think you need to play a very calm and careful game at the moment. The move is underway. It's unstoppable. She purposefully didn't let you and Ned know what was happening until it was too late to prevent it. So you have to watch out. She's very touchy and . . . unpredictable.'

'You know her better than I do,' said Ruth, with a touch of bitter irony in her voice.

'I've known her longer.'

The advantage, thought Ruth, that you always have.

★   ★   ★

The atmosphere at home when she got back was a little less frosty than it had been.

After their argument, neither of them quite knew what to do next, unused as they were to conflict. It hadn't been resolved, and so both

301

went on feeling wounded and owed an apology, but also very much wanted an end to it and for things to return to the cosy, loving warmth they'd grown accustomed to. They were in stalemate for days.

Ruth felt as though she were living two lives: in one, she was normal Ruth, happily married to a man she loved, with a difficult mother-in-law but the comfort of a circle of friends she liked and trusted. When she was making breakfast or arriving at work and going through her day, this was the Ruth she occupied. It was wonderfully calming to be this Ruth, and she felt the relief that came from being able to get on with her life. This Ruth was able to go out shopping for baby clothes with Erin and enjoy the simple normality of it.

The other Ruth came at bad times: in the night, when she woke suddenly in the dark convinced she'd heard something — a step on the stair, the click of the phone going down — and her thoughts began racing hectically. This Ruth was plagued by fear, and felt herself at the centre of some kind of conspiracy to punish her, as though she'd stepped into a gang of villains obsessed with bringing her down. When this Ruth rose to the surface — in the long dark car journey home from work, or sometimes as she lay in the bath — she imagined that Ned had only married her to humiliate her, and that he was creeping about behind her back, being faithless and sly. She mistrusted Erin and was learning to hate her.

She felt pulled between her two selves. Even

though her dark self came less frequently than the other, it wielded greater power and it played on her fear that she was destined to be betrayed, and abandoned to suffering.

And then she looked at Ned, and couldn't believe it. She'd even pulled out all the photographs from the wedding and relived the day in each detail. By the end, she'd been weeping, happily for a change, and convinced that she'd created everything in her own mind. Except that she knew the boxes were sitting upstairs in the wardrobes, with all their written proof and all the unanswered questions they'd stirred up in her mind.

The trip with Erin, though — at the same time as feeding her suspicions and raising new worries, it had reminded her that things were different now. Erin was carrying Tom's child and they had been together ten years or more. This day she and Ruth had shared was exactly the kind of thing two friends did: friends who didn't desire each other's husbands, or betray them behind their backs.

'Hello,' she said, coming in from the coldness of the darkening afternoon to the slightly sultry warmth of the sitting room.

Ned looked up from the sofa. He had showered after his morning's sport, and was fluffy haired and shiny cheeked, his battered old slippers on his feet. A football game was on the television: tiny coloured figures hurtled about on a green background, chasing a white speck.

'Hi there. How was your trip? Successful?' There was still an unfamiliar stiffness in the way

303

he spoke to her. It gave her a faint prickle of resentment.

'Yes, I think so. You can't imagine how much stuff a baby needs. It's like preparing for some kind of royal progress. Bed sheets — four, pure cotton. Night gowns — three, with scratch mitts. Blankets of organic cellular cotton, long-sleeved vests, short-sleeved vests, no-sleeved vests. I had no idea babies were so demanding.' Ruth put down her outdoor things and went through to the kitchen.

Ned grunted and looked back at the screen.

'Would you like some tea?' she called, filling the kettle. The gush of water drowned out his answer but when she turned the tap off, she heard him say:

' — says you were very short with her.'

'What?' She put the kettle into its cradle and switched it on. Then, at the doorway, she said, 'What did you say? I missed it.'

He frowned as he threw a glance away from the screen in her direction. 'Mum was a bit upset about your phone call with her the other night. I spoke to her this morning.'

'Oh. Oh God.' Ruth put a hand to her head. 'Yes. I forgot. She called the other night when we . . . just after . . . you'd gone out. I meant to call her back.'

'She says you hung up on her.'

'No, I didn't,' said Ruth indignantly. 'She hung up on *me*.'

Ned didn't say anything, and she rushed in to defend herself. 'She called up just when I was feeling in a bit of a state and she said 'is this a

304

good time, or should I call back?'. I was feeling so grim that for once I thought I would ask her to call back — I don't usually, you know. I usually always talk to her, no matter how inconvenient it is. So I said something like . . . I can't remember exactly . . . something like 'I'd love to hear all about the move but how about tomorrow' and she said 'I see, sorry to have bothered you' and put the phone down. I thought I'd offended her by not wanting to talk so I didn't call her back that evening. I imagined she wouldn't want me to. And I forgot to ring her last night, and now . . . it's today.'

'She's worked herself up into a state about it,' Ned said flatly. 'You'd better call and apologise.'

'All right.' The kettle came to a rolling boil and switched itself off. 'You do believe me, though, don't you? That she hung up on me?'

Ned sighed. 'For God's sake, don't ask me to pick sides. This is ridiculous.'

'I'm not. But — you do believe *me*, don't you?'

'I suppose so. But it would be much easier if you just do what she wants. Speaking from experience, I've always found it the best way.'

Ruth stood in the doorway, regarding him for a moment. He was focused again on the football game. 'All right,' she said in a small voice. 'I'll call her later.'

★ ★ ★

When the phone was picked up on the other end of the line, an unfamiliar gruff voice answered. ''lo?'

'Mum?' said Ruth, uncertain. Steven never answered the telephone so it must be Ned's mother. Had she called too late? It was only nine thirty in the evening, well before it became rude to telephone. There was no answer for a moment, just a long sigh down the line. 'Is that you, Mum?' She hated saying 'Mum' but now she had started, there seemed no polite way to stop.

'Hello, Ruth.' Jackie's voice was low and deeply weary, as though she could hardly summon the energy to speak even those two words. 'What do you want?'

'Ned said . . . you'd like me to call. And I said I would call.'

'*I* don't want you to call. I don't want you to do anything you don't want to do.'

'I do want to.'

'Do you?' Jackie laughed. 'All right, what do you want to say?'

There was something in her tone that made Ruth wary, and a blurriness around the edges of her words that made her suspect Jackie was not a little drunk.

'I wanted to ask about your move. Moving house. Coming to live here.'

There was another tired sigh, that made Jackie sound as though she were too exhausted even to be irritated. 'It's bloody stressful, selling your house. We've put years into this place. I've got it just the way I like it. Steven loves his garden. So many memories.'

'It must be very draining.' Ruth tried to pour compassion into her voice but she thought bitterly, Why are you leaving then?

'Yes. You're right.' Jackie sighed heavily again. 'Well, it's done and that's one good thing. The people buying it — they're all right, I suppose. She looks like a stuck-up bitch, though, horrible old woman, nosing round my kitchen, asking questions about my washing machine and how long I've had the dishwasher. She can fuck off, for one.' Jackie's voice was gaining energy. 'Stupid woman. Who do these people think they are? Well, they're going to get a surprise when they move in, that's for sure. Because I'm not leaving one thing behind that wasn't in the fitments list. I'm taking the curtain rails, I'm taking the loo seat, I'm taking the sconces in the front room, I'm even taking the bloody light bulbs. Well, they're mine, aren't they? I paid for them, didn't I? If she thinks she's getting anything for free, she can bloody think again. She got five thousand off the price, so she can whistle for the rest. I'll get my money back if I have to take every battery in the place.' She subsided again into throaty breathing.

'And when do you move here?' asked Ruth. She didn't want to get into a discussion about the rights and wrongs of removing the fittings.

'It's three weeks, Tuesday,' said Jackie. 'The Gables. Birch Road. It's a nice house. Not as nice as we've got, the money doesn't go as far where you are. Prices are mad. They're astronomical. It should be illegal.'

Ruth recognised Birch Road, it was in a newish development on the other side of the village. All the roads had been named after trees:

307

Oak Crescent and Ash Way and Fir Close. At least, she thought, it wasn't next door, but her heart sank nevertheless at the thought of the Haskells' imminent arrival.

'I hope you appreciate the sacrifice we're making,' Jackie said. 'It's a lifetime we've invested in our house. I thought I'd never leave it. I hoped to die there.' She sighed mournfully.

I wish you had, was Ruth's silent response, but then she rebuked herself at once for such a wicked thought.

'But we'll do what's necessary. We'll always put family before ourselves, Steven and I.'

'Thank you,' said Ruth.

'Yes, *thank you*,' said Jackie menacingly. 'Yes. Don't you forget this. I'll do anything for my boy. He's chosen you, he's married you. I won't speak my mind, I keep my thoughts to myself, but all I ask is a little consideration. Is that so much to ask? I don't think it is. Am I wrong?'

'Of course not. I'm sorry if you thought I was rude the other night . . . ' Ruth wanted to say her piece, the little diplomatic rebuff she'd practised before she called.

'*Thought* you were rude,' said Jackie, her voice getting thicker and louder. 'Don't fuck around with me. I *knew* you were rude! Have some respect for me, that's all I ask. Now we'll put it behind us. I'll accept your apology.'

Ruth felt at a loss to know how to defend herself. As a rule, she didn't shout at people or swear at them, it wasn't the way she was used to dealing with others. Every time Jackie swore Ruth winced, and the raised voice made her frightened in a way she hadn't experienced since she was little; it felt as though, any minute, Jackie would be round there, threatening to give her a smack.

'Thank you,' she said, at last, wishing she knew how to resist Ned's mother. She had thought she was learning how to handle her, but now she felt herself becoming more impotent each time they spoke. Jackie seemed to be gaining power and growing in strength like some black force that fed on bad feeling and conflict, as Ruth weakened and cowered in front of her.

Jackie was suddenly soft and whispery again. 'You're very welcome, dear. All right? See you soon. Bye bye, bye bye' — and the phone went down, leaving Ruth standing in the spare room with the silent receiver in her hand, wondering what on earth she was going to do.

15

The reconciliation came gradually, and was sealed a few nights later. They watched television together, after Ned had cooked a meal for them both. Mellowed by the bottle of red wine they'd shared, Ned pulled her into the warmth of his chest and held her against him, stroking her hair gently. She breathed in the smell of him like a perfume and savoured everything it brought her: the familiarity, the promise of pleasure to come. After a while, she tilted her face up to him and, in answer, he kissed her.

When they made love, it was urgent and strong as though they'd been parted for weeks and afterwards their intimacy was restored. They whispered in the dark, telling each other how lonely they'd been during the stand-off, and holding each other tightly. Ruth felt the urge to confess what she knew and to ask for the truth, but she held it in. She didn't want Ned to know how she'd fiddled in his past, pawing over his letters and private writing, and she couldn't think of a way to get the answers she craved without asking him directly, in a way that would reveal what she knew.

At the same time as her bond with Ned was regaining its strength, she couldn't help remaining alert to his contact with Erin. Perhaps it was her imagination but there seemed to be more of these private calls, when Erin would speak to

Ruth for only a few minutes before asking for Ned, who would then take the phone away with him and return with it half an hour later.

'What did Erin want?' Ruth would ask.

'Oh, nothing much. Just a chat. You know what she's like,' Ned would reply carelessly. And that was besides those work calls, thought Ruth, the ones Ned had never thought worth mentioning.

A black hatred for Erin began to fill her heart. She grew convinced that Erin was out to sabotage everything she had with Ned, and she began to pick up the phone every time it rang in order to monitor how often Erin called. But it seemed that every time she picked it up, she got Jackie.

'Hi, Mum,' she would say gaily, as her heart sank.

'Are you busy, Ruth? Am I disturbing you?' Jackie would ask sweetly, and Ruth knew that it was more than she dared ever to say 'yes', even when she was up to her elbows in suds from the washing-up, or in the middle of listening to a radio programme she was particularly enjoying, or cooking the dinner. Then Jackie would launch into her house-moving woes, while Ruth tried to hold back her irritation even though she was longing to say 'Why don't you just stay put then? No one wants you to move here.'

It didn't seem the time to broach the subject with Ned. Their rapprochement was still fresh and a little fragile. Ruth sensed Ned's usual reluctance to talk about his family. Even if she introduced the subject casually, he'd grunt and slide his gaze away from her, clamming up on the topic as he always had.

It will be all right, Ruth told herself, even though she felt as though she were living under sentence of execution and counting down the days before the axe fell. There's nothing they can do to us. We're adults with our own lives — we'll just have to put boundaries in place so that we all understand how things are. That's what we'll do.

* * *

She was walking through Oxford in her lunch hour, lost in her thoughts, when she heard someone calling her. A hand grabbed at her coat as a breathless voice said, 'Nurse, nurse!'

She turned and saw Michael Petheridge's mother standing beside her. It had taken a moment to recognise her; her face was more animated and less exhausted than it had been the last time Ruth had seen her in the surgery, the day that she'd been attacked. That was before she and Ned were engaged. It seemed like a lifetime ago. 'Oh — Mrs Petheridge . . . '

'Nurse, I don't want to interrupt your business. I just wanted to say how sorry I was when my boy hit you. I meant to come back but I never did and then the doctor asked us to leave . . . I felt very bad. I hope you weren't badly hurt. Michael was not happy at the time. He's much better now.'

Ruth was startled. 'Please, don't worry. I was fine, just a little bruised. I'm sorry you were taken off the register.'

'Oh,' said the mother sadly, 'it has happened a few times. We're used to it. Michael is not an easy child. I do my best but . . . ' She shrugged, her mouth turned down. 'He's my son. I have to help him.'

'Of course you do. Thank you for your apology.'

'You're welcome.' Mrs Petheridge smiled and walked off down the road.

Ruth watched her go. She was a good woman, a respectable woman. Not the kind of woman who made malicious phone calls, or swore down the line at people. There was only one woman Ruth knew who did that.

⋆ ⋆ ⋆

She came home from work to find Tom sprawled on their sofa, watching television. He had found the comedy channel and an old episode of *M⋆A⋆S⋆H* was playing out.

'Oh, hello,' Ruth said, hanging up her keys. 'Where's Ned?'

'He's gone to the supermarket to get some food.' Tom got up off the sofa casually, coming over and kissing her on the cheek. His stubble brushed against her and she caught the dark smell of his cologne. 'How are you?'

'I'm fine,' she said. 'Have you got a drink? Did Ned get you anything? I'll get you a beer.' She went through to the kitchen. 'Why did Ned go to the supermarket? We've got food.'

'Not enough for three,' Tom called back.

'Are you staying for dinner?'

'If that's all right.'

'Of course it is. You're on your own, are you? Has Erin gone to Germany now?' Ruth knew she had. She'd known that Erin would be leaving on the Sunday night. At nine o'clock, when the flight was scheduled to take off, she'd felt the lightness of a burden being lifted from her. For a little while she was released from her constant observation of the cosy calls to Ned, the summons to her house, the murmured nick-names and private, whispered conversations when they were all together.

'That's right.'

'I can't wait to see the advert on TV,' Ruth said, coming back into the sitting room with a beer for Tom and a glass of wine for herself.

'You won't see it here. It's only going to be shown on the Continent.'

'Oh. What a shame.' She sat down opposite him. He had returned to the sofa, claiming the entire length, his feet propped up on the opposite arm rest. His fair hair, she thought, was getting darker. That was a sign of ageing, too, hair gradually losing its vibrancy: redheads faded from bright ginger to dark copper, blonds went mousy and dark heads lost their depth and lustre to strings of grey. That was what Ruth was finding anyway: she had seen a sprinkling of wiry grey hairs at her parting only that morning. Tom was looking older, she thought. Or perhaps he was in reality just the same as ever, and it was the effect of thinking of him so often as the young, moody-looking

314

student from the photograph albums that made him seem a little dimmed. He was unshaven and his shirt looked crumpled and old. He was wearing glasses too, an old pair of unashamedly heavy-framed spectacles with dusty looking lenses.

Ruth felt ill at ease. She realised that she'd never been on her own with Tom and that, even when they were with others, she'd never found him relaxing company. He had the air of an obstinate schoolboy who enjoyed challenging authority and he was often taciturn, only turning on the charm when it suited him. He looked like he was accustomed to his own way and took pleasure in being contrary.

He needs careful handling, she thought. How does Erin do it? She imagined that life with Tom would be like a game, in which you would soon have to become an arch manipulator to achieve anything. He gave the impression that you would no sooner ask him to do something, when he would not only do the opposite but any chance of his ever doing what you'd asked would have gone. His stubborn nature would not allow you to win the slightest advantage. She could recognise the aura of intensity that made him attractive, although it was not the kind of thing she was drawn to herself.

But Erin is attracted to it. Perhaps she enjoys the games he plays. Perhaps that's what keeps them together — the tension of seeing who will win.

There was a burst of laughter from the television show.

'So — are you looking forward to being a father?' asked Ruth. She tried to sound friendly without being nosy.

Tom turned his gaze from the screen and stared at her quizzically. '*Looking forward* to being a father,' he repeated. 'I don't know.'

'Well — what do you feel about it? You must feel something. Some people feel happy, others apprehensive . . . '

'What do I feel . . . I suppose I feel a bit surprised.'

'Oh . . . you mean, the reality hasn't sunk in yet?'

'Definitely it hasn't.' That seemed to strike Tom particularly. He frowned. 'You can't *imagine* it. It's rather frustrating. I have tried, but it's just pointless. I know that something will arrive here, a person, and I'll have duties to it, but it's a complete stranger.'

'Your baby. You'll love it,' said Ruth, almost soothingly.

'I might. But I might not. It might be distinctly unlovable. We shall see. Erin gets round that by not thinking of it as a person at all. Instead, she fixates on the birth, as though the way she handles those few hours will dictate whether she has a good baby or a bad baby. She says she doesn't want this painkiller, or that procedure, as though if she does, the baby will be cross with her for not trying harder. She's convinced herself that the only thing to do is to push out exactly as nature intended or she won't have been the best mother she can be.'

'That's silly. It's not an exam. She's not going

316

to be given a mark at the end of it. And if pushing it out were that easy, we'd never have invented all the painkillers and interventions.'

'I know,' said Tom, with a strange smile. 'We've forgotten how dangerous childbirth is. I've been reading about it since all this started. Up until very recently, ten per cent of mothers died in or from childbirth. Elizabethan women who fell pregnant used to write little books to their unborn children to be given to them in the event that they died giving birth. I saw one in the Tate — a little handwritten notebook, from a young mother to a baby she would never know. She told the child that she was now in heaven and happy and had fulfilled God's will, and she asked it to be good and learn its prayers. A sad little thing.'

'Did she die?'

'Yes — I suppose that's why the book survived.'

'How awful.' Ruth sat back in her chair. 'You're right. Hardly any mother wonders if she'll die in childbirth these days. It's almost unheard of. How lucky we all are now.'

'So you find other things to fret about,' observed Tom. 'Erin's talking about water births and hypnosis and God knows what else.'

'Well, it's important she's happy and relaxed. And it's not exactly as easy as pie. We may not worry about dying so much, but there is the prospect of overwhelming pain, the possibility of getting into difficulties, and how the baby will cope with being born and whether we'll end up in the operating room having an emergency

317

caesarean. It's a very frightening thing. You'll never have to go through it, after all, so I think you really ought to concentrate on being supportive.'

'Yes, nurse.' Tom grinned.

Ruth laughed a little awkwardly. 'I'm sorry. Do I sound all bossy and professional? I didn't mean to. But I do think you ought to indulge Erin as much as you can.'

'I indulge her enormously, all the time.' Tom waved a hand carelessly. 'She wants for nothing. And that's what she gets. Joke, of course,' he added, seeing Ruth's expression. 'I don't know. Babies, breeding . . . it's full of intimations of mortality, isn't it?'

'You sound like you didn't want a baby at all,' Ruth said a little abruptly. She was feeling cross suddenly. 'Do you think that if you don't have a baby, you'll stay young for longer? Closing your eyes to the prospect of getting older doesn't mean it won't happen, or that you won't die. Anyway, it's only by having a child that you leave anything lasting behind.'

'Unless you write a great novel, or paint a wonderful painting, or compose an undying symphony. Plato believed that the duty of the artist was to refrain from having children and to pour his creative juice into his art.'

'Most of us aren't great artists. And you're a lawyer,' said Ruth, allowing a bite into her words. 'Are you going to leave a great court case behind?'

Tom laughed. 'You like to bring me down to earth, don't you? The point is, I never expected

318

to have a baby so soon.'

'You're thirty-five. When did you want to have it? Pick it up with your bus pass?'

'No, I mean, we'd barely just agreed to have a baby when — boom — Erin was pregnant. She said it would probably take months but it happened immediately. I wasn't quite prepared for how ready her ovaries were.'

'That's lucky. You don't want to delay any more than you have to. All the risks go up after thirty-five.'

Tom sighed and stared at her. 'You're very prosaic, Ruth, aren't you?'

She prickled. 'What do you mean?' He was telling her she was ordinary, just as she had always suspected he thought her.

'Everything is very clear to you. You're lucky. I wish it were as clear to me.'

'It's no more clear to me than anyone.'

'No.' Tom shook his head. 'You seem to grasp practicalities. You don't live in the shadowy, dangerous world the rest of us inhabit.'

She felt offended, as though he were implying she were shallow, unable to discern the light and dark in life. 'That's not true,' she said. She thought of her fears and the bitter but compelling fantasies that swirled round her mind when she thought about Ned and Erin. *Erin*. Tom's partner. Tom's lover. Did he ever think the things that tortured her, or imagine the two of them — his friend and the mother of his child — wrapped round each other on rumpled sheets in an anonymous bedroom the way she did? Perhaps he had an answer for her, perhaps he could shed some light on it, and the images might vanish in it like dreams in the morning. She leaned forward. 'Tom — did you ever — was there ever anything . . . Erin . . . and Ned . . . '

'Oh,' he said, raising his eyebrows. He didn't look in the least surprised at the turn the conversation had taken. 'Don't you mean Curly and Bear? So sweet together, aren't they? I wondered how long it would take before you started asking questions about that. They're the *best* of friends, aren't they? I think you've been extraordinarily tolerant so far, if you want to know the truth. I mean — ' he laughed curtly ' — Erin standing up at your wedding. Faith, hope and love, but the greatest of these is love!' He laughed again. 'Jeremy nudged me pretty hard at that bit, I can tell you.'

'What's the joke?' asked Ruth coldly. 'I'd love you to explain it.'

'No joke. It's no use playing the cool customer with me now. You've just asked me about Erin and Ned. It's obvious you're beginning to see the truth, like the rest of us always have.' He stood up, strode over to the fireplace, and turned towards her. Behind him, the khaki figures on the screen moved about, accompanied by miniature bursts of laughter. 'You're a lovely girl, and I'm sure Ned's very fond of you but unfortunately even you had to see that he's head over heels about my wife. He has been for years. We've all got used to it to such an extent that we hardly even notice it any more. It was quite endearing, the way he doted on her, always following her about, ringing her up. Always on call if she needed him. Then you arrived and suddenly everything changed. That startled all of us. What's he doing with this one? we thought, because it was obvious that you might be the exception to the rule. Before now, Ned's girlfriends have been so comically unsuited to him it was almost pathetic. Every relationship doomed before it even began. Then little Ruth arrives, and Ned is clearly really smitten this time. Is Erin's spell broken? I'm sure everyone was wondering just as I was — is this the end of Erin's unbroken reign as queen of Ned's heart? Surely not! But there it was. And before we know it, you're in the cottage with him and there's talk of engagements and weddings and nothing could be nicer because we all wish the best for our dear friend Ned.' Tom's cynical, sarcastic tone was ugly.

'*Is* he your friend? It doesn't sound like it.'

'Of course he is. We've been bound together for so many years, neither of us have a choice. Did you ever hear about the woman who grew so fat, she could only lie on her sofa? She lay there for seven years and then one day, when she was about fifty stone, she had a heart problem, so they called the ambulance. It took six men to even attempt to lift her off the sofa, and when they did, she shrieked with agony. Her skin and the fabric of the sofa had meshed together and fused so that they couldn't be separated without immense pain and injury. That's me and Ned. The fat woman and her sofa. Or the sofa and its fat woman, whichever way you like to look at it.' Tom stared at her, his blue eyes icy.

'So all this time all of you have known that Ned . . . has feelings for Erin. You seem to take pleasure in telling me this. Don't you think it hurts me? And if it's so important, why didn't anyone tell me before Ned and I got married?' She threw out the questions like challenges. Tom knew things she desperately needed to know as well, and she wanted to provoke him into revealing them.

'You've noticed it for yourself, darling! You brought all this up, not me. And that's the whole point, isn't it? At first it looked as though you'd won. You'd managed to release Ned from his bondage, given him a whole new chance of happiness, something fresh, so he could blow his stale old passion away like so much dust. I was glad for him. We all were. Except one person.'

'Erin.'

'Exactly.' Tom nodded. 'And I can hear from your voice that you've started to realise what she can be like. The mistress of the game. The arch manipulator. The queen who does not like to be toppled from her throne. *You* are the problem, really,' he said, with a cold smile, 'because without you, it would all have gone along just as it always has. But *you*, with your love for Ned and his love for you, started it all up.'

'Me? How can this possibly be my fault?' Indignation rose in her.

'I didn't say it was your fault. But can you blame Erin? No one wants to be told they're not top dog any more. No queen wants to lose her crown. And this particular queen likes nothing quite as much as a challenge.'

322

That's what Jeremy said, thought Ruth miserably.

'Once it's taken away from her, there's nothing she wants more! All these years she could have had poor Ned like that' — he snapped his fingers — 'but she didn't want him then. She wants him *now*. Or she thinks she does, or she pretends she does, or she just can't bloody help herself.' Tom stopped for a moment to swig from his beer bottle and then muttered to himself, 'Or perhaps it's not even about him at all, poor bastard. She only wants to test her power and see if he'll come back to her if she tugs hard enough. She can't tolerate being replaced, and she doesn't think you're any real competition. Jesus, I spend my life trying to work out what game everyone is playing.'

'And — do you think that Ned would go to her if she asked him to?' Ruth asked, trying to sound as though her whole life didn't hang on the answer.

'That's the question, isn't it? You should know, sweetheart. You're the one who's married to him. I don't know how far either of them would go. In a way, I have to give Ned his due — he's played the cleverer hand in the end. He finally worked out a way to get her, just like he always wanted.'

In a small, frightened voice, Ruth said, 'But there can't really be anything going on, can there?' Her imagination had taken her there but still she couldn't accept that it might be true. Not her Ned. Not after everything they'd meant to each other.

Tom's lip curled up on one side, ugly and

distorted. 'You've noticed how they've been over the last few months. It's been so cosy it's made me puke. I don't know how you've put up with it — or perhaps Ned is better at hiding it than Erin is. Phoning each other every day, bestest bestest friends.' He put on a twisted smile and cocked his head in a parody of a caring gesture. He spoke in a falsetto voice, a nasty approximation of a woman. 'Poor Neddy's getting married — is he rushing into it? Is he sure? Is it his mother, do you think? Perhaps he's only trying to escape from her. Is he making a terrible mistake? I must spend lots and lots of time with him to make sure.' In something like his normal voice, he snarled, 'You never bloody wanted to spend time with him before, when he followed you round sick to the gills with his bloody passion for you.'

'So you think that they've been together. That they've s-s-slept together,' she said, stumbling over the words, feeling sick as she said them.

'There's every chance.' He laughed bitterly. 'Ned's certainly had more of an opportunity than he's ever had before. And there could be even more to it. This baby, for example. I'm sure it's occurred to you that it might be his.'

Ruth staggered to her feet. 'What do you mean?' She felt as though she were plunging downwards, falling through a hole in the floor she hadn't seen into a black tunnel. Sickness swilled about in her stomach. 'No ... no ... what are you talking about?' she whispered through the bitter taste in her mouth.

'Come on, Ruth!'

I don't know this man at all, thought Ruth,

what's he doing here? She was almost too dazed to feel anything but was vaguely aware she was frightened, as though she had inadvertently unleashed a dog she thought was friendly but who turned out to be a dangerous beast. Her legs felt weak underneath her but she forced herself to stand and face him. This was it then. She was getting the answers she longed for now, wasn't she? In all their bitter, dreadful reality.

Tom seemed cool but a muscle was twitching near his eye, revealing his tension. 'It only takes a moment of thought to see that of course it might be Ned's. We'll see when the time comes. We'll see what he and Erin decide to do.'

'Oh my God!' Tears sprung to her eyes. 'I can't believe Erin would do this! How could she . . . how could *they* . . . ?' She fought to control herself, worried that if she broke down, she would not be able to recover.

'Do you hate her?' asked Tom coolly.

'Hate her? . . . I don't know . . . ' Then she lifted her head in fury and spat, 'Yes, I hate her! I hate her bloody guts!' She bit her lip and took a breath. 'How can you be so calm about it? Your best friend and your partner . . . '

'I take the long view. I can live with whatever happens.'

'But you think that the baby . . . ' Her voice broke on it. It was too appalling a thought to entertain. It was a thousand times worse than she'd imagined.

Tom's composure seemed to desert him and he suddenly put his face in his hands. She'd never seen him display more emotion than mild amusement. To see him like this was frightening, disorienting, like a child seeing its mother cry for the first time.

'I don't know,' he muttered into his hands. 'All I know is that they were together a lot. Erin said she was worried about him, about how quickly he'd got engaged. She said she needed to talk to him. And then, she was pregnant. I read somewhere once that a woman is more likely to conceive with a lover than with her partner. It just all happened so fast.' He looked at her, his face drawn. 'We'd hardly agreed to have a baby when she told me it was underway. It was so quick . . . I wondered if she was already pregnant, or . . . '

'When was it?'

'Early October.'

'I remember that time. Ned was working late a lot,' whispered Ruth. 'He had a special deadline on.' She felt faint. 'Oh no . . . ' She remembered how happy they'd been that month, how much time they'd spent discussing the wedding. Was Ned really so happy because he'd got what he wanted all along? To have Erin?

Tom laughed grimly. 'I bet he was.'

The phone went, and Ruth answered it automatically. It was Ned.

'Hi, darling. I hope it wasn't too surprising to find Tom on the sofa when you got home.'

'Oh . . . no. It's fine.'

'I'm just on my way home with some dinner for us all. I couldn't decide what to cook so in the end I went to the Indian and got a takeaway. I'm on my way back now. Okay? I'll be home in about twenty minutes.'

'Okay. Bye.' She put the phone down.

Tom seemed calmer now. 'Well, that's effectively blown all our cover, hasn't it? As long as no one mentioned it, we could keep this nicely under wraps, pretend it wasn't happening. But you spoke the fatal words, didn't you? It's out there now, out of our control. I suppose we're going to have to decide what we'll do about this.' He came up close to her suddenly, almost pressing against her. He put an arm around her back and pulled her into him. 'How about getting a bit of our own back, eh? How about it, Ruth? You and me? Shall we have our revenge together?' His beery breath came close to her mouth.

'Get off.' She tried to shout but her voice emerged muffled and squeaky, and she batted at him impotently, feeling weak and stupid as though in a dream. 'Go away.'

He laughed again. 'All right. Don't worry. I'm going now. I don't think I could quite stomach sitting down to dinner with you both at the moment. But do you know what? I bet that in the end we'll be able to forget all this and go back to our old ways. Being friends is the oldest habit we've got. Perhaps not even this will let us break it. We'll see.' He turned to the door, picking up his coat from the back of a chair as he went. 'I don't know what you're going to say to Ned. Let me know what you decide.' He turned back and looked at her as he pulled on his coat. 'Ruth, I'm sorry. I really am. I can see by your face that you really had no idea about all of this.

One of us should have told you, let you know what you were getting yourself in to. I feel bad that you found out about Ned this way. Don't do anything rash, okay? Be careful.'

Ruth wanted to say something but she had no idea what, and just nodded her head silently.

'Bye.' Tom went out of the cottage into the night beyond.

Ruth sank into a chair and waited.

*   *   *

When Ned came home, she was still in her chair, curled up with her feet tucked under her, her cardigan pulled tightly around her, as though she were trying to comfort herself. The cat had come to her, stepping delicately over the sofa cushions, and curled up on her lap to sleep in its warmth.

Ned was carrying a brown paper bag that was piebald with grease spots and smelt of rich spicy food. He looked about as he put it on the table. 'Where's Tom? In the loo?'

'He's gone.' Ruth looked at him, not knowing whether she was glad to see him or furious. She could feel herself shaking with pent-up emotion.

'Gone?' Ned came over, frowning, still holding his car keys. 'Why?' He sat down opposite her and seemed to notice for the first time what kind of state she was in. 'Ruth — are you all right?'

Her voice was tight. It sounded strange, even to her own ears: too high and too precise to be entirely normal. 'No. I'm not all right. I've got something to tell you.'

'What?' He leaned forward, concerned. His

328

eyes, she thought, were so clear and trusting. His whole face was open to her. *You don't have to tell him*, she said to herself. *You don't have to say anything. Nothing needs to change. Leave it — we can have dinner together, go to bed, forget everything else . . .* But she couldn't stop herself.

'You,' she said shakily. 'You and your bloody friends. Do you know how *bizarre* you all are? All of you circling Erin like she's the centre of the universe. Except for Luke — he managed to escape. He's the most normal of all of you. What would it take to break you up?'

Ned wrinkled his nose. 'Ruth, what are you talking about? We're not going to discuss Erin again, are we? I thought that was behind us. Don't let's go there again, please.'

'I'm sorry, Ned, but we must. Didn't you hear me? I've got something to tell you.' She stroked the cat's head. Maisie stretched her head up, her eyes closed into small black slants as the satisfied purr rumbled in her throat. Ruth lost her fingertips in the thick white fur behind the cat's ears, feeling the small skull underneath. 'I was clearing out the spare room, and I found your boxes of things — those papers, and odds and ends — you know, postcards and things. I know I shouldn't have, but I went through one of them and looked in your old school books. I thought that's all they were. Just old books.'

'Yes?' Ned's expression became wary.

She decided there was no gain in wasting time getting to the point. 'I found your diaries. The ones about Erin. I read them, by accident to start with. I found out how you were in love with her.'

Although he didn't stir, it felt as though he had moved backwards, away from her. A series of emotions passed over his face, a flash of surprise, bewilderment and disbelief, followed by anger and upset, and finally his open expression became closed and hard.

He said slowly, 'You've read all my diaries?'

'I read what I found in one box — the years you were at university.'

'I see,' he said. His shoulders slumped downwards and he hunched over, resting his fingertips on his forehead, as though he were struggling to recall what he had written: not just the sense, but the actual words, sentences and paragraphs. Ruth saw a dark flush creeping up his neck and when he looked back at her again, his expression was agonised. 'You read . . . everything?'

She felt low. 'Yes,' she whispered. 'I know all about it.' Is he going to be angry? she wondered. Are we going to fight?

But he didn't say anything for a long time, just stared back at the floor, lost in thought. When he did begin to speak again, it wasn't with anger in his voice but a kind of vulnerability she hadn't heard before.

'It's . . . a shock. I don't know what to say. I haven't read those things for years, I've almost forgotten they were there. I knew I should have got rid of them.'

'Are you — angry?'

'I'm not sure. Yes, I'm angry but I'm also . . . '

His voice tailed off. 'You, looking at those things — it's embarrassing, humiliating. I've never told anyone about what I've written there. Those are my deepest, most private thoughts. I feel as though you've invaded them.'

'You don't need to be embarrassed — ' she began but he cut her off, with a flash of anger in his eyes.

'Don't tell me that. How would you know? Don't you understand what all that means? Besides the simple invasion of my privacy, it's about more than that. She was the girlfriend of one of my best friends and all the time I wanted to betray him. I spent years on the cusp of telling her how I felt, in the hope that she would leave him for me. What does that make me? Don't you see? It's like having my worst faults on display for you to see.'

'Don't be so hard on yourself. You didn't mean it, you couldn't help it.' Ruth, perversely, was overwhelmed with pity for him. He was blaming himself for the passion that had caused him such agony over the years.

'The only thing that helped,' he said quietly, almost to himself, 'was that no one knew, I never told anyone. That's why I spent so many useless hours writing it all down. It was the only way to get it out of my system. I kept it bottled up inside for so long. It's hard living with a secret like that.'

He thinks no one knew, she thought, stricken. He doesn't realise how obvious it was, how they all must have known. I can't tell him! She remembered Tom's words, how he suggested

331

that all of the friends found Ned's devotion to Erin amusing. She had been wanting to throw them in his face, imagining the viciousness with which she could hurt him in the way she felt hurt; but she found that now she couldn't.

'So you did love her.'

He winced. After a while he said, 'Yes. Of course I did. But it brought me nothing but hell.'

'Did you ever tell her?'

He flicked a glance at her. 'I didn't tell her. I don't think she's ever known.'

Of course she has! thought Ruth. We know when we're loved. She remembered the letters, the nicknames, the intimacy. She knew. And she played you pretty well, keeping you just where she wanted you.

'It was the worst time of my life, that period at university, when it was so overpowering I thought it was going to kill me.' Ned spoke in a low voice, almost to himself. 'I sometimes wondered if that would be easier, just to jump off a bridge somewhere and put an end to it. I never really got close to it but sometimes it felt perilously near, that kind of black thinking. And then there was a time — just before she got together with Tom, when I knew it was all coming to an end with Jeremy — I thought I saw my chance. I asked her to meet me one evening, ostensibly to go to a new bar but really so that I could open my heart and ask her to give me a chance. We'd been having strange encounters. Erin was drinking a lot, at parties and gigs and things, and at the end of the evening when she was pissed, she would fall into my arms and

332

stroke my hair, and be sweet with me. We were living together by then — Christ, it was hard.' He ran his hands through his hair. 'She'd lie on the sofa, smoking and blinking at me, running her hands through her curls, singing songs to me in that sultry voice and letting her skirt ride up too far to be strictly decent. I thought she was giving me signals.' He laughed harshly. 'Poor sap! I must be a bloody idiot. And all the time, she was concentrating on something else entirely. One night we came back, and she was pretty drunk, flirting outrageously with me. She came and sat on my knee and told me she loved me — in that sweet way that could mean 'like a brother' — but, my God, my heart soared, it really did.'

He was silent for a moment.

'But I wasn't going to do anything when she was so drunk, so I decided to arrange this night when I'd tell her everything. You should have seen me, it was pathetic. I spent hours deciding what I would wear, what I would say, where we would go for our first kiss.' He laughed again. 'She never turned up, of course. When I got home, she wasn't there either. There was just a note on the kitchen table telling me she'd gone to Tom. He'd gone home to his family to revise, probably to get himself off all the drugs he was so keen on taking. She was always eager to go to Tom's house — a bit of a pushover for that big house they live in, any excuse to stay. So it wasn't all that surprising that she'd decided on a whim to see him. But they came back . . . together. Just like that. Out of the blue.'

'What was it like — when you found out she was with Tom?'

'Incredibly horrible. Like a double betrayal. If anyone knew, or guessed, it was Tom. And I realised that he must have been planning how to get her for months, never saying a word. And despite the way she pretended to confide in me and trust me, she never said a word either. I knew then, really, that it was over, that I'd never really had a chance with her at all.' He shrugged. 'So, after that, I just hoped it would go away, that if I suffered it for long enough, eventually I'd get over it, like coming off drugs cold turkey.'

'And did you?' she whispered.

He closed his eyes and sighed almost irritably. When he opened them, he said, 'Ruth, I had a life before you. I'm sorry if you find that difficult to handle. But we're married now. Of course I got over it. I fell in love with you instead.'

'I know you did. But . . . ' She wished she didn't have to ask but she was certain she would never find peace if she wasn't absolutely sure. 'Is it as good as what you felt for Erin?'

'Ruth, Ruth . . . ' he said, his tone almost begging. 'Why do you have to ask me these things? What is the point?'

'Because I need to know!' she cried. 'I need to know I'm not second best. I need you to tell me that you love me more than you love her.'

'I tell you every day,' he said harshly. 'I married you.'

'I don't know if that's the answer I need.'

'I can't — I won't — give you any more than that. I'm sorry. You have to trust me.'

334

She began to cry. This felt to her like evasion. Why was it so difficult to tell her what she needed to hear?

'I don't understand why this is happening,' he said plaintively. 'It feels incredible to be accused like this. For Christ's sake' — he stood up and paced the room, then turned back to her. 'If you hadn't read my diaries, none of this would have happened. That's why I didn't tell you about it in the first place, because I knew you would be like this when you don't have to. See what you've done?'

Ruth wiped away tears with the back of her hand, sniffing. She thought about Erin's swelling belly, the child she had bought a tiny white cardigan for. She imagined Ned putting his soft lips to Erin's, his hands on her breasts and belly. 'I'm not so sure about that. I don't know if we can just blame me for being nosy.'

He frowned suspiciously. 'What do you mean?'

Shall I ask him? she thought, desperate. Shall I risk this? Can it possibly be true?

The phone went. Ned looked at it for a moment, as though he needed to make the connection between its ringing and what he had to do in response. Then he picked it up.

'Yes? Yes, speaking . . . What? Yes, I know him . . . Oh, God.' He went white. 'I see . . . No, his wife's away. Yes . . . I'll be there right away . . . Is there anything else you can tell me? . . . I understand. Of course. Thank you.'

He put the phone down. 'I have to go.'

'What's happened? Who was it?' asked Ruth, frightened.

'There's been an accident. A car crash. Tom's in hospital. I must get there at once.'

Ruth gasped. 'Oh God. He only left an hour ago. What's happened to him?'

'I don't know. They wouldn't tell me anything. I'd better get going.' Ned strode to the door, taking his coat and the car keys.

'I'll come with you!'

'Don't be stupid. There's nothing you can do. I'll call you when I know anything. You wait here.'

Ruth jumped up and ran to him, putting a hand on his arm. 'Be careful, won't you? Don't speed.'

He looked at her briefly, his mind obviously elsewhere. 'Don't worry. I'll be careful.'

Ruth stood at the window and watched the lights of his car disappear in the blackness.

16

The last time she'd been in church, Ruth realised, was for her wedding. She'd always wanted to be married in church, although she wasn't at all sure whether she believed in its tenets or not. She found it easier to believe in a hazy idea of an omnipotent, benevolent God than in the Bible stories of Adam and Eve, and virgin births and wine turning to water. Ned, like Cordy, considered religion the refuge of weak and superstitious minds and the cause of tension and dissension in the world, and Christianity as something to be vaguely embarrassed about. It was all right to like the hymns and turn up at Christmas for candles and carols, but to show that you might think there was anything more to it than that was to look like a fool. Ruth wasn't sure where she stood, and she certainly didn't have the strength of conviction to argue with anyone on the point, but there seemed to be something essential in it, and she knew that when she came to be married, she wanted it to be in this solemn and beautiful place, where the commitment she was going to vow to Ned was regarded with the kind of reverence she herself felt for it.

She looked about the church now. It was in leafy grounds close to the Thames and not far from Tom's home, and was a mixture of old and new, with familiar Gothic arched windows and a square, battlemented bell tower, but with evidence of restoration in a later century. Inside, in the oldest part of the church, the walls were encrusted with monuments and plaques. A fine funeral monument in black marble boasted weeping cherubs and angels in attitudes of despair, their smooth faces blankly miserable, while the gilded lettering intoned in Latin the reason for their grief.

I wonder what it says, thought Ruth, who had never learned Latin. She'd been taken out of Latin classes along with a handful of others who were considered to be more suited to doing 'classical projects' — drawing pictures of Caesar and Roman villas and writing about how the Romans cooked dormice.

Chinks of coloured light fell from the windows on to the grey plaques, some ornamented with coats of arms declaring lives and deaths of the local rich. Above her head, Ruth read that Margaret Diggory, wife of Thomas Diggory, had died in 1765, the mother of twelve infants who had gone to heaven before her. In the floor were further stones, their ornate lettering rubbed away by footsteps, and brasses smoothed almost flat. In the far corner, near the chapel, were effigies of a knight and his wife lying side by side beneath a stone canopy, their hands stiff in prayer and their eyes closed.

So many weddings and christenings must have taken place here, thought Ruth. But the only things that have lasted are the memorials to death.

She was near the front, waiting for whatever

would happen next. No doubt someone knew what was going on. The front rows were empty, waiting for the family who would come in with the coffin. The organ — invisible, but from the sound of it somewhere high up — played soft, sad music while the congregation waited quietly.

Abigail, in the same pew and also alone, took her hand gently and whispered, 'This is awful, isn't it? How is Ned?'

'Shattered,' whispered Ruth, glad that Abigail was there. Like her, she was accorded her place close to the family only by virtue of marriage. People who had known Tom better were further away.

'Luke too.' Abigail shook her head. Her eyes welled with tears. 'It's so bloody dreadful, isn't it? And poor Erin. I can't imagine what she's going through.' Abigail groped for a handkerchief and sniffed. 'God, I'm sorry.'

Ruth put her arm about her and hugged her, a small part of her envying the other woman her grief. She wished she was able to weep, to show her humanity and her fear of the pity and terror of death, but she couldn't. She was frozen.

She remembered other funerals she had attended: that of a friend from college who had died of cancer so quickly that Ruth hadn't really grasped she was even ill; her grandfather's cremation service, which had felt quick and cold, with one family leaving as they arrived and another following on their heels when they filed out after the coffin had slid jerkily through the purple curtain. And her mother's funeral, of which she had only two or three memories she could pull up before her mind's eye, and which she remembered more as a feeling of horror that still came upon her at moments: a ghastly, ill feeling that soured her whole being and almost overwhelmed her with hopeless dread.

If she could feel something like that now, or anything, she would prefer it to this sense of being sealed over and immune to everything. From the moment she had heard Tom had died, probably instantly when his car veered off the road at speed and collided with an oak tree, it had been like this. It was as though she had plunged downwards too fast, taking only her body with her, and leaving her heart and feelings to catch up with her at some later date.

Why can't I feel anything? Ruth wondered, her arm on Abigail's shaking shoulders. I don't understand.

The organ music stopped abruptly but began again after a beat, this time louder. The congregation turned towards the open doors of the church, and there was the coffin, a smooth pale brown box, carried on the shoulders of grimfaced men: Tom's brothers, Ned, Jeremy, and Luke who, as the shortest, was at the back, half hoisting his end on one of his arms. They advanced down the aisle, followed by the servers — one swinging a fretted silver canister of incense, another carrying the ornamental silver cross high, and two more carrying candles. Behind them were the vicar, in stiff dark purple robes embroidered with silver, and his assistants in their less rich cassocks, and then the family. Erin, her stomach a large and graceful outward curve under her black dress, was supported by someone Ruth assumed was Tom's mother. Both were dry-eyed with white, drawn faces.

The coffin reached the front. The pallbearers manoeuvred it as gracefully as they could on to the catafalque, while the cross and candles went towards the altar and the family edged into their pews.

Ruth stared at the coffin as Ned and Luke took their places beside her. It looked unreal, like a stage prop. The whole thing felt like a pretend, a rehearsal. They weren't ready for death yet, it wasn't supposed to be part of their world.

She had an urge to push past everyone to the coffin on its stand, and knock on it and shout, 'Tom, don't be so silly. Get up out of there and be normal. Can't you see how this behaviour is upsetting everyone?' It was such a strong impulse, she had to bite her lip and clench her fist to stop herself doing it.

The funeral service began. All of Ruth's thoughts focused on Ned standing next to her, his knuckles white as he clutched the service sheet and swayed a little. She glanced up at him as they all began to sing the first hymn, with no gusto and the drag of weak voices. He was staring at the words, his lips moving faintly but with no sound coming out. She put her hand on his arm and squeezed gently but he didn't respond. She was glad he had nothing more to do in the service because she didn't think he would be able to manage anything. Ever since the night he had been summoned to the hospital, to find Tom not injured as he had thought but

341

dead, he had been in a state that veered between the trance of a somnambulist and the racked grief of the newly bereaved. It had been Ned who called Erin the following day, interrupting the action on her film set in Germany, and told her what happened. He and Ruth had driven to Heathrow to meet her return flight; they'd stood at the barrier waiting for her to come through and when she had, Ruth had had to stand back as they embraced, unable to share in the intensity of the loss that bound them.

Funerals are shorter than weddings, thought Ruth, as they moved quickly through the service sheet: there were prayers and then Erin stepped forward and stood at the front before the coffin. There was an almost audible intake of breath from the congregation and the feeling of a collective sigh at the sight of her, so full with the child of the dead man. She stood neatly, feet together and her paper in her hands like a schoolgirl reading at assembly. Her voice lacked the actressy richness it had had at Ned and Ruth's wedding; instead it was quavering and low but infinitely more touching.

'Death, be not proud,' she read, 'though some have called thee mighty and dreadful . . . '

John Donne, thought Ruth. She'd studied his poems at school and remembered liking them. She listened to the words rebuking death and watched Erin, her beauty refined by grief to a point that made it almost hard to look at, so pale and perfect was her face.

'One short sleep past, we wake eternally,' read Erin. She looked up at everyone. 'And death shall be no more. Death — thou shalt die.' She stood for a moment, gazing at the coffin and her hand moved for an instant to her stomach, before she turned gracefully and went back to her seat.

How sad, thought Ruth, but it still felt as though she were shut in a room with invisible walls that cut her off from everyone else.

The vicar spoke, beginning, 'I didn't have the pleasure of knowing Tom personally but I've talked with his family and friends and . . . '

Ruth listened to him try and explain why it was that Tom had to die so senselessly, with a child coming that he would never know, and attempt to draw some good from it. Then one of Tom's brothers spoke, and that's when she could hear the weeping and when Ned's hands shook and she realised that he was crying too, as Tom's brother said what they all really felt: how stupid and pitiful it was for someone to die like this.

At the end, the brother begged, 'Don't forget him. Don't forget Tom, that's all we ask, because the only way he'll live on now is through you all, and through his child. Please come here whenever you can, and visit him. He'll be here a long time.'

Ruth held Ned's hand tightly and tried to will her strength into him; the last hymn, shot through though it was with terrible sadness, gave them time to recover before the vicar led them outside for the interment. The men shouldered their burden again, for the last time, taking the coffin outside to the grave. Ruth filed out of her pew and followed the procession, seeing Jackie and Steven Haskell in their seats further back as she went. She smiled weakly at Jackie, who was in deep black and a large hat, her eyes red with crying and a lace handkerchief pressed to her nose, but her mother-in-law didn't respond.

The grave was at the far end of the churchyard, under a yew tree, a bleak hole in the ground with earth on each side. When they got there, Ruth was surprised at how deep it was: it seemed to go on and on. She stood at the edge of the group of mourners, letting others stand in front, so that she only saw their backs. She didn't want to see the coffin lowered in; she'd seen that happen before and had been so horrified by the cold and darkness of it that she didn't want to witness it again.

As the vicar began his final oration, she realised she was standing next to Jeremy. There was something comforting about his height and the thick fabric of his suit. She wanted to lean against him, draw some strength from him, and she realised vaguely that she'd spent a week or more being as strong as she possibly could for Ned and now she was very tired.

Jeremy looked down at her, and muttered quietly:

'Beneath those rugged elms, that yew-tree's
    shade,
Where heaves the turf in many a moulder-
    ing heap,
Each in his narrow cell for ever laid,
The rude forefathers of the hamlet sleep.'

344

She thought for a moment: the narrow cell. Yes, that was what the grave was like. A tiny, cold prison. She shuddered a little. 'Who wrote that?'

'Thomas Gray. 'Elegy Written in a Country Churchyard'. Part of all that lovely, melancholy stuff so fashionable at the time. It goes on to be quite touching, and rather apt for poor old Tom, cut off before his prime. About lisping children no more being kissed by their father, and flowers born to waste their scent on the desert air.'

They stood side by side for a moment, hearing the vicar's voice float in patches of sound over the heads of the congregation.

'You're managing well,' said Ruth carefully, unable to tell whether Jeremy was untouched by Tom's death, or, like her, unable to reach out and be a part of the funeral.

'I am. Unlike your mother-in-law.' He nodded over to where Jackie was rocking back and forwards as she sobbed, her husband's arms around her as he gently shushed her. 'She's certainly getting her money's worth.' He saw Ruth's expression. 'Now don't be disapproving. I don't see anything wrong with emoting at these ceremonies. That's what they're for. When Mrs Haskell gets in the car to go home she'll feel much better, and an hour later she'll be wondering what to have for dinner and what's on the telly. But the people who aren't crying — Tom's parents, his family — they know that for them, this won't be over when it's time to go home. That's why they're in no hurry to weep and sob. And also, if Tom's mother broke down, what do you think Ned's would do? She's got a bit of a melodramatic streak, hasn't she? Perhaps she'll dive in after the coffin, like Hamlet.'

Ruth wanted to laugh, and it was a relief to feel even the mildest desire to be cheerful after the unrelenting gloom that had blanketed them for the last ten days. 'You wait until she gets on the sherry later,' she said.

Someone in front turned round and frowned. The last prayers were being spoken. The mutter of 'Amen' came towards them like a Chinese whisper.

'Amen,' said Ruth obediently, and it was all over.

Tom is buried, she thought, as they turned and made their way back to the path and round the church. She had a sudden flash of Tom pulling her towards him leerily, alcohol on his breath, and saying, 'Shall we have our revenge together?' A chill of alarm passed through her, and she shook her head to banish the image. She didn't want to think about that.

Instead, she realised that the sun was shining and that the church looked beautiful, and that she felt intensely, amazingly alive. This was how you're supposed to feel after funerals, she thought. She'd read it in an article about bereavement: there was nothing like death to fill the living with the zing of existence. She thought of soldiers and girls whooping and dancing and making love during the Blitz, the wildness in the taverns during times of plague, and she wanted to run and yell herself, but she held it in, instead becoming aware of the movement of the fabric of her clothes against her skin and the lift of the breeze in her hair, and the miracle of inhaling and exhaling.

'Ruth?' Ned was beside her, startling her.

'Yes?'

'I'm going with Mum to the house. Are you coming?' Ned didn't look as though he were feeling the buzz of being alive; he seemed bent and hollow.

She didn't say anything and Jeremy said, 'You could walk up with me, if you want, Ruth. I'm going to take the scenic route and get a breath of air on the way.'

'Yes, I'll do that, if that's all right,' said Ruth, relieved not to have to get into a car with Jackie.

'Whatever,' said Ned, briefly, and disappeared back into the crowd to find his mother.

'This way,' said Jeremy, and led her out of a side gate in the churchyard.

★ ★ ★

They walked along the river, on a path edged by an old stone wall overhung with trees bursting out in their spring colours. The day was fine and clear, the sky a pure blue edged with ruffles of cloud. Ruth felt the heat prickle her skin through her dark wool suit.

Large properties were concealed from them behind the wall, the occasional open gate showing lush green lawns stretching away towards glittering conservatories and prosperous red brick.

'I didn't realise Tom's family were that rich,' said Ruth, as they strolled past.

'Oh yes. It's all inherited, I think. They're distantly connected to really rich people and are merely quite well off.'

'It's all relative, though, isn't it?'

'Well — yes.' Jeremy said casually, 'And how are you coping with all of this?'

'All right. I'm still in a daze really. I can't believe it's happened. What about you?'

'I'm afraid I'm a bit of an enemy of sentiment. People get very gloomy around death, and talk about the dead being robbed of life. I see it the other way round. The chance of having existence at all is so infinitesimally tiny that to be alive for any length of time at all means you're already a winner. Dying in your mid-thirties is late middle age by mediaeval standards. I consider him to have had a good innings.'

'No, I can't agree. You can't possibly say that Tom's was a life complete, can you? It's a life interrupted. He's never even going to know his child.'

'It's all completely immaterial to him. We know all that, but he doesn't because he's dead.' Jeremy shrugged. He took out one of his small roll-ups and lit it. 'I told you. Look, Tom died very quickly without sickness or fear or torture — it's not a bad way to go. A hundred other people have died today as well. A sick child. A father in his forties on a cancer ward. An old person slipping away in their nursing home bed. A young woman driving a car. Someone falling off a ladder or being hit by a bus. A hundred more tomorrow. It happens. There's no mystery to it. Every story has to end. We'll always think of

Tom now as the man destined to die youngish in a car crash. It's only fear of how death will come to us that makes us sad.'

'I don't think that's true,' began Ruth, thinking of how Tom's mother must feel, and of her own mother dying. Jeremy cut her off.

'But you were the last person to see him, weren't you? You and Ned?'

'Not Ned,' said Ruth, without thinking. 'He was out getting dinner.'

Jeremy raised his eyebrows. 'Just the two of you? And Tom left before dinner? What had you been talking about?'

Ruth said nothing for a while, as they kept walking. 'I don't want to discuss it,' she said at last. 'Please, Jeremy. There's no secret — there's nothing to know. Tom decided to go home and that was all there was to it.'

'On such small decisions do our fates hang,' observed Jeremy. 'And I suppose the cause of death was satisfactorily established.'

'The fact that his car was in the shape of a horseshoe afterwards did seem fairly conclusive.' Ruth tried not to sound too sarcastic, but she was frightened by what Jeremy was implying: that she knew of some reason why Tom had died on his way home. It was something she had not been able to face herself and she had dreaded anyone asking her. 'There was no question over how he died.'

'And no alcohol involved?'

Ruth shook her head. 'Ned said the family was told there was nothing significant enough to be assumed as the cause. He had a beer. That was all. It was very straightforward.'

'No inquest?'

'No.'

'May I say something, Ruth? You don't seem yourself.'

She glanced up at him. 'Don't I? Is that so strange? No one seems themselves today, or hadn't you noticed?'

'I may be speaking completely out of turn. Ignore me if so. I'd like to ask you something first. Did Tom . . . say anything to you? Tell you anything you didn't know? Shock you?'

She didn't answer for a moment and they walked on quietly. She longed to confide in someone but she didn't trust Jeremy. She was sure he had ulterior motives of some sort, though she couldn't guess at what they were. 'No,' she said at last. 'He didn't.'

'There's no reason, of course, why you should tell me if he did. Why should you wish to confide in me? I'm sure you think I'm a slippery character, that's why I'm going to tell you this now, all right? It might not be the most tasteful of times, what with it being Tom's funeral, but I can't help that.' He stopped walking and grabbed Ruth's hand, pulling her round to face him. 'Whatever you think of me, Tom was a million times worse. If you think I'm evasive or manipulative, Tom was the master. He was the true game player among us. He loved it, he was addicted to it. He thought he could push us about, like pieces on a chess board, making us win or lose as he desired. We were his puppets, made to dance whenever he wished it. And his destructive streak sometimes got the better of him.' He let go of Ruth's hand, turned back to the path, and started walking again, examining the stony ground as he went. 'I don't know what he said to you that night but I would caution you, beg you to beware. He thought he would be here to carry on pulling strings, altering outcomes. But he's not now. He's not here to stop whatever dangerous games he set in motion.'

'Why should I trust you?' blurted out Ruth. 'Why shouldn't *you* be the games master, trying to manipulate me, like a bluff within a bluff? And it's very convenient now, isn't it, now that Tom isn't here to defend himself or challenge you.'

'That's a perfectly reasonable point. But all I can say is that you've got it wrong. Surely it makes sense to you now I've said it? I'll leave it to you to think about.' They'd reached the back gate of Tom's family home. It squeaked on its hinges as Jeremy pulled it open. 'After you.'

Most of the mourners were already there for the wake and had spilled out of the house on to the lawn. Ruth threaded her way among them. The mood had lightened outside, and people were drinking wine and talking almost cheerily. In the house, it was a different matter. She found Ned with Tom's family and the rest of his closest friends in the drawing room. In the largest chair, Erin sat like a queen surrounded by courtiers, her feet up on a stool and a table at her side laden with untouched food and drink. She seemed tired and washed out and the weight of her full stomach, which she usually carried with such grace, pulled her down.

Ruth stayed only a moment, going to Ned and whispering to him that she would be outside, though he hardly heard her. She couldn't take the stifling atmosphere of grief another moment. Perhaps it wouldn't have been so bad if she shared it as intensely as the others did, but she couldn't. Right now she needed light, so she went back out into the spring sunshine and walked on to the lawn, wishing she could take her shoes and stockings off and squish the cool green grass between her toes.

It was strange to see this side of Tom's life, to be let into it now that he was gone. The whole thing was still unreal, but now this, the funeral, had made it immediate. The reality that Tom was dead was beginning to hit home. Gazing out at the muddy brown river and a family of ducks carried past on the current, Ruth allowed herself for a moment to think the things that she had tried to forbid herself from entertaining in her mind.

Tom is dead. The last thing he said to me was 'be careful'. He told me not to do anything rash. He said whatever happened, he could live with it. Are those the words of a man who is about to run himself into a tree deliberately? I can't believe he would do it. I can't believe that our conversation was strong enough to drive a man to suicide. He didn't know, he wasn't sure — about any of it. Not sure enough to die for it. No. I'm certain it was an accident.

She thought about what Jeremy had said, that Tom had been the worst of all of them. So it wasn't Jeremy, or Erin, but Tom who directed the action . . . did she believe him? Would Tom really have risked lying about something so important as the father of Erin's child, about Ned and Ruth's marriage? Could he really have done that?

Surely not, thought Ruth. She didn't want to think about Jeremy anyway. She didn't want to start deciding who she trusted and who she didn't. Instead, she was drawn back to her deepest fear, the thing that had been obsessing her.

Everything that had happened since she'd opened that cursed box and read those papers seemed to be building up a cast-iron case: the letters themselves, everything Tom had said, and the things that Ned could not bring himself to say. They all pointed to one thing: that Ned's passion for Erin was not extinguished and that since she, Ruth, had come along, Erin's own territorial nature had been provoked into wanting to reawaken its flames and fan it with promises of returning his love. That was the obvious consequence, surely. And perhaps he had given in to her. Perhaps they'd got carried away. Perhaps even to the extent that Erin's pregnancy was the result. The thought made her turn cold.

But as long as there was Tom, there was a natural brake on the whole thing. Now he was gone, the way was clear for them, wasn't it?

Almost since the moment she'd heard about Tom's death, Ruth now realised as she stood alone at the bottom of the garden, she'd been waiting for the axe to fall, waiting for Ned to tell her that now he and Erin would be together. It hadn't yet. But it was just a matter of time. She was certain of it.

17

A few months ago, Ruth thought, I considered Ned and myself a radiant example of a wonderful marriage. Now look at us.

The cottage, once full of talk and laughter, the home she had yearned for every time she was away from it, was a silent and strained place. Ned was a shadow of himself, a man who had closed down to the outside world entirely so that he could concentrate on his inner turmoil. Ruth wanted so desperately to help him, to give him the love she thought he needed, but not only was his back turned towards her in bed, she was also becoming increasingly convinced that he no longer needed her.

They were perfectly civil to each other, except when little things triggered sniping and irritation. This rarely blew up into a row but the constant biting at each other was tiring and depressing.

If that wasn't enough to cope with, there was now the added pressure of Ned's parents being in such close proximity. They'd moved in the week after Tom's funeral; Ruth and Ned had been at work on the actual moving day, and Jackie had refused to let them visit before she'd had a chance to get straight. They went down on the Saturday to see it.

'It's still a mess,' warned Jackie, as she let them in through the front door. 'I haven't had time to make it the way I like it.'

But to Ruth's eyes it was immaculate, the previous house recreated almost exactly in the placing of furniture and ornaments, with the same stiff, decorous formality. There was something almost Victorian about the amount of silk and hangings and tassels, and the clusters of objects arranged on every surface that sat strangely with the modernity of the house: its low ceilings, UPVC windows and spotlights.

'Do you like it, Steven?' Ruth asked, as they sat in the lounge, going through the usual routine with the metal tea tray on legs. She always made an effort to include him, or he would not open his mouth from saying hello to taking his leave.

'Oh, aye. I can't pretend I don't miss the old place, though.'

'The people,' put in Jackie. 'The people are very snotty here. The old woman next door gave me a look like you wouldn't believe. But that's southerners for you. We'll see if they lighten up at all.'

'And the garden?' asked Ruth. 'Does it have any potential?'

Steven said, 'I'm looking forward to getting started on it, though there won't be time to do much this late — '

'He's got big plans,' said Jackie. 'A gazebo. A rockery. A place for us to have drinks in the evening when it's warm. A vegetable garden at the back.'

She won't let him say anything for himself, thought Ruth. *She won't even allow him a conversation.* She'd begun to think about the way Jackie treated her husband, and to wonder if this was why Ned was so reticent in his mother's presence; why bother speaking if your thoughts were always hijacked? She watched now as Jackie turned to Ned and whispered, 'How are you, son?' A mournful expression came over her face. 'Are you still feeling bad about poor Tom?'

'I'm all right,' Ned said shortly. His foot started jiggling. *He's cross,* thought Ruth.

'I'm still in pieces,' declared Jackie softly. 'I'm ripped up about it. He was so young! And with a baby on the way. It's tragic. I couldn't sleep last night, could I, Steven? I cry whenever I think about it.'

That's her other trick. No matter how bad things are for you, they're worse for her.

'Now, Edward, you've got to promise me you'll take care in that car of yours. I don't want it happening to me. Losing a son. I've got no one to take your place, have I?'

Typical. It's all about her.

'It's Erin I feel sorry for,' Jackie continued. 'When is the baby due?'

'Next month.'

'Oh! That poor girl. I'm going to go round to see her as soon as I can.'

I bet you are, thought Ruth. *Get the inside story under the guise of your sickly sympathy.*

'She's away,' said Ned. Ruth tried not to show her surprise. Neither of them had mentioned Erin's name since the funeral. It hung between them, unspoken, but both painfully aware of it. Ruth's anger and hatred towards her had

357

become fear. When would she swoop in and take Ned away? 'She's gone home to her family for a while. She might even have the baby there.'

'That would be best,' said Jackie, nodding, and holding her tea cup with exaggerated delicacy as though the subject demanded extra formality. 'Stay among loved ones. After all, what's she got around here now? An empty house.' She leaned towards her son. 'But she's got you, love, hasn't she? You'll stand by her, won't you? I saw how you were towards her at the funeral, always looking out to make sure she was all right. You're the best friend she could ask for.' She smiled at Ned, cocking her head on one side in the way she had to express her caring side.

They walked all over the house, obediently admiring it. When they left, Jackie said, 'I'll be up later, I expect. All right?'

'Yes, see you later,' said Ned, and Ruth trailed along behind him as they walked down the drive.

'I didn't know Erin had gone,' she ventured, increasing her pace so that she could trot alongside him.

'Well, she has. She might be back, I don't know.' Ned thrust his hands in his pockets and pushed his chin downwards in the neck of his jumper, as if to signify that he wouldn't be speaking any longer.

Ruth wanted to ask him what he thought about his mother's new house, and her arrival in the village. She wanted them to talk about it, laugh about it, unite in the face of all the irritation and the biting-of-tongues that was no doubt to come. But this wall was between them, an obstacle she was beginning to wonder if they would ever overcome.

★ ★ ★

Ruth could speak to no one about how she could feel her marriage disintegrating around her. It was humiliating: married six months and somehow she had managed to ruin it. Ned remained taciturn — polite, but speaking only when strictly necessary. He went out for long walks and when she offered to come with him, he said gruffly that he'd rather be on his own. She suspected that he took his mobile with him to make calls to Erin with no fear of being overheard.

It was ironic, she thought, that she was seeing Jackie almost more than she was seeing Ned. Jackie had got into the habit of strolling up in the evenings to visit. Ruth was growing to dread the journey home from work in case she saw her mother-in-law, as she often did, waiting on the doorstep. She would come in and start bustling about immediately, tidying up and doing some of the housework as Ruth struggled to be constantly polite and interested in her babble.

It ought to be helpful, she thought, as she saw that Jackie had been upstairs and emptied the laundry basket of clothes, and was coming down with an armful of dirty washing, but it wasn't. It drove her mad. It was annoying like nothing she had ever known. And what was worse — she clenched her teeth as Jackie went to the washing machine, opened the door and began putting the clothes in — Jackie had carefully separated Ned's clothes from Ruth's and was only putting her son's in to wash.

'Ladies like to do their own washing, don't they?' said Jackie as her only explanation. Then, with Ned's underpants circling in the froth, she would set about ironing his shirts, or pairing his socks, tidying away his things and asking Ruth if she should start getting Ned's dinner ready. When Ned arrived home, she would be joyously animated, chatting away to him non-stop although Ned only grunted in return. When she finally left, usually around ten o'clock, the silence was so welcome that there was little for Ned and Ruth to do but talk desultorily as they washed up and went up to bed. They were both, thought Ruth, at Jackie's mercy, somehow, and she couldn't summon the strength to fight her.

She came downstairs one evening, having disappeared up there not long after Ruth let her in. Ruth, tired and depressed that Jackie was round yet again, had gone to make tea in the kitchen, and was flicking through the paper when Jackie got back down.

'I've just scrubbed your lavatory,' she announced triumphantly. 'If you don't mind me saying, Ruth, it was in a state. I know I have high standards, but really — you'll be getting Ned some kind of infection if you're not careful. A virus or something. It can happen.'

Ruth's mental conversations with Jackie were her only retaliation, and while she said, 'Thanks, Mum, but you really shouldn't have, there's no need', she was thinking *you stupid old bag,* whoever heard of that? I'm a nurse for God's sake, I know about hygiene. That loo was fine.

'I brought my own bleach.' Jackie plonked a big yellow bottle on the counter. 'Yours won't do the job.'

'Mine is biodegradable.' And I bet you just poured enough bleach down there to kill off most of the marine life between here and the North Sea, you idiot.

'Bio-useless,' said Jackie and laughed. 'I like things clean,' she said with satisfaction. 'And no one's ever had sickness in their lives in my house.' Jackie went into the sitting room to start rearranging Ned's magazines and books.

'This cat,' she called to Ruth, who came in with her tea. She eyed Maisie distrustfully. 'Does it ever move?'

Maisie was curled into a tabby cushion, her head tucked under her paws, asleep on the sofa.

'She's old, so she sleeps most of the time,' said Ruth.

'I don't like animals. They carry dirt and germs and fleas. I wouldn't have one in my house.'

Oh God, don't dunk her in bleach, will you? 'Maisie's all right. She hardly goes outside any more.'

'And look at the hair!' Jackie shuddered. 'The sofa's covered in it. If Erin brings that baby round, you'll have to lock that cat in a bedroom. Cats kill babies. It's well known. They like to sleep on their faces.'

You'll believe anything, won't you? You really are a fool. Ruth hid her irritation as best she

361

could. 'I think any baby would be able to best Maisie, and she'd sooner sleep on a cushion. Less wriggling.'

Jackie sat herself down on the sofa, at the far end from Maisie and said, 'Is there any news from Erin? Is the baby here?'

'No, still not here.' Ruth wished Ned would come home so that they could at least share the burden of talking to his mother.

'Oh, Erin. I love that girl. She's like a daughter to me.' Jackie sighed. 'I've adored her since Ned first introduced her to me. I won't lie to you, Ruth.' She sent a sideways glance in Ruth's direction, and her voice dropped to that sinister whisper. 'You don't mind me saying, do you? Only I always secretly hoped that she and Ned would marry. Of course, when she started courting with Tom, I realised it was unlikely.' There was that sickly false smile. 'And then *you* came along. People've said to me what a quick wedding you had. A few have said 'marry in haste, repent at leisure'. I've always told them that my Ned knows his mind and what's good enough for him is good enough for me. If he's chosen you, well, I'll stand by his choice no matter how I feel about it, and whether or not his father and I think he could be ruining his life.'

Ruth smiled back stiffly. She had no idea how to react to this kind of thinly veiled insult, especially when it was delivered in such a tender manner.

'The sad thing is,' Jackie said, in sweeter tones than ever, 'if he'd only waited a few months, he could have had her after all, couldn't he? And with a little baby too. I think they would have been a very nice little family. It's almost a shame, isn't it? But what's done is done. And I'm sure you'll have a baby in time, and that will make up for it.'

Ruth sat in astonished silence, feeling like cold water had been thrown over her. Jackie was speaking out loud her own most private thoughts: and if it was so clear to Jackie, perhaps it was clear to everyone. Perhaps all of them were saying to each other, 'such a pity he got married so quickly! If he hadn't, it could all have worked out very nicely. But now there's Ruth . . .'

Those people didn't even know that the baby might be Ned's anyway. All the more reason for them to be together.

I'm a burden, she thought. *I'm in the way. They'd all be very happy if it weren't for me.*

Self-pity fell on her like a heavy, dark blanket. She had a sudden clear vision of Ned and Erin, cooing over a perfect baby, Jackie in the background beaming with joy. The other friends — Luke and Abigail, Jeremy — came in and congratulated them and said how, in the circumstances, it was the best thing that could have happened. Tom's family arrived and said how, if it had to be anyone, they were delighted it was Ned who'd be bringing up Tom's child. His oldest friend. His best friend.

There was no place for Ruth in the picture. *Oh God, what a mess,* she thought miserably. *What an awful bloody mess.*

'Now, what's my boy having for his dinner?'

asked Jackie brightly. 'Would you like me to make a start? He'll be back soon, won't he?'

★ ★ ★

When Jackie left that evening, Ruth went upstairs, leaving Ned on the sofa watching television, with Maisie curled on his lap. She went up the stairs slowly and heavily, trying to recall the good times. She remembered when she'd first moved in, exclaiming and laughing over all of Ned's mess; the giant heap of clothes in the corner of the bedroom, the stack of empty mugs by the bed, and the collection of old sports sections underneath it. She remembered how, when they'd released Maisie from her travelling cage, the cat had had a burst of youthful energy and whisked upstairs before they could catch her. They'd spent hours trying to find her, and it was Ned who got up in the night when he thought he'd heard her; Ruth found him, naked to the waist, lying on the floor, trying to tempt the cat out from behind the bookshelf with butter and a tin of tuna.

She recalled their urgent lovemaking, the way they'd christened every room in the house, though the kitchen had been the least enjoyable because she'd seen all the old food under the stove from her vantage point and hadn't been able to stop thinking about it, in between worrying whether the neighbours could see in the window from their garden.

It had been weeks since they'd touched each other, aside from a few swift pecks on the lips.

She remembered leaving here the night before her wedding, with the dress in its cover, so excited she could barely think. In her washbag, she'd found a note from Ned, placed there so she would find it last thing before she went to bed. In it he said how happy she had made him, how much he was looking forward to their life together. He said many sweet and tender things that brought such sadness to her now, she stopped herself thinking about it with an act of iron will.

In the bedroom, she looked about for a while, then took her travel bag from under the bed and started to put some clothes in it. When it was packed, and she'd collected her wash things and some books, she carried it downstairs and put it in the hall. Then she took her car keys from the rack and went in to the sitting room.

'Ned,' she began in a soft voice. He looked up at her briefly and then back at the television. 'Ned,' she said again, a little more loudly. 'I've been thinking.'

He looked up at her again and something in her face made him pay attention. Turning the television off with the remote control, he said, 'Thinking about what?'

He looks so different now, she thought. It was hard to imagine the old Ned, with his sparkling eyes and warm smile and the strength of his body against hers. Now he seemed older, and had lost weight. His mouth seemed to be permanently set in a grim line. It was a long time since she'd heard him laugh.

She sat down opposite him, hunched over her

knees with her hands clutched together, and talked very fast. 'Ned, I think I'm going to go home for a while. To stay there. We've not talked about it but there's no point in pretending that things haven't been bad between us. I know I'm to blame in a lot of ways. Things haven't been the same since the night Tom . . . had his accident. I should never have done what I did, but in a way I can't regret it because it has made things clearer.

'Oh God, I don't know what I'm trying to say really, except that I don't know how much longer we can go on like this, just existing in the same house, not talking, with nothing really between us. I know you're still in a bad way because of Tom and I've tried to help you but there doesn't seem to be anything I can do. Instead, we have your mother here almost every night, we never talk, we never have sex, and it's just not working, is it? I'm not making you better and you're not able to talk to me. I think . . . I can't see how things can get any better unless we have some time apart. I don't think I can stay here the way things are. Maybe it would help if we had a breather.

'I'm only going home, I won't be far. You can reach me if you need me. But . . . I think it's for the best.'

She stared at the floor and waited. It was only now that she realised how much she wanted Ned to tell her not to be so stupid, and not to go. That he loved her and couldn't bear it if she went. *Please say something*, she begged silently.

When she looked up, Ned's head was bowed.

He looked defeated. *Is he crying?* she wondered, and had the urge to jump up, go to him and throw her arms around him. Instead, she clasped her hands more tightly and dug her elbows into her thighs.

Finally, he looked up. 'Is this what you want?'

'I think it might be for the best.'

There was a long pause. They stared at each other, trying to read in the other's face what it was that they really thought. But they saw only their own desperation mirrored back at them.

'I won't stand in the way of whatever you want to do,' he said in a low voice.

'Then . . . ' She waited a moment to give him the opportunity to change his mind and to break in and stop her. More than anything she did not want to walk out the door. She could see that by packing her bag, and holding her car keys, she'd taken a gamble. She wanted him to leap up, grab the keys, throw them down and shout, 'No! You're not to go!' And if he didn't, then she'd know for sure that it would be best for all of them — Ned, Erin, the baby, Jackie, all of them — if she went on her way. 'Will you look after Maisie for me?' she asked. 'I don't want to confuse her by taking her home again.'

'Of course I will,' Ned said, and put his hands over his face.

'What is it?' she whispered. It would take only a tiny thing to let her back down and tell him she didn't mean it, and that she'd stay.

For a long moment he kept his face covered. Then he put his hands down, and said, 'If this is what you want, I won't stand in your way. Maybe you're right. It could be for the best. I haven't been easy to live with. I know that. It will probably do you good to go home.'

Ruth stood up slowly. 'I'll go then.'

'Will you call me soon?'

'Of course.' She picked up a shawl, although the night was warm, and went to the door. 'Good night, then.'

He stood up and came to the door with her, standing so close it was hard to resist the temptation to touch him. Leaning over, he kissed her cheek softly. 'Take care, Ruthy. Won't you?'

'Yes,' she said, misery settling on her. 'You too. Good bye.' And she walked to the car with her bag.

* * *

'Ruth, what are you doing here?' asked her father, surprised, when she walked in at the back door. He was stirring a foul-smelling mixture at the stove. 'Here, do you know if one should add salt and pepper to nettle soup?'

'I don't know, I'm afraid,' said Ruth.

'What are you doing here?' asked Silas again, this time putting down his wooden spoon and giving her his full attention. 'You look awful. Is everything all right?' He opened his arms to her for a hug. 'Come here, little girl.'

She went to him and started to cry as he rocked her slightly.

'There, there. It's all right,' he soothed. 'You're going to be all right.'

18

To Ruth's surprise, her father was not very sympathetic. When she explained that she'd come to stay for a while, he was genuinely shocked.

'What about Ned?' he asked. 'Is he coming?'

Ruth had thought in the back of her mind that her father would be delighted by her coming home. After all, wasn't he always trying to get her and Cordy back on their own, so they could relive the old times? Didn't he always want her to be a little girl again? Well, here she was, ready to be treated like a little girl again, comforted and cherished like she used to be. She'd always been at the centre of Silas's world and that's what she wanted now: to feel important to someone.

'Ned and I think we need to have some time apart,' she explained. After she'd calmed down, they'd gone into the study and Silas had poured out some of his treasured thirty-year-old Laphroaig. They sat now, in the battered leather armchairs, sipping the smoky malt.

Silas frowned. 'Time apart?' he echoed. 'What on earth are you talking about? You've only been married five minutes. Why have you come home?'

'Things haven't been very good lately,' began Ruth hesitantly.

'Good? Good? What's good?' Silas looked

quite angry. 'What do you mean? Has he stopped laying a chocolate on your pillow every night or something?'

'Well — you know that Ned's friend Tom died, and his girlfriend Erin is going to have a baby . . . ' she couldn't quite bring herself to add 'that Tom and I thought might be Ned's' ' . . . and Ned's parents have moved to be close to us — '

'Excuse me, but what's that got to do with the price of fish?' demanded Silas. 'I'm sure it's very sad that Ned's friend died, but it doesn't explain why you need to move out.'

'Dad, you don't understand — '

'You're right, I don't. I'm sorry, Ruth. I thought you had more sticking power than this. I didn't expect you to jump ship at the first sign of trouble.'

'It's more complicated than that,' Ruth said, defensive.

'I should hope so, otherwise this is a very poor show indeed. What are these other complications?'

'I don't want to talk about it at the moment.' Ruth felt tears stinging her eyes, and willed them back. 'You wouldn't understand.'

'Perhaps I would, perhaps I wouldn't. One thing I do understand, though, is that you shouldn't be rushing back here anytime you're feeling out of sorts. I'm not going to turn you away, you know that. But I don't want you thinking this is your home, because it isn't. When I walked you down the aisle, this stopped being your home. Of course, in a manner of speaking, it will always be that — but your proper home, your permanent home is now with Ned. You'd better bear that in mind.'

Ruth stared into her glass and said nothing, but she was thinking, *what if Ned doesn't want me? What then?*

* * *

It was strange driving to work the old way. She kept the windows open so that the stiff breeze came in and chilled her cheeks. It was a hot morning. It seemed that summer had decided to arrive after this baggy, damp spring they'd been having. The day gave the first intimation of long hours of daylight and the warming of the air.

My summer clothes are at home, she thought. Then felt confused because she meant the cottage, not the Old Rectory. I'll get something new in town today.

Ned called at lunchtime, when she was at her desk updating the computer system from the notes of the patients she'd seen that morning. He was friendly: 'How are you? Did you get home all right?' But there was nothing of importance to say, it seemed.

'I haven't told Mum yet. That you've gone home,' he said just before they said goodbye. 'I'm going to wait. Spin it out for as long as I can.'

'Okay,' said Ruth, thinking how pleased Jackie would be. She waited for him to ask her when she'd be back. She wanted to tell him what Silas had said to her. But instead they finished their

371

brief conversation and put the phone down. Does Ned feel this bad? wondered Ruth, as she closed her eyes against how awful being apart from him made her feel. Can he? I suppose he can't, or he would say something.

She and Silas resolutely avoided talk about the state of her marriage, and instead had a happy time nosing round the cellar where he explained his plans to turn it into a music and games room.

'You know how I like to listen to my old rock 'n' roll records. Down here, I won't disturb anyone.' As though there was anyone upstairs to care whether he played his Rolling Stones at top volume or not.

At the weekend, Cordy arrived — at the instigation, Ruth had no doubt, of Silas. Cordy suggested a walk around the village in the afternoon, so they ambled up the main road. Cordy carefully steered her in the opposite direction to the church, where an early summer wedding was taking place, and instead they browsed in the bookshop and bought liquorice and pear drops at the post office stores, and ended up on the village green, where they sat on swings and went idly back and forth while they ate their sweets.

'Dad tells me you've decided to take a break from married life,' said Cordy at last. Ruth had been wondering when she would broach the subject.

Ruth nodded. 'It's a difficult situation at the moment.'

'Want to talk about it?'

Ruth realised that she was desperate to talk about it, and that Cordy was the best person she could possibly ask for: she wouldn't judge in the way others would. She wouldn't see anything wrong in what Ruth had done, so she told it all, including finding Ned's diaries and reading them.

'So, let me see if I've got this right,' said Cordy, her cheek bulging round a pear drop. 'You've discovered that years ago, Ned was in love with this Erin. You're convinced they've been carrying on behind your back, and Tom's back. And you both thought this baby that Erin's going to have might be Tom's. I mean, Ned's. God, they all sound the same, don't they? That's rough. That really is. Did you face Ned down about it?'

'I asked him if he loved me more than her.'

'But you didn't come out and say, 'Have you been having an affair? Tom says the baby might be yours'?'

'No.'

'So what did he say when you asked if he loved her et cetera . . . ?'

'He wouldn't really answer. He said he'd married me and that was the answer.'

Cordelia whistled as well as she could round the pear drop. 'Tricky. That sounds like a dodge, doesn't it? Why couldn't he say 'I love you more and I don't love her anymore'?'

'Exactly.' Ruth tried to remember precisely what they'd said but couldn't get the exact words. 'He asked me to trust him. But it's hard — he lied to me once. He told me he'd never loved Erin, but he had.'

'So did you ask him why he lied?'

'He said it was to avoid all this — that he'd known I'd react this way.'

'Well, that sounds plausible enough to me. But I can see that it would damage your trust in him. When did he tell you the lie?'

'When we first met Erin — I asked him about her. We'd only just got engaged.'

'I can understand that wasn't the best time for him to start telling you about how he'd once been crazy about her. Poor old Ned. Must have been one of those spur-of-the-moment decisions to lie. But if it's damaged your trust in him . . . '

'I don't know if it has! I think . . . you know, I would have trusted him if he'd said he loved me better than he'd loved Erin. And if Tom hadn't said that about the baby. And if Ned had tried to stop me when I left.'

'So you keep setting little tests for him, and he keeps failing.'

The words stung. She flushed. 'Well, I don't know if I would say that. Anyway, I'll know the truth,' Ruth said simply. 'I'll know that if he doesn't ask me to come back, and if he goes to Erin, that I was right all along, and that he made a terrible mistake marrying me and wants to divorce me.' She felt sick at the thought. She'd never said the word 'divorce' before, or even thought it. Now it had dropped like a stone from her mouth. She stopped her swing moving, hoping that would quell the nausea rising in her stomach.

'If that's the way you want to do things,'

replied Cordelia diplomatically. 'I know I bang on about the evils of marriage and all its attendant ills, but I really believe you and Ned are a good thing. It would a terrible waste if you two split up, and I'm not convinced about this affair theory you've got. I can see how you've got all het up about it but you know what? It doesn't ring true to me. None of it.'

'But Ned's papers, his diaries . . . '

'Do you remember who I loved when I was eighteen? John Powell! Remember? I adored him! His hands virtually skimmed the pavement when he walked, he was so Neanderthal.'

They both laughed.

Ruth said, 'He could hardly string two words together — such an idiot.'

'Yes,' said Cordy, 'but I thought he was wonderful. I'd run a mile before I spent a minute with him now.'

Ruth was reluctant to accept that the two situations were at all similar. 'It's different. Ned's loved Erin for ages.'

'Says who?'

'Jeremy. Tom.'

'And those two are oracles of truth, are they? You trust them over Ned, do you?'

Ruth thought about it, recalling what they'd said to her at various times. They'd always sounded so plausible. 'But why would they lie?'

'Why not? They've always seemed like a queer lot to me, to be honest. There's something about that group that's not entirely healthy.' Cordy swung back and forth on her swing for a while. 'How is the evil Ma Haskell?'

Ruth was glad they'd changed the subject, so that she didn't have to think about the doubts that Cordy had set swirling round her mind. 'Awful. As bad as I could have expected.' Ruth told her a few of the more choice stories of what Jackie did — 'she even washes up only Ned's dishes, and leaves mine for me' — and recounted how Jackie had admitted she'd wished all along Ned had married Erin.

'Wicked old witch,' cried Cordy, outraged. 'How dare she? You mustn't listen to her, Ruth. You really mustn't. She's trying to poison your mind. She's the last person you should let influence you.'

'It's hard. Perhaps she's only saying what everybody thinks.'

'I mean it, Ruth.' Cordy flushed with anger. 'It's bad enough she thinks it's all right to turn up at your house virtually every night, poking her nose in and acting as though Ned's still her property. Don't give in to her. You won't, will you?'

'I'll do my best but she's not easy,' said Ruth, surprised at Cordy's vehemence.

'I said earlier you should try some plain speaking, and I'm going to do a bit of my own, so don't be hurt, all right? Ever since Mummy died, you've been desperately trying to find love and approval from anyone who'll give it to you. Don't interrupt me, let me finish,' she said quickly, seeing Ruth's expression. 'It's completely understandable, but it's made you vulnerable to people who want to use you and manipulate you and hurt you. It's made you gullible and credulous. That woman is very clever and very destructive. She's not happy and she can't see why anyone else should be, least of all you. She's obviously got terrible problems — drinking too much is probably the least of it. It was her who called that night I was there, wasn't it?'

'I think so,' replied Ruth unhappily.

Cordy nodded. 'I think she's the kind of person who'll stop at nothing to get her way and you mustn't let her do it. You mustn't. Do you understand?'

'What am I supposed to do?'

'Fight her,' said Cordy determinedly. 'Take her on. But don't do it alone; she knows all your weaknesses. You and Ned will need to do it together.'

'I'm not strong like you, Cordy,' said Ruth. Exhaustion engulfed her. 'I don't think I can do it. And the way Ned and I are at the moment . . . '

'Of course you can. You know you can.' Cordy grinned at her. 'You're stronger than you think.'

★   ★   ★

On Sunday morning, lying in her childhood bed and staring at the pattern of twisting roses on the wallpaper that she knew so well, she woke up to the familiar sounds of the bells announcing the morning service.

When she got up, the house was deserted. Cordy had gone to the hospital and Silas was out for his Sunday run, when he loped out down the lane for a couple of miles, and back. 'Keeps me young,' he would say, when he got back red-faced and puffed out.

Ruth moped about, making herself coffee and wondering what Ned was doing. When the phone rang, she scooped it up, hoping that it would be him. Perhaps he was also thinking of her, and they had produced a synchronicity between them.

'Hello?'

'I hope you're satisfied!' came a bellow down the phone.

Ruth began to tremble and her mouth was dry. She had been hoping that this confrontation would not come. She remembered Cordy's words. *I must stand up to her*, she thought. 'Hello, Mum — ' she began.

'Don't you bloody dare call me Mum! You traitorous bitch!' The growl at the end of the word reminded her of the anonymous phone call. Somehow she'd known all along that it was Jackie, angry at being crossed. Now, here she was again but this time she had words pouring out of her. 'You've got no right. When I think of what you've done to my son, my boy! He's in pieces! You've wrecked his life, walking out on him for no reason when his best friend's just died. I told him all along you were no good. I told him he'd made a mistake, going with a stuck-up little cow like you. Right from the start, I've seen it and don't think I haven't. Looking down your nose at us! Because we're not educated like you are! I've given you everything, every chance. I welcomed you like you were my own daughter. I gave up my own home to be near you, and near your family, to help you. And this is the thanks we get!' Jackie was nearly screaming. Then her voice dropped low again. 'Listen to me. He's *glad* you're gone. He knows it's for the best. He told me. He never wants to see you again, understand? You're just like all the rest, wanting to break up our family. Well, you won't succeed, do you hear me? We never want to see you again!' The phone slammed down.

Ruth stood shaking for a while. A mechanical voice down the handset began requesting that she hang up. After a few minutes, she shook herself and put down the phone.

* * *

Somehow she got through lunch with her father. He saw that something was wrong but didn't press it. When she said she was going out for a walk, he didn't try to stop her, or suggest joining her. It was a sunny day, so she dressed lightly in jeans and a tee-shirt and some turquoise flip-flops that always cheered her up, and wandered out in to the road.

She turned towards the church and the outskirts of the village. Walking past the new rectory, she saw a sleek black Jaguar parked in front of it, and guessed that the rich man who owned it was staying for one of his weekends. He was hardly ever there these days. Perhaps one day he'd sell it again. It would probably be made into luxury flats. The graceful façade of the house seemed to promise a better life within,

379

unmarred by trouble, need or quarrels. As a child, Ruth had fantasised about being allowed inside, perhaps meeting a boy there who would turn out to be the owner's son, and they would fall in love — perhaps he would save her from a falling tree or a fire — and live there happily ever after, raising children. Fourteen or fifteen, she could never decide how many exactly she wanted. As it was, the owner didn't appear to have a son and Ruth had never met him, let alone been inside.

She went past slowly and skirted round the churchyard. Stopping at the lych-gate, she saw the scattering of rose-petal confetti, the remains of yesterday's wedding, trod into the gravel by the Sunday morning congregation. On impulse she walked up the path towards the heavy iron-hinged and studded oak door of the church, which was closed. The morning service was over. There would be no activity now until Evensong.

Inside there was an atmosphere of fusty quiet, with a sense of the organ only recently having been quieted. She walked in, her flip-flops clacking against her heels. The last time she'd been here, she'd been in that dress, wearing those silver-heeled slippers, surrounded by her family and friends — exchanging her marriage vows. She looked down at her wedding ring, sitting tightly below her engagement ring. So far it had never occurred to her to take it off. Perhaps she should. Was her marriage really over?

According to Jackie Haskell, it was.

But Cordy had made her promise not to listen

to her . . . It was so hard, though! The words kept echoing in her mind, fulfilling her worst fears so completely it was hard not to accept them.

She slid into a pew and sat down on the hard wooden seat, looking up towards the altar.

I won't call Ned again, she decided. I'll let him come to me. If Jackie's right, he won't call me. And if she's wrong, he will. But if she's telling the truth and he really doesn't want to see me again . . . well, I can't ring. It would be too awful.

The idea of Ned telling her those things himself made her cold all over.

'Ruth?' The voice echoed through the empty church. 'Ruth, is that you?'

She jumped and turned to where the voice seemed to be coming from but the acoustics were deceptive and she was surprised to see the vicar emerging from near the organ loft, clutching an enormous hymn book. She got up, feeling this was the polite thing to do when a vicar entered the room. Even though she'd known him for as long as she could remember, she couldn't help feeling shy and formal in his presence. 'Yes, hello.'

He came towards her with a welcoming smile. 'How are you, my dear? Are you visiting us?'

'Well, not exactly — '

'And how is married life? I remember that beautiful day, one of the loveliest weddings I've done. The choir said the same.' He reached her, took her hands and kissed her cheek.

She wanted to lie, and say, 'Oh vicar, it's all

fabulous, I'm ecstatic!' but she couldn't, and her silence said more than she wanted to.

'My dear child,' he said, looking more closely at her, concerned. 'Are you all right?'

What *is* it about vicars? she thought, as she sat sobbing in the church pew, the vicar next to her, his kindly air making her cry even harder. Perhaps not all vicars shared this quality, but this one made her want to tell him her life story, so that he could give her answers and explain everything to her: that it had a pattern and a meaning and, most important of all, a happy ending.

'I think it's all over. I've spoiled it. Ned doesn't want to be married to me anymore.'

'That's terrible. Are you sure? Tell me what has happened.'

She explained everything that happened. The words came easily since she had described almost the same events to Cordy the day before. The vicar listened carefully and then said, 'His mother has told you that he no longer wants to see you?'

'Because I've left him in his hour of need.'

'Well, there is something in that.'

'Really?' Ruth felt her worst fears confirmed. 'You mean Ned's mother is right?'

'The first thing is, you need to stop running round in circles after yourself. There is an answer for you — it's right there, if you can only stand back for a moment. Everything you've told me is based on assumption and supposition, and very little on fact. Now, Ruth, I'm going to talk to you plainly. It may sound harsh though I don't mean it to be. I only want to help, and I think you're in here for a reason. I think you came looking for help, and I want to give it to you. So here it is.

'You must stop putting yourself at the centre of everything. This doesn't all revolve around you — there are other people and their lives and private connections involved. The second thing is, that you must think about what you've undertaken. You are married. Remember our classes, what I told you about what you were doing? You've made a commitment that doesn't allow you to run away when you don't like what's happening, or withdraw your love because you don't feel you're getting your fair share back. It would be different if something serious were happening — if Ned were abusing you — but he isn't doing that, is he? What has he done?'

'Well . . . ' Ruth faltered. Now she was on the spot, she could bring almost nothing to mind. Everything that had been so important, obsessed her over the last few months, seemed to melt away.

'You found out a part of his past which he has told you is over and done. You must trust him, unless his behaviour shows you otherwise.'

'But that's the thing,' burst out Ruth. 'He may have been having an affair with the woman he loved all along.'

'Yes, I agree, that's bad. But you've only told me what you think, not what you know. If he is unfaithful, then that of course puts a different light on things. But are you sure?'

'No. I'm not sure.'

'That is what I'm trying to tell you, my dear.

You must establish the facts. Have you asked him directly about this other woman?'

'No.'

'Then that is the first thing you must do.'

'But his mother says he doesn't want to see me any more.'

'His mother? That's ridiculous, if I may say so. Married couples do not communicate through their mothers, fathers, aunts or whoever. They talk to each other. Without that, it's all hopeless.' He put a hand on her arm. 'Ruth, I've been married thirty-two years, and I'm not talking from some fluffy, sentimental point of view, but from the knowledge that this takes hard work, and effort. But to approach it at all, you have to be clear-eyed. It seems to me that you are making yourself the victim of your own delusions. You have an idea of what may have happened, or be happening, and you are basing everything you think and do on that. In the meantime, you are taking no action at all, except to run away from a difficult and painful situation.'

Ruth started to cry again. Why was everyone acting as though this was all her fault? It was unfair.

'Listen to me,' said the vicar, his voice serious. 'You've been tested. But it's not too late. There is still time to repair the damage, but the only thing is to remember what love is — the deep, giving and forgiving love you promised Ned just a few weeks ago right here in this very place. You have a duty, not a choice, but a duty to do your best to make this right. You know that, really, don't you? And you wouldn't really expect me to say anything else, would you?

'If what you are assuming is true, and Ned has been carrying on with someone else, then you must make sure you are absolutely certain. Until then, you owe him more than this, Ruth, don't you?'

★ ★ ★

It was like jumping and expecting a soft landing, only to find you'd landed in brambles, Ruth reflected. She'd come home to be comforted and everyone said the same thing: that she had to go back and sort things out. In a way, it was a relief. She felt calmer now, after her little pep talk from the vicar. There was a new resolve forming in her mind. Tonight she would ring Ned, perhaps even go and visit him, and they would sit down together and talk this whole thing through and start again, if that was what they both wanted. She hoped so much that it was. Facing life alone, without him, seemed like the bleakest thing she could imagine, and suddenly, she felt foolish for ever having left him at all, for opening the door to the possibility that their marriage could be over.

I'll put it right, she vowed. I'm sure I can.

★ ★ ★

For the rest of the afternoon, she watched the clock moving slowly round towards evening. She would ring him at nine o'clock, she'd decided.

That seemed like the time to call. In the meantime, she was more cheerful and her father was noticeably relieved to see her smile a little and generally behave a bit more like her old self.

At seven thirty, she heard her mobile ringing from the depths of her handbag, and scrabbled to find it before it cut off.

'Hello?'

'Ruth?' A small, frightened, breathless voice.

'Yes.'

'It's Erin.'

She was startled. She hadn't recognised the voice at all, and had picked up the phone too quickly to register the number. 'Oh. Hi. How are you?'

'I'm at home. I came back this morning to do some clearing out. The thing is, I'm having some contractions, and I know you're not a maternity nurse or anything but you're the only one I can think of to ask. The surgery's closed.'

'When are you due?' asked Ruth, thinking fast.

'Not for two weeks yet. They came on a while ago, but I wasn't too concerned. I thought that they might be Braxton Hicks, and would just wear off. Everyone tells me that first babies are late, so I'm not expecting it to come, and the contractions are quite far apart — twenty minutes sometimes. It's just . . . they're getting stronger and . . . ' On cue, Erin stopped talking and made a gritting, growling sound that grew fainter as she took the phone away from her face. Ruth could hear her groaning, and then she came back on the line again, breathless with the exertion. 'See, that was twenty minutes since the

386

last one. The hospital said not to phone or go in unless my waters had broken, or the contractions were five minutes apart, and neither of those things has happened so . . . ' Erin began to sound panicked. 'I just don't know what to do! You're the only person I could think of to call. I'm so glad you're on your mobile. When there was no answer at the house, I was frightened you were away. You're not, are you?'

'No, I'm at my father's. Are you on your own?'

'Yes.'

'It sounds pretty much like you're in labour to me, but if the contractions are so far apart, it could be ages before you need to go into hospital. Where are you booked in?'

'The Radcliffe.'

'Listen, I'm going to come straight over. That way I'll be there if you need me. And if they wear off, and are just Braxton Hicks after all, we'll be the none the worse. All right?'

'Thank you, Ruth.' Relief flooded Erin's voice. 'Thank you. If you're sure it's all right . . . '

'Don't be silly. Of course it is.'

The drive from the Old Rectory to Erin's house was just over thirty minutes. Time for Erin to fit in about two contractions. That wasn't so bad. As she drove through the soft evening light, the shadows of the hedges long across the road, she tried to remember what she could of what she'd been taught about labour and birth. It seemed very long ago, but from what she could remember there should be plenty of time. With a first baby, Erin could be in labour for days, if she were unlucky. The chances were that she had a good few hours to go, her waters would break, and they could head into the hospital with lots of time in hand. The baby possibly wouldn't make an appearance until late on Monday or even in the early hours of Tuesday. And that was assuming this was real labour — although Ruth knew very well that first babies could appear at any time, despite everyone assuming they would be late. And two weeks before the due date was quite normal: the chances were that the baby was ready to be born and that this wasn't a premature labour.

But poor Erin to be on her own at a time like this. Ruth subtly increased her speed. She didn't want to leave her on her own any longer than she had to. All her nursing instincts were to the fore, and she resolutely pushed all other thoughts out of her head. There would be plenty of time for that later.

19

Ruth made good time to the house. The roads were clear in a lazy, sunny Sunday evening kind of way, as though everyone had decided to take it easy and not cram themselves and their screaming families in the car to head out for some kind of entertainment.

Ruth pulled into the driveway and went to the front door. She rang a couple of times but there was no answer, so she went round to the back door, which was unlocked, and let herself in to the deserted kitchen.

'Erin?' she called. She frowned, looking about for signs of life, and walked into the hall, calling again. A faint sound came from above; she ran up to the upstairs landing. 'Erin, are you there?'

A moan came from one of the bedrooms. The door was ajar; Ruth pushed it open further and looked inside. She hadn't been in Tom and Erin's room before. It was dominated by a magnificent Thirties walnut bedhead with flowing curves and twisted carved columns on either side, the bed itself covered in a white lace counterpane. A period glass dressing table was nestled into the bow window, covered in cut glass scent bottles and a silver hairdressing set. It was a glamorous room, almost like a film set with its attention to fitting the furniture to the period of the house. Beside the enormous walnut wardrobe was a door open to the bathroom.

Ruth skirted the bed and saw a body on the black and white tiled bathroom floor.

'Erin,' she called, fearing the worst as she darted forward.

Erin lifted her head from the floor. She was lying on her side, her stomach vast in front of her, her maternity dress unbuttoned. Her face was a ghastly shade of white, tinged with grey and green and glistening with sweat, and her hair was damp. Her eyes were dull and dazed but they came to life when she saw Ruth.

'Thank God, you're here,' she said weakly. 'It's all gone a bit crazy. Oh God, here it comes again.' Her face contorted in agony and she pulled her knees up towards her belly, her fists clenching and cried out, even though she was trying to stifle it as best she could. It lasted, as far as Ruth could tell, about a minute. As it eased off, Erin's face cleared. 'Bloody hell. I think I'm going to be sick. This is like the worst hangover I've ever had.'

'These are not Braxton Hicks,' declared Ruth, kneeling beside her and holding her hand, which was clammy. 'How long has it been like this?'

'Um . . . I don't know really,' she gasped. 'I was timing them and then suddenly it all went a bit mad. Now I just don't know. I kept trying to time them but I couldn't read the clock anymore.'

'And have your waters broken?'

'No. But I went to the loo and there was blood.'

Blood, thought Ruth, panicked as well but trying to hide it. Is that normal? I think it's all

right and sometimes the waters don't break at all
. . . She racked her memory for what she'd
learned in college, and the cases she'd worked
with on the maternity ward years before.

Erin moaned again. 'Oh no . . . ' She
convulsed and shrieked as the pain took hold of
her, clenching her whole body so that she was
almost retching.

'That was about three minutes since the last
one.' Ruth spoke fast. 'I need to examine you,
Erin, to see how dilated you are.'

'Three minutes?' gasped Erin. 'It was eight last
time I timed them.'

'You've gone from eight minutes to three
minutes, just like that. Okay. It's happening quite
fast now, isn't it? Just hang in there, you're going
to be absolutely fine. Everything's proceeding
completely normally. I'm going to examine you
and I'll call an ambulance as well, because I
don't think we should go in the car when you're
like this. All right?'

'Yes, yes,' said Erin gratefully. 'I'm so glad
you're here.'

'Okay, now, try and kneel up for me. Rest on
the loo. When the next one comes, it might help
if you push down on the loo, okay? But don't
push down on your cervix — you don't feel like
you want to, do you?'

'No. I just feel absolutely awful. This is
horrible!' Erin's eyes were frightened. 'How long
is it going to be like this? They never said . . . no
one said it was going to hurt this much. Oh
Christ, not again!' She clutched Ruth's arm and
dug her fingers in while the pain gripped her.

Ruth was almost as pleased as Erin was when it passed, but she didn't say anything. She helped Erin to the loo, and then went to wash her hands. When she'd thoroughly scrubbed them, she went over and helped Erin raise her dress over her vast bump, and carried out the examination, testing with her fingertips the extent that the cervix had dilated.

Pretend you're in the surgery, she told herself. Come on, now, business as usual. 'All right. Erin, you're about six centimetres, so you're over halfway. Well done you. Clever girl. You're doing everything absolutely right. Keep riding the pain and breathing the way you learned in your class. Remember? Remember your yoga: deep breath in, pant out.' Erin obediently pulled in a breath and puffed it out in little streams between her pursed lips. 'Good, that's it. Now, the best thing would be to get to the hospital because we don't know how quickly you're dilating. You could reach ten centimetres quite soon, or you might take another few hours. So I'm going to call for an ambulance now to be on the safe side. All right?'

Erin just moaned as the pain began to take hold again, clenching her jaw and screaming through her closed teeth as her body shook with the contraction.

I'd better be prepared, thought Ruth, calm now as her nursing persona took over. Blankets. A waterproof sheet, if they've got one. Or I could tear open bin bags and put them over the bed. I can sterilise the scissors and a bowl, which would give me sterilised water too. While she was thinking this, she dialled on her mobile for an ambulance, calmly explained the situation and asked for it to come as soon as possible.

She stared at the phone for a moment, and then swiftly rang Ned, first at the cottage and then on the mobile. There was no reply from either. The ambulance will be here soon, she thought. We'll be fine on our own. There's not much he could do anyway.

Now that Ruth was here, Erin had surrendered all responsibility for the situation and was concentrating only on what was happening to her body. Her mind had focused itself inside, shutting out everything but the extraordinary event that was possessing her.

Ruth told her gently that she would leave her on her own now, but only for a short time while she went downstairs to get some things, repeating that Erin should use her breathing and pushing on the loo seat to help ride the pain. Running down to the kitchen, she looked quickly through drawers and cupboards to find what she needed, putting a saucepan of water on the stove to boil so that she could sterilise some equipment. She grabbed bin bags, kitchen roll and string, and found a first aid kit. She took the wodge of cotton wool from it and threw it into the saucepan along with a bowl and the scissors, and took the rest of the things upstairs. In the linen cupboard, she found towels, a sheet, some clean face-cloths, and a hot-water bottle. She put everything in the bedroom, looked in on Erin and then went back downstairs to boil the kettle, check on her saucepan and find some squash she could give Erin to keep her blood sugar up. When the kettle had boiled, she filled the hot water bottle for Erin to press against her stomach to help relieve the pain; when the time came, she would also use it to warm towels and compresses.

Please, please don't let me have to deliver the baby, she thought. But she knew she must be prepared just in case. All the things I don't have! No painkillers, no syringes, no oxygen or blood, no stethoscope, nothing for suturing. I can't even read her blood pressure. For the first time she felt really frightened, and the responsibility appeared almost overwhelming. But, she told herself, women have given birth like this for thousands of years. It's got to be possible. I must think positively.

In the bathroom, Erin was making a weak attempt to undress herself. 'The bath,' she gasped when she saw Ruth. 'I want to go in the bath. Can I?'

'Yes, of course. That's a good idea — it can help ease the pain. I'll run it for you.' She set the taps gushing. The clouds of steam that rose from the hot tap were comforting and made everything seem normal for a moment, before Erin's groans from behind her reminded her that things were far from normal. But they had to get on with it — it would be at least twenty minutes before the ambulance arrived.

When the bath was half full of warm water, she helped Erin take off her dress and supported her weight while she climbed unsteadily into the water and gingerly set herself down. Almost at once, the water calmed her and she lay there, her stomach ballooning massively above the surface and her knees apart, her face resting on the cool porcelain of the tub.

'That's better,' she murmured, and seemed to fall asleep. Then she came to, her eyes widened and she tensed as another wave of pain took hold. 'Chr . . . rist! Oh my God, oh my God,' she screamed while it had her, and then fell back again, exhausted as it left her. 'I'm so tired,' she moaned. 'I just want to sleep. Can I sleep? If I can have a little break to have a rest, I know I can come back and try harder afterwards. Can I?'

'Rest as much as you can between the contractions,' said Ruth softly.

'We can't stop it, can we? Can't we turn it off for a while?'

'The baby's coming, Erin. It'll be here before too long.'

Erin moaned again, and drifted away into a semi-sleep, getting some blessed relief while she could. The contractions came and went, each one leaving Erin even more limp and tired. Then a massive one came, making her bellow out without words, and Ruth saw Erin's belly rising upwards and then, to her astonishment, she saw a powerful ripple as the muscles inside gathered up and clenched downwards.

'I'm pushing!' shouted Erin, panicked. 'I'm trying not to but . . . SHIT!'

'Good girl, you're doing well. You're doing brilliantly. But try not to push, if you can help it. If you push before everything is ready, you'll make it more difficult at the end.'

Erin ignored her, dozing again. Ruth gave her some squash, which she drank through her stupor. Then, when the next one came, Ruth saw again how the belly rose up and, as though an enormous, invisible fist was squeezing it, pushed downwards.

'Try not to push,' warned Ruth.

'I'm trying,' yelled Erin, furious. 'For Christ's sake, I can't HELP it.'

'Good girl.'

'What the fuck do you mean, *good girl?* You're telling me not to push, and I'm pushing. How is that good?'

Ruth sat beside her, holding her hand, passing her the squash in between the enormous contractions, praying that the ambulance would be here soon. She would ring again in five minutes. Checking her watch, she saw that she'd been there for over two hours. It had gone by so fast — though not for poor Erin, labouring away under her agonising pangs that came every few minutes.

After ten minutes, she went into the bedroom and called again. The emergency switchboard reassured her that the ambulance was on its way and would arrive at any moment.

'Please hurry,' begged Ruth, and went back into the bathroom to check on Erin. She was lying stiller than before, her eyes shut, seemingly fast asleep. It seemed strange that she was able to relax so completely between her contractions: perhaps it was the body's way of allowing some respite so that it could summon up the strength to fight on in the great effort of pushing out the baby.

Fifteen minutes went by and Erin did not have another contraction.

Oh no, thought Ruth. What's happening now? Has labour stopped? She racked her brains to remember all the various possibilities during a normal labour. It was quite possible for labour to stop, but that might mean the baby was in danger. Where was the bloody ambulance? It would have been quicker to drive Erin herself at this rate.

Erin slept on, the bath water cooling around her. Another five minutes went by, and still no contraction. It was odd to be wishing back the howling and pain of the previous hours, but this stillness was chilling.

Erin's eyes opened suddenly. 'I want to get out,' she announced. 'I'm cold.' Immediately she started shivering. 'Brrr, it's freezing.' She lifted up her arms and Ruth took her weight as Erin heaved herself up and hauled herself over the edge of the bath. Ruth wrapped a towel round her and they went into the bedroom where Ruth had removed the counterpane, spread out the bin bags and covered them with towels and then a sheet.

'Bed,' said Erin, in tones of great longing, and went to lie down, sinking gratefully on to the mattress. On the bedside table, a photograph of Tom and Erin embracing on a beach, smiling into the camera, looked out over the bed.

'I'm going to check your dilation again in a minute,' said Ruth. A word had floated into her

397

mind and she'd remembered suddenly that transition came between the first and second stages of labour. In the first stage, the cervix dilated. In the second, the baby was pushed down the birth canal, now able to press through the open neck of the womb. In between the two could come a period of strange calm. Some women experienced great anger or fear in transition; others wanted to get up and demanded to go home. Others, like Erin, were tired, and low, wishing only that it might all be over. Erin hadn't mentioned the baby once; it was as though she couldn't even remember what all this pain was in aid of.

Ruth steeled herself. The ambulance wasn't coming. Perhaps it was lost, perhaps the message hadn't been passed on properly. It didn't matter. She would be delivering the baby. Downstairs, she collected the sterilized equipment, talking herself through what she had to do: I must keep her pushing, keep her going, tell her how to use each contraction to push down. When the baby crowns, there'll only be a few pushes to go, and once it's out, I must make sure of its vital signs, check the airways, suck out any meconium, tie off the cord, cut it . . . and deliver the placenta and check it's intact. Ha! Easy. And that's if there're no complications.

If only she had a stethoscope, she could at least check the baby's heartbeat. She didn't even know what position it was lying in. She could try palpating but wasn't sure she'd be able to tell whether it was breech or not, and whether it was too late at this stage anyway.

I'll just do what I can. The ambulance must come eventually.

In the bedroom, Ruth said, 'We must get labour going again, if we can.' She had checked the dilation again and Erin was now at the full ten centimetres. 'I know it's nice lying down but I need you to get up now, and move about a bit, to help stimulate everything to start up.'

'I don't want to,' said Erin mulishly. 'I like it here.'

'I know, but you've got to. Come on.' She pulled Erin into a sitting position and then made her swing her legs over the bed. 'Come on, now, here we go.' She pulled her up, and they started walking together about the room.

'Am I going to have the baby here?' asked Erin, almost in her normal voice.

'I don't know. You might.'

Erin looked about, almost happily. 'That would be . . . you know . . . fitting. After all, it was made in this room. That was a happy night. The funny thing is, we knew exactly what we were doing. We said 'Let's make a baby! Right here, right now.' And we did. Don't you think that's odd? All the way through, I've been able to tell the midwives the exact date of conception. But they never believed me.'

'So . . . you both knew the date that you conceived? Tom did, too?'

'Oh yes. We often talked about it.' She looked at Ruth. 'I wish Tom was here. He was going to be with me all the way, he said. He didn't want to be one of those fathers who stay in the pub and wait to get a text message. He wanted to be

399

with me all the time, and see our baby born.'

Sadness seemed to fall upon the room. *Erin's low*, thought Ruth. *This is taking it out of her*. Erin's certainty that both she and Tom knew the date of the pregnancy seemed to lift a weight from Ruth, making her feel stronger. 'Perhaps Tom *is* here,' she said warmly.

Erin laughed. 'I don't really believe in all that. But it would be nice to think that there's some vestige of him here, in our bedroom. Although, Tom, if you are here, can I just say, you are a bloody idiot, getting yourself killed and leaving me to do this all on my own.' After a pause, she added, 'They said I was too old for a home birth.'

They walked around the room again slowly.

'Tom was a peculiar man,' Erin said dreamily. 'I didn't ever truly understand him. He could do the strangest things sometimes, and never be able to explain why.' Then she breathed in sharply. 'Oh Christ, here we go again.' She grabbed at Ruth's hand. 'Before it all kicks off, I just want to say thank you. Thanks for being here, and helping me. And if it all goes wrong and something happens to me, you'll make sure the little one's all right, won't you?'

They stared into each other's eyes for a moment.

'You'll be fine,' said Ruth fiercely, 'it's all going to be fine' and, as she spoke, the contraction kicked in and Erin fell heavily against her.

This is it, she thought. *Now the baby is on its way*. Then she was aware that a buzzing noise she'd been hearing for a while had resolved itself

400

into a wail and that the ambulance was coming down the high street towards the house.

★ ★ ★

Erin begged Ruth to go with her, so she drove to the hospital, getting there some time behind the ambulance. By the time she arrived, Erin was in the final stages of her labour. Ruth was allowed in, as there was no one else there to be the birth partner, and she held Erin's hand as she went through the last of her contractions, pushing down with all her might each time the muscles seized, to get the baby out.

Just after one in the morning, the baby was born, tiny and bluish white, slithery with blood and mucus. It was a little girl, put into Erin's arms after being thoroughly checked and given her Vitamin K injection. After the endlessness of what had gone before, the immediate post-birth period felt oddly quick. It seemed no time before Erin was clean and in a fresh hospital gown, the baby pinking up inside its borrowed clothes and blanket, and they were left alone.

Erin held her baby with an air of detached surprise, as though she couldn't quite believe that it was all over, and that this was her daughter. The baby's eyes were closed, its little mouth half open, and one fist tightly balled while the other tiny hand wrapped itself around Erin's finger as she lay against her mother's chest.

'Have you planned any names?' asked Ruth. The infant was perfect and she herself was full of amazement at the sight of her. A few hours ago, this little thing had been curled up inside Erin. Now it had spent its first few sleepy minutes in the outside world it would inhabit until death. The miracle of birth, she thought. Gets you every time.

'We had two for a girl — Dolly or Violet.'

'Those are both nice,' Ruth said politely, although she didn't much like Dolly.

'So I think — Violet. Violet Gwendoline, after Tom's mother.'

Tom's mother, thought Ruth. She looked at the baby, to see if there was a sign of who might be its father, but the little squashed face, chinless with the over-large nose of the newborn, looked like no one she could recognise. She remembered what Erin had said in the bedroom, about knowing when she and Tom had made the baby. It hadn't sounded like a lie. She knew at once and with absolute certainty that this wasn't Ned's baby. And as soon as she knew that, she also realised that she had never believed it was, that she'd been frightening herself with the idea of it, like a child conjuring up pictures of vampires.

'Ruth,' said Erin hesitantly.

'Yes. What can I do? Call your family? There must be someone wondering where on earth you are.'

'Yes, yes, I'll need to borrow your mobile. Mine's in my car back at the house. No, it's something else. I want to apologise to you.'

Ruth looked at her properly for the first time since the baby had been born. She was pale and tired-looking, her hair pulled back into a

402

ponytail, and pinned down with kirby grips. Her lips were still tinged with blue from the last great efforts she had made to give birth. Were new mothers supposed to be elated? Erin seemed quite calm and not quite aware of it all. But her eyes were earnest as she gazed at Ruth.

'What do you want to apologise for?' Ruth felt her heart quicken.

'Well . . . I . . . this is hard. I don't know quite how to put it.' She laughed nervously. 'I've behaved badly towards you, and I'm sorry. You've been so marvellous today, and I didn't deserve it, and you and I both know it.'

'I don't know what you mean.'

'Oh yes, you do. I've got to admit something I didn't even admit to myself until just recently. When you started going out with Ned, I was jealous. It's so stupid, isn't it? I was used to him loving me best, no matter how many girlfriends he'd had. But when you came along, it was different and I could see that, and I got a touch of the green-eyed monster, even though I was perfectly happy with Tom. I don't know how to explain it — and I really didn't think I was causing any harm. I thought I was doing what was right for Ned, making sure he was certain about everything with you. But I can see now I wasn't. I was trying to make him stay in love with me. Because he used to have a crush on me when we were younger — I expect he told you. I always found it very flattering — well, who wouldn't? And when I thought it was over, I got a bit nettled.' Erin looked down at the baby in her arms and adjusted the blanket so that the little head, dusted in brown hair, was covered. 'It was very wrong.'

'Wh — ' Ruth cleared her throat. 'What did Ned do?'

'He was confused, that was clear. Not about you. About me. He couldn't understand why I was doing what I was doing, calling him up all the time, arranging to meet. But he went along with it because he's always done anything I asked. It's a habit with him, I suppose. He's been doing it for over ten years, it's not that easy to break a habit like that.' Erin flushed. 'I hope you don't mind me talking like this.'

'Of course not,' said Ruth fervently. 'Tell me everything.'

'Well, there's not much to tell. Just that I did what I could to convince myself that it was me he liked best. But it soon became apparent that it was no longer the case, though he'd never be anything but my best friend in the world, after Tom.'

'So . . . so . . . you never . . . he never . . . nothing ever went on.'

Erin raised her eyes to Ruth, her gaze clear and candid. 'Oh no. What makes you think that? There was never anything.' She laughed lightly. 'I'm sure I gave a few signals that there could be if he wanted. I don't know if I'd have gone through with it. But he never responded.'

Ruth felt light, warmed by the kind of happiness that she hadn't known for weeks. Alongside it came something else: a fury towards Tom, that he'd involved her in his unfathomable, nasty little games. Then it was replaced by pity;

he'd died too young without the chance to put things right. He'd never know his baby now. He'd never realise how much Erin had truly loved him — that is, if he'd ever doubted it.

'I saw Ned yesterday,' Erin went on. 'He told me you'd gone to stay with your father. I felt very bad because I was afraid I'd had something to do with it. I was going to find you and tell you this anyway — it's just happened a little sooner than I expected.' She grinned wryly. 'And not quite in the circumstances I imagined.'

Ruth took her hand. 'I need to say sorry, too. I've thought some very bad things about you.'

'I thought you might have. I'm glad we've sorted it out. Do you hate me now?'

'No,' said Ruth honestly. She was too relieved to feel angry.

'You've seen me at my weakest. There's a bond between us now. There aren't many friends of mine who've checked my dilation and seen me naked and screaming in the bath.'

'I don't suppose there are.' Ruth smiled at her. 'Thanks for telling me.'

'I think you ought to go to Ned as soon as you can,' Erin said. 'I really do.'

20

The day seemed to be a charmed one. Although she should have been exhausted from the events of the day before, Ruth was full of energy and her heart was light. She realised how listless and depressed she had been now that she could feel hope and happiness again. Her journey into work was delightful, the day a fabulous specimen of the early English summer: golden and blue with a light breeze, and everything touched by the lushness of new life. Aeroplanes made pretty white tramlines as they streaked across the sky. The traffic, even in Oxford, was unusually clear and she even found her favourite parking spot was empty when she arrived.

This all bodes well, she thought. Strolling to work, and earlier than usual, she took a detour down Little Clarendon Street, looking in the windows of the expensive shops. She ought to get a present for Erin: something for the baby. A toy, or a rattle, or something sweet to wear. Perhaps she would come back and have a look at lunchtime.

As she approached the surgery, she went over her plan. She would call Ned during her break, and suggest she go over and cook dinner for him. She would take a bottle of wine, some steaks from the expensive butcher in the Covered Market, and maybe a gift for him; there would certainly be time to go into the bookshop and pick something he would like. Then, after work, she'd get to the cottage before he arrived and have time to bathe, change and get ready before he got back. She would stop being a dowdy old married woman, and dress up for him. She would wear red lipstick and stockings and high heels, and remind him of the Ruth he had fallen in love with, and, she hoped, still desired.

She grinned, and hugged her scheme to herself. If everything went as she hoped, they would spend the night together. She felt a pleasant tingle of anticipation when she thought about it: it had been a long time and her body was ripe for a night with her lover.

In the surgery, Rhonda was in a good mood as well, and although the phones were already ringing constantly, there was not a great deal on for Ruth that morning.

She took the opportunity to phone Ned between patients, when a vaccination failed to turn up and the asthma patient she was advising about ongoing care postponed the appointment for a week. Her heart was racing as she dialled Ned's work number and she swallowed hard as it rang, preparing herself to sound as normal as possible.

Amazing to be so nervous calling my own husband! she thought, and then felt deflated when the line went to his answer machine, even though it was a pleasure even to hear his recorded voice saying, 'Hi, this is Ned Haskell . . . '

She left a quick message. 'It's Ruth. I wondered if we could have a chat — I'd love to talk to you. By the way, did you know Erin's had her baby? It's a little girl called Violet. So . . . that's nice, isn't it? Er . . . ring me if you can.'

Then she tried his mobile, but it was off.

I'll just ring again later, she thought. At lunchtime, she went out and did her shopping and came back laden with her bags. She tried Ned again, but there was still no answer. This time she left a message on his mobile, asking him to call.

Beginning to feel nervous by mid-afternoon when he still hadn't called her, Ruth scanned the rest of her appointments. There was nothing urgent and after she'd done a baby MMR immunisation, with the mother almost threatening her with legal action if anything should happen to the child as a result, she decided to ask Rhonda to call and cancel the last two appointments so that she could leave early. Rhonda, still in her good mood, obligingly said she would and that Ruth deserved to have a bit of time off because she'd looked so down recently.

On her way out, she was startled when Dr Fletcher popped out of her office and said, 'Ruth, can I have a word?'

As Ruth couldn't say that actually she was sneaking off early, she smiled and said of course and went in. Dr Fletcher said that the doctors had been discussing Ruth's progress at their monthly meeting. They had agreed that she was doing very well, and it was time to ask her if she would consider some further training with a view to taking over some clinics and generally having more to do with planning strategy and implementing policies and so forth, which was really a promotion and would mean a pay rise.

Ruth, her heart rising at this further good omen, said that she would be delighted to have more responsibility.

Dr Fletcher said that was excellent and they should schedule a time to talk about the practicalities, but she'd pass on the good news to the other doctors.

Ruth left the surgery, almost skipping down the street. Then she remembered that she hadn't heard from Ned all day and crossed her fingers. 'Please let it be all right,' she whispered to herself. There's no need to panic. Everything will be fine.

★ ★ ★

At the crossroads outside Oxford, she almost took the turn for the Old Rectory without thinking. It was worrying how quickly she'd fallen back into the habit of going back the old way.

I haven't been gone that long, she reminded herself as she drove back into the village, although it felt like an age. Nothing had changed, she was glad to see. When she got to the cottage, Ned's car wasn't there. Good. There would be time to have her bath and get changed before he arrived home.

As soon as she let herself in through the door, she could hear scrabbling about upstairs. 'Hello?'

she called. 'Is anyone there?'

She walked to the bottom of the stairs and looked up. Jackie's face appeared over the banister and stared at her for a moment.

'Oh, it's you,' she said shortly, and then disappeared back onto the landing.

Ruth's heart fell. She'd forgotten all about Jackie. Of course, she was likely to turn up — after all, hadn't she taken to coming up almost every night? — but she hadn't expected to see her here during the day. Ned must have given her a key. How was she going to get her out of the house?

Jackie's face appeared again, flushed and angry looking. 'Perhaps it's a good thing you're here,' she announced. 'You can take this away with you.'

A black bin bag knotted at the top came plummeting down from upstairs, landing in a heap at Ruth's feet.

Ruth looked at it for a moment. 'What's this?' she asked.

'Have a look.' Jackie vanished again.

Ruth untied the bag and saw that some of her clothes were inside. She left the bag and pounded up the stairs into the bedroom where Jackie was still busy in the wardrobe, a half-full bin bag beside her. She pulled down another armful of hangers with Ruth's clothes loaded on them and started to stuff them into the bag.

'What are you doing?' demanded Ruth, her voice trembling slightly. She had never been any good at confronting Jackie, but she couldn't stand by and watch her doing this.

'What does it look like?'

'Why are you putting my things into those bags?'

'Why do you think?' Jackie laughed roughly. She pulled out another couple of hangers, one with a favourite dress of Ruth's on it, a silk wrap dress she'd bought for a wedding. It began to slide off the hanger and Jackie grabbed it, scrunched it into a ball and tossed it into the bag.

Ruth's hands were shaking as she advanced. 'Stop that!' she cried. 'Stop doing that at once!'

'I'm doing a clear out,' said Jackie in a menacing low voice. 'Keep out of my way.'

'Those are my things.'

'You should have thought about that before you walked out on my son.'

'You don't know anything about it.'

'I know all I need to know. I've seen him here, crying his heart out for his best friend. And where's his wife? Eh? Well? I'll tell you — she's pissed off, because she can't be bothered.' Jackie turned to face her. 'You've had your chance. You've messed it up. Now get out.'

'I need to talk to Ned,' Ruth said, struggling to control herself. 'Where is he?'

'Not here,' spat Jackie. Then she smiled. 'He's at the hospital, visiting Erin and her little baby.'

'Will he be back tonight?'

Jackie shrugged. 'I s'pose so. I've put a pie in for his dinner.'

Ruth put all the menace she could gather into her voice. 'Don't you dare touch anything else. Those are my things, and they belong here.'

Jackie stared at her impassively, her eyes magnified by the lenses of her spectacles.

Ruth left her there, and went downstairs to phone Ned again. He'd been unavailable all day; he couldn't have been at the hospital all that time. His mobile, though, was still off. He would surely be on his way home by now. She went to the window and looked down the road as far as she could, hoping to see Ned's car but there was no sign of him.

What am I going to do? she wondered. She could hear Jackie at her work again upstairs, defying Ruth, clearly not in the least frightened of her. She knew she should do what Cordy said and stand up to her, but it was impossible. The atmosphere was poisoned while Jackie was here. How could she have her bath or get changed or get dinner ready — especially when there was a pie or something underway for Ned? There was nothing to do but wait until Ned got home and ask him to make his mother leave.

She went to the sofa and sat down, wondering how long she would have to wait. The sofa was empty of its usual slumbering tabby cushion, with only a smattering of white and grey hairs to show that she had been there. Ruth got up.

'Maisie! Maisie!' she called, looking about. There was no sign of the cat, so she went into the kitchen and opened the back door. Maisie rarely went outside now — perhaps once or twice a day — so it would be unusual to see her in the garden. She preferred the warmth of the patch of sunlight on the sitting room carpet when she wasn't curled up on the sofa. She

412

called again from the back door, hoping to see Maisie answering her name, stepping elegantly towards her across the lawn, but there was nothing.

She shut the back door and turned back into the kitchen. 'Where is she?' she wondered aloud, and looked down to check that the cat's bowls had enough food and water in them. They were gone.

'Maisie, Maisie!' she called, her voice urgent now. She ran out of the kitchen to the stairs and shouted up, 'Where is she? Where's Maisie?'

Jackie was already standing at the top, and she came down the stairs slowly, her face calm but her eyebrows a little too raised for her to be entirely at ease.

'You mean that cat?'

'Of course I do. Where is she?'

Jackie reached the bottom and the two of them stood facing each other, Ruth taller by half a head, the other woman blinking behind her glasses. Jackie said, 'She was very ill.'

'What?'

'She was ill. It was obvious. It was the kindest thing to do.'

'She's not ill!' shouted Ruth, fearful. 'She's just old. What have you done with her?' But she already knew.

Jackie sighed and turned her eyes away, shrugging lightly. 'She was old and sick and it was just cruelty keeping her going, poor mite. So I took her to the vet and they put her to sleep. She didn't suffer. I told you — it was the kindest thing to do.'

'No,' whispered Ruth. 'I can't believe you would do such a thing.'

'I don't know why you're so upset. It was just a mangy cat. You can get another one if you're so desperate, though why you would want another pest-ridden animal in the house is beyond me. The air's been a lot fresher since that cat's been gone.'

Ruth felt herself wilting. Maisie had felt like a vital connection with her mother; she had arrived as a kitten before Ruth and Cordy had even known their mother was ill. Looking back, she could see now that her parents had got the kitten on purpose, to distract the children from the ordeal to come, to give them something to care for and focus on when the grief became too much. Ruth remembered taking Maisie into her bed at night, although it was forbidden, and listening to her purr rumbling away while Ruth told her how terrible it was, the things that were happening to her mother: the sickness, the treatments that seemed worse than the cancer, the knowledge that she would soon be leaving them.

Everything built up in her, all the tensions from the last few weeks, from Tom's funeral to caring for Erin through her labour, mixed with the fear that it was too late to make things up with Ned.

She began to cry. *Don't be so weak*, she admonished herself, *don't let her see you like this*. But she couldn't help it, and when she thought of poor Maisie, being put in her travel cage by Jackie and taken down to the vet, unaware of what was going to happen, it made her weep even harder.

Jackie looked uncomfortable. 'Oh, now, don't start all that,' she said. 'Don't get emotional on me.' Then she seemed to become exasperated. 'What are you crying for? For goodness' sake, you think you've got things to cry about? What about *me*? I'm the one dealing with all the stress! It's not been easy, you know, moving house. It's one of the most stressful experiences you can have. You don't see me wailing about it, though, do you? I just get on with things and I don't complain. I keep a lot inside and that's why I get these chest pains.'

'Shut up, you selfish old woman!' cried Ruth, crouching down to grope for a tissue in her bag. She blew her nose and then stood up. She'd stopped crying; instead, her whole being went icy with rage. 'I want you out! Get out of my house!' She ran to the front door and opened it. 'Get out!'

'Your house? You mean Ned's house,' declared Jackie, putting her hands on her hips as though squaring up for a fight. This, she understood. Confrontation was what she thrived on.

'No, I don't. This is *my* house. What you don't seem to understand is that Ned married me. I'm his wife. You have no right to be here if we don't want you. And we don't. So get out.'

Jackie's mouth fell open. 'Well, of all the . . . ungrateful cow!'

'You heard me. Please leave at once.' A great calm came over Ruth. She felt her spine stiffen and straighten. She wasn't going to shout, or swear, or do any of the things Jackie would understand. Instead, she found an authority she'd never known when dealing with her mother-in-law. She stood there and waited.

Jackie pursed her lips into a tight, wrinkled circle, and narrowed her eyes. She seemed to be sizing up the situation. Then she said, 'All right. I'm going. But you needn't think you've won. No one's ever come between me and my boy. Do you hear? And you're no different.'

'You're wrong,' said Ruth clearly, as Jackie strutted past her with as much dignity as she could muster, her head high. 'I *am* different. And the sooner you realise that, the better.'

★ ★ ★

When Ned came back, it was not at all the scenario she'd envisaged earlier in the day. She'd expected to be poised and glamorous with freshly washed hair, make-up and a pretty dress, her wine open on the table and dinner almost ready. Instead, she was sitting cross-legged on the sofa, her eyes red and a bunch of damp tissues next to her.

'Ruth!' he said, astonished, as he came through the door. 'What are you doing here? I thought I must have left a light on when I went out this morning.'

'Didn't you get my messages?'

He shook his head. 'We've been out at our summer awayday. I went down there yesterday so that I didn't have to fight the early traffic. Mobiles off, by order of David. I forgot to turn it

416

on again, now you mention it.' He came over, almost tentative, but smiling. 'It's good to see you. Are you all right? You've been crying.' He looked apprehensive.

She felt her lip wobble. 'Ned, how could you let her? How could you let her do that to Maisie?'

'What are you talking about?'

'Your mother! She took Maisie to the vet and had her put down.' Tears started up again but she tried to repress them.

Ned sat down beside her, looking puzzled. 'No. She's taken her in for a check-up. She said Maisie had been sick in the kitchen and she wanted to get her looked over. The vet kept her in for observation. I'm sure she's fine.'

'She's not. She's had her put to sleep. She told me.'

Ned sat silently for a moment taking this in, his face paling. 'When did you talk to her?'

'This evening.'

He frowned. 'What was she doing in here? How did she get in?'

'Didn't you give her a key?'

'No. She must have nicked the spare one and got a copy cut. Christ!' His eyes flashed. Ruth could tell he was getting angry. 'I can't believe she's starting all this again. I thought we'd got off too easy. I know she's been difficult but it's nothing like what she's done in the past. Every time I think it will be different. But now, she's gone too far.' He took her hand and held it hard. 'If she really has done what you say, it's unforgivable. I suppose she was planning to spin me a story about Maisie getting ill and dying at the vet's. I'm so, so sorry. My God . . . ' He let go her hand, stood up and started pacing about. He saw the bin bag spilling its contents at the bottom of the stairs. 'What's that?'

'My clothes,' said Ruth. 'I came back to see you, to tell you how sorry I am and to see if we can start again, if you want to. I found your mother here. She was getting rid of all my things. She told me you never wanted to see me again. Did you ask her to do it? Is it true you don't want me back?' Her voice quavered on the last words.

Ned made a sound like a snort, halfway between a laugh and an exclamation of fury. He strode over to her and put out his hand. 'Come on.'

It was a warm evening, which was lucky as they hadn't stopped to put on jackets in the dash out of the house. Together they walked through the village, Ned marching ahead, his face set and his eyes terrifying in their fury. They went past the village green, where a gang of children was squealing and shouting as they clambered over the climbing frames and swung high in the air on the swings. Outside the pub, couples and lone drinkers sat enjoying the summer evening, glasses on the wooden tables, cigarettes burning in the ashtrays. Windows were open as they strode past the cottages along the High Street, letting the sounds of evening television, the clanking of pots and pans and the smell of cooking escape on to the road. As they went down the hill towards the Haskells' house, a man

418

was washing his car, sending streams of soapy water down his drive and on to the pavement, while a radio blasted out. A woman stood in her garden sending a spray of water over her plants, as her husband clipped the hedge at the side of their house.

An ordinary village evening, thought Ruth. Except that it's not ordinary for us. Adrenaline was coursing through her. What was Ned going to say? How would Jackie take it? For once, she didn't feel afraid of her mother-in-law. They were going to face her together, and together they were strong enough to take her on, and win. It was exhilarating. It felt, for the first time in a long time, as though she and Ned were a team again.

When they reached the house, Ned rang on the doorbell and knocked on the door almost simultaneously, as though he was impatient to confront his mother while his rage was still hot. A moment later, Jackie opened the door, beaming when she saw Ned.

'Hello, son!' she said merrily, and then her face dropped when she spotted Ruth. 'Oh.'

'Let me in,' Ned said, pushing open the door and going in to the house.

'Don't mind me,' said Jackie sarcastically. 'I'm just your mother, after all.'

Ned ignored her and went to the sitting room, Jackie following him, and Ruth behind them. The television was on, and Steven was sitting in an armchair, a paper open on his lap with the sudoku puzzle half completed. 'What's going on?' he asked, startled, as they all came into the room.

'I want you to hear this, Dad. I want you both to hear this.'

'If it's about that cat,' began Jackie, 'there's been a misunderstanding. I thought Ruth *wanted* me to take her to the vet. That's what she said.'

'You might as well shut up right now,' said Ned. Ruth could tell that he was having trouble controlling himself and staying calm. 'I don't want to hear any more of your lies. Your atrocious bloody lies. I'm tired of you trying to wreck my life. I'm tired of the way you've tried to sabotage every relationship I've ever had. Do you remember Madeline? Do you remember what you did to her? Poor girl. She never got over having you shouting in the street, calling her a whore in the middle of York. She'd only been going out with me for a month!

'I've tried to put up with you. I've tried to tolerate you, and do you know why? Because I'm sorry for you. I'm sorry for you that your father died when you were young, and that you're drinking yourself stupid all the time, because I honestly believe you can't help it, and that you can't change your ways no matter how miserable you make yourself. I think about you as a sad old woman with no friends, incapable of having a normal relationship with anyone and I actually pity you. But not any more. I've had enough.'

'What are you talking about?' said Jackie in an indignant squeal. 'I've got friends!'

'You've got people you go to your club with, spend a merry evening with, but you've got no real friends. You don't even know what it means.

Even the friends you've got, you spend half the time bitching about them: how awful their houses are, how badly they run their lives, how terrible they look, as if you've got anything to boast about. And what about your family? You've feuded with just about all of them. There's no one you're actually on speaking terms with any more, is there? Look at Uncle George. You had a row with him about who should pay what on the bill when we went out for lunch, and you haven't spoken to him since. That was ten years ago! Is that normal?'

Jackie said, 'He wanted me to pay for a share of the red wine and I told him that neither your father nor I touched the stuff, and I couldn't see why I should pay for it.'

'You see!' shouted Ned. 'Even now, you can't see how . . . bloody pathetic that is.' His voice dropped to a pleading tone. 'Can't you see how ridiculous it is? How mean?'

'I won't be taken advantage of!' declared Jackie. 'I'm no one's mug.'

'You're no one's anything.' Ned turned his back on her and went over to the fireplace, leaning against it as though to regain his strength.

'Now,' said Steven, trying to calm things down. 'What's this all about?'

Jackie turned round and jerked a finger in Ruth's direction. '*Her*,' she spat. 'She's spreading lies, turning Ned against me. After everything I've done for her.'

Ned turned round. 'Dad, you know what it's about. It's the same old thing. I don't know why

421

you stand up for her. I don't know how you can bear being with her, if it comes to that. I don't know why you've ruined your life staying with her.'

'Don't talk like that,' said Steven warningly. 'That's your mother you're speaking about.'

'You think I don't know that?' Ned ran a hand through his hair, and sighed. 'My God! You know, Susie did the right thing. She just got as far away from you as she possibly could.'

'Susie's an ungrateful little miss,' said Jackie nastily.

'Everyone's ungrateful, aren't they? Don't you ever think it's a bit odd, the way the whole world is ungrateful and out to get you, and you're the only perfect one? Doesn't it ever strike you as strange that everyone who knows you ends up disliking you, fighting with you, being frozen out by you? Because if I were you, I'd start asking myself some damn hard questions.'

'You're being so rude,' sniffed Jackie. 'It's that girl's influence.' She nodded towards Ruth.

Ned walked over to Ruth and took her hand. 'This is my wife,' he said clearly. 'She's the most important person in my life. You've done everything you can to make her life difficult — don't think I haven't noticed. You want to get rid of her like you have all the others, because you can't stand anyone being more important to me than you. But you'd better understand something. We're together. Our life and happiness comes first. *She* comes first. If you lie to her, or abuse her, or do anything to her, you're doing it to me. Understand? I'll always trust her over

422

you. I'll always favour her over you.' He looked at his father. 'Dad's done the same. He's stuck with you through everything, no matter what you've done, because he married you and that's that. He's let you alienate his daughter so that he barely sees her any more. He's let you uproot him from the home he loved and move him down here so you could pursue your stupid agenda. He'd even let you get rid of Ruth, if you could. Well . . . our relationship is nothing like that, Ruth and me. We're good together. We're a family. We can shut you out if we want, and we won't shed a tear. You'd better think about it, all right? From now on, our life is our own. You won't be dropping in every night. You can come when you're invited, when we feel like seeing you, if we ever do again after what you've done. Is that clear? You may be my mother, but you don't have a right to my love. You have to earn it. Understand?'

Jackie crossed her arms and sniffed.

Ned continued. 'I hope I've made myself clear. If I haven't, feel free to ask me about it anytime, and I'll explain it again. Okay? Come on, Ruth. We're leaving.'

★ ★ ★

As they marched together up the hill, back towards the cottage, Ruth was too exhilarated to speak for a while. When they reached the brow and were alongside the village green, she stopped Ned, holding both his arms, and looking into his

423

eyes. 'Did you mean that? Did you really mean it all?'

'Of course.'

'But after what I did . . . '

'What did you do?'

'I read your diaries! I thought you were having an affair with Erin! I left you.'

'You thought I was having an affair with Erin?' He laughed disbelievingly. 'You never said that.'

'I know — but I thought it.'

'Why didn't you say anything?'

'I don't know . . . ' She didn't want to tell him about what Tom had said. There was no point now in blackening his name. She wasn't going to blight Ned's memory of his friend over something that couldn't be changed.

Ned said, 'You kept asking me if I loved you better than I used to love Erin. It was an unanswerable question — I was a different person then. It was completely different, impossible to compare. I was hurt that you wanted me to say such a thing and that you didn't see how much I loved you. But I never imagined that you thought it was still going on.'

'But it was because . . . ' Ruth took a deep breath and gazed up into his eyes. They were worried and earnest; it made her want to weep when she realised how much she loved him and how close she had come to losing him. 'You lied to me that time. You told me you'd never loved Erin.'

'I know.' An agonised look passed over his face. 'I wish I'd told you but I honestly thought it would only cause more trouble. I thought that there was no way you'd ever find out because I'd never told anyone. But I can see it was stupid. I hated the fact I hadn't come clean. I never lied to you again after that. I'm so sorry.'

'You didn't lie again, but you were evasive. You talked so carefully — picking your words so that you wouldn't be telling an untruth. I could tell what you were doing and it only made me more suspicious.'

'Oh, Ruth. I'm so sorry. Can you trust me again?' He pulled her in close and hugged her. She hugged him back and then looked up at him.

'I know you didn't have an affair with Erin. It was all in my head — almost. I can see that now. I should've talked to you about it, I should've come clean.'

'You silly girl.' Ned pulled her close and kissed the top of her head. 'You can say anything to me, you know that. If you'd only told me what you were thinking . . . but it's not all your fault, I know that. We were both idiots.'

'And it wasn't just us — the others had their parts to play too, didn't they? Tom, Erin and Jeremy . . . '

Ruth and Ned looked at each other for a moment without speaking, acknowledging something that had lain between them all this time.

'My friends,' he said softly at last. 'It's not all laughing and games, I know that. I'm sorry.'

'But I was the one who walked out. I didn't want to. Even while I was going, I was telling myself not to be so stupid. I should never have gone.'

'Do you think I blamed you? I've been impossible to live with for ages. You didn't talk to me because I shut you out, I know that. And when Tom died . . . I felt so guilty for so many reasons, things going back years. It was hard to live with and I dealt with it by turning off. I know I do it when things get hard. I didn't blame you at all when you wanted to go. I thought that since you'd read my diaries, you thought less of me, that you'd seen how pathetic I really was. And then with my bloody awful mother making your life hell, and my silent act . . . I'd have left me, if I could.'

'Oh Ned,' she said, choked. 'I can't believe this has all happened.'

Ned laughed as well. 'It seems that all we had to do was open the lines of communication.'

'It means so much to me — what you said in there. To your parents. About us being a family, and me coming first. Did you really mean it?'

'Of course. I've always meant it. You're my wife now — not a teenage crush, or a girlfriend, or someone I fancy shacking up with for a bit. You're the real thing. I meant it when I promised that it was for life.'

They kissed and Ned pulled away, staring down at Ruth earnestly.

'I'm sorry about my mother. She's put you through hell, I know that. And I didn't do anything about it, just hoped it would all go away. I should have stood up to her at the very beginning when she started with all her rubbish. I'm sorry I didn't, I mean it. I won't make the same mistake again.'

'I forgive you. And I do understand — she's a . . . complex woman.' Ruth grinned. Suddenly Jackie seemed very small and unimportant. A loser. While she, Ruth, was a winner, with her gorgeous husband and beautiful home. All the hatred and anger vanished and instead, she felt sorry for her mother-in-law. *Oh no you don't!* she warned herself. *None of that bleeding heart stuff, that's what got you into all this trouble in the first place. No more looking for Mummy substitutes. You're an adult now.*

'Complex is one way of putting it. Well, I meant what I said. There won't be any more nonsense. We come first — you and me. It's our life and we should live it the way we want. Mum forfeited just about all her maternal privileges years ago.' He held her hand tightly. 'Listen, we can move away if you want. In fact, I think we should. The cottage is almost too small for us as it is.'

Ruth laughed. 'Away from your mother? That'll make her happy, after all the trouble she went to moving here.'

Ned shrugged and smiled. 'Who cares?'

'And what about Luke and Abigail, and Jeremy, and Erin? Don't you want to stay close to them?'

'It's nice being close to my old friends, but one of these days we'll have more important things to think about. Kids, maybe. New friends. Life doesn't have to stand still, does it?'

'No. No, it doesn't.'

'Is there any chance we can stop talking now? I'd quite like to kiss you again.'

'You started it,' said Ruth, jokily indignant, but she couldn't say any more because Ned's lips were on hers, and she could feel herself melting into the delicious kiss she knew so well.

The children playing on the village green stopped their antics, whooped and screamed and gave them a round of applause as encouragement.

21

Weddings, funerals, christenings, thought Ruth. The milestones of our lives are marked by these events.

A different church, a modern one this time. The altar and pulpit were of polished oak and the glass windows zigzags of colour in abstract patterns. The service had lots of congregation participation, and the music was provided by a group of guitars, flutes and tambourines alongside an electric piano. This was not quite how she'd envisaged Erin would like Violet's christening, but it had a festival air that was hard to resist. The baby herself was adorable. The dark brown fuzz she'd been born with had disappeared, replaced by a thick, fair mop not unlike Tom's. She was plump and pink-cheeked, and seemed content to sleep through most of the goings-on. When she did open her eyes, she revealed the same dark blue saucers that Erin had.

After the sermon, the priest summoned Erin, the baby's grandparents, and Ruth and Ned to the front.

'Wow,' he said. He was a friendly, bearded man, who had earlier introduced himself as Mike. 'What a great day for all of us, as we celebrate Violet's christening and her entry into our great family, the Church. In a minute, we're going to do the formal thing, have some answers and responses, take Violet down to the font and baptise her. But first I want to say a few words to welcome you today. We're all so pleased to have you here, Violet and Erin's friends and relations.' Mike smiled round at them all, his regular congregation and the visitors, who tried to hide any awkwardness they were feeling in this supremely relaxed environment. 'Please join us all after the service. Refreshments will be served in the Refectory, so come and say hi and have a cup of tea with us. Before we get going, I want to say a few words, and this baptism wouldn't be complete if I didn't say them. Around Violet are her loving family and godparents, the people who are going to take care of her in the future, bring her up, educate her, show her how to be a productive, responsible, loving member of society. One person is missing. That's Violet's father, who was tragically killed in a car accident only a few months ago. He never got to meet his beautiful daughter.'

Oh dear, thought Ruth. Don't go on about it too much. We're all desperate to be happy today, of all days.

'But,' continued Mike, 'he would be overjoyed to see you all today, ready to take on the responsibility of caring for his little girl. He lives on in this child. You can show your love for Tom in the way you love his family. Be there — for *him*. And let's rejoice today! Let's lift up our hearts and say 'Yeah! Alleluia! All *right*!' Okay?'

Ned squeezed Ruth's hand, and she looked over at him. He was biting his lower lip in an effort not to laugh.

Sometimes it's the only way to deal with things like this, she thought. To laugh.

'All righty,' said Mike with a broad grin, spreading his hands out towards the congregation. 'Let's get this kid in the font!'

★ ★ ★

Afterwards there was a party at Erin's parents' house.

Ruth and Ned were standing together in the sitting room, each holding a plate of the delicious food Erin's mother had made. These days, they found it hard to be apart, and could not seem to resist gravitating back towards each other no matter where they were. Now, even though Ned was talking to a relation of Erin's, he was close to Ruth, his arm almost touching hers. They'd spend hours together, talking through everything that had happened, that had almost created the disaster of their splitting up. It terrified Ruth, how close she'd come to losing him. Ned was the same, simultaneously grateful that their love had been restored, and horrified at how he'd nearly allowed it to be wrecked.

Erin came into the room, her eyes searching the people there. When she saw Ruth, she came over, smiling. She was looking radiant in a houndstooth suit and military style boots that laced tightly to her knees.

'You look all together too good for someone who gave birth four months ago,' announced Ruth. 'I suddenly have no appetite for this delicious food.'

'Ah, come on, now,' said Erin in an Irish brogue, 'it's our traditional stew wit dumplins, so 'tis. Don't you complain now, just enjoy.' Then, in her normal voice she added, 'It's the demands of the job, dear. That and breastfeeding. It's all falling off me.'

'Where's Violet?'

'I'm very unlikely to see Violet ever again. She's been taken prisoner and is being suffocated by ten of my closest relatives who are determined to hug and kiss her to death.' Erin grinned. 'Honestly, they're fighting over her like mother hens. It's quite sweet.'

'You'll be glad of them one day, I suppose.'

'I'm glad of them now.'

'Have you had a good day?'

'Yes, it's been wonderful. And so many lovely gifts for the baby. Thank you so much for yours — it's terribly generous.'

'Well, it's from both of us — her godmother and her godfather.'

'Her whole godfamily.' Erin smiled at her. 'Thank you.'

'It's nothing . . . '

'No — I mean, for everything. For being there when I needed you.'

'You know it's fine.' They looked at each other. We'll always be connected by that day, thought Ruth. Through Violet, too. But also through what happened on her birth day. It's bonded us somehow.

'And how are you?' she asked, bridging the moment.

'Up and down,' said Erin. 'Some days it's

432

unbearable. At night, when I'm getting up to feed Violet, and I'm all alone . . . or she sniffs or coughs and I want to turn to someone and say 'do *you* think it's serious or am I being a mad mother?' . . . or when she smiled for the first time, or started kicking in the bath . . . ' She smiled again. 'It's strange, because sometimes the good times are worse than the bad ones. It's the happy ones that make me cry, when I think about what Tom's missing. When she won't sleep and is wailing and wailing and I'm at my wit's end, I think 'lucky bastard, missing *this*.' It's the smiles and the sweetness and the fact that she's growing out of all her baby clothes so fast that curdle me up.'

Ruth laid a hand on her arm.

'Oh, I know, it will get better,' said Erin. 'One day at a time. But look at you and Ned. Things seem to be good.'

'They are,' Ruth said simply. 'It's all . . . very good. I feel like we're having the married bliss we should have had after the wedding now.'

'And the cottage?'

'We've had lots of viewings and some good offers. It's just a question of deciding which one to accept.'

'Does that mean you'll get the place you want? You found one you liked, didn't you?'

'Yes — on the other side of Oxford. It's a beautiful house, Victorian, with four bedrooms and a garden. There's a good chance we'll get it. Now that I've had my promotion.'

'I didn't know about that! Congratulations,' said Erin warmly.

'Thank you. It's very exciting. And it means more money, so we can afford a bigger mortgage. But we've got other plans as well. We might rent it out at some point and go travelling, see something of the world. Live in London for a while, or Edinburgh. Try out city life. Spend a year in Sydney.'

Erin laughed. 'Wow. Big plans. I think that's great. We've all been a bit intense for too long. It will do all of us good to expand our horizons. I'm thinking of similar plans myself. I might take Violet to London for a bit while she's small, see if I can do a bit of stage work, providing I can find a good nanny.' She shot Ruth a mischievous look. 'I bet Jackie isn't too thrilled.'

'She's been quiet as a mouse. I mean it, we haven't heard a squeak from her for months. Ned is still freezing her out. He says that if she never gets in touch again, he could live with it. But I'm sure she will, eventually.'

'Well done, both of you, for cutting loose. It's about time. And I've never seen Ned look so happy. So there you are — you must be doing something right.'

★　★　★

It was Ruth's birthday at the end of November, and she and Ned were invited to the Old Rectory for a celebration lunch on a balmy Autumn Sunday.

'Be careful,' she warned on the way over, 'my father can't cook and he's very proud of the fact.'

But they were greeted by the sight of Silas proudly turning his roasting potatoes over in their fat, and telling them importantly that the beef was resting.

'Priscilla's been giving me some cooking lessons,' he explained, 'and I've been showing her how to work her boiler. Fair exchange, trading, you know. I've got this meal down pat.'

'How often are you eating roast beef, then, Dad?' asked Ruth, giving him a kiss on the cheek.

'At least once a week.'

'That must be expensive,' remarked Ned.

'It is,' admitted Silas. 'So I'm thinking of breeding cows in the back garden. Slaughtering one a year should see me through most of the time.'

'Or,' said Ruth, 'you could learn to cook something else . . . ? It might be easier and cheaper than raising cattle just to kill them for their meat.'

'Humph,' replied Silas. 'It took me quite a long time to learn this. You know how it is, Ruth. I'm a man. Cooking is woman's work. I can see that roasting a good haunch of meat is not unlike something a Viking warrior would have done, but you're not going to find me faffing about with aprons and butter and measuring flour and all that. I just couldn't do it, I've got to be honest. We men haven't got the eyes for it. Have we, Ned?' he appealed, as he passed Ned a bottle of ale from the larder.

'Well, I don't know,' said Ned amiably. 'I quite like cooking actually.'

435

'Do you?' Silas was surprised. 'What do you make?'

'My favourite recipe is a kind of herby salmon, with crème fraîche and a mixture of tarragon, parsley and dill. It's really delicious with steamed vegetables. Or you can't beat good sausages and decent onion gravy over mash. Potatoes are best with sausage but when I make my shepherd's pie, I prefer parsnip mash. There's just something about it . . . the sweetness, I think. Have you tried that?'

Silas eyed him a little suspiciously as though he thought Ned might be teasing him but he seemed quite serious. 'Hmm. Parsnip mash? No, I can't say I have. Doesn't sound too difficult. Do you think it would go with beef?'

*   *   *

Cordy arrived late, as usual, though she didn't have the hospital to blame this time.

'Sleep,' she announced. 'I'm not going to apologise. Blissful sleep.'

'You deserve it,' said Ruth.

'Thank you, sister dear,' said Cordelia, putting out her cheek to be kissed. When Ruth got close, she muttered, 'Post-coital sleep. Best there is. Don't tell Dad, I don't want the Inquisition,' and grinned conspiratorially.

'As long as you tell me later,' replied Ruth.

'Course I will. Ah, Ned! Pleasure to see you, as usual,' said Cordy, hugging her brother-in-law. 'Now, Dad, let me guess. Could that delicious smell *possibly* be roast beef?'

They ate in the dining room — Silas had cleared the junk off the table for once — and a birthday cake, courtesy of Mrs Jackson, was produced at the end of the meal, complete with candles and the word 'Ruth' spelt out in pink icing.

'Oh, how nice of her!' exclaimed Ruth. 'I must thank her.'

'We can go round after lunch if you like,' remarked Silas. 'Take her a slice. Not that she needs it. She claims to be slimming again, though she looks just as elephantine as usual to me.'

'Oh. Oh, that would be nice.' Ruth cut into the thick icing. 'But perhaps we should stay just family today. Look at this buttercream — yum.'

'Make a birthday wish!' called Cordy.

Ruth shut her eyes obediently and thought of something. 'There. Now, who's for some of this?'

They ate their cake, and then set out on a walk to work off the excesses of Sunday lunch. Silas took Ned on ahead while Cordy and Ruth followed behind. The day had begun gently enough with sunshine but now the skies were greying and a brisk wind was picking the fallen leaves and whirling them about.

'So,' said Ruth, 'who is this chap?'

'Just a bloke I know,' said Cordy airily. 'It might be nothing but, honestly, it's been so long since I've had a shag I was frightened I wouldn't remember how. I was worried I might say, 'Goodness, what an odd appendage! What *are* you planning to do with that?'. Luckily it all came back to me in the nick of time.'

Ruth laughed.

'But,' continued Cordy, 'it does my old heart good to see you and Ned so happy. It's like you used to be, when you first met.'

'Yes.' Ruth looked at him as he walked beside her father, his tall figure and the way he had his hands stuffed in his pockets. 'We are. We came through. It was touch and go for a bit.'

'You managed to get the better of that awful woman, then. His mother. I'm proud of you.'

'Yes. Well, Ned did.'

'Sounds like you both did. She's a grim old bag, isn't she?'

'Well, you know . . . ' Ruth shrugged.

'Oh, Ruth!' cried Cordy, outraged. 'You're not to feel sorry for her! Honestly, you and your soft heart . . . '

'Ned's sister came down to supper with us the other night. She told me some of the things that Jackie had done to *her*, which rather put my complaints in the shade. I'm not kidding, it would make your hair stand on end.'

'God, she's unbelievable.'

'But she also told me how Jackie's father committed suicide when she was young. It devastated the whole family, but Jackie most of all. She never really recovered. She had a weirdly close relationship with her mother that veered between deep affection and dreadful hatred. She's been compulsively controlling all her life, and Susie thinks that's why. Terrified of being left again, or perhaps she's even afraid she drove her father to it, so she's desperate to be loved.'

'Mmm,' said Cordy carefully. 'That is a sad

438

story but it doesn't excuse her: people have to take responsibility for themselves in the end, you know that. You lost your mother but it doesn't mean you scream and shout and expect the world to revolve around you.'

'She's got that alcohol problem.'

'Then she needs to take responsibility for that too. I'm sorry if it sounds harsh, but she does.'

They walked along in silence for a moment. Then Ruth said, 'You know, the strange thing was, I was completely mistaken about the whole thing. I was afraid of Ned's friends, of them coming between us somehow; and I was scared of the past he shared with them, because no matter how hard I tried, I could never be a part of that. I could sit there and listen to all their stories but I just hadn't been *there*. I got so hung up on it. I thought all that was more important to Ned than his future with me. I honestly felt that if Ned could, he would go back in time and live endlessly in his tight little gang, when of course he couldn't be happier to have found a life outside them all. I can see now that when I came along it gave him a way out of that stifling little circle for the first time. Not that he wasn't — and isn't — enormously fond of them all. But you can't live off friends alone, can you? In the end, you need something more.'

Cordelia nodded her agreement, kicking up some leaves that were heaped in her path.

'I focused all my fear on his old love for Erin. It was the outlet for all my insecurity, and it made me imagine that it was all still going on.'

'When really, the danger was from quite a

439

different direction,' remarked Cordy.

Ruth frowned. 'I knew his mother was difficult, but it never occurred to me that she would try and break us up. I didn't realise that, if I let her, she had the power to do it.'

'I wouldn't shoulder all the blame, if I were you. You couldn't stand up to her on your own, could you?'

'Exactly. It was something that Ned and I could only do together. I hadn't realised it. It seems so stupid now. And it was precisely because we weren't talking to each other properly that she was able to wriggle in between us and start manipulating everything the way she wanted.'

'You had some bad luck there. I can't believe that there are many in-laws as awful as Jackie.'

'I hope not.'

'But,' Cordy threw her a sidelong glance, 'I hope you're taking notes about how not to do it. You'll probably be a mother yourself one of these days, won't you?'

'Maybe,' said Ruth, smiling.

'I'd be surprised if you weren't.'

'I've got my new promotion to think of. I've only just started taking on my new responsibilities. And then there's the house move. We'll be completing on the sale in a month, and I've got movers and a million different things to organise . . . And we've got plans to travel.'

'Excuses, excuses . . . babies are portable, you know. All the same, I'll put my money on an announcement soon.'

'We'll see,' said Ruth, blandly. 'We'll see.'

'You'd better make Dad a grandfather soon,' said Cordy, 'before he goes completely dotty. Cows in the back garden! Whatever next? He needs a new interest — some impressionable little child to show his mad schemes to.'

'He'll be a terrific grandfather. No one at school will believe he really exists.'

They both looked fondly at their father, who was gesticulating dramatically to Ned as they walked. They heard him say, 'But that's the whole point of mass murderers, isn't it? They kill masses of people! They're not going to waste their talent on me on my own. I told Priscilla that, when she said I shouldn't go camping alone in the New Forest in case I met a mass murderer. It doesn't make sense, I told her. I need to be frightened of the lone schizophrenic who's been hearing voices telling him to murder old men in tents. And what are the chances of that?'

'Very low,' replied Ned.

'Exactly,' said Silas with satisfaction.

Cordy took Ruth's hand. 'You've got a good one. Anyone who can put up with Dad is a solid fellow.'

'I know,' said Ruth happily. 'I know.'

They carried on down the lane, back towards the house.

Acknowledgements

With grateful thanks to my editor Jane Wood and everyone at Orion, particularly Susan Lamb, Lisa Milton, Sara O'Keeffe, Juliet Ewers, Jenny Page, Gaby Young and Bea Hemming, as well as the fantastic sales team and rights department and everyone else. They all do a wonderful job.

Huge thanks to Lizzy Kremer, my agent, and all at David Higham Associates.

A big thank you to my friends, none of whom are like the friends in this book (well, not much anyway), and to my family.

And particular thanks to my parents-in-law, Judy and David Crawford, who are immensely kind and supportive and provided me with a bolt hole when I needed one, and who are *nothing* at all like the parents-in-law in this book!

We do hope that you have enjoyed reading this large print book.

Did you know that all of our titles are available for purchase?

We publish a wide range of high quality large print books including:
Romances, Mysteries, Classics
General Fiction
Non Fiction and Westerns

Special interest titles available in large print are:
The Little Oxford Dictionary
Music Book
Song Book
Hymn Book
Service Book

Also available from us courtesy of Oxford University Press:
Young Readers' Dictionary
(large print edition)
Young Readers' Thesaurus
(large print edition)

For further information or a free brochure, please contact us at:
Ulverscroft Large Print Books Ltd.,
The Green, Bradgate Road, Anstey,
Leicester, LE7 7FU, England.
Tel: (00 44) 0116 236 4325
Fax: (00 44) 0116 234 0205

OTHER WOMEN

Kirsty Crawford

Since the death of her husband Theo, Jane Fielding has tried to keep Rawlston House, despite her inherited money problems. Selling off property has helped: there are new people next door and in the lodge. But Jane is beset with new anxieties . . . Sam Clarke becomes aware that her husband Ben's life is more of a mystery to her than she realised . . . The lives of the other women throw a harsh spotlight on Bella Balfour, as the cracks in her marriage to her husband Iain turn into unbridgeable chasms . . . Each woman is drawn into the lives of the others, whether she likes it or not.

GANG OF FOUR

Liz Byrski

They have been friends for two decades, supporting each other through so many crises — parents dying, children leaving home, job changes, diets and bad haircuts. Now the 'gang of four', Isabel, Sally, Robin and Grace, are all facing fifty-something, successful . . . and restless. Isabel makes the first move, taking a year away from her family to follow her mother's footsteps across Europe. Soon Sally is on her way too — to San Francisco to come face to face with a guilty secret. Robin, in the wake of a clandestine relationship, heads for isolation in the country. And Grace? Well, Grace would never go away for an entire year, but she thinks she might take a short holiday in England. Once there she bumps into someone she hardly knows — herself.

THIRTEEN MOONS

Charles Frazier

Will Cooper's search for identity and home begins at the age of twelve, when he is given a horse, a key and a map, and sent to the edge of the Cherokee Nation to run a trading post as a bound boy. Between a Cherokee chief named Bear and the mysterious and beautiful Claire Featherstone, Will finds the passionate connections and the complications of manhood that will forge his character and shape his life. As his fate becomes intertwined with the destiny of the Cherokee, Will travels to Washington City to fight against the Removal of the Indians from their land and to protect Bear's people, their culture, and way of life.

WATERSHED

Maggie Makepeace

Jonathan arrives on the Somerset Levels and shuts himself away in a lonely cottage to write about his obsession — water. He poses an irresistible challenge for Pamela, a forceful pillar of the community. But why is Jonathan so resistant to her blandishments — and so *rude*? Only Vinny, Pamela's long-suffering companion, has the desire and the sensitivity to get to the bottom of Jonathan's strange behaviour. But she herself is trapped by emotional blackmail. Will Jonathan prove to be her saviour, as much as she is his? Vinny is forced to make a difficult decision, and comes to her own personal watershed. Storms, fire and floods suddenly raise the stakes for everyone. As the waters rise, emotions are also set to burst their bounds.

A SCENT OF BLUEBELLS

Meg Henderson

They called her Auld Nally — a moneylender in one of Glasgow's roughest areas, Inchcraig. Once, though, she'd been Alice McInally from Belfast, beautiful and beloved by her childhood sweetheart. But his family was Catholic and hers Protestant, and opposition to their marriage plans meant they must leave Ireland and their well-to-do families. However, their dream for their future founders in war-torn Glasgow, and Alice struggles to make ends meet. To protect the children in her care, she relies on the man Inchcraig knows as 'him', and lives among people far from her background; people she admires and doesn't want to leave. Every day, though, she must live with a lie that could destroy everything — unless she can find the exact time to put it right . . .